THE LEGACY OF THE BONES

Dolores Redondo was born in Donostia-San Sebastián in 1969, where she studied Law and Gastronomy. Her novel, *The Invisible Guardian*, was published in Spain in 2013, with rights sold in thirty-one languages. It was chosen as 'Best Crime Novel of the Year' by the major Spanish newspaper *La Vanguardia* and over 1,000,000 readers turned the Detective Inspector Amaia Salazar series into one of Spain's biggest literary successes in recent years. *The Legacy of the Bones* is the second book in the series and went straight to No.1 in Spain. The film adaptation is currently being developed by the producer of *The Killing* and Stieg Larsson's Millennium Trilogy.

Dolores Redondo currently lives and writes in the Ribera Navarra area of Spain.

DOLORES REDONDO

The Legacy of the Bones

Translated from the Spanish by Nick Caistor and
Lorenza García

HarperCollins*Publishers*

HarperCollins*Publishers*
1 London Bridge Street
London SE1 9GF

www.harpercollins.co.uk

Published by HarperCollins*Publishers* 2016
1

Originally published in 2013 by Ediciones Destino,
Spain, as *Legado en los huesos*

A catalogue record for this book
is available from the British Library

ISBN: 978-0-00-816559-8

Set in Sabon LT Std by Palimpsest Book Production Limited,
Falkirk, Stirlingshire

Printed and bound in Great Britain by
Clays Ltd, St Ives plc

MIX
Paper from
responsible sources
FSC **FSC™ C007454**
www.fsc.org

Find out more about HarperCollins and the environment at
www.harpercollins.co.uk/green

For Eduardo, every word.

Has this fellow no feeling of his business?
He sings at grave-making.

William Shakespeare

Often the sepulchre encloses, unawares,
Two hearts in the same coffin.

Alphonse De Lamartine

Pain when inside is stronger
It isn't eased by sharing.

Alejandro Sanz, *'Si Hay Dios'*

Itxusuria

Following the line traced by rainwater dripping from the eaves, the grave was easy to find. The figure knelt, fumbling among its clothes for a trowel and a small pick to scrape off the hard surface of the dark soil. It crumbled into soft, moist clods that gave off a rich smell of wood and moss.

A careful scraping of a few centimetres revealed blackened shreds of decayed cloth mixed with the earth.

The figure tugged away the cloth, still recognisable as a cot blanket, to reveal the oilskin enshrouding the body. Only fragments of the rope securing the bundle remained; where it had been pulled tight a deep mark was left on the canvas. Pushing aside the shreds of rope, the figure groped blindly for the edge of the cloth, and could feel it had been wrapped round several times. Tearing at the end of the bundle, the shroud fell open as though cut with a knife.

The baby lay buried face down, cradled in the earth; the bones, like the oilcloth itself, appeared well preserved, although stained by the black earth of Baztán. Stretching out a hand that almost completely covered the tiny form, the figure pressed the baby's chest further into the earth and pulled the right arm out of its socket. As it came loose, the collarbone snapped with a soft crack. It sounded like a sigh from the tomb, a lament for the sacrilege. Suddenly uneasy, the shadowy figure recoiled and stood up, tucked the bones under its clothes, then cast one last glance at the body before scuffing the soil back into the grave.

1

The atmosphere in the courthouse was stifling. The damp from rain-soaked overcoats was starting to evaporate, mixing with the breath of the hundreds of people thronging the corridors outside the various courtrooms. Amaia undid her jacket as she greeted Lieutenant Padua, who made his way towards her through the waiting crowd, after speaking briefly to the woman accompanying him and ushering her into the courtroom.

'Good to see you, Inspector,' he said. 'How are you? I wasn't sure you'd make it here today,' he added, pointing to her swollen belly.

Amaia raised a hand to her midriff, heavy from the late stages of pregnancy.

'Well, she seems to be behaving herself for the moment. Have you seen Johana's mother?'

'Yes, she's pretty nervous. She's inside with her family. They've just called from downstairs to tell me the van transporting Jasón Medina has arrived,' he said, heading for the lift.

Amaia entered the courtroom and sat down on one of the benches at the back. From there she was able to glimpse Johana's mother, dressed in mourning and considerably thinner than at her daughter's funeral. As though sensing her presence, the woman turned to look, greeting her with a brief nod. Amaia tried unsuccessfully to smile as she contemplated the haggard features of the woman, who was tormented by the knowledge that she had been powerless to protect her daughter from the monster she herself had brought into their home. As the court clerk began to call out the names of the witnesses, Amaia couldn't help noticing the woman's face stiffen when she heard her husband's name.

'Jasón Medina,' the clerk repeated. 'Jasón Medina.'

A uniformed officer entered the courtroom, approached the clerk and whispered something in his ear. He in turn leaned over to speak to the judge, who listened to what he said then nodded, before calling the prosecution and defence barristers to the bench. He spoke to them briefly then rose to his feet.

'The trial is adjourned; if necessary, you will be summoned again.' And without another word, he left the courtroom.

Johana's mother cried out, turning to Amaia for an explanation.

'No!' she screamed. 'Why?'

The women with her tried helplessly to comfort her.

Another officer walked over to Amaia.

'Inspector Salazar, Lieutenant Padua has asked if you would go down to the holding cells.'

As she stepped out of the lift, she saw a group of police officers gathered outside the toilet door. The guard accompanying her motioned to her to enter. Inside, a prison officer and a policeman stood propped against the wall, their faces distraught. Padua was leaning into one of the cubicles, his feet at the edge of a pool of still fresh blood seeping under the partition walls. When he saw the inspector arrive, he stepped aside.

'He told the guard he needed to use the toilet. As you can see, he was handcuffed, yet he managed to slit his own

4

throat. It all happened very fast, the officer didn't move from here, heard him cough and went in, but there was nothing he could do.'

Amaia went in to survey the scene. Jasón Medina was sitting on the toilet, head tilted back. His throat was gaping from a deep, dark gash. His shirtfront was drenched in blood, which oozed like red mucus between his legs, staining everything in its path. His body still radiated warmth, and the air was tainted with the smell of recent death.

'What did he use?' asked Amaia, who couldn't see any object.

'A box cutter. He dropped it as the strength drained out of him. It's in the next-door toilet,' he said, pushing open the door to the adjacent cubicle.

'How did he get it through security? The metal would have set the alarm off.'

'He didn't. Look,' said Padua, pointing. 'See that piece of duct tape on the handle? Somebody went to a lot of trouble to hide the cutter in here, no doubt behind the cistern. All Medina had to do was peel it off.'

Amaia sighed.

'And there's more,' said Padua, with a look of distaste. 'This was sticking out of his pocket,' he said, holding up a white envelope in his gloved hand.

'A suicide note?' ventured Amaia.

'Not exactly,' said Padua, handing her a pair of gloves and the envelope. 'It's addressed to you.'

'To me?' Amaia frowned.

She pulled on the gloves and took the envelope.

'May I?'

'Go ahead.'

The adhesive strip opened easily without her needing to tear the paper. Inside was a card; in the middle of it a single word was printed.

'*Tarttalo*.'

Amaia felt a sharp twinge in her belly and held her breath to disguise the pain. She turned the card over to make sure nothing was written on the back, before returning it to Padua.

'What does it mean?'

'I was hoping you'd tell me.'

'Well, I've no idea, Lieutenant Padua,' she replied, puzzled. 'It doesn't make much sense to me.'

'A *tarttalo* is a mythological creature, isn't it?'

'Yes, as far as I know it's a kind of Cyclops. It exists in both Graeco-Roman and Basque mythology. What are you getting at?'

'You worked on the *basajaun* case. The *basajaun* was also a mythological creature, and now Johana Márquez's confessed murderer, who tried to copy one of the *basajaun* crimes to conceal his own, kills himself and leaves a note that says: "*Tarttalo*". You must admit it's curious, to say the least.'

'You're right.' Amaia sighed. 'It's strange. However, at the time we proved beyond doubt that Jasón Medina raped and murdered his stepdaughter, then made a clumsy attempt to pass it off as one of the *basajaun* crimes. Not only that, he made a full confession. Are you suggesting he wasn't the murderer?'

'I don't doubt it for a minute,' said Padua, glancing at the corpse. 'But there's the question of the severed arm, and the girl's bones turning up in the Arri Zahar cave. And now this. I was hoping you might . . .'

'I've no idea what this means, or why he addressed it to me.'

Padua gave a sigh, his eyes fixed on her.

'Of course not, Inspector.'

Amaia headed for the rear exit, anxious not to bump into Johana's mother. What could she say to the woman: that it was all over, or that her husband, like the rat he was, had escaped to the next world? She flashed her ID at the security

6

guards; it came as a relief to be free at last of the atmosphere inside. The rain had stopped and the bright yet hesitant sunlight, typical in Pamplona between showers, emerged through the clouds, making her eyes water as she rummaged in her bag for her dark glasses. As ever when it was raining, finding a taxi to take her to the courthouse during the morning rush hour had been almost impossible; but now several of them sat idling at the rank, while the city's inhabitants chose to walk. She hesitated for a moment beside the first car. No, she wasn't quite ready to go home; the prospect of Clarice running around, bombarding her with questions was decidedly unappealing. Since her in-laws had arrived a fortnight earlier, Amaia's idea of home had been seriously challenged. She gazed towards the enticing windows of the cafés across from the courthouse and at the other end of Calle San Roque, where she could see the trees in Media Luna Park. Working out that it was roughly one and a half kilometres to her house, she set off on foot. She could always hail a taxi if she felt tired.

Leaving behind the roar of traffic as she entered the park gave her an instant sense of relief. The fresh scent of wet grass replaced the exhaust fumes, and Amaia instinctively slackened her pace as she crossed one of the stone paths that cut through the perfect greenness. She took deep breaths, exhaling with deliberate slowness. *What a morning*, she thought; Jasón Medina perfectly fitted the profile of the criminal who commits suicide in jail. Accused of raping and killing his wife's daughter, he had been put in solitary confinement pending his trial; no doubt he'd been terrified at the prospect of having to mix with other prisoners after being sentenced. She remembered him from the interrogations nine months earlier, when they were investigating the *basajaun* case: a snivelling coward, weeping and wailing as he confessed his atrocities.

The two cases weren't connected, but Lieutenant Padua of the *Guardia Civil* had invited her to sit in, because of Medina's clumsy attempts to imitate the modus operandi of the serial killer she was chasing, based on what he had read in the newspapers. That was nine months ago, just when she became pregnant. Since then, a lot of things had changed.

'Haven't they, little one?' she whispered, stroking her belly.

A violent contraction caused her to pull up short. Leaning on her umbrella for support, she doubled over, enduring the terrible spasm in her lower abdomen, which spread in a ripple down her inner thighs, wrenching a cry from her, more of surprise at the intensity than of pain. The sensation subsided as quickly as it had arisen.

So that's how it felt. Countless times she had wondered what it would feel like to go into labour, whether she would recognise the signs, or be one of those women who arrived at the hospital with the baby already crowning, or who gave birth in the taxi.

'Oh, my little one!' Amaia spoke to her sweetly. 'You still have another week. Are you sure you want to come out now?'

The pain had vanished, as if it had never happened. She felt an immense joy, accompanied by a twinge of anxiety at the imminence of her baby's arrival. She smiled, glancing about as if she wished she could share her pleasure. But the moist, cool park was deserted and its emerald green colours, still more radiant and beautiful in the dazzling light seeping through the clouds above Pamplona, reminded her of the sense of discovery she always felt in Baztán, which in the city seemed like an unexpected gift. She continued on her way, transported now to that magical forest and the amber eyes of the lord of that domain. Only nine months previously she had been investigating a case there, in the place where she was born, the place she had always wanted to flee, the place where she had gone to hunt down a killer, and where she conceived her baby girl.

The knowledge that her daughter was growing inside her had brought the soothing calm and serenity to her life that she had always dreamt of. At that time it had been the only thing that helped her cope with the terrible events she had lived through, which a few months earlier would have been the death of her. Returning to Elizondo, dredging up her past, and, most of all, Víctor's death, had turned her world and that of her entire family upside down. Aunt Engrasi was the only one unaffected, reading her tarot cards, playing poker with her women friends every afternoon, smiling like someone who has seen everything before. Overnight, Flora had moved to Zarautz, on the pretext of recording her daily programme on baking for national television, and, who would have believed it, had handed over the running of Mantecadas Salazar to Ros. Much to Flora's astonishment – and confirming Amaia's intuitions – Ros had turned out to be a first-class manager, if a little overwhelmed to begin with. Amaia had offered to help her out and for the past few months had been spending almost every weekend in Elizondo, even after she realised that Ros no longer needed her support. And yet she continued to go there, to eat with them, to sleep at her aunt's house, feeling at home. From the moment her baby girl started to grow inside her, she'd begun to rediscover a feeling of home, of roots, of belonging, that for years she thought she had lost for ever.

As she came out into Calle Mayor it began to drizzle again. She opened her umbrella, picking her way between the shoppers and a few pedestrians who had no protection and were scurrying along beneath the eaves of the buildings and shop awnings. She paused in front of the colourful window of a store selling children's clothes and contemplated the little pink smocks embroidered with tiny flowers. Clarice was probably right, she ought to buy something like that for her baby. She sighed, all of a sudden irritated, as she thought of the room Clarice had decorated for her child. James's parents had come over from the States for the birth and after only ten days in Pamplona his mother had more than fulfilled Amaia's worst expectations of what a meddlesome mother-in-law could be like. From the very first day, she voiced her bewilderment about there being no nursery despite all the spare rooms they had.

Amaia had salvaged an antique hardwood cot from her Aunt Engrasi's sitting room, where for years it had been used as a log basket. James had sanded it down to the grain before applying a fresh coat of varnish, while Engrasi's friends had made an exquisite valance and a white bedcover that accentuated the craftsmanship and character of the cot. There was plenty of space in their large bedroom; besides, despite what the experts said, Amaia wasn't convinced about the merits of her baby having a separate room; for the first few months, while she was breastfeeding, having the baby nearby would make it easier to feed her during the night, and knowing that she could hear her if she cried or had a problem would reassure her . . .

Clarice had raised the roof. 'The baby must have her own room, with all her things around her. Believe you me, both mother and baby will sleep better. If you have her next to you, you'll be listening for her every breath and movement; she needs her space and you need yours. Anyway, it's not healthy for a baby to share its parents' bedroom, children become used to it and won't be taken to their own room.'

Amaia had also read the advice of a host of celebrated paediatricians determined to indoctrinate an entire new generation of children into the ways of suffering: don't pick them up too often, let them sleep alone from birth, don't comfort them when they have a tantrum because they need to learn to be independent, to cope with their fears and failures. Such stupidity made Amaia's stomach churn. It occurred to her that if any of these distinguished doctors had been obliged since birth to 'cope' with fear the way she had, they would have an entirely different view of the world. If her daughter wanted to sleep in their bedroom until she was three years old, that was fine by her: she would comfort her, listen to her, take seriously and allay her childish fears, because as she herself knew only too well, they could loom large in a child's mind. But evidently Clarice had her own ideas about how things should be done, which she didn't hesitate to share with everybody else.

Three days earlier, Amaia had arrived home to discover that her mother-in-law had given them a surprise gift: a magnificent nursery complete with wardrobes, a changer, chest of drawers, rugs, and lamps. A superabundance of pink fleecy clouds and little lambs, all wreathed in ribbons and lace. Amaia had been alarmed enough when James had opened the door, given her a kiss and whispered apologetically: 'She means well.' But when she was confronted by this profusion of pinkness, her smile froze as she realised she was being made to feel like a stranger in her own home. Clarice, on the other hand, was thrilled, gliding amidst the furniture like a TV presenter, while Amaia's father-in-law, impassive as always when faced with his wife's enthusiasm, carried on calmly reading the newspaper in the sitting room. Amaia found it difficult to reconcile the image of Thomas at the helm of a financial empire with the way he behaved towards his wife, with a mixture of submissiveness and apathy that never ceased to amaze her. If only because she knew how uncomfortable James felt, Amaia did her best to keep her composure while his mother extolled the marvels of the nursery she had bought for them.

'Look at this lovely wardrobe, all her clothes will fit in there, and there is room in the changer for nappies as well as everything else. Aren't the rugs cute? And over here,' she said, grinning smugly, 'the pièce de résistance: a cot fit for a princess.'

Amaia had to admit that the huge pink cot was indeed majestic, and big enough for her daughter to sleep in until she was at least four years old.

'Very pretty,' she forced herself to say.

'It's beautiful, so now you can give your aunt back her log basket.'

Amaia left the nursery without a word and went into her bedroom to wait for James.

'Oh, I'm sorry, sweetheart, she doesn't mean to interfere, it's just how she is. They'll only be here a few more days. I know you're being incredibly patient, and I promise you that after they've gone we'll get rid of everything you don't like.'

She had agreed for James's sake and because she didn't have the strength to argue with Clarice. James was right: she was being incredibly patient, even though it went against her nature. This was possibly the first time she had ever let anyone control her, but in this final stage of pregnancy, she had noticed a change come over her. For days now she had been feeling unwell; all the energy she had enjoyed during the first months had given way to an apathy that was unusual in her. Clarice's domineering presence only brought that fragility to the fore. Amaia glanced again at the baby clothes in the shop window and decided they had quite enough with every-thing her mother-in-law had bought. Clarice's extravagances as a first-time grandmother made Amaia feel queasy, but there was something else: secretly she would have given anything to have the same intoxicating love affair with pink that afflicted her mother-in-law.

Since she had become pregnant, all she had bought for her daughter was a pair of bootees, a few T-shirts, some leggings, and a set of Babygros in neutral colours. She told herself that pink wasn't her favourite colour. When she browsed the shop windows and saw frocks, cardigans and skirts bedecked with ribbons and embroidered flowers, she thought they looked lovely, perfect for a little princess, but no sooner did she have them in her hand than she felt an intense aversion towards all those tasteless frills and ended up walking out, confused and irritated, without buying anything. She could have done with some of the enthusiasm shown by Clarice, who would dissolve into raptures at the sight of a frock and matching shoes. Amaia knew that she couldn't have been happier, that she had always loved this baby, from the time when she herself had been a brooding, unhappy child dreaming of being a mother one day, a real mother, a desire that had crystallised when she met James. And when motherhood threatened to elude her, assailed with fears and doubts, she had considered undergoing IVF treatment. But then, nine months ago, while investigating the most important case of her career, she had become pregnant.

Amaia was happy, or at least thought she was, and that puzzled her even more. Until recently she had felt fulfilled, contented, self-assured in a way that she hadn't for years; yet over the past few weeks, fresh fears, which were actually as old as time, had started creeping back, infiltrating her dreams, whispering familiar words she wished she didn't recognise.

Another contraction, less painful but more drawn-out, gripped her. She checked her watch. Twenty minutes since the last one in the park.

She headed towards the restaurant where they had arranged to meet. Clarice didn't approve of James cooking all the time, and kept hinting that they needed staff. Half-expecting to arrive home one day to find they had an English butler, she and James had decided they should lunch and dine out every day.

James had chosen a modern restaurant in the street next to Calle Mercaderes, where they lived. When she arrived, Clarice and the taciturn Thomas were both sipping martinis. James stood up as soon as he saw her.

'Hi, Amaia, how are you, my love?' he said, planting a kiss on her lips and pulling out a chair for her.

'Fine,' she said, wondering whether to mention the contractions. She glanced at Clarice and decided to keep quiet.

'And the little one?' James smiled, resting his hand on her belly.

'The little one,' repeated Clarice derisively. 'Do you think it's normal that a week before your daughter's birth you still haven't chosen a name for her?'

Amaia pretended to browse the menu while looking askance at James.

'Oh, Mom, not that again. We like several, but we can't decide, so we're waiting until the baby arrives. The moment we see her little face we'll know what to call her.'

'Oh!' Clarice perked up. 'So, you *have* thought of some names. Is one of them Clarice, maybe?' Amaia heaved a sigh. 'Seriously, though what names are you thinking of?' Clarice persisted.

Amaia glanced up from the menu as a fresh contraction gripped her belly for a few seconds. She looked at her watch again and smiled.

'Actually, I've already chosen one,' she lied, 'only I want it to be a surprise. What I can tell you is that she won't be called Clarice: I don't like names repeated within families, I think each person should have their own identity.'

Clarice grimaced.

The baby's name was another missile Clarice fired at her whenever she got the opportunity. James's mother had harped on about it so much that he had even suggested they choose one just to shut her up. Amaia had snapped. That was the last straw: why should she be forced to choose a name simply to make Clarice happy?

'Not to make her happy, Amaia, but because we have to call her something, and you don't seem to want to think about choosing a name at all.'

As with the clothes, she knew they were right. Having researched the subject, she'd become so concerned about it that she consulted Aunt Engrasi.

'Well, not having had babies myself, I can't speak from personal experience, but at a clinical level, I gather it's fairly common among first-time mothers and fathers in particular.

14

Once you've had a baby, you know what to expect, there are no surprises, but with a first pregnancy some mothers, despite their swollen bellies, find it hard to relate the changes in their body to the realities of having a child. Nowadays with ultrasound and listening to the baby's heartbeat, knowing if it's a boy or a girl, expectant parents have more of a sense that their baby is real, whereas in the past you couldn't see a baby until it was born; most people only realised they had a child when they were cradling it in their arms and gazing into its little face. Your misgivings are perfectly natural,' she said, placing her hand on Amaia's belly. 'Believe me, no one is prepared for parenthood, although some people like to pretend that they are.'

Amaia ordered fish, which she hardly touched. She noticed that the contractions were less frequent and less intense when she was still.

As soon as they'd finished their meal, Clarice returned to the offensive.

'Have you looked at crèches?'

'No, Mom, we haven't,' said James, setting his cup down on the table and gazing at her wearily. 'Because we're not putting the baby in a crèche.'

'I see, so you'll find a child-minder when Amaia goes back to work.'

'When Amaia goes back to work, I'll look after my daughter myself.'

Clarice's eyes opened wide. She looked to her husband for support, but received none from Thomas, who smiled and shook his head as he sipped his rooibos.

'Clarice . . .' he cautioned. These gentle repetitions of his wife's name in a tone of reproach were the closest Thomas ever came to protesting.

She ignored him.

'You can't be serious. How are you going to look after her? You don't know the first thing about babies.'

'I'll learn,' James replied, smiling.

'Learn? For goodness' sake! You're gonna need help.'

'We have a cleaner who comes regularly.'

'I'm not talking about a cleaner four hours a week, I'm talking about a nanny, a child-minder, someone who'll take care of the child.'

'I'll take care of her. We'll take care of her together, that's what we have decided.'

James seemed amused, and, judging from his expression, so did Thomas. Clarice sighed, smiled wanly and adopted a calm tone, as though making a supreme effort to be reasonable and patient.

'Yes, I know all about this modern parenting stuff – breastfeeding children until they grow teeth, having them sleep in your bed, dispensing with a nanny – but, son, you have to work too, your career is at a critical stage, and during the baby's first year, you'll scarcely have time to draw breath.'

'I've just finished a forty-eight-piece collection for the exhibition at the Guggenheim next year, and I have enough works in reserve to enable me to devote myself to my daughter. Besides, Amaia isn't always busy. Yes, she has periods of intense activity in her job, but she often comes home early.'

Amaia could feel her belly tense beneath her blouse, more painfully now. She breathed slowly, dissimulating as she glanced at the clock. Fifteen minutes.

'You look pale, Amaia, are you feeling OK?'

'I'm tired. I think I'll go home and lie down for a while.'

'Good, Thomas and I are going shopping,' announced Clarice, 'otherwise you'll be using vine leaves instead of baby blankets. Shall we meet back here for dinner?'

'No,' Amaia protested. 'I'll make something light at home, and try to rest. I was thinking of going shopping tomorrow; I found a store where they sell cute dresses.'

Clarice took the bait: the prospect of a shopping spree with her daughter-in-law instantly made her relax, and she beamed contentedly.

16

'Oh, of course, my dear, we'll have a wonderful time, you'll see. I've seen so many gorgeous things since I came. You have a rest, dear,' she said, making her way towards the exit.

Thomas stooped to give Amaia a peck before he left.

'Well played,' he whispered, winking at her.

Their house in Calle Mercaderes revealed none of its splendours from the outside: the tall ceilings, large windows, wood panelling, the wonderful mouldings that ornamented most of the rooms and the ground floor, which had once been an umbrella factory and where James now had his studio.

Amaia took a shower then stretched out on the sofa, pamphlet in one hand and watch in the other.

'You look more tired today than usual. I noticed that during lunch you weren't paying as much attention to my mother's foolishness.'

Amaia grinned.

'Is it because of something that happened at the courthouse? You mentioned that the trial had been adjourned, but you didn't say why?'

'Jasón Medina killed himself this morning in the courthouse toilets. It'll be in all the papers tomorrow.'

'Well,' James shrugged. 'I can't say I'm sorry.'

'Me neither. He's no great loss, but I imagine the girl's family must be a bit disappointed that he won't be standing trial. On the other hand, they'll be spared the ordeal of having to listen to all the gory details.'

James nodded thoughtfully.

Amaia considered telling him about the note Medina had left for her, but decided it would only upset him. She didn't want to ruin this special moment by bringing that up.

'But, yes, I am more tired today, and my mind is on other things.'

'Such as?' he asked.

'At twelve thirty I started having contractions every

17

twenty-five minutes. At first, they only lasted a few seconds, now they're getting stronger and I'm having them every twelve minutes.'

'Oh, Amaia, why didn't you tell me before? Were you suffering all through lunch? Are they really painful?'

'Not really,' she said, smiling. 'It's more like an intense pressure, besides I didn't want your mother going hysterical on me. I need a bit of calm now. I'll rest and keep checking the frequency of the contractions. When I'm ready, we can go to the hospital.'

The skies above Pamplona were still overcast, and the distant twinkle of winter stars was barely visible.

James was asleep face down, sprawled over a larger area of the bed than he was entitled to, in that peaceful, relaxed way of his that Amaia had always envied. At first he had hesitated about going to bed at all, but she had persuaded him to rest while he could because she'd need him awake later on.

'Are you sure you'll be OK?' he had insisted.

'I'm sure, James. I only need to check the frequency of the contractions. When it's time to go I'll let you know.'

He had fallen asleep as soon as his head touched the pillow, and the house was silent save for his steady breathing and the soft rustle as she turned the pages of her book.

She broke off reading as she felt another contraction. Gasping, she clutched the arms of the rocking chair she'd been sitting in for the past hour, and waited for it to subside.

Frustrated, she put down the book without bothering to mark her page, realising that, although she'd read quite a lot, she hadn't taken any of it in. In the past half-hour the contractions had grown more painful, almost making her cry out. Even so, she decided to wait a little longer. She leaned out of the window gazing down into the street, which was quite busy that Friday night, despite the cold, the occasional drizzle, and the fact that it was well past midnight.

She heard a noise in the hallway and went over to listen at the bedroom door.

It was her in-laws, returning after dinner and a stroll. She glanced at the soft glow coming from the reading lamp she had switched on and thought about turning it off, but there was no need; although Clarice meddled in virtually every area of their lives, she wouldn't dare barge into their bedroom.

Continuing to check the increasing frequency of the contractions, she listened to the sounds in the house, to James's parents going to bed, and how everything stopped, giving way to a silence troubled only by the creaks and whispers that inhabited the enormous building, as familiar to her as her own breath. She had nothing to worry about now; Thomas was a heavy sleeper, while Clarice took tablets every night, so she wouldn't be awake before dawn.

The next contraction was truly terrible, and despite concentrating on breathing in and out the way she'd been taught in her prenatal classes, she felt as if she was wearing a steel corset that was squeezing her kidneys and lungs so tight it made her panic. What frightened her wasn't so much giving birth, although she admitted feeling some trepidation about it, whilst being aware that this was perfectly normal. No, she knew that what frightened her was something far more profound and deep-seated, because this wasn't the first time she had confronted fear. She had carried it around with her for years like an unwanted, invisible traveller that only appeared when she was at her lowest ebb.

Fear was an old vampire looming above her bed while she slept, hidden in the darkness, filling her dreams with terrifying shadows. Suddenly she remembered her grandmother Juanita's word for it: *gaueko*: 'the night visitor'. A visitor who retreated into the darkness whenever she succeeded in opening a breach in her own defences, a breach that let in the light of understanding, only to reveal the cruelty of the terrible events that had marked her life for ever, and which through sheer willpower she kept buried deep in her soul. The first step had been to comprehend, to identify the truth and to confront it. And yet, even in that instant of euphoria when she believed she had triumphed over her fear for the first time, she realised she hadn't won the war, only a battle – a glorious one, but a battle all the same. From then on she had worked hard to keep that breach open, allowing the light that flooded in to strengthen her relationship with James, as well as the image of herself she had built up over the years. And as a postscript, this pregnancy, the little being growing inside her, brought her a feeling of serenity she could never before have imagined. Throughout her pregnancy she had felt amazing: no morning sickness, no discomfort, her sleep was restful and serene, free from nightmares or sudden jolts; she had so much energy during the day that she even surprised herself. The perfect pregnancy, until a week ago, the night that evil returned.

She had been going in to the police station every day as usual; they were investigating the case of a missing woman, whose partner was the chief suspect. For months the disappearance had been regarded as intentional, but her daughters' insistence that their mother hadn't left of her own accord had aroused Amaia's interest, and she had reopened the investigation. Besides her two daughters and three grandchildren, the middle-aged woman was a catechist at her local church and paid daily visits to the care home where her elderly mother lived. Too many commitments for her to vanish without a word. They had established early on that suitcases, clothes, personal documents and money were missing from her house. Even so, when Amaia decided to take over the investigation, she insisted on going back there. Lucía Aguirre's house was as neat and tidy as the photograph of its smiling owner, which had pride of place in the hallway. In the tiny sitting room, a piece of crochet lay on a coffee table covered with photographs of her grandchildren.

Amaia searched the kitchen and bathroom, which were

spotlessly clean. In the master bedroom, the bed was made and there were few clothes in the wardrobe and chest of drawers. In the spare room were twin beds.

'Jonan, do you notice something strange here?'

'The bedcovers are different,' said Deputy Inspector Etxaide.

'We noticed that the first time around. The matching counterpane is in the wardrobe,' explained the accompanying officer, checking his notes.

Amaia opened the wardrobe to find the blue counterpane matching one of those on the bed neatly folded in a see-through plastic pouch.

'And didn't it strike you as odd that this neat, house-proud woman wouldn't take the trouble to use matching bedspreads, when she had them to hand?'

'Why start changing bedspreads if she was planning to disappear?' the officer said with a shrug.

'Because we're slaves to our nature. Did you know that some women from East Berlin mopped the floors of their houses before fleeing to West Germany? They were abandoning their country, but they didn't want anyone saying they weren't good housewives.'

Amaia pulled the bulky package out of the wardrobe and put it on one of the beds before unzipping it. The sharp odour of bleach permeated the room. With one gloved hand, she tugged at the edge of the counterpane, unfolding it to reveal a yellowish stain in the middle where the bleach had eaten away the colour.

'You see, officer, it doesn't fit,' she said, turning towards the policeman, who nodded, speechless.

'Our murderer has seen enough TV programmes about crime scene investigations to know that bleach gets rid of bloodstains, but he's a terrible house husband because he didn't take into account that it also removes the colour. Call in Forensics to do a blood search – this stain is enormous.'

After a thorough search by the forensic team, traces had

been found, which, despite the attempted clean-up, revealed amounts of lost blood that would have resulted in loss of life: the human body contains five litres of blood; losing five hundred millilitres is sufficient to cause fainting, and the tests suggested more than two litres had been spilled. They had arrested the suspect the same day: a vain, cocky individual, his overly long hair streaked with grey, and his shirt unbuttoned halfway down his chest. Amaia suppressed a laugh when she saw what he looked like from the adjoining room.

'The return of El Macho,' said Deputy Inspector Extaide. 'Who's going to question him?'

'Inspector Fernández, they've been working on the case from the beginning . . .'

'I assumed it would be us, now that this is a murder inquiry. If it hadn't been for you, they'd still be waiting for her to send a postcard from Cancún.'

'It's a matter of courtesy, Jonan. Besides, I can't interrogate suspects in this state,' she said, pointing to her belly.

Inspector Fernández entered the interview room and Jonan switched on the recorder.

'Good morning, Mr Quiralte. My name's Detective Inspector Fer—'

'Wait a minute,' interrupted Quiralte. He raised his cuffed hands, accompanying the gesture with a flick of his hair worthy of a diva in a celebrity magazine. 'Don't I get to be interrogated by the star cop?'

'Who do you mean?'

'You know, that inspector woman from the FBI?'

'How do you know about that?' asked Fernández, taken aback. Amaia clicked her tongue in annoyance. Quiralte smirked.

'Because I'm smarter than you.'

Fernández looked nervous. He had little experience interrogating murderers, and the suspect had already succeeded in unsettling him.

'Don't let him get the upper hand,' muttered Amaia.

As if he could hear her, Fernández took control of the interview.

'Why do you want her to interrogate you?'

'Because they tell me she's hot, and I'd rather be questioned by a pretty woman inspector than by you any day,' he said, settling back in his chair.

'Well, you'll have to make do with me. The inspector you are referring to is on leave.'

Sneering, Quiralte turned towards the two-way mirror as if he could see through it.

'Well, that's a shame, I'll just have to wait until she gets back.'

'You don't intend to give a statement?'

'Of course I do.' He was clearly enjoying himself. 'Don't pull that face, if the star cop isn't here, take me before the judge and I'll tell him I killed that stupid cow.'

And that was precisely what he did. He confessed straight away, only to remind the magistrate impudently that without a body there was no crime, and that for the moment he had no intention of telling them where it was. One of the youngest magistrates on the circuit, Judge Markina's chiselled looks and stonewashed jeans occasionally fooled some felons into giving too much away, as had been the case with Quiralte. He gave the man one of those dazzling smiles that wrought havoc among the female clerks, before ordering his detention.

'So, no body, eh, Mr Quiralte? Well, then we'll just have to wait until it appears. I'm afraid you've been watching too many American movies. The fact of admitting that you know where the body is while refusing to divulge this information is reason enough to detain you indefinitely. Moreover you've confessed to a murder. A spell in jail might refresh your memory. I'll talk to you again when you have something to tell me. Until then . . .'

Amaia had walked home, trying to thrust the details of the

23

case from her mind, as an exercise in self-control but also to get herself in the mood for celebrating her final day at work with James. The baby was due in two weeks' time, and although she felt perfectly capable of working right up until the last moment, James had persuaded her to take some annual leave because his parents were due to arrive the following day. After dinner, she had fallen into bed, exhausted, and gone to sleep without realising it. All she remembered was that one minute she was talking to James and then, nothing.

She heard the woman first, before she saw her. She was shivering with cold; the sound of her teeth chattering bone against bone was so loud it caused Amaia to open her eyes. Lucía Aguirre was wearing the same red-and-white knitted sweater as in the photograph in her hallway, a gold crucifix round her neck, short fair hair, no doubt dyed to mask the grey. Nothing else about her appearance resembled the cheerful, self-possessed woman who was smiling at the camera. Lucía Aguirre wasn't weeping, wailing or sobbing, yet there was a deep, distressing pain in her blue eyes that gave her face an air of profound bewilderment, as if she understood nothing, as if she couldn't accept what was happening to her. She stood quietly, disoriented, rocked by a relentless wind that seemed to blow from every direction and made her sway rhythmically, adding to her air of helplessness. Her left arm was clasped about her waist, in a self-protective gesture that afforded her little comfort, and every now and then her eyes would cast about like searching probes, until they met Amaia's gaze. She opened her mouth, surprised, like a little girl on her birthday, before starting to speak. Amaia watched the woman's lips, blue with cold, but no sound emerged. She sat up in bed, concentrating as hard as she could, trying to understand what the woman was saying, but she was far away and the deafening wind carried off the muted sounds emerging from her lips, intoning over and over words that Amaia couldn't hear. She woke up in a daze, infected by the woman's anguish, and her own increasing sense of despair. This dream, this phantom-like apparition, had shattered her state of grace, the freedom from fear she had enjoyed since conceiving her daughter, a time of peace when all the nightmares, the *gauekos*, the ghosts had been exiled to another world.

Some years earlier, in New Orleans, sitting one evening with a cold beer in a bar on St Louis Street, a jovial agent from the FBI had asked her:

'So, tell me, Inspector Salazar, do murder victims appear at the foot of your bed during the night?'

Amaia's eyes had gaped in astonishment.

'Don't try to fool me, Salazar; I can tell a police officer who sees ghosts from one who doesn't.'

Amaia stared at him in silence, trying to decide whether he was joking or not, but the agent went on talking, an inscrutable smile playing on his lips.

'I know, because they've been doing the same to me for years.'

Amaia smiled, but Special Agent Aloisius Dupree looked her straight in the eye and she knew he was serious.

'You mean . . .'

'I mean, Inspector, waking up in the middle of the night and seeing the victim of the crime you are investigating standing beside your bed.' Dupree's smile had vanished.

She gazed at him uneasily.

'Don't let me down, Salazar. Are you going to tell me you don't see ghosts? I'd be disappointed.'

She was alarmed, but not enough to run the risk of looking like a fool.

'Agent Dupree, ghosts don't exist,' she said, raising her glass in a silent toast.

'Of course they don't, Inspector, but if I'm not mistaken – and I'm not – more than once you've awoken in the middle of the night having sensed the presence of one of those lost victims at the foot of your bed. Am I mistaken?'

Amaia took a sip of beer, determined not to tell him anything, but inviting him to go on.

'You shouldn't feel ashamed, Inspector . . . Would you prefer me to say that you "dream" about your victims?'

Amaia sighed. 'I'm afraid that sounds just as disturbing, dubious and deranged.'

'Aye, there's the rub, Inspector: labelling it as deranged.'

'Explain that to the FBI shrink or his equivalent in the Navarre police,' she retorted.

'Oh, come on, Salazar! Neither of us would be foolish enough to expose ourselves to the scrutiny of a shrink when we both know this is something he or she would be incapable of understanding. Most people would think that a cop who has nightmares about a case is at the very least stressed out or, at worst, if you push me, emotionally over-involved.'

He paused, draining the dregs of his glass then raised his arm to order another two beers. Amaia was about to protest, but the stifling New Orleans heat, the soft tones of a piano whose keys someone was stroking at the far end of the room, and an old timepiece stopped at ten o'clock which took pride of place above the bar, made her change her mind. Dupree waited until the barman had set down two fresh glasses in front of them.

'The first few times it scares the pants off you, to the point where you think you're starting to go crazy. But that's not true, Salazar. On the contrary, a good homicide detective doesn't possess a simple mind, or simple thought processes. We spend hours trying to figure out how a murderer's mind works, how he thinks, what he wants, how he feels. Next, we go to the morgue, where we view his work, hoping the body will tell us why, because once we know the killer's motive, we have a chance of catching him. But in the majority of cases the body isn't enough, because a dead body is just a broken shell. For too long perhaps, criminal investigations have been more focused on understanding the mind of the

26

criminal than that of the victim. For years, murder victims have been seen as little more than the end products of a sinister process, but at last victimology is coming into its own, showing that the choice of victim is never random, even when it's made to appear so, that too can provide clues. In dreaming about victims, we are accessing images projected by our subconscious, but that doesn't make them any less significant. It's simply another form of thought-processing. For a while those apparitions of victims by my bed tormented me. I used to wake up drenched in sweat, terrified and anxious. I'd feel that way for hours, while I tried to figure out to what extent I was losing my mind. I was a rookie agent back then, partnered with a veteran. Once, during a long, tedious stakeout, I woke up suddenly in the middle of one of those nightmares. "You look like you've seen a ghost," my partner said. I froze. "Maybe I did," I replied. "So, you see ghosts too?" he said. "Well, next time you should pay more attention to what they say instead of hollering and trying to resist." That was good advice. Over the years, I've learned that when I dream about a victim, part of my brain is projecting information which is already there, but which I haven't been able to see.'

Amaia nodded slowly. 'So, are they ghosts or projections inside the investigator's mind?'

'Projections, of course. Although . . .'

'Although what?'

Agent Dupree didn't reply. He raised his glass and drank.

She roused James, trying not to alarm him. He sat up in bed with a start, rubbing his eyes.

'Is it time to go to the hospital?'

Amaia bobbed her head, her face pallid as she gave a weak smile.

James pulled on the pair of jeans and jumper that he had laid out in readiness on the end of the bed.

'Call my aunt, will you? I promised I'd let her know.'

'Are my parents home yet?'

'Yes, but please don't tell them, James. It's two in the morning. I'm not going to give birth straight away. Besides, they probably won't be allowed in. I don't want them to have to sit for hours in the waiting room.'

'So, it's OK to tell your auntie, but not my parents?'

'James, you know perfectly well that Aunt Engrasi won't come here, she hasn't left the valley in years. I promised I'd tell her when the time came, that's all.'

Dr Villa was about fifty, with prematurely grey hair that she wore in a bob, which fell across her face whenever she leant forward. Recognising Amaia, she approached the side of her bed.

'Well, Amaia, we have some good news and some not-so-good news.'

Amaia waited for her to continue, reaching out for James, who clasped her hand between his.

'The good news is that you're now in labour, the baby is fine, the umbilical cord is not wrapped round her, her heartbeat is nice and strong even during the contractions. The not-so-good news is that, despite the length of time you've been having contractions, your labour isn't very advanced. There's some dilation, but the baby isn't properly positioned in the birth canal. What most concerns me though is that you look tired. Have you been sleeping well?'

'No, not too well these past few days.'

This was an understatement. Since the nightmares had returned, Amaia had been sleeping on and off for a few minutes before drifting into a semiconscious state from which she would awake exhausted and irritable.

'We're going to keep you in, Amaia, but I don't want you to lie down. I need you to walk – it will help the baby's head engage. When you feel a contraction coming, try to squat; that will ease your discomfort and help you dilate.'

28

She gave a subdued sigh.

'I know you're tired,' Dr Villa went on, 'but it won't be long now. This is when your daughter needs your help.'

Amaia nodded.

For the next two hours she made herself pace up and down the hospital corridor, which was empty at this hour of the morning. By her side, James seemed completely lost, distraught at how impotent he felt watching her suffer without being able to do anything.

For the first few minutes, he had kept asking if she was all right, whether he could help, or did she want him to bring her something, anything. She scarcely replied, intent upon keeping a degree of control over her body, which no longer felt like it belonged to her. This strong, healthy body that had always given her a secret feeling of pleasant self-assurance, was now no more than a mound of aching flesh. She almost laughed at the absurdity of her long-held belief that she had a high pain threshold.

In the end, James had given up and decided to remain silent. She was relieved. She had been making a superhuman effort not tell him to go to hell each time he asked her if it was hurting. Pain produced a visceral anger in her, which, coupled with her exhaustion and lack of sleep, was beginning to cloud her mind, until the only thought she could focus on was: I just want this to be over.

Dr Villa threw away her gloves, satisfied.

'Good work, Amaia, you need to dilate a little more, but the baby is in position, so it's all a matter of contractions and time.'

'How long?' she asked, anxiously.

'As a first-time mother, it could take minutes or hours, but you can lie down now – you'll be more comfortable. We'll monitor you and prepare you for labour.'

The moment Amaia lay down, sleep overwhelmed her like a heavy stone slab closing eyes she could no longer keep open.

'Amaia, Amaia, wake up.'

Opening her eyes, she saw her sister Rosaura aged ten, hair dishevelled, wearing a pink nightie.

'It's nearly morning, Amaia, go to bed. If *Ama* finds you here she'll scold us both.'

Clumsily drawing back the blankets, Amaia placed her small five-year-old feet on the cold floor. She managed to open her eyes enough to make out the pale shape of her own bed amid the shadows, the bed she didn't want to sleep in, because if she did, *she* would come in the night, to watch her with those cold black eyes, her mouth twisted in a grimace of loathing. Even without opening her eyes, Amaia could see her with absolute clarity, sensing the stifled hatred in her measured breath as she watched her feigning sleep, well aware that she was awake. Then, just when she felt herself weakening, when her muscles started to go stiff from the pent-up tension, when her tiny bladder threatened to empty its contents between her legs, eyes shut tight, she would become aware of her mother leaning slowly over her strained face, and a prayer, like an incantation, would echo in her head, over and over, preventing her even in those moments of darkest dread from falling into the temptation to disobey the command.

Don'topenyoureyesdon'topenyoureyesdon'topenyoureyesdon'topenyoureyesdon'topenyoureyes.

She wouldn't open them, yet even with them closed she could sense the slow advance, the precision of her mother's approach, the icy smile forming on her lips as she whispered:

'Sleep, little bitch. *Ama* won't eat you today.'

Amaia knew she wouldn't come near if she slept with her sisters. Which was why, every night, when her parents went to bed, she would plead with her sisters, promise to do anything for them if only they would let her sleep in their bed. Flora seldom indulged her, or only in exchange for her servitude the following day, whereas Rosaura would relent when she saw Amaia cry; crying was easy when you were scared out of your wits.

She groped her way across the darkened room, vaguely aware of the outline of the bed, which seemed to recede even as the ground softened beneath her feet, and the smell of floor polish changed into a different, more pungent, earthy odour of dank forest floor. She threaded her way through the trees, protected as if by ancient columns, as she heard nearby the babbling waters of the River Baztán flowing freely. Approaching its stony banks, she whispered: *the river*. And her voice became an echo that bounced off the age-old rock framing the river's path. *The river*, she whispered once again.

And then she saw the body. A young girl of about fifteen lay dead on the rounded pebbles of the riverbank. Eyes staring into infinity, hair spread in two perfect tresses on either side of her head, hands like claws in a parody of offering, palms turned upwards, showing the void.

'No,' cried Amaia.

And as she glanced about her, she saw not one but dozens of bodies ranged on either side of the river, like the macabre blossoms of some infernal spring.

'No,' she repeated, in a voice that was now a plea.

The hands of the corpses rose up as one, their fingers pointing at her belly.

A shudder brought her halfway back to consciousness for as long as the contraction lasted . . . then she was back beside the river.

The bodies were immobile again, but a strong breeze that seemed to be coming from the river itself tousled their locks, lifting them into the air like kite strings, while it whipped the limpid surface of the water into white, frothy swirls. Above the roaring wind, Amaia could hear the sobs of the little girl, who was her, mingling with others that seemed to come from the corpses. Drawing closer, she saw that this was true. The

31

girls were weeping profusely, their tears leaving silvery tracks on their cheeks that glinted in the moonlight.

The suffering of those souls tore at her little girl's heart.

'There's nothing I can do,' she cried helplessly.

The wind suddenly died down, and the riverbed was plunged into an impossible silence. Then came a watery, rhythmic, tap-tapping.

Splash, splash, splash . . .

Like slow rhythmic applause from the river. Splash, splash, splash.

Like when she would run through the puddles left by the rain. After the first sounds, more followed.

Splash, splash, splash, splash, splash . . .

And more. Splash, splash, splash . . . and yet more, until it was like a hailstorm, or as if the river water were boiling.

'There's nothing I can do,' she cried again, wild with fear.

'Cleanse the river,' shouted a voice.

'The river.'

'The river.'

'The river.' Other voices echoed.

She tried desperately to find the source of the voices clamouring from the waters.

The clouds parted over Baztán, and the silvery moonlight seeped through once more, illuminating the maidens who sat on the overhanging rocks, tapping their webbed feet on the water's surface, long tresses swaying, their furious incantation rising from red, full-lipped mouths filled with needle-sharp teeth.

'Cleanse the river.'

'Cleanse the river.'

'The river, the river, the river.'

'Amaia, Amaia, wake up!' The midwife's strident voice brought her back to reality. 'Come on, Amaia, the baby is here. Now it's your turn.'

But Amaia couldn't hear, for above the midwife's voice, the maidens' clamour still filled her ears.

'I can't,' she cried.

But it was no use; they didn't listen, only commanded.

'Cleanse the river, cleanse the valley, wash away the crime . . .' they cried, their voices merging with the cry issuing from her own throat as she felt the stabbing pain of another contraction.

'Amaia, I need you here,' said the midwife. 'When the next one comes, you have to push, and depending how hard you push you can do this in two or in ten contractions. It's up to you, two or ten.'

Amaia grasped the bars to heave herself up, while James stood behind, supporting her, silent and nervous, but reliable.

'Excellent,' the midwife said encouragingly. 'Are you ready?'

Amaia nodded.

'Right, here comes another,' she said, her eye on the monitor. 'Push, my dear.'

She pressed down as hard as she could, holding her breath as she felt something tear inside her.

'It's finished. Well done, Amaia, very good. Except that you need to breathe, for your sake and that of your baby. Next time, breathe – believe me, it'll be over much more quickly.'

Amaia agreed obediently, while James wiped the sweat from her face.

'Good, here comes another. Push, Amaia, let's finish this, help your baby, bring her out.'

Two or ten, two or ten, a voice inside her head repeated.

'Not ten,' she whispered.

Concentrating on her breathing, she kept pushing until she felt as if her soul were draining out of her, and an overwhelming sensation of emptiness seized her entire body.

Perhaps I'm bleeding to death, she thought. And she reflected that, if she were, she wouldn't care, because to bleed was peaceful and sweet. She had never bled like this, but Agent Dupree had nearly died from a bullet in the chest; he had told her that, although being shot was agonising, to bleed felt peaceful and sweet, like turning into oil and trickling away. And the more you bled, the less you cared.

Then she heard the wail. Strong and powerful, a genuine statement of intent.

'Oh my goodness, what a beautiful boy!' the nurse exclaimed.

'And he's blond, like you,' added the midwife.

Amaia turned to look at James, who was as bewildered as she was.

'A boy?' she said.

The nurse's voice reached them from the side of the room.

'Yes, indeed, a boy who weighs 3.2 kilos and is pretty as a picture.'

'But . . . they told us it was a girl,' stammered Amaia.

'Well, they were wrong. It happens occasionally, but usually the other way round, girls who look like boys because of where the umbilical cord is.'

'Are you sure?' insisted James, who was still supporting Amaia from behind.

Amaia felt the warmth of the tiny body the nurse had just placed on top of her, wrapped in a towel and wriggling vigorously.

'A boy, no doubt about it,' said the nurse, raising the towel to reveal the baby's naked body.

Amaia was in shock.

Her son's little face twisted in exaggerated grimaces; he was squirming as though searching for something. Raising a tiny fist to his mouth, he sucked at it hard, then half-opened his eyes and stared.

'Oh my God, James, it's a boy,' she managed to say.

Her husband reached out and stroked the infant's soft cheek with his fingers.

'He's beautiful, Amaia . . .' he said with a catch in his voice, as he leaned over to kiss her. The tears ran down his face and his lips tasted salty.

'Well done, my darling.'

'Well done to you, too, *Aita*,' she said, gazing at the baby, who appeared fascinated by the overhead lights, eyes wide open.

'You really had no idea it was a boy?' the midwife asked, surprised. 'I was sure you did, because you kept repeating his name during the birth. Ibai, Ibai. Is that what you're going to call him?'

'Ibai . . . the river,' whispered Amaia.

She gazed at James, who was beaming, then at her son.

'Yes, yes!' she declared. 'Ibai, that's his name.' And then she burst out laughing.

James looked at her, grinning at her contentment.

'Why are you laughing?'

She was giggling uncontrollably and couldn't stop.

'I'm . . . I'm imagining your mother's face when she finds out she has to take everything back.'

2

Three months later

Amaia thought she recognised the song that reached her, scarcely a whisper, from the living room. She had just finished clearing away the lunch things, and, drying her hands on a kitchen towel, she walked over to the door, the better to hear the lullaby her aunt was singing to Ibai in a soft, soothing voice. Yes, it was the same one. Although she hadn't heard it for years, she recognised the song her *Amatxi* Juanita used to sing to her when she was little. The memory brought back her adored and much-lamented Juanita, wrapped in her widow's weeds, hair swept up in a bun, fastened with silver combs that could barely contain her unruly white curls; her grandmother, the only woman who had cradled her as an infant:

> *Txitxo politori*
> *zu nere laztana,*
> *katiatu ninduzun,*
> *libria nintzana.*
>
> *Libriak libre dira,*
> *zu ta ni katig,*

librerik oba dana,
biok dakigu.[1]

Sitting in the armchair near the blazing fire, Engrasi held the tiny Ibai in her arms, eyes fixed on his little face as she recited the old verses of that mournful lullaby. She was smiling, although Amaia distinctly remembered her grandmother weeping as she sang it to her. She wondered why, reflecting that perhaps Juanita already understood the suffering in her granddaughter's soul, and shared her fears.

Nire laztana laztango
Kalian negarrez dago,
Aren negarra gozoago da
Askoren barrea baiño.[2]

When the song finished, Juanita would dry her tears with the spotless handkerchief embroidered with her initials and those of her husband, the grandfather Amaia had never known, gazing down at her from the faded portrait that presided over the dining room.

'Why are you crying, *Amatxi*? Does the song make you sad?'

'Take no notice, my love, your *amatxi* is a silly old woman.'

And yet she sighed, clasping the girl still more tightly in her arms, holding her a little longer, although Amaia was happy to stay.

She stood listening to the end of the lullaby, relishing the pleasure of recalling the words just before her aunt sang them. In the air lingered an aroma of stew, burning logs and the

---

[1] Beautiful baby girl / You are my love, / I who was free, / Am bound by you. // Those who are free are free, / You and I are captives, / Although we both know, / That it's better to be free.

[2] My love, my little love / You are weeping in the street, / Your tears are sweeter / Than the laughter of many.

wax on Engrasi's furniture. James had fallen asleep on the sofa, and although the room wasn't cold, Amaia went over, covering him as best she could with a small, red rug. He opened his eyes for an instant, blew her a kiss and carried on dozing. Amaia pulled up a chair next to her aunt and sat contemplating her: the old lady had stopped singing, yet she continued to gaze in awe at the face of the sleeping child. Engrasi looked at her niece, smiling as she held the child out for her to take. Amaia kissed him gently on the head before putting him in his cot.

'Is James asleep?' Engrasi asked.

'Yes, we hardly slept a wink. Ibai sometimes has cholic after a feed, especially at night, so James was up in the small hours, pacing round the house with him.'

Engrasi turned to look at James. 'He's a good father,' she said.

'The best.'

'What about you, aren't you tired?'

'No, you know me. I'm fine with a few hours' sleep.'

Engrasi seemed to reflect, her face clouding for an instant, but then she smiled once more and gestured towards the cot.

'He's beautiful, Amaia, the most beautiful baby I've ever seen, and I'm not just saying that because he's ours; there's something special about Ibai.'

'You can say that again!' declared Amaia. 'The baby boy who was supposed to be a girl but changed his mind at the last minute.'

Engrasi pulled a serious face. 'That's exactly what I think happened.'

Amaia looked puzzled.

'I did a reading when you first became pregnant – just to make sure everything was all right – and it was obvious then that the baby was a girl. Over the following months, I consulted the cards several times, but never looked into the question of the baby's sex again because it was something I

38

already knew. Towards the end, when you were acting strangely, saying you felt unable to choose a name for the baby or to buy her clothes, I came up with a plausible psychological explanation,' she said with a smile, 'but I also consulted the cards. I must confess that, for a while, I feared the worst; that this uncertainty you felt, this paralysis, was a sign that your child would never be born. Mothers sometimes have premonitions like that, and they always reflect something real. But on that occasion, no matter how many times I consulted the cards about the baby's sex, they wouldn't tell me – and you know what I always say about the things the cards won't tell us: if the cards won't tell, then we're not meant to know. Some things will never be revealed to us, because their nature is to remain mysterious; other things will be revealed when the time is right. When James called me early that morning, the cards couldn't have been clearer. A boy.'

'Are you saying you think I was going to have a girl but in the last month she turned into a boy? That's physically impossible.'

'Yes, I think you were going to have a daughter, I think you probably will have her one day, but I also believe this wasn't the right time for her, that someone left the decision until the last moment and then decided you'd have Ibai.'

'And who do you think took that decision?'

'Perhaps the same one who gave him to you.'

Amaia stood up, exasperated.

'I'm going to make some coffee. Do you want a cup?'

Aunt Engrasi ignored the question. 'You're wrong to deny it was a miracle.'

'I'm not denying it, Auntie,' she protested, 'it's just that . . .'

'Don't believe in them, don't deny their existence,' said Engrasi, invoking the old incantation against witches that had been popular as recently as a century earlier.

'Least of all me,' whispered Amaia, recalling those amber eyes, the fleeting, high-pitched whistle that had guided her through the forest in the middle of the night as she struggled with the feeling of being in a dream while at the same time experiencing something real.

She remained silent until her aunt spoke again.

'When are you going back to work?'

'Next Monday.'

'How do you feel about it?'

'Well, Auntie, you know I like my job, but I have to admit that going back has never felt this hard, not after the holidays, or after our honeymoon. Everything's different now, now there's Ibai,' she said, glancing at his cot. 'It feels too soon to be leaving him.'

Engrasi nodded, smiling.

'Did you know that in the past in Baztán women had to stay at home for a month after they gave birth? That was the period the Church deemed sufficient to ensure the baby's health and survival. Only then was the mother allowed out to take the baby to the church to be baptised. But every law has its loophole. The women of Baztán were known for getting things done. A month was a long time, considering most of them were obliged to work, they had other children, livestock and crops to tend, cows to milk. So whenever they had to leave the house, they would send their husbands up to the roof to fetch a tile. Then they tied it tightly on their head with a scarf. That way the women were able to carry out their chores, while continuing to observe the custom, because as you know, in Baztán your roof is your home.'

Amaia grinned. 'I can't quite see myself with a tile on my head, but I'd happily wear one if that meant I could take my house with me.'

'How did your mother-in-law react when you told her about Ibai?'

'Much as you'd imagine: she began by railing against the doctors and their prenatal screening methods, insisting such things never happen in the States. She was fine with the baby, although clearly a little disappointed, probably because she wasn't able to smother him in ribbons and lace. Overnight she lost all desire to go shopping, changed the nursery from pink to white, and swapped the baby outfits for vouchers, which will enable me to clothe Ibai until he's four.'

'What a woman!' chuckled Engrasi.

'Thomas, on the other hand, was thrilled with Ibai. He cradled him in his arms all day, covered him in kisses and took countless photos of him. He's even opened a college trust fund for him! Clarice grew bored once she stopped shopping. She began to talk about going home, about her many commitments there – she's president of a couple of clubs for society ladies, how she missed playing golf, and she started to pester us about getting Ibai baptised. James stood up to her, because he always wanted our baby to be baptised at the San Fermín Chapel, but you know how long the waiting list is – a year, at least. So, Clarice showed up at the chapel, spoke to the chaplain, made a generous donation, and managed to get a date next week,' Amaia said, laughing.

'Money talks,' said Engrasi.

'It's a shame you won't be coming, Auntie.'

Engrasi clicked her tongue. 'You know, Amaia . . .'

'I know, you never leave the valley.'

'I'm happy here,' said Engrasi, her words embracing a whole philosophy of life.

'We're all happy here,' said Amaia, dreamily. 'When I was small, I only ever felt relaxed in this house,' she added all of a sudden. Amaia was gazing into the fire, mesmerised, her voice, at once soft and shrill, was that of a little girl.

'I scarcely slept at home – because I had to keep watch, and when I could no longer stay awake, when sleep came, it was never deep or restful, it was the sleep of those condemned to death, waiting for their executioner's face to loom over them because their time has come.'

'Amaia . . .' Engrasi said softly.

'If you stay awake she won't get you, you can cry out, wake the others and she won't be able to—'

'Amaia . . .'

She turned away from the fire, looked at her aunt and smiled.

'This house has always been a refuge for everyone, hasn't it? Including Ros. She hasn't been back to her own place since what happened to Freddy.'

'No, she goes round there regularly, but sleeps here.'

They heard a soft knock at the door. Ros appeared in the entrance, pulling off her colourful woollen hat.

'*Kaixo*,' she said. 'It's freezing outside! How *cosy* you are in here,' she added, peeling off several layers of clothing.

Amaia studied her sister; she knew her well enough to notice how thin she was, that despite her luminous smile her face had lost its glow. Poor Ros, her anxieties and the sadness she carried around inside had become such a constant part of her life that Amaia could scarcely recall the last time she saw her sister truly happy, despite the success she had made of managing the bakery. Yes, there had been the problems of the past few months, her separation from Freddy, Víctor's death . . . But more than anything, the sadness was part of her character. She was one of those people for whom life is more painful, who make you think they might take the easy way out if things get too difficult.

'Sit here, I'm going to make coffee.' Amaia rose to offer Ros her chair. As she clasped her sister's hand, she saw that her nails were flecked with white. 'Have you been painting?'

'Just a few bits and bobs in the bakery.'

Amaia hugged Ros, feeling her thinness even more starkly.

'Sit down by the fire, you're freezing,' she urged.

'I will, but first I want to see the little prince.'

'Don't wake him up,' whispered Amaia, coming over.

Ros gazed at Ibai, frowning.

'I can't believe it! Doesn't this child do anything other than

42

sleep? When is he going to wake up so that his auntie can give him a cuddle?'

'Try coming to my place between eleven p.m. and five a.m. and you'll see that, not only is he wide awake but nature has blessed him with a fine pair of lungs, and a cry that threatens to burst your eardrums. You're welcome to come round and cuddle him anytime.'

'I might take you up on that – or are you trying to scare me off?'

'You'd last one night, then you'd hand him straight back to me.'

'Woman of little faith,' said Ros, pretending to take umbrage. 'If you lived here, I'd show you.'

'Right, go and buy some earplugs; you're on duty tonight – we're sleeping over.'

'What a shame,' said Ros, feigning disappointment. 'It just so happens I have other plans.'

They all laughed.

3

Winter 1979

He reached out his hand, seeking his wife's warm presence, but found only an empty space where the heat from her body had long since evaporated.

Alarmed, he sat up, slid his legs out of bed and listened intently for any tell-tale sounds that his wife was in the house.

Barefoot, he searched every room. He entered the bedroom where the two girls lay asleep in twin beds, the kitchen, the bathroom. He even checked the balcony to make sure she hadn't collapsed after she got up, and was lying on the floor unable to cry for help. Part of him wished this were true, rather than knowing that she had waited until he was asleep to steal out of the house, to go . . . He had no idea where or with whom, only that she would return before dawn, that the cold which had seeped into her flesh would take a while to ease, lingering between them, an invisible, insurmountable barrier, as she fell into a deep sleep while he lay there motionless. He went back to the bedroom, stroked the soft pillowcase, instinctively leaning over to breathe in the scent of his wife's hair. A guttural cry of despair rose from his throat as he struggled once more to understand what had happened

44

to them. 'Rosario,' he whispered, 'Rosario.' His proud wife, the young woman from San Sebastián who had come to Elizondo on holiday, with whom he had fallen in love the moment he saw her, the woman who had given him two daughters, and was carrying a third in her belly, the woman who had worked alongside him every day, devoting herself to the bakery, who undoubtedly had a better head for commerce than he, who had helped him raise the business beyond his wildest dreams. The elegant woman who never left the house without looking immaculate; a wonderful wife and a loving mother towards Flora and Rosaura, so distinguished and sophisticated that other women looked like housemaids in comparison. Standoffish towards their neighbours, she oozed charm in the bakery, but avoided contact with other mothers. Apart from him, her only friend was Elena. And then a few months ago the two women had stopped speaking to each other. When he bumped into Elena in the street one day and asked her why, all she could say was: 'Rosario is no longer my friend, I've lost her.' This made all the more puzzling her nocturnal escapades, the long walks she insisted on taking alone, her absences at all hours of the day or night, her silences. Where did she go? At first when he had questioned her, her replies were evasive: 'Out walking, thinking.' Once, half in jest, he had said: 'Can't you think here with me, or at least let me go with you?'

She had shot him a strange, angry glance, then replied with alarming coldness:

'That's completely out of the question.'

Juan considered himself a simple man; he realised that he was lucky to be married to a woman like Rosario, that he knew little about the female psyche, and so, filled with misgivings and guilt for what he saw as an act of betrayal, he sought advice from their local doctor. After all, the doctor was the only other person in Elizondo who knew Rosario relatively well. He had looked after her during her two previous pregnancies and attended the births. That was all, though: Rosario was a strong woman who rarely complained.

'She sneaks out at night, lies to you about going to the bakery, is uncommunicative and wants to be left alone. What you're describing sounds to me like depression. Sadly, here in the valley, that kind of affliction is commonplace. Rosario is from the coast, from the seaside, where the light is different even when it rains. The greyness here eventually takes its toll, we've had a lot of rain this year, and the suicide rate has reached alarming levels. I suspect that Rosario is slightly depressed. The fact that she showed no symptoms during her previous pregnancies means nothing. Rosario is a very demanding woman, but she makes great demands on herself too; I'm sure she's a wonderful wife and mother, she looks after both the house and the bakery, is always impeccably turned out, but this pregnancy is more difficult for her because she's no longer young. Hardy women like her see motherhood as another chore, another self-imposed responsibility. So, although she wants this baby, it has created a conflict between her need to be perfect in everything she does, and her fear of falling short. If I'm not mistaken, this will only get worse after the birth. You must be patient with her, shower her with affection and try to ease her burden. Take the older girls off her hands, hire an extra hand at the bakery, or find a home help.'

Rosario refused even to discuss the matter.

'That's all I need, one of those village gossips snooping around my house so she can tell people what I have and don't have. What's this all about? Have I been neglecting the house or the girls? Have I stopped going to the bakery every morning?'

He had felt overwhelmed, scarcely able to reply.

'Of course not, Rosario, I'm not saying that, I just thought that while you are pregnant, you could do with some help.'

'I'm more than capable of running my house without any

46

help, so stop interfering unless you want me to go back to San Sebastián. I refuse to discuss the matter again, you've insulted me simply by mentioning it.'

She had sulked for days, barely speaking to him, until gradually things returned to normal; she would slip out virtually every night while he lay awake until she came back cold and silent, vowing he would speak to her in the morning, even though he knew full well he would put it off to avoid confronting her.

Deep down, he felt like a coward. A fearful child before a mother superior. And realising that what he feared most was her reaction made him feel still worse. Each time he heard her key in the latch, he would heave a sigh of relief, postponing once more the discussion that would never take place.

4

The desecration of a church wasn't the sort of incident that usually got her out of bed in the early hours to drive fifty kilometres north, but the urgency in Inspector Iriarte's voice had left her no choice.

'Inspector Salazar, forgive me for waking you, but I think you need to see this.'

'Is it a body?'

'Not exactly. Someone has desecrated a church, but . . . well, I think you should come and see for yourself.'

'In Elizondo?'

'No, a few kilometres away, in Arizkun.'

She hung up and checked the time. One minute past four. She waited, holding her breath for a few seconds until she heard the slight movement, the imperceptible rustle, followed by a sweet, tiny sigh that announced her son was waking up, punctually, for his next feed. She switched on the bedside lamp, draped with a scarf to diffuse the light, and leant over the cot. She picked up the warm bundle in her arms and inhaled the soft smell of his scalp. Placing him on her breast, she gave a start as she felt the force of his suction. She smiled at James, who was propped up on his elbow, watching her.

'Work?' he asked.

'Yes, I have to go, but I'll be back before his next feed.'

'Don't worry, Amaia, he'll be fine. If for any reason you're late, I'll make up a bottle.'

'I'll be back in time,' she said, stroking her son's head and planting a kiss on the soft spot on his crown.

In the early hours of that winter morning, lights were shining inside the church of San Juan Bautista in Arizkun, contrasting sharply with the gloomy bell tower that stood narrow and erect, like a silent sentinel. Several uniformed police officers were busy examining the lock on the door to the south entrance to the chapel with their torches.

Amaia parked in the street and woke up Deputy Inspector Etxaide, who was dozing on the passenger seat beside her. Locking the car, she walked around it, stepping over the low wall that surrounded the churchyard.

She greeted a few of the officers and entered the chapel. She stretched her hand towards the font but pulled up short when she became aware of a smell of burning in the air that reminded her of freshly ironed clothes and singed fabric. She recognised Inspector Iriarte, who was speaking with two priests, who stood aghast, hands clasped to their mouths, eyes fixed on the altar. Amaia held back, observing the commotion caused by the arrival of the pathologist, Dr San Martín, and the legal secretary, as she wondered what they were doing there.

Iriarte hurried across to them.

'Thank you for coming, Inspector Salazar; hello, Jonan,' he said. 'It seems that several desecrations have taken place in the chapel in the past few weeks. First of all, someone broke into the church in the middle of the night and smashed up the baptismal font. A week later they took an axe to one of the front pews. And now this,' he said, pointing towards the altar, which showed signs of an arson attempt. 'Someone set fire to the altar cloths, only luckily they're made of linen and burn slowly. Since all this started, the chaplain, who lives nearby, has been keeping an eye on the church. He noticed a light inside and called the emergency services. By the time the patrol cars arrived the fire had gone out, and the culprit or culprits had scarpered.'

Amaia looked at him expectantly. She pursed her lips, puzzled.

'Right, so, an act of vandalism, desecration or whatever you want to call it – I don't see how we can help.'

Iriarte raised his eyebrows theatrically.

'Come and see for yourselves.'

They approached the altar, where the inspector crouched down and lifted a sheet to reveal what looked like a stem of dry, yellow bamboo cane, charred at one end where it had been set alight.

Bewildered, Amaia glanced at San Martín, who leant over to inspect it more closely.

'Good Lord!' he said with surprise.

'What is it?' asked Amaia.

'A *mairu-beso*,' he whispered.

'A what?'

San Martín drew back the sheet, revealing another piece of broken cane and the tiny bones of a hand.

'Good God, it's a child's arm,' said Amaia.

'A child's arm bones, to be precise,' San Martín corrected her. 'Probably less than a year old; the bones are tiny.'

'I'll be . . .'

'A *mairu*, Inspector Salazar, a *mairu-beso* is a baby's arm bone.'

Amaia looked at Jonan, seeking confirmation of what the doctor had said. She saw that his face had turned visibly white as he contemplated the charred little bones.

'Etxaide?'

'Yes,' he said in a hushed voice, 'it's a *mairu-beso*. For it

50

to be genuine, it has to come from a child that died before being baptised. In the olden days, it was believed they had magical powers that protected people when used as torches; the smoke they gave off could put to sleep the inhabitants of a house or an entire village, while the bearers carried out their "sorcery".'

'So, what we have here is not only the desecration of a church but of a grave as well,' declared Iriarte.

'In the best-case scenario,' whispered Jonan Etxaide.

It didn't escape Amaia, the way Iriarte drew Jonan aside, their uneasy conversation coupled with furtive glances towards the altar. In the meantime she went on listening to Deputy Inspector Zabalza's observations:

'As with suicides, desecrations carried out on human remains aren't usually made public, due to their social consequences and because of the possible copycat effect, but they occur more often than is reported in the media. Since the arrival of immigrants from Haiti, the Dominican Republic and Cuba, as well as parts of Africa, religious practices that originated in those countries have gained acceptance among Europeans. *Santería*, for example, has become more popular in recent years; in some of its rituals, human bones are used to summon the spirits of the dead – as a result, desecrations of tombs and niches have increased significantly. A year ago, during a routine drugs search, a car was intercepted on its way to Paris containing fifteen human skulls stolen from various cemeteries along the Costa del Sol. Apparently, they fetch a good price on the black market.'

'So, these bones could have come from anywhere,' ventured San Martín.

'No, not from anywhere,' Jonan said, rejoining the group. 'I'm convinced they were stolen here in Arizkun, or in one of the surrounding villages. It's true that human bones are used in many religious rituals, but *mairu-beso* are limited to the Spanish and French Basque Country, and Navarre. As soon as Dr San Martín has dated the bones, we'll know where to look.'

He turned round and walked towards the far end of the nave, while Amaia gazed after him bemused. She had known Jonan Etxaide for three years, and in the last two her respect and admiration for him had grown in leaps and bounds. Jonan had joined the police force after finishing his studies – he held a twin degree in anthropology and archaeology – and although he wasn't a typical cop, Amaia appreciated his somewhat romantic viewpoint and his discreet, non-confrontational approach. She was all the more surprised, therefore, by his somewhat stubborn insistence about where to steer the case. Concealing her unease, she said goodbye to the pathologist, still puzzling over the way Iriarte had nodded while Jonan spoke, the two of them casting anxious glances at the walls of the chapel.

She could hear Ibai as soon as she turned the key in the lock. Leaning back against the door to close it, she hurried upstairs, slipping off her coat. Guided by his urgent cries, she burst into the bedroom to find her son screaming his lungs out in his cot. She glanced around, a knot of anger clenching her stomach.

'James,' she yelled, as she lifted the baby out of the cot. He walked in carrying a feeding bottle.

'How could you leave him to cry like that? He was desperate. What on earth were you doing?'

James stopped in his tracks, holding up the bottle.

'He's fine, Amaia. He's crying because he's hungry, which is what I was trying to deal with. It's time for his feed, you know how punctual he is. I waited a few minutes, but when you didn't arrive, he started getting louder . . .'

Amaia bit her tongue. She knew James' words weren't meant as a reproach, but they felt like a slap in the face. She turned away, sat down on the rocking chair and lifted the baby to her.

'Throw that muck away,' she ordered.

She heard him sigh good-naturedly as he walked out.

Grilles, railings, and French windows: the flat, three-storey façade of the Archbishop's palace, whose weather-worn oak door gave on to Plaza Santa María. Inside, a priest dressed in a smart suit and clerical collar introduced himself as the Archbishop's secretary, then led them up a wide staircase to the first floor. After ushering them into a room, he asked them to wait while he announced their arrival, then disappeared noiselessly behind a hanging tapestry. Within seconds he was back.

'This way, please.'

The Archbishop received them in a magnificent room, which Jonan estimated must have spanned the entire length of the first floor. Four windows, which opened on to balconies with close-set railings, were closed against the bitter morning cold of Pamplona. The Archbishop greeted them standing beside his desk, proffering a firm handshake as the police commissioner made the introductions.

'Monsignor Landero, this is Inspector Salazar who heads the murder squad at the Navarre regional police, and Deputy Inspector Etxaide. I believe you've already met Father Lokin, the parish priest at Arizkun.'

Amaia noticed a middle-aged man standing gazing out of the nearest balcony window. He wore a dark suit that made the secretary's look shoddy in comparison.

'Allow me to introduce Father Sarasola. He is attending this meeting in an advisory capacity.'

Sarasola walked over, shook hands with them while staring straight at Amaia.

'I've heard a great deal about you, Inspector.'

Amaia didn't reply, but bobbed her head by way of greeting, before taking a seat. Sarasola returned to the window where he stood with his back to the room.

Monsignor Landero was one of those people who can't keep their hands still while they speak. Picking up a pen, he began to twirl it in his pale, slender fingers, until all eyes were focused on him. However, to everyone's astonishment, Father Sarasola spoke first.

'I'm grateful for your interest in this case, which both involves and concerns us,' he said, turning to face the company, without moving from the window. 'I'm aware that you went to Arizkun yesterday when the, shall we say "attack", took place, so I assume you've been informed about the spate of previous incidents. All the same, permit me to run through them once more with you. Two weeks ago, in the dead of night, exactly like yesterday, somebody broke into the chapel through the sacristy door. It's an ordinary door with a simple lock and no alarm, so it didn't present much of a problem. However, instead of behaving like common thieves, pilfering money from the donation box, the intruders with a single blow, split in two the baptismal font: a work of art over four centuries old. Last Sunday night, they broke in again, took an axe to one of the pews, reducing it to a pile of fragments the size of my hand. And yesterday they desecrated the temple a third time, setting fire to the altar, and placing beneath it that atrocious offering.'

Amaia noticed the parish priest fidgeting anxiously in his seat, while Deputy Inspector Etxaide wore the same frown she had seen the morning before.

'We live in turbulent times,' Sarasola went on, 'and of course, more often than we would like, churches suffer acts of desecration, most of which go unreported to avoid any copycat crime. Although the way some of them are staged is quite spectacular, few possess such a dangerous element as in this latest case.'

Amaia listened carefully, suppressing the urge to interrupt. Try as she might, she couldn't understand what importance all this had, beyond the destruction of a four-hundred-year-old liturgical object. And yet she was curious to see what direction this unusual meeting would take; the attendance of the city's highest police and Church authorities was an indication of how seriously they viewed these incidents. And this priest, Father Sarasola, was seemingly in control, despite the presence of the Archbishop, to whom he scarcely paid any attention.

'We believe that these acts demonstrate a hatred towards the Church based on a misinterpretation of historical concepts. The fact that the most recent attack entailed the use of human remains leaves us in no doubt as to the complexity of the case. Needless to say, we count on your discretion; in our experience, nothing good ever comes of giving publicity to such matters. Not to mention the concern this would arouse among the parishioners of San Juan Bautista, who are shrewd enough to understand the significance of these attacks and liable to be very disturbed by this sort of thing.'

The Commissioner took the floor:

'You have my assurance that we shall proceed with the utmost care and discretion. Inspector Salazar's abilities as a detective and her knowledge of the area make her the best person to lead this investigation; she will look into the case with her team.'

Amaia glanced uneasily at her boss, barely managing to stifle a protest.

'I'm sure you will,' Father Sarasola replied, turning to Amaia. 'I've heard excellent things about you. I know you were born in the valley and that you're the right person to investigate this case. I trust you will proceed with sensitivity and care while resolving this delicate matter.'

Amaia didn't reply, but took the opportunity to examine more closely this Armani-suited priest, who impressed her less by what he knew about her than by the influence he seemed to wield over the company, including the Archbishop, who had agreed with all Father Sarasola's statements, without the priest having turned to him once to seek his approval.

55

As soon as they stepped through the door into Plaza Santa María, Amaia addressed her superior.

'Commissioner, I think—'

'I'm sorry, Salazar,' he interrupted. 'I know what you're going to say, but my hands are tied. Father Sarasola holds a senior position at the Vatican. So get to the bottom of this as quickly as possible and move on.'

'I understand that, sir, but I have no idea where to start or what to expect. I simply don't think this case is right for my team.'

'You heard what he said, they want you.'

He climbed into his car, leaving her with a frown on her face, gazing at Jonan, who was chuckling.

'Can you believe it?' she exclaimed. 'Inspector Salazar's skills as a detective and her knowledge of the area make her the best person to investigate this case of vandalism *vulgaris*. Can someone explain to me what went on in there?'

Jonan was still chuckling as they walked over to the patrol car.

'It's not that simple, chief. What's more, this VIP from the Vatican specifically asked for you. Father Sarasola, also known as Dr Sarasola, is attaché to the Vatican in defence of the faith.'

'You mean he's an inquisitor.'

'I don't think they like to be called that nowadays. Shall I drive or will you?'

'I'll drive. I want you to tell me more about this Dr Sarasola. Doctor of what, exactly?'

'Psychiatry, I think; possibly other things. I know he's a prelate of Opus Dei with a lot of influence in Rome, where he worked for many years with Pope John Paul II, as well as being advisor to his predecessor when he was still a cardinal.'

'Why would an attaché to the Vatican in defence of the faith take such an interest in a local affair like this? And how did he hear about me?'

'As I said before, he's an important member of Opus Dei, so he receives regular reports about everything that goes on in Navarre. As for his interest in the case, perhaps that can be explained, like he said, by the concern that there's an element of hatred or vengeance towards the Church due to, how did he put it, the misinterpretation of a historical concept.'

'A concept you appear to agree with . . .'

Jonan looked at her, taken aback.

'I noticed the way you and Inspector Iriarte responded to this yesterday morning. You seemed more worried than the parish priest and the chaplain.'

'That's because Iriarte's mother is from Arizkun, as is my grandmother, and anyone who comes from there takes what happened in the church very seriously . . .'

'Yes, I heard what Sarasola said about parishioners understanding the significance and being disturbed, but what did he mean?'

'You're from the valley, you must have heard of the *agotes*.'

'The *agotes*? You mean the people who lived in Bozate?'

'They lived all over the Baztán Valley and in Roncal, but mostly they were concentrated in a ghetto in Arizkun, which is now part of the Bozate neighbourhood. What else do you know about them?'

'Not much, to be honest. They were artisans and they were never really assimilated.'

'Pull over,' Jonan ordered.

Amaia looked at him in surprise, but said nothing. She found a space by the roadside, stopped the car and turned round in her seat to study Deputy Inspector Etxaide, who gave a loud sigh before beginning:

'Historians disagree about where the *agotes* came from originally. They were thought to have crossed the Pyrenees into Navarre during the Middle Ages, fleeing war, famine, plague and religious persecution. The most widely accepted theory is that they were Cathars, members of a religious sect

57

persecuted by the Inquisition. Another theory suggests they were deserters from the Visigoth armies who sought refuge in the leprosy colonies of southern France and became infected with the disease themselves – one of the reasons why they were so feared. A third explanation is that they were bandits and social outcasts, forced into serfdom by the feudal lord of the area, who at that time was Pedro de Ursua. The remains of one of his fortresses still exist to this day in Arizkun. And that would explain why most of the *agotes* lived in Bozate.'

'Yes, that's more or less what I thought: a group of social outcasts, lepers or fleeing Cathars who settled in the valley in medieval times. But what does this have to do with the desecration of the church in Arizkun?'

'A great deal. The *agotes* lived in Bozate for centuries and were never allowed to integrate into society. Treated as second-class citizens, they were prohibited from settling outside Bozate, running businesses or marrying outside their group. As artisans they worked with wood and hides, because those trades were seen as dirty and dangerous. They were obliged to wear identifying markings sewn into their clothes, even to ring a bell, like lepers, to warn passers-by of their presence. And, in common with many periods throughout history, the Church, far from encouraging their integration, did the exact opposite. We know they were Christians and observed and respected Catholic rites, yet the Church treated them like pariahs. They had a separate baptismal font, and the holy water they used was thrown away. They were forbidden from approaching the altar, often forced to remain at the back of the nave and to enter the church through a different, smaller door. In Arizkun, they were kept apart from the other parishioners by a grille, which was later removed in recognition of the deep shame the recollection of this treatment arouses in the people of Arizkun even to this day.'

'Let's see if I've got this right. You're telling me that the exclusion of a racial group in the Middle Ages is the historical misunderstanding Father Sarasola referred to in his attempt to explain the current desecration of the church in Arizkun?'

'Yes.' Jonan nodded.

'The same exclusion suffered by Jews, Moors, Gypsies, women, witch doctors, the poor, etc. If as you say, on top of everything else, they were suspected of spreading leprosy, then it's hardly surprising they were excluded. The mere mention of that dread disease must have been enough to strike terror into the hearts of the entire population. I know that dozens of women in the Baztán Valley were accused of witchcraft and burnt at the stake, many of them denounced by their neighbours – and those were women who'd been born and bred in the valley. Anything that deviated from the norm was thought to be the work of the devil, for which count-less minorities and ethnic groups throughout Europe suffered as a consequence. No country's history is free of such episodes. I'm no historian, Jonan, but I know that during the Middle Ages the whole of Europe reeked of human flesh, burnt at the stake.'

'That's right, but the *agotes* were excluded for centuries. Generation after generation were deprived of the most basic rights; in fact, they suffered such ill treatment for so long that a papal decree was issued in Rome granting them equal rights and demanding the cessation of all discrimination. But the evil had already been done; tradition and belief are stubbornly resistant to logic and reason, thus the *agotes* continued to be subjected to discrimination for many years.'

'Yes, things take a long time to change in the Baztán Valley. It feels like a privilege to live there now, but life must have been tough back then. Even so . . .'

'Chief, the desecrated objects are clear references to the exclusion of the *agotes*: the baptismal font they couldn't be baptised in; a pew at the front of the church, reserved for nobles and off limits to the *agotes*. The cloth on the altar they were forbidden to approach—'

'What about the bones? The *mairu-beso*?'

'That's an old piece of witchcraft, also associated with the *agotes*.'

'Yes, of course, witchcraft . . . In any case, it sounds far-fetched to me. I won't deny that this matter of the bones sets the latest incident apart, but the previous acts were sheer vandalism. You'll see, in a few days' time, we'll arrest a couple of stoned teenagers who broke into the church as a prank, and things got out of hand. What intrigues me is that even the Archbishop is taking an interest in this.'

'That's the point. If anyone can and should recognise a crime with a historical motive, it's the Church. You saw the look on the parish priest's face: he was beside himself.'

Amaia sighed, irritably.

'You could be right, but you know how much I hate all this stuff about the valley's dark past. There always seems to be somebody eager to exploit it,' she said, glancing at her watch.

'We've got plenty of time,' Jonan reassured her.

'Not really – I have to stop off at my place first, Ibai needs his feed,' she said with a smile.

5

Amaia spotted Lieutenant Padua as soon as she entered Bar Iruña in Plaza del Castillo, a stone's throw from her house. He was the only man sitting alone, and although he had his back turned, she recognised the tell-tale dampness of his raincoat.

'Raining in Baztán, is it, Lieutenant?' she said by way of greeting.

'As always, Inspector, as always.'

Taking a seat opposite him, she ordered a decaf and a small bottle of water. She waited for the barman to put her drinks down on the table.

'So, tell me what you wanted to talk to me about.'

'About the Johana Márquez case,' said Lieutenant Padua, without preamble. 'Or rather, the Jasón Medina case, because we all agree that he alone was responsible for the girl's murder. It's been nearly four months since Jasón Medina took his own life in the courthouse toilets the day his trial was due to start.' Amaia nodded. 'As is customary with these incidents, we carried out a routine inquiry, which would have ended there, had I not received a visit a few days later from the prison guard who'd accompanied Medina from the jail. Perhaps you remember him? He was downstairs in the toilets, white as a sheet.'

'Yes, I remember a prison guard as well as a policeman.'

'That's the guy, Luis Rodríguez. He came to see me, visibly upset, implored me to make it clear in my conclusions that he was absolved of any responsibility, especially over the box cutter Medina used to kill himself, which a third party must have brought into the courthouse. He was extremely worried, he said, because this was the second time a prisoner had committed suicide on his watch. The first time was three years ago: a prisoner hanged himself in his cell during the night. On that occasion the prison authorities admitted responsibility for having failed to activate the suicide prevention protocol by placing two guards on watch, but Rodríguez was afraid this latest suicide might lead to his being suspended or possibly dismissed. I reassured him then casually asked about this other guy. He had murdered his wife and then mutilated her body by severing one of her arms. Rodríguez didn't know whether the limb had been recovered or not, so imagine my surprise when I call the Logroño police, who investigated the case, and they tell me, yes, this guy had murdered his estranged wife, who'd taken out a restraining order following a previous attack. The kind of story we hear about every day on the news, nothing more to it. He rang her bell and, when she opened the door, he pushed her against the wall, knocked her unconscious, then stabbed her twice in the stomach. Afterwards, he ransacked the house, even heating up a plate of stew, which he ate in the kitchen while he watched her bleed to death. Then he left without bothering to close the door. A neighbour found the dead woman. Two hours later they arrested the husband in a local bar, drunk and still covered in his wife's blood. He immediately confessed to her murder, but when asked about the mutilation denied all knowledge of it.'

Padua gave a sigh. 'Amputation at the elbow, using a sharp, serrated object, such as an electric carving knife or a compass saw. What do you think of that, Inspector?'

Amaia clasped her hands together, pressed both forefingers to her lips, and remained silent for a few moments before replying.

'What I think, for now, is that this is a coincidence. He could have severed her arm to remove items of jewellery, a wedding ring, or to try to conceal her identity – although, given she was in her own house, that wouldn't make much sense. Unless there's something else . . .'

'There is,' Padua affirmed. 'I went to Logroño and spoke to the two police officers who led the investigation. What they told me bore even more resemblance to the Johana Márquez case: the crime had been violent and gruesome, the house was a mess, even the blood-soaked knife they found next to his wife's body was taken from her kitchen. During the attack, he cut his hand, but rather than bandage it, he left his bloody fingerprints all over the house. He even urinated in the toilet and didn't bother to flush. His actions were brutal and chaotic, like the man himself. Yet the amputation was carried out post-mortem, with no significant loss of blood, neatly severed at the elbow. Neither the limb nor the sharp blade used to carry out the amputation were ever recovered.'

Amaia nodded, absorbed.

'I spoke to the prison governor, who informed me that the prisoner had only been there a matter of days before he killed himself, and had shown neither remorse nor depression – which is unusual in cases of this nature. He was calm, relaxed, had a good appetite, and slept like a baby. As he was still adapting to prison life, he spent most of the time alone in his cell, where he received no visits from relatives or friends. Then suddenly one night, despite never having shown any inclination to self-harm, he hanged himself in his cell. And trust me, it must have taken a supreme effort, because there's nothing in those cubicles high enough for a person to hang themselves from. He basically sat on the floor and strangled himself, which requires enormous willpower. The guard heard him struggling to breathe and sounded the alarm. He was still alive when they entered the cell, but died before the ambulance arrived.'

'Did he leave a suicide note?'

'I asked the governor about that. He said "sort of".'

'*Sort of?*'

'He told me the guy had carved some gibberish into the plaster on the wall with the tip of his toothbrush,' said Padua, sliding a photograph out of an envelope he laid on the table. He swivelled it until the image was facing her.

It had been painted over, although they hadn't bothered to plaster over the grooves. The photograph had been taken at an angle so that the flash clearly highlighted the bold lettering. A single, perfectly legible word:

'*TARTTALO.*'

Amaia raised her eyes in astonishment, gazing at Padua searchingly. The lieutenant grinned, pleased with himself, as he leant back in his chair.

'I can see this has piqued your interest, Inspector. *Tarttalo,* spelled the same way as in the note Medina left for you,' he said. He dropped a plastic folder on to the table. Inside was an envelope addressed to Inspector Salazar.

Amaia remained silent, considering everything Lieutenant Padua had told her during the past hour. Despite her best efforts, she could find no logical, satisfactory explanation as to how two ordinary, bungling, disorganised killers could have performed identical mutilations on their victims without leaving any clues as to how they did it, when the rest of the crime scene was littered with evidence; or why they had used the exact same word to sign their crime, a word that was anything but commonplace.

'Well, Lieutenant, I see where you're going with this. What I don't understand is why you're telling me about it. After all, the Johana Márquez affair is the *Guardia Civil*'s responsibility, as are prisoner transports. The case, if there is one, is yours,' she said, sliding the photographs back towards Padua.

He picked them up, gazed at them in silence, then heaved a loud sigh.

'The problem, Inspector Salazar, is that there isn't going to be a case. I looked into this on my own, based on what Rodríguez told me. The Logroño case was handled by the police there and is officially closed, as is that of Johana Márquez, now that her confessed killer is dead. I presented everything I told you to my superiors, but they say there's insufficient cause to open an investigation.'

Head in hand, Amaia listened intently, chewing on her bottom lip.

'What do you want *me* to do, Padua?'

'What I want, Inspector, is to be sure that the two crimes aren't related, but my hands are tied . . . In any event, at the end of the day, you're already involved. And this,' he added, sliding the envelope back to her, 'is yours.'

Amaia ran her finger over the shiny plastic folder and along the edge of the envelope that bore her name in small, neat handwriting.

'Have you visited Medina's cell at the prison?'

'How did you guess!' Padua laughed and shook his head. 'I went there this morning before I called you.'

Leaning to one side, he took a file out of his bag. 'Page eight,' he said, placing it on the table.

Amaia instantly recognised the file: an autopsy report. She had seen hundreds of them, the name and number printed on the cover.

'Medina's autopsy report, but we already know how he died.'

'Page eight,' Padua insisted.

While Amaia started to read, the lieutenant reeled off the passage as if he knew it by heart.

'The index finger on Jasón Medina's right hand showed significant damage. The nail was missing, and the skin flayed so that the flesh was showing. The prison governor let me go through Medina's personal effects. His wife doesn't want them, and no one else has claimed them, so they're still at the prison. As far as I can see, Medina was quite a simple fellow. No books, no photographs, no real possessions, just a few back issues of a glossy magazine and a sports journal. His personal hygiene was basic; he didn't even own a toothbrush. I asked to see his cell, which at first glance appeared unremarkable. Other inmates have occupied it over the past four months. But I had a hunch, so I sprayed the walls with Luminol and the place lit up like a Christmas tree. Inspector, the night before his trial Jasón Medina scraped his finger practically down to the bone to write in blood on his cell wall the same word as the prisoner in Logroño. And afterwards, like his predecessor, he took his own life, the only difference being that Medina did so outside the prison, because he had to give you this,' he said, pointing to the envelope.

Amaia picked it up without looking at it and slipped it into her pocket before leaving the bar. As she made her way home, she could feel its ominous presence, pressed against her side like a warm poultice. She took out her mobile phone and punched in Deputy Inspector Etxaide's number.

'Hello, chief.'

'Good evening, Jonan, forgive me for calling you at home . . .'

'How can I help?'

'I want you to find out everything you can about the mythological creature *tarttalo*, or any references to something spelled t-a-r-t-t-a-l-o.'

'No problem, I'll have it for you tomorrow. Was there anything else?'

'No, that's all. Thanks a lot, Jonan.'

'My pleasure, chief. See you tomorrow.'

Hanging up, she realised how late she was; Ibai had been due his feed nearly three-quarters of an hour earlier. Anxious to get home, she broke into a run, dodging the few pedestrians who had braved the chilly Pamplona weather. As she ran, she couldn't help thinking about how punctual Ibai was with his feeds, how he woke up demanding to be fed every four hours, practically to the minute. She glimpsed her house halfway along the street. Still running, she fumbled in the pocket of her quilted jacket for her key, and, as though performing a perfect bullfighter's lunge, inserted it in the lock and opened the door. The baby's hoarse cries reached her like a wave of despair from the first floor. She bounded up the stairs without taking off her coat, her mind filling with absurd images of Ibai left to cry in his cot while James lay asleep, or of James staring at the baby, incapable of consoling him.

But James wasn't asleep. Rushing into the kitchen, Amaia found him rocking Ibai on his shoulder, singing in an effort to calm him.

'For heaven's sake, James, haven't you given him the bottle?' she asked, reflecting on her own ambiguous feelings about the matter.

'Hi, Amaia, I did try,' he said, gesturing towards a feeding bottle full of milk languishing on the table, 'but he doesn't want to know,' he added, smiling sheepishly.

'Are you sure you mixed it properly?' she said, looking askance at him and shaking the bottle.

'Yes, I'm sure,' James replied good-naturedly, still rocking the baby. 'Fifty millilitres of water to two level scoops of formula.'

Amaia slipped off her coat and tossed it on to a chair.

'Give him to me,' she said.

'Relax, Amaia,' said James, trying to calm her. 'Ibai is fine,

67

he's just a bit grouchy, that's all. I've been holding him all this time, he hasn't been crying long.'

She all but snatched the baby from James, walked into the sitting room and sank into an armchair as his wails crescendoed.

'How long is not long?' she demanded, crossly. 'Half an hour, an hour? If you'd fed him on time, he would never have got into this state.'

James's smile faded.

'Less than ten minutes, Amaia. When you didn't come home, I prepared the bottle in time for his feed. But he didn't want it, because he prefers breast milk, the artificial stuff tastes funny. I'm sure if you hadn't come back when you did, he would have ended up taking the bottle.'

'I wasn't late out of choice,' she snapped. 'I was working.'

James looked at her, bewildered. 'No one is saying otherwise.'

Ibai was still crying, moving his head from side to side frantically in search of her tantalisingly close nipple. She felt the intense, painful suction, as the wailing ceased, leaving a deafening silence in the room.

Distraught, Amaia closed her eyes. It was her fault. She had been out too long. Carelessly, she'd lost track of time, while her son was crying to be fed. She placed a trembling hand on his tiny head and stroked his downy hair. A tear rolled down her cheek and fell on to her child's face. Oblivious to his mother's anguish, he was suckling softly now as sleep overtook him and his eyelids closed.

'Amaia,' whispered James, drying the wet streaks on his wife's face with his fingers. 'It's no big deal, my love. He didn't suffer, I promise. And he only started hollering a few minutes before you arrived. Don't fret, Amaia, he isn't the first baby to start taking formula. I'm sure the others protested just as loudly.'

By now Ibai was sound asleep. Amaia buttoned up her blouse, handed the baby to James, and fled the room. He could hear her throwing up.

She hadn't been aware of falling asleep, which usually happened when she was exhausted. She woke up with a start, convinced she'd heard a loud sigh from her son in his sleep, after the terrible tantrum he'd had earlier. But the room was quiet, and, raising herself up a little, she could see, or rather sense in the dim light, that her son was sleeping peacefully. She turned towards James, who was also asleep, face down, right arm crooked under his pillow. She leant over without thinking and kissed his head. He fumbled for her hand with his free arm, in a mutual gesture they both made several times each night unconsciously. Reassured, she closed her eyes and went back to sleep.

Until she was woken by the wind. The deafening gusts howled in her ears, roaring magnificently. She opened her eyes and saw her. Lucía Aguirre was staring at Amaia from the banks of the River Baztán. She was wearing her red-and-white pullover, which looked oddly festive, her left arm clasped about her waist. Lucía's mournful gaze reached her like an enchanted bridge spanning the turbulent waters of the river; Amaia could see in the woman's eyes all her fear, her pain, but most of all, in the despairing look she gave Amaia, her infinite sadness as she accepted an eternity of wind and solitude. Suppressing her own fear, Amaia sat up in bed, held the woman's gaze, then nodded, encouraging her to speak. And Lucía spoke, but her words were snatched away by the wind before Amaia could make out a single sound. She seemed to be shrieking, desperate to be heard, until her strength failed her and she sank to her knees, her face hidden momentarily. When she looked up again, her lips were moving rhythmically, repeating what sounded like just one word: 'tar . . . trap . . . rat . . . rat . . .'

'I will,' Amaia whispered. 'I'll trap the rat.'

But Lucía Aguirre was no longer looking at her. She simply shook her head, even as her face sank into the river.

6

She had spent longer than usual saying goodbye to Ibai. Holding the baby in her arms, she had dawdled, pacing from room to room, whispering sweet nothings in his ear while putting off getting dressed and leaving for work. And now, an hour later, she couldn't shrug off the imprint of his fragile little body in her arms. She yearned for him in a way that was almost painful; she had never missed anyone like that before. His smell, his touch enchanted her, arousing in her feelings so rooted in her being they felt like memories. She thought of the soft curve of his cheek, his clear eyes – the same blue as hers – and the way he gazed at her, studying her face as if, inside him, instead of a child, there was the serene spirit of a sage.

Jonan held out a mug of milky coffee, which Amaia took from him, cupping it in her hand in an easy gesture that had become part of her routine, but which today gave her no comfort.

'Did Ibai give you a hard night?' he asked, noticing the dark rings around her eyes.

'No. Well, sort of . . .' she said, evasively.

Jonan had worked with Inspector Salazar long enough to know that her silences spoke volumes.

'I have that information you asked me for yesterday,' he said, his gaze wandering back to his desk. She seemed puzzled for an instant.

'Oh, yes. That was quick.'

'I said it wouldn't be a problem.'

'Read it to me,' she said, inviting him to talk while she sat next to him at the desk, sipping her coffee.

He opened the document on his computer and began reading out loud.

'*Tarttalo*, also known as *tártaro* and *torto*, is a mythological creature from the Basque region of Navarre, a one-eyed giant, exceptionally strong and aggressive, that feeds on sheep, young girls and shepherds, although in some references the *tarttalo* is portrayed as a shepherd with its own flock, but in any event, always as a devourer of Christians. There are similar references to Cyclops all over Europe, in Ancient Greece and Rome. They figure prominently in the Basque Country, among the ancient tribe of the Vascones, although accounts of them were recorded well into the twentieth century. They are solitary creatures that dwell in caves, whose locations may vary according to the area, but not in such remote places as the goddess-genie Mari. Instead they prefer to stay close to the valleys, where they can stockpile enough food to satisfy their voracious appetite for blood. They are distinguished by a single eye in the centre of the forehead, and, of course, bones, mounds of them stacked outside their cave entrances, the fruits of their depravity. I'm attaching a couple of popular tales about their encounters with shepherds, more than one of whom was gobbled up. And here's one about a Cyclops that drowned in a well after being blinded by a shepherd – you're going to love this:

'In Zegama, the *tarttalo* was a hideous one-eyed ogre who lived in a place called *Tartaloetxeta* ("*tarttalo's* house"), near Mount Sadar. From there he roamed the nearby valleys and mountains, stealing sheep and men that he would roast and then eat.

'On one occasion, two brothers were walking along a path on their way home from a fair in a neighbouring village, where they had sold their sheep and had a good time. They were chatting happily when suddenly they stopped in their tracks: they had seen the *tarttalo*.

'They tried to flee, but the ogre seized them both with one hand and carried them back to his cave. When he got there, he flung them into a corner and started to build a huge fire with oak branches. When he'd finished, he placed a big roasting spit over the fire. The two brothers watched, quaking with fear. The ogre picked up the fatter of the two, killed him with a single blow and stuck him on the spit. The other shepherd wept bitter tears as he witnessed the ogre devouring his brother's body. When it had finished its gruesome meal, the ogre picked up the other lad and threw him on to a pile of sheepskins.

'"You need fattening up," he said contemptuously, his sadistic laughter echoing off the walls of the cave. Then he added: "But to stop you from running away, I'm going to put this ring on your finger."

'And with that he slipped a magic ring on to the lad's finger. It had a human voice that cried out incessantly: "Here I am! Here I am!"

'After that, the *tarttalo* fell soundly asleep.

'Rather than wait to be fattened up and eaten by the ogre, the shepherd resolved to escape, come what may. And so, crawling over to the fire, he picked up a spit and held it over the flames until it was red-hot. Then, clutching the end firmly, he made his way over to where the *tarttalo* was snoring, and drove it into the one eye on his forehead.

'The monster, crazed with pain and rage, rose to his feet, letting out savage roars and sweeping the air with his huge paws in search of the shepherd who had stabbed him in the eye.

'But the youth dodged his assailant's frenzied attacks, nimbly clambering over the sheep huddled inside the cave and covering himself in an animal hide to try to sneak past the ogre, who was now blocking the mouth to the cave.

'The lad managed to get past him, but the magic ring started to cry out:

'"Here I am! Here I am!"

'Guided by the ring, the *tarttalo*, despite his vast size, bounded like a deer after his prey.

'The young shepherd feared he would never escape. Though he ran and ran, trying to hide in the forest, each time the ring led the ogre to him with its resounding cry:

'"Here I am! Here I am!"

'Realising he would be caught – and terrified by the ogre's angry howls and curses – the shepherd made a brave decision: he tore off the finger with the tell-tale ring on it and threw it down a well.

'"Here I am! Here I am!"

'Following the ring's calls, the *tarttalo* leapt head-first down the well and drowned.'

'You're right,' Amaia said, grinning. 'It's a great story – and I can tell you're in your element here.'

'Well, it isn't all myth and fable. In a more modern context, *tarttalo* is the name given by some terrorist groups to a type of bomb: a box with no visible wiring, containing an LDR photoelectric cell – in effect, a single, light-sensitive eye; hence *tarttalo*. As soon as the box is opened, the light detonates the explosive device.'

'Yes, I've heard of that, but I don't think it's relevant. What more do you have?'

'A small film production company called Tarttalo, plus half a dozen restaurants in various parts of the Basque Country. On the Internet I came across various references to the fables, animation shorts about ogres, silkscreens for T-shirts, a village where they bring out an effigy of the *tart-talo* during local fiestas. Then there are a handful of blogs that either use the name *Tarttalo*, or make references to it. I'll send you the links. Ah, and it seems the spelling you mentioned, with two "t"s, is the old way of writing it. And then there are José Miguel de Barandiarán's books on Basque mythology.'

At that moment, the telephone on Jonan's desk rang, interrupting his explanations. He apologised, picking up the receiver and listened briefly before gesturing to her as he hung up.

'The Commissioner wants to see you, chief.'

The Commissioner was on the phone when she entered his office. She murmured an apology and turned towards the door, but he raised his hand, motioning for her to wait.

He hung up and sat staring at her. Amaia assumed he was being leant on by the Archbishop, and was about to tell him they hadn't come up with anything yet, when he took her by surprise.

'You aren't going to believe this – that was Judge Markina. He called to tell me that the man being held for the murder of Lucía Aguirre has been in touch to tell him that if you go to see him in prison, he'll tell you where to find the victim's body.'

Amaia drove out to Santa Lucía hill, where the new Pamplona prison was situated, flashed her badge at security and was immediately shown into an office where the prison governor, whom she had met before, was waiting for her. So too were Judge Markina and a legal secretary. As she entered, the judge rose to greet her.

'Inspector, I've not had the pleasure of greeting you in person, as I was appointed when you were on maternity leave; thank you for coming. This morning Quiralte asked to see the governor. He told him that if you agreed to see him he would tell you where Lucía Aguirre's body is.'

'And do you think he will?' she asked.

'The truth is, I don't know what to think. Quiralte is a

75

cocky individual who bragged about his crime then refused to say where he had hidden the body. According to the director, he's like a pig in clover. He eats well, sleeps well, is sociable and active.'

'He seems in his element,' agreed the governor.

'So this could be a trick, or perhaps he means it. Either way, he insisted it had to be you and no one else.'

Amaia recalled the day they had arrested him and the way he had stared at the two-way mirror while another officer was interrogating him.

'Yes, he asked to talk to me when we arrested him as well, but the reasons he gave seemed like a joke. Back then I was about to go on leave, so he was questioned by the team that had been working on the case.'

Quiralte had been waiting for ten minutes when Amaia and the judge entered the interview room. He was sitting slumped in an upright chair by the table, his prison uniform unbuttoned halfway to the waist. He gave a forced smile that revealed whitish, overly long gums.

'The return of El Macho, indeed,' thought Amaia, recalling Jonan's comment the day they had first arrested him.

Quiralte waited for them to install themselves on the other side of the table, then sat up straight and proffered his hand to Amaia.

'So you've finally condescended to see me, Inspector. It's been a long wait, but I must say it's worth it. How are you? How's your baby boy?'

Amaia ignored his outstretched hand. After a few moments he lowered his arm.

'Señor Quiralte, the only reason I came here today is because you promised to reveal the whereabouts of Lucía Aguirre's remains.'

'As you wish, Inspector, you're the boss, but the truth is I thought you might be a little friendlier, seeing as I'm helping raise your profile as star cop,' he said, grinning.

'Señor Quiralte—' Markina began.

'Shut up,' Quiralte hissed. Markina looked daggers at him. 'If you don't stay quiet, your honour, I won't say a word. In fact, what the hell are you doing here? Wasn't I clear enough about only wanting to speak to Inspector Salazar? You should be grateful I let you stay.'

Judge Markina pulled his arms away from the table, stiffening as though ready to pounce on the prisoner if necessary. Amaia could almost hear his muscles crack with indignation; nevertheless, he remained silent.

Quiralte's wolfish grin returned, and, ignoring Markina, he addressed Amaia once more.

'I've been waiting a long time, four whole months. I wanted to get this over with sooner – it's entirely your fault that the situation dragged on, Inspector. As I'm sure you know, I asked to speak to you when I was arrested. If you hadn't refused, you would have that slut's body by now, and I wouldn't have been forced to rot away in prison all this time.'

'That's where you're wrong,' said Amaia.

Quiralte shook his head, grinning. It occurred to her that he was enjoying himself.

'So?' she asked.

'Do you like to drink *patxaran*, Inspector?'

'Not all that much.'

'No, you don't seem like that kind of woman. I'll bet you didn't drink at all while you were pregnant. A wise choice, otherwise you'd end up with kids like me.' He guffawed. 'And you're breastfeeding now, right?' he added.

Amaia concealed her surprise by feigning irritation, turning towards the door and pushing her chair back to stand up.

'Hold your horses, Inspector, I'm getting there. My father used to brew *patxaran* at home, you see. It was nothing special, but it was drinkable. He worked for a well-known liqueur company in a small village called Azanza. When the sloe harvest was finished, employees were allowed to pick any leftover berries. My father used to take me with him out to the countryside. Those blackthorn trees are lethal, if you prick your finger it always goes septic and the pain lasts for days. I thought the ideal place for her would be among those bushes.'

'You buried her there?'

'Yes.'

'Right,' said Judge Markina, 'you'll be coming with us to point out the exact spot.'

'I'm not going anywhere! The last thing I want is to see that bitch again, she'll be disgusting by now, anyway. I can tell you which field she's in, but the rest is up to you. I've kept my side of the bargain and, once this is over, I intend to go back to my cell to rest.' He leant back in his chair again, beaming. 'I'm feeling quite tired after all this excitement,' he said, staring straight at the judge.

'That's not how this works,' said Markina. 'We didn't come here so that you could play cat and mouse with us. You'll show us the place in situ. Verbal directions could make the search difficult. In addition, it's been a while, so there won't be any visible signs. Even you might have difficulty remembering the exact spot.'

Quiralte interrupted Markina's monologue.

'Oh, for God's sake! This guy's a bore. Give me a pen and paper and I'll show you, Inspector.'

Amaia handed them to him, while Markina carried on protesting:

'A clumsy drawing doesn't make a reliable map; in a plantation all trees look alike.'

Amaia watched Quiralte, who gave the judge a knowing smile, then started to write.

'Don't worry, your honour,' he said patronisingly, 'I'm not doing a drawing.' And he handed them the piece of paper with a brief series of numbers and letters, which left Markina puzzling.

'What on earth is this?'

'Coordinates, your honour,' Amaia explained.

'Longitude and latitude, your honour – didn't I tell you I was in the Foreign Legion?' Quiralte added jauntily. 'Or maybe you'd prefer a little drawing?'

Azanza turned out to be a small village on the outskirts of Estella, whose main industry was devoted to producing the sloe-flavoured liqueur called *patxaran*. By the time they managed to summon the whole team and find the location, it was growing late. The fading light seemed to be held for an instant by the millions of little white flowers, that, despite the remoteness of spring, adorned the tree branches and gave the impression of a palace corridor rather than a burial spot improvised by a cruel brute.

Amaia looked carefully around her while the forensic team installed spotlights and a tent, which she had insisted they put up regardless of the hurry they were in; although there was no real chance of rain, she didn't want to risk clues at the site of the grave being destroyed by a downpour.

Judge Markina came over and stood next to her.

'You look sceptical, Inspector. Do you doubt that we'll find the body there?'

'No, I'm pretty certain we will,' she said.

'Then what is bothering you? . . . Allow me,' he said, raising his hand towards her face. She shrank back in surprise. 'You've got something in your hair.' He picked out a little white flower and held it to his nose.

Amaia saw Jonan glance at her from the far side of the tent.

'Tell me, what doesn't convince you?'

'Quiralte's behaviour doesn't convince me. He's a textbook thug, court-martialled from the army, a drunk, arrogant, violent, and yet . . .'

'I know, I also find it hard to understand what made a

charming woman like Lucía Aguirre associate with a man like that.'

'Well, *that* I can help you with. She fits the profile perfectly. Sweet-natured, altruistic, devoted to helping others, pious and empathic to a fault. She was a catechist, helped out at a soup kitchen, babysat her grandchildren, regularly visited her elderly mother . . . but she was single. For a woman like that, life has no meaning unless she is caring for others, even though at the same time she dreams of someone who will come and take care of her. She yearned to feel like a woman; not a sister, a mother, or a friend, but a woman. Her mistake was to believe that to achieve this she needed a man at any price.'

'Well, Inspector, without wishing to appear sexist, I don't see anything wrong with a woman needing a man by her side in order to feel whole, in matters of love, at any rate.'

Jonan stopped taking notes. Keeping his head down, he grinned, his attention split between the technicians digging the pit and his superior.

'Your honour, Quiralte isn't a man. He's a specimen of the male sex. There's a big difference.'

The diggers raised the alarm as they started to uncover some black plastic sheeting. Amaia approached the grave, but not without turning to Markina to say:

'I'm sure Lucía Aguirre also realised that, which is why she reported him. Too late.'

When the bundle was completely exposed, it was clear the murderer had placed the woman's body inside two bin liners, top and tail, which he had then fastened at the waist with Sellotape. The tape had come unstuck and was fluttering in the breeze, creating an eerie sensation of movement, as if the victim were writhing in her grave, clamouring to be let out. A sudden gust revealed the victim's red-and-white pullover among the folds of the bag. Amaia recognised it from her dream. A shiver ran down her spine.

'I want this photographed from every angle,' she ordered. While waiting for the photographers to do their work, she stepped back a few paces, crossed herself, and, lowering her head, said another prayer for the victim.

Judge Markina stood gaping at her, as Dr San Martín approached.

'It's just another way of distancing oneself from the dead,' he murmured to Markina, who looked away, shamefaced.

Stepping over the grave, Dr San Martín took a pair of nail scissors from his bag, then glanced at Markina, who gave a nod of approval. With a single movement, he snipped the plastic lengthways, exposing the top half of the body.

The corpse lay fully outstretched, tilted slightly on its right side. Decomposition was relatively advanced, although somewhat delayed by the cold, dry soil. The flesh looked sunken and shrivelled, above all on the face.

'Fortunately, because of the recent cold weather, the degree of decomposition is less than you'd expect after five months,' San Martín explained. 'At first glance, the corpse presents a deep gash to the throat. Bloodstains on the pullover indicate the victim was still alive when this was done to her. The wound is deep and straight, indicating an extremely sharp blade and a clear intent to cause death. There is no sign of hesitation; what's more, the wound travels from left to right, suggesting her assailant was right-handed. Blood loss was extreme, so that despite being well wrapped up in relatively dry ground, there is abundant evidence of insect activity in the initial phase.'

Amaia approached the head of the grave and crouched down. Tilting her head slightly to one side, she remained like that for a few moments, as if she were feeling dizzy.

Judge Markina looked at her with concern. He moved towards her, but Jonan restrained him with a gesture, then whispered something in his ear.

'That mark on her eyebrow, is it from a blow?' asked Amaia.

'Well spotted,' said San Martín, beaming with the pride of a teacher who has trained his pupil well, 'and it would appear to be post-mortem, because there's an indentation but no bleeding.'

'Look,' said Amaia, pointing, 'there seem to be others all over her head.'

'Yes.' San Martín nodded, leaning closer. 'There's some hair missing here, which isn't due to decomposition.'

'Jonan, take a photograph from here, will you?' asked Amaia.

Markina crouched down beside Amaia, so close that he brushed her with his jacket sleeve.

He murmured an apology, then asked San Martín if the body had been there the entire time or if it had been brought there immediately after death. San Martín said he thought it had, explaining that the maggots' remains corresponded to early stage soil fauna typical of the area, but that he would only know for sure when he had carried out all the relevant tests.

Markina stood up and walked over to the judicial clerk, who was busy taking notes at a discreet distance.

Amaia remained kneeling for a few seconds, puzzling over the body.

Jonan gazed expectantly at her.

'Can we take it away now?' one of the technicians asked.

'Not yet,' said Amaia, raising her hand without looking round. 'Your honour,' she called out.

Markina turned towards her and obediently made his way back.

'Quiralte said that if he'd spoken to me sooner he wouldn't have had to rot in jail for four months, didn't he?'

'Yes, he did, although having confessed to the crime, I'm not quite sure how he imagined that would happen.'

82

'I think I do . . .' she whispered, pensive.

Markina held out his hand, which she frowned at, rising to her feet and circling the grave.

'Doctor, could you cut through more of the bag, please?'

'Certainly.'

He went to work with the scissors again, this time opening the lower half of the bag down to the knees.

The skirt Lucía Aguirre had been wearing with her striped pullover appeared hitched up, and her underclothes were missing.

'I assumed we would find evidence of sexual aggression – it's common in cases like these. I wouldn't be surprised if it occurred post-mortem,' said the pathologist.

'Yes, like a furious unleashing of all his fantasies – but that's not what I'm looking for.'

Gingerly, she peeled away the bag on either side.

'Jonan, come here a minute. Keep the plastic taut so the mud doesn't get in.'

Jonan nodded and passed the camera to one of the technicians. He knelt down and clasped the two bits of plastic firmly in both hands.

Crouching beside him, Amaia fumbled for the victim's right shoulder, slowly feeling her way down the arm, which was partially obscured by the body leaning slightly on to its side. Using both hands, she dug her fingers underneath the body at the level of the bicep, and pulled gently to reveal the arm.

Jonan gave a start, lost his balance and fell on to his backside, still clinging to the plastic sheet.

The arm appeared to have been severed from the elbow in a clean, neat incision; the absence of any blood made it easy to see the tip of the arm bone and the atrophied flesh surrounding it.

A terrible shiver coursed through Amaia's whole body. For an instant all the cold in the universe converged on her backbone, making her judder as if she'd received an electric shock.

'Chief . . .' Jonan's voice brought her back to reality.

She looked straight at him and he nodded.

'Come on, Jonan,' she ordered, tearing off her gloves and starting to run towards the car.

She stopped in her tracks, wheeling round to address Markina:

'Your honour, call the prison and tell them to keep Quiralte under strict surveillance. If necessary, they should put a guard inside his cell.'

Markina was already clutching his mobile.

'Why?' he asked with a shrug.

'Because he's going to kill himself.'

She had let Jonan take the wheel – she always did when she needed to think and was in a hurry. He was a good driver, managing to achieve the right balance between safety and the impulse to put his foot down on the accelerator, which she would have yielded to. The journey from Azanza to Pamplona took them less than thirty minutes. In the end the rain had held off, but the overcast skies had led to a starless, moonless night that seemed to dampen even the city lights. As they turned into the prison car park, they saw an ambulance with its lights extinguished.

'Shit,' she whispered.

An officer was waiting for them at the door and ushered them into a corridor so they didn't have to go through security. As they hurried along the passageway, he brought them up to date:

'The paramedics and the prison doctor are with him now. He seems to have swallowed something, rat poison probably. A fellow inmate on cleaning duty must have sold it to him. They usually put it in each other's food or cut drugs with it; in small doses it causes stomach cramps and nausea. When you gave the alert, he was already unconscious, lying in a pool of his own blood and vomit; I reckon he's puked his guts out. He regained consciousness, but I don't think he even knows where he is.'

Pale and worried-looking, the prison governor was waiting for them outside Quiralte's cell.

'We had no way of knowing . . .'

Amaia walked straight past him and peered into the cell. There was a pervading stench of faeces and vomit, and in the middle of it lay Quiralte, motionless on his bunk and with several tubes sticking out of him. Even with the oxygen mask on, she could see the severe blistering around his nose and mouth. One of the paramedics was taking notes, while the other quietly gathered up their equipment.

The prison doctor, who was an old acquaintance, wheeled around, removing his gloves before shaking Amaia's hand.

'Inspector Salazar, this was a tough one,' he said arching his bushy eyebrows. 'I got here first because I was still in the building. The paramedics arrived a few minutes later. We did our best, but we couldn't save him. Ingesting this type of toxic substance seldom ends happily, still less when it's self-administered.' The doctor pointed to a discarded cyclist's water bottle in the corner and continued: 'As soon as he returned to his cell, he prepared the cocktail and drank it. He must have been in agony, but he didn't make a sound or call for help.' He contemplated the dead man once more. 'One of the most horrific deaths I've ever encountered.'

'Do you know if he left a letter or a note?' Amaia asked, glancing about.

'He left this,' said the doctor, gesturing towards the bunk beds behind her.

She turned, stooping slightly to read what Quiralte had written on the wall of the lower bunk.

Jonan did so too, wrinkling his nose.

'He's written it in . . .'

'Faeces,' confirmed the doctor, behind him. 'Using it to write with is a common protest tradition in prisons. As for the word, I've no idea what it means.'

7

Whenever Amaia called a meeting, she tried to make sure she'd be the first to arrive. She would remain for a few minutes staring through the windows looking out over Pamplona, collecting her thoughts, lulled by the growing murmur of voices behind her. Only Jonan would approach her, quietly, with a mug of coffee, which she always accepted, though it would often be left untouched after she had warmed her hands on it.

When she heard Inspector Iriarte's voice cheerily greeting the assembled company, she turned to face the room. Accompanying him was Deputy Inspector Zabalza, who nodded and said something under his breath as he sat down next to Iriarte. She waited until they were all seated, and was about to begin talking when the door swung open and the Commissioner entered. He stood with his arms folded, leaning against the wall, offering his apologies before inviting her to carry on.

'Pretend I'm not here,' he said.

'Good morning, everyone. As I'm sure you've already gathered, the aim of this meeting is to establish a plan of action for investigating the desecrations that have been taking place at the church in Arizkun. The results of preliminary tests carried out on the bones show they belong to a human infant of less than a year old, but otherwise don't shed much light on the matter. Dr San Martín will keep us informed of his progress as and when further results come in, but in the meantime I want to begin by looking at what constitutes an act of desecration and why this particular case falls unmistakably into that category . . .' She got to her feet and walked over behind Deputy Inspector Etxaide.

'Desecration is the act of depriving something of its sacred character, despoiling and treating with contempt objects that should be respected. Based on this premise, and bearing in mind these acts were perpetrated in a place of worship and involved the use of human remains, we would seem to be dealing with an act of desecration. However, before deciding how we take the case forward, there are a few things worth clarifying. As with every type of criminal behaviour, desecration takes many forms. Understanding the mechanics of desecration will give us a profile of the sort of person we're looking for.

'The most common type of desecration is vandalistic in nature, generally associated with urban gangs and marginal groups, who express their hatred of society by attacking its sacred and religious symbols. They might choose to attack a monument or a library, to burn a flag or smash the windows of a large department store. This type of desecration is the easiest to identify, because it shows clear signs of irrational violence.

'The second type concerns people who desecrate churches and cemeteries, gangs or groups of criminals whose sole aim is to steal valuable objects, to strip the church of microphones, sound or lighting equipment, anything made of silver or gold, tabernacles, candlesticks, chalices, even gravediggers' tools. In the most heinous cases, they may steal jewellery or even gold teeth from corpses. Recently, a gang was arrested for stealing the platinum frames from the photographs of the deceased that adorn many graves. Some of these delinquents admit to staging their crimes to look like satanic rituals in order to throw the police off the scent, directing the blame at sects and spreading fear among the locals. In such cases, it's important not to be duped, to remember that satanists aren't usually interested in pocketing a priest's mobile phone. And this brings us to the third type of desecration, the esoteric kind. Jonan . . .'

Jonan stood up and walked over to the whiteboard.

'These are magic rituals that derive from various cultures. The majority of these so-called desecrations are in fact religious rituals used in santería, Haitian voodoo, Brazilian candomblé or the Cuban palo mayombé,' he said, writing the words on the whiteboard.

'These rituals are associated with death and spiritism and are habitually performed in cemeteries rather than in churches and temples. Only satanists choose places of Christian worship, because besides being devil-worshippers, their aim is to offend God. Satanic desecrations are rare, although at yesterday's meeting with the Archbishop it was suggested that such acts are often hushed up in order to deter copycat crimes. Most frequently we find sacred symbols being soiled with faeces, vomit, urine, animal blood, and ashes, with the aim of creating a spectacle: decapitated saints, virgins with phallic symbols scrawled on them, inverted crucifixes, that kind of thing. A few years ago, a group of satanists broke down the door of a tiny chapel at A Lanzada in Galicia with an axe. They chopped the hands off a statue of the Virgin that was much revered in the region and tossed them over a cliff. This is a typical example of the theatrical gesture: they could have simply forced open the door, which was sturdy but had an ancient lock and no alarm; they could have taken away the whole statue, but what they did was much more spectacular and offensive.'

Amaia took the floor again.

'Lastly we have desecration as social protest, or so the perpetrators claim. I had the opportunity to study this type of behaviour close up while working alongside the FBI in the United States. This consists of vandalising graves, digging up bodies of specific people and performing amputations and mutilations, the sole aim of which is to shock. Individuals who perform such acts harbour strong feelings of hatred towards society, and profilers consider them extremely dangerous, because desecration is simply a starting point for their actions, which may go on to target living people. A well-known case occurred when a police officer was killed in an explosion during a raid on a safe house in Leganés where terrorists were hiding out after the 11-M atrocity in Madrid. After the funeral, a group dug up his body, mutilated it and then set it alight. It is worth pointing out that in the Muslim faith, fire signifies the total annihilation of the dead person's soul, making their resurrection to eternal life impossible.

'Studies of criminal behaviour consider this type of conduct as a stage of psychopathy. Subjects often have a history of torturing animals, arson, bed-wetting, extreme backwardness at school, abuse . . . There is often a significant psychosexual element, because of the difficulties they have in relating normally to the opposite sex.

'To begin with, I must admit that I favoured the vandalistic theory – and I haven't entirely ruled it out. However, there are aspects of the history of Arizkun – for those of you unfamiliar with it, Jonan has prepared a report explaining the possible historical motive – which mean we can't dismiss the possibility that these attacks are a form of social protest, albeit in an embryonic phase.

'Another kind of desecration which we have ruled out is art theft. Perpetrators enter a church they have previously identified, causing minimum damage, and remove only the most valuable objects. These people are usually working for someone else, are never opportunistic or disorganised.'

'Good,' the Commissioner chimed in. 'Now, tell me what you've done so far?'

Iriarte opened his notebook and read out loud:

'For the moment we have a round-the-clock patrol car outside the church; that seems to have gone some way towards reassuring the locals; a few of them have been over to thank the officers. No further incidents have taken place.'

'Have you questioned people living in the immediate vicinity?' asked Amaia.

'Yes, but, even though Arizkun is quiet as the grave at night, no one saw or heard anything. Chopping up the pew with an axe must have made quite a din.'

'That church has solid walls, which would have muffled the blows, not to mention the walls of the houses themselves. And on a cold winter night, people's doors and windows would have been firmly shut.'

Iriarte nodded. 'We've also looked into local teenage gangs with antisocial tendencies, but drawn a blank. On the whole, young people in Arizkun are pretty laid-back, a bit national-istic, but that's about it. The majority, practising or not, see the church as a symbol of the village.'

'What about the issue of the *agotes*?' asked Amaia.

Iriarte sighed. 'That's an extremely sensitive subject, chief. And one most people in Arizkun prefer not to talk about. I can assure you that, until recently, an outsider coming to Arizkun asking about them would encounter an impenetrable wall of silence.'

'There are a couple of odd stories about that,' Zabalza chimed in. 'I heard that some years ago, a well-known author arrived in Arizkun intending to write about the *agotes*, but was forced to abandon his project, because everyone he asked played dumb, or pretended they'd never heard of them. They all assured him the *agotes* were a myth and no one believed they had really existed. Apparently the novelist Camilo José

91

Cela was interested in them too, and was given the same treatment.'

'Those are my people you're talking about,' said Amaia, smiling. 'Things must be different among the younger generation. They're usually proud of their roots, but don't feel the guilt the older generations carry around. As I was saying to Jonan yesterday, the story of the *agotes* is similar to that of the Jews or Muslims in Spain; people were treated differently because of their religion, gender, ancestry, wealth: the same as now, more or less . . . Even noblewomen were forced to marry or confined in convents.'

'You're probably right. For most young people, anything that happened before the civil war is prehistoric. Nevertheless, we need to avoid treading on people's toes.'

'We will,' Amaia assured him. 'This afternoon I'm heading off to Elizondo for a few days to take charge of the investigation.'

The Commissioner nodded, so she went on:

'Jonan is going to look at anti-Catholic action groups and everything relating to the *agotes*, as well as the desecrated objects. I'd like someone to arrange for me to meet separately with the parish priest and the chaplain at Arizkun: we can't rule out the possibility that this is an act of revenge against one of them. Don't forget the recent theft of the Codex Calixtinus, which turned out to be part of a personal vendetta against the dean of Santiago Cathedral by a former employee. In other words, before we start developing any historical or mystical theories, we should do a bit of digging on the people involved, as we would with any other case. I have a few ideas I want to follow up. That's all for now,' she said, rising and following the Commissioner out of the room. 'See you there tomorrow morning.'

The report, which had kept her awake until three in the morning, was lying on the Commissioner's desk. She examined the cover for any sign that he had read it.

'Sir, have you had a chance to look at my report?'

The Commissioner turned and gazed at her pensively for a few moments before responding.

'Yes, I have, Salazar. It's exhaustive.'

Amaia scanned his inscrutable face, wondering whether for him exhaustive was a good or a bad thing.

After a brief silence, to her astonishment he added:

'Exhaustive and extremely interesting. I can understand why all this caught your attention. I can also see why Lieutenant Padua might consider it merits further investigation, but I agree with his superiors. If you'd brought me this report a week ago, I would have told you exactly what they told him. The similarities are somewhat far-fetched and could be a coincidence. The fact that prisoners communicate amongst themselves or with people who admire their crimes is commoner than people think.'

He broke off and sat down facing her.

'Of course, yesterday's events cast a different light on things. Quiralte directly involved you by deciding to tell you where the body was. I've given it a lot of thought, but I'm still not sure. These cases are all officially closed. The killers are all dead, by their own hand. Separate cases, in different provinces, run by different forces, and you're asking me to open an investigation.'

Amaia remained silent, holding his gaze.

'I have faith in you, Salazar, I trust your instinct. I know there must be something there to have aroused your interest. However, I don't consider there's enough evidence to authorise opening an official investigation, which would only stir up rivalries between the different forces.'

He fell silent, while Amaia held her breath.

'Unless there's something else you aren't telling me . . .'

Amaia smiled. Not for nothing was he commissioner. She slipped the plastic sheath out of her pocket and handed it to him.

'Jasón Medina was carrying this envelope the day he killed himself in the courthouse toilets.'

He took it from her, examining the contents through the plastic. 'It's addressed to you,' he said, surprised. He opened his desk drawer, searching for gloves.

'You can touch it, it's been tested for fingerprints – they didn't find a single one.'

The Commissioner took the envelope out of the plastic sheath and read the card inside before looking up at Amaia.

'All right,' he said. 'I'm authorising an investigation based on the fact that the two murderers addressed themselves exclusively to you.'

Amaia nodded.

'Do your best not to tread on any toes – and before you proceed you'll need to secure Markina's blessing, although I doubt he'll be a problem. He seems to have the greatest respect for you as a detective. Why, only this morning he called to discuss the Aguirre case and was singing your praises. I don't want any run-ins with the other forces, so I'm asking you to be polite and treat them with kid gloves.' He paused for effect. 'And in return, I expect to see some progress on the desecrations at Arizkun.'

Amaia pulled a weary face.

'I know your thoughts on the matter, but it's imperative we solve the case as soon as possible. The Mayor was on the phone earlier. He sounded extremely concerned.'

'I'm sure the culprits will turn out to be some young tearaways.'

'Well then, arrest them and give me some names; that'll get the Archbishop off my back. They're in a panic over this and, while it's true that they're inclined to exaggerate when it comes to Church affairs, I've not seen them this stirred up over other, more sensational cases of desecration.'

'Don't worry. I'll do all I can. As you know, we have a patrol car stationed outside the church. That should reassure them, and maybe they'll stop pestering you.'

'I hope so,' he said.

Amaia stood up and walked towards the door.

'Thank you, sir.'

'Hold on, Salazar, there's one more thing.'

Amaia stopped in her tracks and waited.

'It's been a year since Inspector Montes was suspended after what happened during your investigation of the *basajaun* murders. Having looked into the matter, Internal Affairs recommend he be reinstated. As I'm sure you're aware, that will only happen if the other officers involved – in this case, yourself and Inspector Iriarte – give Montes a favourable report.'

Amaia kept quiet, waiting to see where the Commissioner was going with this.

'Things have changed. Then you were the detective leading the investigation, now you're head of the murder squad. If Inspector Montes is reinstated, he'll be under your command like everyone else. I have the last word over whether to assign him to your team or not, but your team is one short, so if you don't want Montes, I'll have to assign another permanent officer.'

'I'll think about it,' she said frostily.

The Commissioner sensed her animosity.

'I'm not trying to influence your decision, Inspector, I'm merely keeping you informed.'

'Thank you, sir,' she replied.

'You can go now.'

Amaia closed the door behind her and whispered:

'No, of course you aren't.'

The Navarre Institute of Forensic Medicine was deserted at midday. Between showers, a hesitant sun shone on surfaces glistening from the recent rain; the number of spaces in the car park showed it was lunchtime. Even so, Amaia wasn't surprised to see two women throw away the cigarettes they had been smoking and walk over to her as soon as they saw her. She found herself resorting to a memory cue, as she struggled with their names: 'Lazaro's sisters'.

'Marta, María,' she greeted them. 'You shouldn't be here,' she said, knowing full well that there was no obvious place for family members to go, and that they would either remain in the doorway or in the tiny waiting room until their loved one was released. 'You'd be better off at home, I'll let you know as soon as the . . .' She always found the word *autopsy*, with its sinister connotations, impossible to pronounce in the presence of family members. It was just another word; they all knew why they were there; some of them even used it themselves. But, knowing what it entailed, for her it was as painful as the scalpel making a Y-shaped incision on the corpse of their loved one. '. . . As soon as they've finished all the tests,' Amaia said.

'Inspector.' It was the older sister who spoke, Marta or María, she could never be sure. 'We realise there has to be an autopsy because our mother was the victim of a violent crime, but they told us today that it could be a few more days before they release her . . . well, her body.'

The younger sister burst out crying. As she attempted to stifle her tears, she gasped as if she were choking.

'Why?' demanded the older sister. 'They already know who killed her. They know it was that animal. But now he's dead and, God forgive me, I'm glad, because he died like the filthy rat that he was.'

Tears started to stream down her face too. She wiped them away furiously, for unlike her sister's, they were tears of rage.

'. . . And yet at the same time I wish he was still alive, locked up, rotting in prison. Can you understand that? I wish I could strangle him with my bare hands, I wish I could do everything to him that he did to our mother.'

Amaia nodded. 'And even then, you wouldn't feel any better.'

'I don't want to feel better, Inspector. I doubt anything in the world would make me feel good right now. I just wish I could hurt him, it's as simple as that.'

'Don't talk that way,' her sister implored.

Amaia laid her hand on the angry woman's shoulder.

'No, you wouldn't. I know you think that's what you want – and to some extent it's normal, but you couldn't do anything like that to anyone, I know you couldn't.'

The woman stared at her. Amaia could see she was close to breaking down.

'How can you be so sure?'

'Because to do the things he did, you'd need to be like him.'

The woman clasped her hands to her mouth; from the horror on her face, Amaia saw that she had understood. Her younger sister, who had appeared the more fragile and defence-less of the two, placed one arm around her older sister, and encountered no resistance as with her free hand she gently tilted the woman's head on to her own shoulder, in a gesture of reassurance and affection which Amaia was sure she had learned from their mother.

'We assumed we'd get her back after the autopsy. Why is it taking longer?'

'Our mother lay abandoned for five months in a frozen field. Now we need time with her, time to say our goodbyes, to bury her.'

Amaia studied them, assessing how resilient they were. Against all the odds, and despite evidence to the contrary, relatives of missing people show great resilience, which is nourished by the belief that their loved ones are still alive. But the moment the body appears, all the energy that has been keeping them going collapses like a sandcastle in a storm.

'All right, now listen to me, but bear in mind that what I'm about to tell you relates to an ongoing investigation, so I'm counting on you to be discreet.'

The two women looked at her expectantly.

'I've been honest with you from the start, from the day you

asked me to authorise a search for your mother because you were convinced she hadn't disappeared voluntarily. I've kept you informed every step of the way. And now I need you to carry on trusting me. We've established that Quiralte killed your mother. However, it's possible he wasn't the only person involved.'

Their anticipation gave way to astonishment.

'You mean he had an accomplice?'

'I'm not sure yet, but this case resembles another one I worked on in an advisory role, where a possible second culprit was also suspected. A different force was in charge of that investigation and so comparing the different elements and evidence will be a more complex and time-consuming process. We've been given the green light, but this could take hours, possibly days, I can't say for sure. I know this has been very hard for you, but your mother is no longer in a frozen field, she's here. And the reason why she's here is so that she can help us to solve the crime of which she herself was the victim. I'll be in there with her, and I promise you that no one respects the smallest detail she might be able to tell us more than these pathologists. Believe me, they are the voice of the victims.'

She could tell from the look of acceptance on their faces that she had convinced them. Whilst she didn't need their consent, there was nothing to be gained from having irate relatives getting in the way of her work.

'At least we'll be able to hold a Mass for her soul,' murmured Marta.

'Yes. That'll do you good. You know she would have liked that.' Amaia proffered a firm hand, which both women shook. 'I'll do my best to speed things up. I promise to call you.'

Amaia swapped her coat for a gown and entered the autopsy room. Dr San Martín, stooped over a stainless steel worktop, was showing something on the computer to a couple of assistants.

'Good morning,' she said. 'Or should that be good afternoon?'

'For us it's good afternoon, we've already had lunch,' replied one of the assistants.

Amaia suppressed the look of disbelief spreading across her face. She had a fairly strong stomach, but the idea of those three eating before an autopsy seemed . . . improper.

San Martín started to pull on his gloves.

'So, Inspector, which of the two do you want us to start on?'

'Which of what two?' she asked, puzzled.

'Lucía Aguirre,' he said pointing to the body draped with a sheet on a nearby slab, 'or Ramon Quiralte,' he added, signalling a table further away, on which she could make out a large shape still zipped inside a body bag.

Amaia looked at him quizzically.

'Both autopsies are scheduled for today, so we can start with whichever one you like.'

Amaia walked over to the mound made by Quiralte's body on the table, unzipped the bag and studied his face. Death had erased any vestige of good looks he might once have possessed. Around his eyes, dark purple spots had formed where small capillary veins had burst from the strain of vomiting. His half-open mouth, frozen in the middle of a spasm, revealed his teeth and the tip of his white-coated tongue, which protruded like a third lip. His swollen lips were covered in acid burns, and still streaked with vomit, which had trickled into his ear and formed rank clots in his hair. Amaia looked over to where the woman lay and shook her head. Only two metres separated victim and executioner; it was quite conceivable they would use the same scalpel to cut open both bodies.

'He shouldn't be here,' she said, thinking out loud.

'Pardon?' replied San Martín.

'He shouldn't be here . . . Not with her.' The assistants

99

stared at her, bemused. 'Not together,' she added, gesturing towards Lucía's corpse.

'I doubt whether either of them care at this point, don't you think?'

She realised that, even if she could explain, they wouldn't understand.

'I'm not so sure about that,' she muttered to herself.

'Right, then, which one do you want first?'

'I'm not interested in him,' she replied coldly. 'Suicide, end of story.'

She zipped up the bag, and Quiralte's face disappeared.

The pathologist shrugged as he uncovered Lucía Aguirre's body. Approaching the slab, Amaia came to a halt, bowed her head in a fleeting prayer, then finally looked up. Stripped of her red-and-white pullover, Amaia barely recognised the cheerful woman whose smiling face presided over the entrance to her house. The corpse had been washed, but the multiple blows, scratches, and bruises she had suffered made the woman appear soiled.

'Doctor,' said Amaia, moving closer to him, 'I wanted to ask you a favour. I know you follow strict procedures, but, as you can imagine, what really interests me is the amputation. I managed to get hold of photos of the skeletal remains the *Guardia Civil* discovered in the cave at Elizondo,' she said, showing San Martín a thick envelope. 'This is all they've given me so far. What I need you to do is compare the two sections where the bones were cut through. If we could establish a link between this and the Johana Márquez case, Judge Markina would authorise further measures that might enable us to make headway in the case. I'm meeting him later today – I was hoping I could take along something a little more convincing than mere theories.'

San Martín nodded. 'All right, let's get started.'

Switching on a powerful lamp above the body, he held a magnifying glass above the severed limb and photographed the lesion. Then he leaned in so close his nose almost touched the mutilated arm.

'A clean, post-mortem incision. The heart had already stopped, and the blood was clotting. It was made with a serrated object similar to an electric saw, yet different; this is reminiscent of the Johana Márquez case, where the direction of the incision also suggested an electric knife or angle grinder. Since in the Márquez case it was assumed the culprit was the stepfather, no further inquiries were made into the object he might have used; a few tools from the house and his car were examined, but no matches found.'

Amaia lined up the photographs Padua had given her on the negatoscope and switched on the light, while San Martín placed the one the printer had just spat out next to them.

He studied the images at length, rearranging and occasionally superimposing them, giving low, rhythmical grunts that set Amaia's teeth on edge and brought joking remarks from his assistants.

'In your opinion, were the incisions made with the same object?' Amaia asked, interrupting San Martín's musings.

'Ah!' he exclaimed. 'Now that would be saying a lot. But what I can confirm is that the same technique was used for all of them; they were made by a right-handed person who was very assured and also very strong.'

Amaia gazed at him, wanting more.

San Martín went on, grinning at the glimmer of hope he saw in the inspector's eye:

'Although I can confirm that the bones all belonged to adults, without any tissue attached, it's impossible to pinpoint their exact age or sex from looking at the photos, still less whether these limbs were surgical amputations or taken from a desecrated tomb. It's obvious at first glance that the incisions resemble one another, that the bones are all forearms . . . However, in order to be one hundred per cent certain, I'd need to examine the instrument that was used. We could make moulds of the bones themselves to scan and compare them. I'm sorry, Inspector, but that's the best I can do, based on photographic evidence. It would be different if we had the actual samples.'

'The *Guardia Civil* have their own laboratories – that's where the samples are kept. You know how reticent their top brass is about sharing information. I've been saying for years that until we set up an independent criminal investigation unit, with members from all the different forces, including Interpol, working together in the same laboratories, investigations like this one will continue to grope in the dark,' complained Amaia. 'Thank heavens for officers like Padua, who are genuinely interested in solving crimes, not in scoring points.'

Amaia walked back to the body, leaning over as San Martín had done to take a closer look at the wound.

The flesh looked withered and cracked, dried out. The skin had a pale, faintly washed-out quality compared to the rest of the body. Seeing the tiny serrations the blade had made on the bone, she suddenly thought she could make out a dark, pointed object embedded in the flesh.

'Come over here will you, Doctor? What do you think this could be?' she asked, stepping aside so he could look through the magnifier.

He glanced up, surprised.

'I didn't see that. Well done, Salazar,' he complimented her. 'I expect it's a bit of bone that broke off during the amputation,' he explained, extracting the fragment with a pair of tweezers. He examined the tiny triangle beneath the magnifier before placing it on a tray, where it made a definite metallic tinkle. He carried it swiftly over to the microscope, then raised his eyes with a grin as he made room for her. 'Inspector Salazar, what we have here is the tooth of a metal saw – the saw used to amputate the victim's arm. If we make a mock-up from this one tooth, we'll have a good chance of establishing

102

approximately what type of saw it was. And if you're clever enough to persuade Judge Markina, we should be able to carry out tests to ascertain whether the same instrument was used on the bones discovered in the cave in Elizondo. And now, if you don't mind, I'll get on with the autopsy,' he said, handing the tray containing the sample to his assistant, who immediately set to work.

8

Inmaculada Herranz was one of those women who earned people's trust by appearing at once friendly and anxious to please. With her slight build and discreet gestures, Amaia had always thought of her as an ugly geisha; her soft voice and hooded eyelids disguised the stern expression on her face something upset her. Amaia had never warmed to her, despite, or perhaps because of, her affected politeness. For six years, Inmaculada had been Judge Estébanez's efficient and ever-willing personal assistant, but the judge had no qualms about leaving her behind when she was promoted to her new post on the High Court in Madrid, even though Inmaculada was unmarried and had no children.

Inmaculada's dismay soon gave way to glee when Judge Markina filled the vacant post, although from then on she was obliged to spend more of her salary on clothes and perfume in an effort to make Markina notice her. And she wasn't the only one; there was a joke doing the rounds of the courtrooms about the increased expenditure on lipstick and hairdressers among female staff.

Amaia had dialled Markina's number on her way to her car. Searching her pockets for a pair of sunglasses to ward off the dazzling light reflected in the rain puddles, she waited to hear his secretary's mellifluous voice.

'Good afternoon, Inmaculada, this is Inspector Salazar from the murder squad at the Navarre Police Department. Could I speak to Judge Markina, please?'

Her icy response took Amaia by surprise.

'It's two-thirty in the afternoon and, as you can imagine, the judge isn't here.'

'Yes, I know what time it is. I've just come from an autopsy, the results of which Judge Markina is waiting to hear. He asked me to call him . . .'

'I see . . .' replied the secretary.

'I find it hard to believe he would forget. Do you know if he's coming back later?'

'No, he isn't coming back, and of course he hasn't forgotten.' She paused for a few seconds, then added: 'He left a number for you to call.'

Amaia waited in silence, amused at her blatant hostility. She sighed loudly to make it clear her patience was wearing thin, then asked:

'So, Inmaculada, are you going to give me that number, or do I need a court order? Ah, no, wait, I already have one from the judge himself.'

She didn't respond, but even over the telephone, Amaia could sense the woman pursing her lips and narrowing her eyes in that prudish way so typical of mousy women like her. She read the number out once then hung up without saying goodbye.

Amaia looked at her mobile in amazement. *What a long streak of misery!* she thought. She punched in the numbers from memory and waited.

Judge Markina replied after one ring tone.

'I thought it might be you, Salazar. I see my secretary relayed my message.'

'Sorry to bother you, your honour, but I've just come from

Lucía Aguirre's autopsy. The forensic report is conclusive, we have fresh evidence, which in my opinion warrants further investigation.'

'Are you talking about reopening the case?' Markina asked, hesitantly.

Amaia forced herself to be more cautious.

'I wouldn't presume to tell you how to do your job, your honour. However, this fresh evidence points to a new line of investigation, without prejudice to the initial one. Neither we nor the pathologist are questioning Quiralte's guilt, but—'

'Very well,' the judge interrupted her, seeming to reflect for a moment. His tone suggested she had aroused his interest. 'Come and talk me through it in person, and remember to bring the pathologist's report.'

Amaia glanced at her watch.

'Will you be in your office this afternoon?' she asked.

'No, I'm out of town, but I'll be dining at El Rodero tonight at nine, come there and we can talk.'

She hung up, glancing again at her watch. The pathologist's report would be ready by then, but if they were to arrive at a reasonable hour James would have to go on ahead to Elizondo with Ibai. She could join them there after her meeting with the judge. She sighed as she climbed into the car, thinking to herself that if she hurried she might make it home in time to give her son his three o'clock feed.

Ibai was crying erratically, alternating gasps and wails to show his annoyance. Between protests, he sucked at the bottle James was struggling to keep in his mouth, cradling him in his arms. He grinned sheepishly when he saw her.

'We've been doing this for twenty minutes and so far I've only managed to make him take twenty millilitres, but we're slowly getting there.'

'Come to *Ama, maitia*,' she said, spreading her arms wide as James passed the baby to her. 'Did you miss me, my love?'

she added, kissing his face and giggling when he started to suck her chin. 'Oh, my darling, I'm so sorry, *Ama* is very late, but I'm here now.'

She sat down in an armchair, folding the baby in her arms, then devoted the next half-hour to him. Ibai's fretfulness slowly faded, he relaxed and grew calm as Amaia caressed his head, tracing with her forefinger his perfect, tiny features, marvelling at the clear, bright eyes gazing back at her with the intensity and wonderment of an audacious lover.

When she had finished breastfeeding him, she took Ibai to the room Clarice had decorated for him, changed his nappy, reluctantly acknowledging that the furnishings were comfortable and practical, although the baby still slept with them in their bedroom. Afterwards, she cradled him in her arms, singing softly to him until he fell asleep.

'It's not good for him to get into the habit of falling asleep like that,' James whispered behind her. 'You should leave him in the cot so he learns to relax and goes off on his own.'

'He has the rest of his life to do that,' she said rather brusquely. Then she reflected, and added in a softer voice: 'Let me pamper him a little, James. You're right, I know, but I miss him so much . . . And I suppose I'm afraid he'll stop missing me.'

'Of course he won't, silly,' said James, picking the sleeping child up and moving him to his cot. He arranged a blanket over him and looked again at his wife. 'I miss you too, Amaia.'

Their eyes met, and for an instant she felt the urge to fling herself into his arms, into that embrace, which, over time, had become the unequivocal symbol of their union, their love for one another. An embrace that always made her feel protected and understood. But the urge didn't last. She was seized by a sudden frustration. She was tired, she'd skipped lunch, and had just come from an autopsy . . . For the love of God! She was forced to rush from one side of the city to the other, she scarcely had time to be with her son, but all James could think of was that he missed her. She missed herself! She couldn't remember the last time she'd had five minutes to herself. She hated him for looking at her with those mournful, dead sheep's eyes. It didn't help; no, it didn't help one bit. She left the room, overwhelmed by feelings of anger and remorse. James was a darling, a wonderful father and the most tolerant man any woman could wish for, but he was a man, and therefore light years away from understanding how she felt, which drove her crazy.

She went into the kitchen. Sensing him behind her, she avoided his gaze while she made herself a cup of coffee.

'Have you had lunch? Do you want me to make you something?' he asked, going over to the fridge.

'No, James, don't bother,' she said, sitting down with her milky coffee at the head of the table. 'Look, James, a meeting has come up with the judge in charge of the case I'm investigating. I can't put it off and he can only see me this evening, which is when I'll have the autopsy report. It's extremely important . . .'

He nodded.

'We could drive up to Elizondo tomorrow morning.'

'No, I want to be there first thing, so we'd have to get up very early. I think it's best if you go on ahead with Ibai and install yourselves at my aunt's house. I'll feed him before you leave, and be there for the next one.'

James started to chew his upper lip – a gesture she knew he only did when he was anxious.

'Amaia, I wanted to talk to you about that . . .'

She gazed at him in silence.

'I think that slavishly following this schedule to keep him breastfeeding . . .' she saw he was searching for the right words, '. . . isn't really compatible with your work. Maybe it's time for you seriously to consider weaning him off breast milk completely.'

Amaia looked at her husband wishing she could express

everything that was bubbling inside her. She was trying, trying as hard as she could. She wanted to succeed, for Ibai's sake, but above all for herself, for the sake of the child she once was, the daughter of a bad mother. She wanted to be a good mother, she needed to be, otherwise she would be bad, like her own mother. And suddenly she found herself wondering how much of Rosario was in *her*. Wasn't the frustration she felt a sign that perhaps something wasn't right? Where was the joy all those manuals on motherhood promised? Where was the perfect fulfilment a mother was supposed to feel? Why did she only feel exhaustion and a sense of failure?

Instead she said:

'I already had this job when you met me, James. You accepted that I was and always would be a police officer. If you thought my job would prevent me from being a good wife and mother, you should have said so then.' She stood up and deposited her cup in the sink, adding as she brushed past him: 'I don't need to tell you, this is a marriage, not a life sentence. If you don't like it . . .'

James pulled an incredulous face.

'For heaven's sake, Amaia! Don't be so melodramatic,' he said, rising and following her down the corridor.

She wheeled around, pressing a finger to her lips.

'You'll wake up Ibai.' She went into the bathroom, leaving James standing in the middle of the corridor, shaking his head in disbelief.

She couldn't fall asleep, and spent the next two hours tossing and turning on the bed, trying unsuccessfully to relax enough to get some rest, while the murmur of the TV James was watching floated in from the living room.

She knew she was behaving like a shrew, being unfair on James, yet somehow she couldn't help feeling he deserved it . . . Why? Simply for being understanding? Loving? She wasn't quite sure what she wanted from him, only that she felt bad

109

inside, and wished he wouldn't simplify things so much, that he could unburden her, reassure her, but above all understand her. She would have given anything for him to understand her, to realise it had to be this way. Reaching out to touch the empty half of the bed, she dragged James's pillow towards her, pressing her face into it to find his smell. Why was she making such a mess of things? She felt the urge to go to him . . . to tell him . . . to tell him . . . she wasn't sure what, maybe that she was sorry.

She climbed out of bed and padded barefoot across the oak floorboards, which creaked underfoot. Poking her head round the door, she saw that James was asleep, propped up on his side, while a succession of adverts illuminated the room where the natural light had faded a while ago. She studied his peaceful expression, reflected in the TV screen. As she approached him, she stopped in her tracks. She had always envied his ability to fall asleep anytime, anywhere, but suddenly, the fact that he could do that when he was supposed to be upset, at least as upset as she was . . . What the hell! They'd had probably their worst argument ever, and he went off to sleep, as relaxed as if he'd just got out of the sauna. *Two* million light years away. She glanced at her watch: they still had to pack all the things Ibai would need in Elizondo. Leaving the room, she called out as she walked away:

'James.'

After loading the car as if they were about to climb Everest rather than spend a few days fifty kilometres from home, she gave James a dozen instructions about Ibai, his clothes, how to dress him so he wouldn't catch cold but wouldn't sweat too much, then kissed the baby, who gazed at her from his car seat, content after his feed. He had slept all afternoon and would probably stay awake all the way to Elizondo, but he wouldn't cry. He liked being in the car with its soft purring sound, and seemed to love the music James played, a little too loud, she thought, so that even if he didn't sleep, he would enjoy a relaxed journey.

'I'll be there in time for his next feed.'

'. . . And if not, I'll give him the bottle,' replied James, installed behind the wheel.

She was about to answer back, but wanted to avoid another argument with him. Partly out of superstition, she didn't want them to part on an angry note. As a police officer she had witnessed all too often the responses of relatives when told that a loved one had died, how much deeper their grief was if at the time of that person's death they weren't on speaking terms because of a usually trivial argument that would resonate for evermore like a life sentence. She leant through the open window and kissed James tentatively on the lips.

'I love you, Amaia,' he said, making it sound like a warning, as he turned the key in the ignition.

I know you do, she thought to herself, stepping back. *And I'm only kissing and making up because I couldn't bear you to die in an accident when you were mad at me*. She gave a half-hearted wave, which he didn't see, and stood, arms clasped around herself to try to alleviate the remorse she felt. She watched the car roll slowly down the street, which was pedestrian-only at that time of day except for residents, until the red tail-lights vanished out of sight.

Shivering in the chilly Pamplona evening, she went back inside, glancing at the envelope that had been sitting in the hallway since a police officer delivered it an hour ago. More than anything she longed to soak in a hot bath. She opened the bathroom door and caught sight of herself in the mirror: eyes ringed in dark circles; hair dull and straw-like with split ends – she couldn't remember the last time she had been to a hairdresser. She checked the time, felt a flash of anger as she postponed the longed-for bath and climbed into the shower. She let the hot water run until the screen misted up and she could no longer see out. Then she started to cry, as if some inner barrier had given way and a rising tide threatened to drown her from within. Miserable and helpless, she stood there, her tears mingling with the scalding water.

The restaurant El Rodero wasn't far from her house. When she and James dined there, they usually walked, so that they could have a drink without worrying about driving. This time she took the car, in order to be able to leave for Elizondo as soon as she finished talking to the judge. She parked at an angle opposite Media Luna Park, crossed the street and walked beneath the arcade where El Rodero was located. The large, brightly lit windows and the understated décor of the façade were a promise of the excellent cuisine that had earned the restaurant a Michelin star. The dark wood floor and cherry-wood chairs with cushioned backs contrasted with the beige panelling that reached up to the ceiling. The mirrors that lined the walls, combined with the pristine white tablecloths and crockery, added a touch of brightness, accentuated by the floral decorations floating in crystal bowls on the tables.

A waitress greeted her as she entered, offering to take her coat. Amaia declined.

'Good evening,' she said. 'I'm meeting one of your diners, could you tell him I'm here?'

'Yes, of course.'

Amaia hesitated, unsure whether the judge used his title outside of work.

'Mr Markina.'

The young girl smiled.

'Judge Markina is expecting you. Follow me, please,' she said, escorting her to the far end of the restaurant.

They passed through the room Amaia had assumed they would be meeting in, and the waitress pointed her to one of the best tables beside the chef's personal library. Five chairs stood around it but only two places were set. Markina rose to greet her, extending his hand.

112

'Good evening, Salazar,' he said, avoiding using her rank.

The approving look the waitress gave the handsome judge didn't escape her.

'Please, take a seat,' he said.

Amaia paused for a moment, gazing at the chair he was indicating. She disliked sitting with her back to the door (a professional quirk), but she did as Markina suggested, and sat facing him.

'Your honour,' she began, 'forgive me for bothering you . . .'

'It's no bother, providing you agree to join me. I've already ordered, but I'd feel most uncomfortable if you were to sit and watch me eat.'

His tone brooked no argument, and Amaia became uneasy.

'But . . .' she protested, pointing to the place set for a second person.

'That's for you. As I told you, I hate people watching me eat. I took the liberty. I hope you don't mind,' he said, although it didn't sound as if he cared much whether she minded or not. She observed his body language as he shook open his napkin and placed it on his knees.

So that explained why Markina's secretary was so hostile. Amaia could just imagine her making the reservation that morning with her cloying voice, lips set in a thin straight line. Recalling Inmaculada's words, it dawned on her that Markina had made the reservation even before she called with the results of the autopsy. He knew she would ring him as soon as she got out, and had arranged the dinner in advance. She wondered how far in advance, whether Markina had even been out of town at midday. She couldn't prove anything. It was equally possible he'd made a reservation for one and asked them to lay another place when he arrived.

'This won't take long, your honour, then I'll let you dine in peace. In fact, if you don't mind, I'll start right away.'

She reached into her bag and fished out a brown file that

she placed on the table, just as the waiter approached with a bottle of Navarrese Chardonnay.

'Who would like to taste the wine?'

'Mademoiselle,' replied the judge.

'Madam,' she retorted, 'and I won't have any wine, I'm driving.'

Markina grinned:

'Water for the lady, then, and wine for me, alas.'

As soon as the waiter moved away, Amaia opened the file.

'Not now,' said Markina, sharply. 'Please,' he added, in a more conciliatory tone. 'One look at that and I'll lose my appetite completely. There are some things one never gets used to.'

'Your honour . . .' she protested.

The waiter placed two dishes in front of them, both containing a small golden-brown parcel adorned with green and red sprouts and leaves.

'Truffles and mushrooms in a golden parcel. Enjoy your meal, sir, madam,' he said, withdrawing.

'Your honour . . .' she protested once more.

'Please, call me Javier.'

Amaia's anger rose as she started to feel like the victim of an ambush, a blind date meticulously planned by this cretin, who even had the nerve to order for her, and now he wanted her to call him by his first name.

Amaia pushed back her chair.

'Your honour, I think it's better if we talk later, once you've finished your meal. In the meantime, I'll wait for you outside.'

He gave a smile that seemed at once sincere and guilty.

'Salazar, please don't feel uncomfortable. I still don't know many people in Pamplona. I love gourmet cooking, and I'm a regular here. I always let the chef decide what I eat, but if the dish isn't to your liking, I'll ask them to bring you the menu. Just because we're meeting as colleagues, it doesn't mean we can't enjoy a good meal. Would you have felt more comfortable if we'd met at McDonald's for a hamburger? I know I wouldn't.'

Amaia looked askance at him.

'Please, eat while you tell me about the case, only let's leave the photos until last.'

She was hungry. She hadn't eaten anything solid since breakfast, she never did when attending an autopsy, and the aroma of mushroom and truffle from the crispy golden parcel was making her stomach rumble.

'Very well,' she said. They would dine if he insisted, but they'd do so in record time.

They ate the first course in silence, Amaia realising how ravenous she had been.

The waiter removed the plates and replaced them with two more.

'Pearly soup with shellfish, seafood and seaweed,' he said before withdrawing.

'One of my favourites,' said Markina.

'And mine,' she echoed.

'Do you eat at this restaurant?' he asked, trying to conceal his surprise.

A cretin and arrogant with it, she thought.

'Yes, but we usually reserve a more intimate table.'

'I like this one, looking at the other diners . . .'

And being looked at, thought Amaia.

'Browsing the library,' he explained. 'Luis Rodero has a fine collection of books on cuisine from all over the world.'

Amaia glanced at the spines of a few, among them *The Challenge of Spanish Cuisine*, a thick, dark volume by El Bulli, as well as the splendid cover of *Spanish Cuisine* by Cándido.

The waiter placed a fish dish before them.

'Hake in *velouté* with crab jelly, hints of vanilla, pepper and lime.'

Amaia tucked in, only half able to savour the subtleties of

the dish between glancing at the time and listening to Markina making small talk.

When at last the table was cleared, Amaia declined dessert and ordered coffee. The judge did the same, but with visible reluctance. She waited until the coffee was on the table before once more producing the documents and placing them in front of him.

She saw him pull a face, but went ahead. She sat up straight, instantly sure of herself, on her own ground. Turning her chair slightly to one side so that she could see the door, she felt relaxed for the first time since she'd arrived.

'During the autopsy, we found clues indicating that the Lucía Aguirre case is probably related to at least one other murder that took place a year ago near Lekaroz,' she said, picking out one of the files to show to him. 'Johana Márquez was raped and strangled by her stepfather. He confessed to the crime when he was arrested, but the girl's body presented the same type of mutilation as that of Lucía Aguirre: amputation of the forearm at the elbow. Both Johana Márquez's and Lucía Aguirre's killers took their own lives and left behind identical messages.'

She showed Markina the photographs of the wall in Quiralte's cell and the note Medina had left for her.

He nodded, his curiosity aroused.

'Do you think the two men knew each other?'

'I doubt it, but we could find out for sure if you authorised an investigation.'

He looked at her uncertainly.

'There's something else,' she said, 'which might be unrelated, but I'm pursuing a lead that suggests a similar amputation was carried out in a crime that took place nearly three years ago in Logroño. As with these two cases, the murder itself was a messy affair, yet the corpse was subjected to a text-book amputation and the severed limb was nowhere to be found.'

'In all three cases?' Markina said, alarmed, rifling through the papers.

'Yes, three so far, but I have a hunch there could be more.'

'Explain to me exactly what we're looking for here. A bizarre fraternity of bungling killers who decide to imitate a macabre procedure they possibly read about in the newspapers?'

'Perhaps, although I don't think the press gave sufficient details of the amputation to enable someone to imitate it so precisely. In the Johana Márquez case, that information was withheld. What I can confirm is that the perpetrator in Logroño killed himself in his cell, leaving behind the same message on the wall: *TARTTALO*, with two "t"s. This in itself is noteworthy, because the usual spelling is with one "t". This leads me to think that their actions are so specific that in themselves they point to a clear identity, the hallmark of a single individual. It's improbable, to say the least, that the behaviour of these animals would diverge so substantially from the pattern of abusers who kill. The cases I've been able to look at tick all the profile boxes: connection to the victim, prolonged abuse, alcoholism or drugs, violent, impulsive personality. The only element that clashed at the crime scenes was the postmortem amputation of the forearm – the same arm in each case – and the fact that the limb was missing.'

Markina flicked through one of the reports in his hand.

'I myself questioned Johana Márquez's stepfather,' she went on. 'He denied all knowledge of the severed limb, insisting he had nothing to do with the amputation, despite having confessed to charges of harassment, murder, rape, and necrophilia . . .'

Amaia watched Markina, who ran his hand absentmindedly over his chin as he pondered the information with a wistful expression that made him appear older and more attractive. From afar, the waitress who had accompanied her to the table was standing by the lectern at the entrance, also observing him intently.

'So, what do you think?'

'I think we're looking at an accomplice, a fourth person who could be the link between these three perpetrators and their crimes.'

Markina remained silent, his eyes moving between the documents and Amaia. For the first time that evening she was beginning to feel truly at ease. Finally, she saw on Markina's face that familiar expression, which she frequently encountered on the faces of her colleagues as well as her superiors, when putting forward her arguments: interest, the kind of interest that generated questions, a thorough analysis of the facts and theories that would trigger an investigation. Markina's eyes grew steelier while he was thinking, his undeniably handsome face acquiring an air of intelligence that she found extremely attractive. She contemplated the perfect outline of his lips, reflecting that it was no surprise that half the female secretaries in the courtroom were vying for his attention. The thought made her smile, breaking Markina's concentration.

'What's so funny?'

'Nothing, sorry,' she said, smiling again. 'Honestly, it's nothing . . . I was just remembering something. It isn't important.'

He looked at her, his curiosity piqued.

'That's the first time I've seen you smile.'

'What?' she replied, slightly taken aback by the observation.

He continued to stare at her, his expression serious again. She held his gaze for a few seconds then lowered her eyes towards the manila file. She cleared her throat.

'So?' she said, looking up, in control once more.

He nodded.

'I think you might be on to something . . . I'm going to give you my authorisation. But be discreet and keep it low-key: we don't want the press getting hold of this. Theoretically, these cases are closed, so we need to avoid causing the victims' families any unnecessary suffering. Keep me abreast of your progress. And if you need anything don't hesitate to ask me,' he added, looking straight at her again.

She didn't allow herself to be intimidated.

'OK, I'll take things slowly. I'm working on another case with my team, so there won't be much to report in the next few days.'

'Whenever you're ready,' he replied.

She started to gather up the various papers spread over the table. Markina reached out and touched her hand for a split second.

'You'll stay for another coffee, won't you? . . .'

She paused.

'Yes, I have to drive, it'll keep me awake.'

He raised his hand to order two coffees, while she hurriedly collected the papers.

'I thought you lived in the old quarter?'

You're well informed, your honour, she thought as the waiter brought over their coffees.

'I do, but I have to travel to Baztán because of the investigation I mentioned.'

'You're from there originally, aren't you?'

'Yes,' she replied.

'I've heard the food is excellent. Perhaps you could recommend a restaurant . . .'

Four or five names instantly came into her head.

'I'm afraid not. The fact is, I seldom go there,' she lied, 'and when I do, I tend to eat with my relatives.'

He smiled in disbelief, raising an eyebrow. Amaia took the opportunity to drink her coffee and put the files back in her bag.

'And now, if you'll excuse me, your honour, I really must go,' she said, pushing back her chair.

Markina rose to his feet.

'Where's your car?'

'Oh, not far, I'm parked right outside.'

'Wait,' he said grabbing his coat. 'I'll accompany you.'

'There's no need.'

'I insist.'

He hovered while the waiter brought his card, then took her coat and held it up for her to put on.

'Thanks,' she said, snatching it from him, 'but I never wear it when I'm driving, I find it bothersome,' she added, her tone making it unclear whether she was referring to the coat or to all Markina's attentions.

Markina's expression clouded slightly as they made their way to the door. She held it open until he caught up with her. The temperature outside was several degrees colder, and the moisture in the air had condensed into mist above the thick cluster of trees in the park. This only occurred in that part of the city, causing the orange light from the streetlamps to form hazy circles in the floating mist.

They walked out from under the arcades and crossed the street, which was lined with parked cars, although there was little traffic at that time of night. Amaia pressed the remote, and turned to Markina.

'Thank you, your honour, I'll keep you informed,' she said, keeping her tone professional.

But he stepped around her and opened the car door.

She sighed, trying not to lose her patience.

'Thank you.'

She flung her coat inside and clambered into the driver's seat. She was no fool; she had seen what Markina was up to hours ago and was determined to repel all his advances.

'Good night, your honour,' she said, grabbing the handle to close the door and turning the key in the ignition.

'Salazar . . .' he whispered. '. . . Amaia.'

Uh oh, a warning voice echoed in her head, as she looked up to find his eyes flashing at her with a mixture of entreaty and desire.

Markina reached out, caressing with the back of his hand

a stray lock of hair tumbling on to her shoulder. Feeling her stiffen, he took his hand away, embarrassed.

'Inspector Salazar,' she said brusquely.

'I'm sorry?' he said, bewildered.

'That's how you should address me: Inspector Salazar, Chief Salazar, or just plain Salazar.'

He nodded, and Amaia thought she saw him flush. The light was poor.

'Good night, Judge Markina.' She closed the door and reversed on to the road. 'What a jerk!' she cried, glancing in her rear-view mirror at Markina, who hadn't moved.

There was nothing to be gained from making enemies with a judge, she reflected, sincerely hoping that she had managed with her parting remark to establish the boundaries of their relationship – which was purely professional – without wounding Markina's male pride. She recognised that puppy-dog look in his eyes: she had seen it in other men, and it invariably led to problems, problems that could hamper an investigation. She hoped he didn't feel snubbed. He had gone out of his way to set up their meeting, and she was sure that a good-looking guy like him wasn't used to being rejected.

'There's always a first time,' she said out loud.

She imagined that the efforts of the female staff at the courthouse, headed by the obsequious, self-sacrificing Inmaculada Herranz would pay off, and that one of them would turn Markina's head in next to no time.

She glanced at her reflection in the rear-view mirror.

'Oh my, but he's such a hunk!' she laughed, instinctively raising a hand to where he had touched her hair, and smiling. She switched on the radio as she took the Baztán road, humming along to a tune she only knew from hearing it in the car.

Entering the vast Baztán forest at night is like being cast adrift on the high seas in pitch darkness, not a star in sight. The pale moonlight barely filtering through the clouds did not help much, only the powerful headlights cut through the gloom, throwing a shaft of light on the bends in the road and bisecting the darkness. Amaia slowed down: if her car veered off on one of those bends it would be impossible to see it from the road. The forest, like some age-old black-mawed beast, would swallow it up. Even in daylight a black off-roader like hers would be difficult to spot among the thick under-growth. A shiver ran down her spine.

'Much loved, much feared,' she whispered.

As she passed the Hotel Baztán, she glanced towards the car park, poorly lit by four streetlamps and the faint glow spilling from the windows of the café, which looked full even at that late hour. She couldn't help remembering Fermín Montes brandishing his police firearm, aiming it first at Flora, then pressing it to his own head; the image of him sprawled on the tarmac as Inspector Iriarte restrained him, tears mingling with the dusty ground of the car park. The Commissioner's words echoed in her head: 'I'm not trying to influence your decision, I'm merely informing you.'

She reached the old quarter of Elizondo, drove along Calle Santiago, then turned left, feeling the bounce of cobblestones beneath the tyres as she descended to the Muniartea Bridge. She crossed, took a left and parked outside her aunt's house, which had been home to her from the age of nine until she left Elizondo. She searched for the key on her key ring and unlocked the door. Warm and vibrant, the house welcomed her with the energy of its inhabitant, the eternal drone of the TV humming in the background.

'Hello, Amaia,' Engrasi called out from her chair by the fire in the living room.

Amaia felt a wave of tenderness the moment she saw her aunt, with her silver hair swept up into a loose bun that gave her the air of a romantic heroine in an English novel, sitting upright in an elegant posture as if she were taking tea with the queen.

'Don't get up, Auntie,' she said, leaning over to give her a kiss. 'How are you, beautiful?'

Engrasi chuckled. 'I doubt I look beautiful in this old thing,' she said, tweaking the lapel of her flannel robe.

'You'll always be the fairest in my eyes.'

'My dear child,' she said, embracing her.

Amaia glanced around the room, drinking in its familiar atmosphere. This was one of her rituals when she came home; part inspection, part declaration, as if she were saying: 'Here I am, I'm back!' She wasn't sure where the compulsion came from, but she'd stopped wondering why she felt that way when she was there, preferring simply to enjoy it.

'And my little man?'

'Asleep. He went out like a light after after his feed about half an hour ago. James took him upstairs to bed, but I think he must have dozed off himself, it's been quiet up there for a while,' she said, pointing to the baby monitor, whose garish colours jarred with Engrasi's wooden table.

Slipping out of her leather boots, Amaia climbed the stairs, feeling the wood beneath her bare feet. She repressed the urge to run up, the way she used to as a child.

In the bluish glow spilling from the bedside lamp James had left on, she could see that he had set up Ibai's travel cot by the window and was lying asleep on his side, his outstretched arm resting on the edge of the cot. She walked around the bed to find Ibai sleeping peacefully in his warm Babygro. Switching off the monitor, she slipped out of her pullover, pushed her jeans down to the floor and leapt into bed. Pressing herself against James's back, she grinned mischievously as she noticed him tremble at the touch of her cold body.

'You're freezing, my love,' he whispered sleepily.

'Will you warm me up?' she said coquettishly, nestling closer.

'All you want,' he replied, slightly more awake.

'I want it all.'

As James turned over, she used the chance to kiss him, greedily exploring his mouth.

He recoiled in surprise.

'Are you sure?' he said, pointing at the cot.

Since Ibai's birth, Amaia had been reticent about having sex with the baby in the room.

'I'm sure,' she replied, kissing him again.

They made love without any hurry, gazing at one another in disbelief, as if they'd met for the first time that night and were marvelling at their good fortune, beaming with the contentment and relief of those who know they have just salvaged something precious, something they'd thought lost. Afterwards, they lay in silence until James clasped her hand and turned to look at her.

'I'm glad you're back,' he said. 'Things haven't been great between us lately.'

A faint rustle from the cot obliged him to sit up and look at Ibai, who had started to fidget, giving soft moans that heralded a bout of crying.

'He's hungry,' he said, looking at her.

'I was here in time for his feed, but Engrasi told me you'd already given him the bottle,' she said, trying not to make it sound like a reproach.

'Well, I read somewhere that you should feed babies on demand, and he was getting agitated. I see no harm in giving him the bottle if he's hungry before you get there. Besides, he had less than fifteen millilitres.'

'I don't think it's good to be feeding him all day. You heard what the paediatrician said: it's important to stick to a schedule.'

'I'm not to blame if we don't stick to a schedule . . .' he replied.

'And you're suggesting I am? I told you, I was here on time.'

'Amaia, the child isn't a clock. Arriving on time once isn't enough. What about the last time? And next time? Can you guarantee you'll be here?'

She said nothing. Gathering Ibai in her arms, she sat up in bed to feed him. James lay next to her, stroking the baby's neck with his finger. He closed his eyes. Less than two minutes later, Amaia could tell from his steady breathing that he was fast asleep. *Sometimes he drives me crazy*, she thought, as she tried to relax. She'd read somewhere that a mother can pass on her anxiety to her baby and give him colic.

When Ibai had finished feeding, she propped him against her shoulder until he burped, then cradled him in her arms until she felt his delicate body slacken as sleep claimed him. Leaning over him, she breathed in the rich fragrance from his little head and smiled. Even before Ibai was born, before he was even in her belly, she had loved him. She had loved him ever since as a little girl she played at being a mother, a good mother. And this pained her now, for deep in her heart she felt that all her love was not enough, that she was doing everything wrong, that she didn't deserve to be a mother. Perhaps that instinct was missing from the women in her family. And possibly along with those genes she had inherited something darker and more cruel.

She clasped one of Ibai's tiny hands, splayed out like a starfish now that he was sated. Her water baby, her river baby, who like the river itself had come to claim its territory, overflowing its banks, flooding the land, like a king returning from the crusades. She raised the tiny hand to her lips and kissed it reverentially.

'I'm doing my best, Ibai,' she whispered, as the sleeping child responded with a deep sigh that scented the air about him.

9

Dawn broke at seven thirty, and although it wasn't raining, a blanket of cloud seemed to cascade down the mountains, like foam spilling out of a gigantic bathtub, encircling the valley. As she saw it descending the slopes, thick and white, she knew that within half an hour driving would be difficult.

Amaia kept the car in second gear as she rolled through the narrow streets of the Txokoto neighbourhood, having decided to have coffee with her sister at the bakery before going on to the police station. Driving past the darkened windows, she turned left into the car park at the back then stepped on the brake in surprise. The main wall of the bakery was covered in a huge graffiti sprayed in black paint. Brush in hand, Ros was busy painting over the dark lines, but underneath could still be read: 'MURDERING WHORE'.

Amaia stepped out of the car and watched from a distance.

'Well, apparently not everyone in the village sees Flora as a heroine,' she said, walking over, eyes still fixed on the graffiti.

'Apparently not.' Ros smiled sheepishly. 'Good morning, little sister.' She left the brush on the paint pot, as she went to give Amaia a kiss.

'I was wondering whether you might make me one of those wonderful coffees with your Italian machine.'

'My pleasure,' she said, following her into the bakery.

As she entered, Amaia took a deep breath, the way she had always done as far back as she could remember. That morning she inhaled the aroma of anisette.

'We're making donuts today,' explained Ros.

Amaia didn't reply straight away. The smell she would forever associate with her mother had stirred her memory, transporting her back in time.

'It smells of . . .'

Ros said nothing. She set out the plates and cups, switching on the grinder to make freshly ground coffee for two. They didn't speak until Ros turned the machine off.

'Sorry not to wait up for you last night, I was exhausted . . .'

'Don't worry. In the end, Aunt Engrasi was the only one who stayed awake. James and Ibai were both dead to the world when I arrived.'

Amaia noticed at once: Ros barely raised her head as she took small sips of coffee from her cup, which she cradled in both hands, keeping it level with her face, like a wall she could hide behind.

'Are you OK, Ros?' Amaia asked, searching her face.

'Yes, of course, I'm OK,' she blurted.

'Are you sure?'

'Don't do this.'

'Don't do what?'

'Interrogate me, Amaia.'

Her reaction made Amaia all the more curious. She knew her older sister, the middle child, the most kind-hearted of the three sisters, the one who always seemed to carry the weight of the world on her shoulders, and was less able to cope with stress, the one who preferred to keep quiet, to bury her problems beneath layers of silence and make-up in an effort to conceal her anxiety.

127

The assistants started turning up for work and the manager, Ernesto, poked his head round the office door to say hello. Amaia noticed her sister's look of relief as she entered into discussions about the day's tasks, like someone avoiding a painful conversation. Placing her empty cup on the draining board, Amaia walked out of the bakery, lingering briefly outside to observe traces of even older graffiti beneath the layers of white paint.

With its modernist straight lines, the Elizondo police station could not have contrasted more with the rest of the architecture in the valley. It was so out of place it resembled a strange artefact left behind by aliens from outer space. Even so, Amaia couldn't help but admire the building's pragmatism, with its huge picture windows designed to act as a magnifying glass, trapping the meagre Baztán sun in winter. As she went up in the lift, she sketched out a mental plan of her day. The doors slid open and the jovial atmosphere of male camaraderie greeted her. She took in the group of police officers chatting next to the coffee machine; Deputy Inspector Zabalza and Inspector Iriarte seemed to be enjoying themselves in the company of Fermín Montes, who was evidently telling them a story, accompanied by an assortment of hand gestures. She walked past without stopping.

'Good morning, gentlemen.'

The conversation broke off abruptly.

'Good morning,' they replied as one, Montes following her to the office door.

'Salazar.' She stopped. 'Do you have a moment?'

'Actually, I don't, Montes, I'm due to leave in one minute to investigate a case we're working on,' she said, glancing over at the other two officers, who instantly straightened up. 'Perhaps if you'd warned me beforehand . . .'

She went into the office and closed the door, leaving Montes outside looking peevish. Inside, Deputy Inspector

Jonan Etxaide looked up from his computer. She greeted him cheerily.

'What's up? Why aren't you with the Vikings around the coffee machine?'

'I don't really drink coffee, chief. At least, not with them.'

Amaia looked at him, surprised.

'Don't you get along with them?'

'It's not that. I guess they don't feel completely at ease with me.'

'Why?' asked Amaia. 'Surely not because . . .?'

Jonan grinned.

'Well, being gay doesn't exactly help, but I'm not sure that's the reason. In any case, don't worry about it. I don't.'

'"Loyalty has a calm heart",' she quoted.

'Do you read Shakespeare, chief?'

She sighed in mock despair.

'The only books I get to read these days are written by renowned paediatricians, educationalists and child psychologists.'

There was a knock on the door and Iriarte and Zabalza walked in.

'Good morning, gentlemen.' Amaia immediately launched into what she had to say: 'Today we're going to pursue two distinct lines of inquiry: Inspector Iriarte and I will visit the chaplain and the priest at Arizkun, while Jonan will carry on checking out anti-Catholic websites and forums, as well as any sites relating to the *agotes* here in the valley. Zabalza, you can help him.'

The three men made to get up.

'One other thing. May I remind you that Inspector Fermín is still suspended from duty, and should be treated the same way as any other visitor here at the police station. Also, he is strictly forbidden from entering working areas, which includes the archive room, and the firearms unit . . . and from having access to any information regarding the case we are working on. Is that clear?'

'Yes.' Iriarte nodded, while Zabalza murmured his assent, blushing to the roots of his hair.

'Let's get to work, gentlemen.'

The chaplain wasn't much help. Extremely hard of hearing, he crossed himself a dozen times as he tottered with tiny, swift steps around the chapel. Iriarte turned to Amaia and grinned as they struggled to keep up with the fellow, who gesticulated wildly as he showed them the remains of the baptismal font in the sacristy and the splintered pew. It gave off the familiar scent of aged wood that reminded Amaia of her grandmother Juanita's furniture.

'Look at this outrage!' exclaimed the chaplain, gazing forlornly at the two halves of the ruined font.

His face froze in an exaggerated grimace, bordering on comical, his eyes filling with tears, as he lifted the front of his flowing, black cassock and rummaged in one of his pockets for a starched white handkerchief to wipe away his tears.

'Forgive me,' he boomed, 'but you can't deny that only a scoundrel would do something like this.'

Amaia glanced at Iriarte, gesturing towards the exit.

'Thank you,' said Iriarte, 'you've been most helpful.'

'Pardon?' said the chaplain, cupping his ear.

'I said you've been most helpful,' bellowed the inspector, his voice echoing round the empty chapel.

The chaplain thanked them loudly, and Amaia winced slightly, grinning as she glanced at Iriarte once more.

Strong gusts of wind had swept away any lingering clouds over Arizkun. Perched on a hill, it was one of those towns where time seemed to have stood still, open to the skies and the extraordinary light much missed in other villages in the valley. The emerald meadows glistened with the perfection of idyllic splendour, and beneath each cobblestone lurked whispers from a past that was still present. They walked from the church to the presbytery, which was in the next street. A tinkle reached them from behind the solid door as they rang the bell.

Beside the front step Amaia noticed the squashed, dried-out body of a small bird, barely recognisable. She wondered whether a car or gust of wind had dashed it to the ground.

'What a pretty town,' said Iriarte, gazing up at the carved wooden eaves of the neighbouring houses, a typical feature of Arizkun architecture.

'And cruel,' murmured Amaia.

The door was opened by a woman of about sixty who guided them to the far end of the house down a long hallway that smelled of wax polish, its shiny floor glinting at them. Father Lokin received them in his study, where Amaia could see that his demeanour and colour hadn't improved since their meeting with the Archbishop. He extended a cold, trembling hand, showing an ugly bruise on his swollen inflamed wrist.

'Oh, I suffer from haemarthrosis, one of the many inconveniences of being a haemophiliac,' he said, stepping out from behind his desk and ushering them into a small adjoining room with uncomfortable ladder-back chairs.

Before sitting down, he offered them coffee, which they both declined.

Iriarte sat next to him, while Amaia waited until they were both installed before taking a seat opposite them.

'What can I do for you?' asked the priest, spreading his hands.

'Father Lokin,' Iriarte began, pretending to consult his notes, 'in your statement you said that the first attack, when the font was destroyed, took place seventeen days ago . . .'

The priest nodded.

'I'd like you to think back a few weeks, possibly a month. Did you notice anyone loitering around the church who looked odd or suspicious, any strangers . . .'

'Well, as you know, we get a lot of tourists and backpackers

131

coming to the village, and naturally most of them visit our splendid church,' he said, beaming with pride.

'Have you carried out any recent repairs or refurbishments to the church?'

'No, the last repairs were to the cornice in the south transept, but that was almost two years ago.'

'Have you quarrelled, or had any differences of opinion with any of your parishioners?'

'No.'

'Or with your neighbours?'

'No. Do you think this could be a personal vendetta?'

'We can't rule that out.'

'You're mistaken,' he said, giving Amaia an icy look, even though she hadn't said a word.

'Who helps out with the tasks in the church?'

'The chaplain, a couple of altar boys – usually young boys waiting to get confirmed in the spring – who do alternate Sundays, a group of catechists . . .' He raised a hand to his brow, as though remembering something. 'Carmen, the woman who opened the door to you, does the cleaning here and in the chapel. She sees to the flowers, occasionally with the help of one of the catechists.'

'Have any of these people taken over the tasks previously done by another individual who left for some reason?'

'I'm afraid that, apart from the chaplain and the altar boys, the others are all women from Arizkun who have been carrying out these tasks for years. Indeed,' he added, smiling for the first time, as he gazed benevolently at Amaia, 'the church owes a great deal to women in general. Without their help, the majority of priests would be unable to perform their duties. For example, here in Ariz—'

Amaia interrupted him with a question: 'How many people live in Arizkun?'

'I don't know the precise number, six hundred, six hundred and twenty.'

132

'Are you sure you know all your parishioners?'

'Yes. In such a small village, everybody knows everyone.' He grinned smugly.

'So you would have noticed if any new parishioners joined recently.'

The priest's smile froze.

'Yes,' he replied, startled. 'I would.'

'Any young lads?' asked Amaia.

'One, a young boy from the village, Beñat Zaldúa. I know his family; his father doesn't come to church, he's a rather coarse fellow – although I'm not criticising him, we each respond to grief in our own way. The mother used to attend, but she died six months ago. Cancer. Tragic.'

'And how long has the boy been coming?'

'A couple of months. But he's a good lad, serious, keeps his nose clean, avoids mixing with the . . . you know what I mean, with other boys who are more . . . Although I haven't seen him in church since his First Communion. I used to bump into him in the library. He gets good marks at school, he told me once he wanted to study history . . .'

'I'll wager he always sits on his own at the back, slightly apart from the others.'

Father Lokin's face grew even paler.

'You're right, but how did you know that?'

'And he never receives the host,' added Amaia.

When they came out of the presbytery, the wind had got up and was sweeping through the streets, lashing the house fronts, from where a few neighbours were watching them through a crack in their doors. Iriarte saved his question until they were in the car.

'Why do you think it's significant that the kid sits at the back of the church? That's where I sit. As for not receiving the host, maybe he's not ready yet, or he might even feel self-conscious. For a lapsed Catholic, coming back to church can be unsettling.'

133

Amaia heard him out, then replied, 'All those things are possible. Or it could be that he's re-enacting a period in history when *agotes* were forbidden to approach the altar, or to receive the host from the same tabernacle as the other parishioners, when they had to remain at the back of the chapel, where a grille separated them from the others – a symbolic grille this lad might be projecting in his mind.'

'I thought you didn't support Deputy Inspector Etxaide's theory about this being an *agote* vendetta.'

'I'm not convinced, nor am I ruling it out until we come up with a better one. If you'd read the report he prepared, you would know what I'm talking about.'

Iriarte remained silent for a moment, absorbing the rebuke.

'So the kid is behaving as if he were an *agote*?'

'He thinks he *is* an *agote*. He fits the profile perfectly. He doesn't get on with his dad, whom Father Lokin said is rather coarse and doesn't accompany his son to church. He's intelligent, knowledgeable and curious; even his interest in history fits. His mother's death could have been the trigger. A small town like Arizkun can feel oppressive to a teenager with an enquiring mind – I know that from experience. Pain and loneliness in adolescence are like a loaded gun.'

Iriarte appeared to mull this over.

'Even so, I don't think a single adolescent did this. This is too explicit, too staged for one kid acting on his own.'

'I agree. Beñat Zaldúa must be trying to impress someone.'

'And who does a teenage boy want to impress?'

'A girl, or his father, or he wants to show the whole of society how clever he is. But in that case, we're talking about psychopathic tendencies,' Amaia said doubtfully.

'Do you want to pay him a visit?' Iriarte suggested, inserting the key into the ignition and starting the engine.

'Just like that? Without any evidence? If he's half as clever as I think, Zaldúa will simply clam up. Etxaide can search for him online and see what he comes up with.'

As they drove past the church, Iriarte waved to the cops guarding the church from their patrol car.

The rain came on at midday, bucketing down for half an hour before giving way to *txirimiri* – a fine, cold drizzle that fell slowly, suspended in the air like sparkling motes of dust. It settled, dew-like, on people's overcoats and penetrated the bones, bringing with it the damp mountain chill and causing the temperature to drop several degrees. The aroma of soup and fresh bread pervaded her aunt's house, and despite having decided on the way home that she wasn't hungry, Amaia's stomach started to growl rebelliously, prompted by the smells wafting from the kitchen. After feeding Ibai, they sat down to eat at the table by the window, commenting on political events in the news.

Amaia noticed that James looked tired.

'Why don't you lie down for a while? You could do with a nap.'

'If Ibai lets me.'

'Go and lie down, don't worry about the baby. I won't go to the station this afternoon, I'll take Ibai out instead, it's hardly raining now,' she said, gazing through the window at the leaden sky. 'Besides, I need you to be fresh for tonight.'

James smiled obediently, as he shuffled over to the stairs.

'Take an umbrella with you,' he said, still smiling as he went up. 'I reckon there'll be another downpour soon.'

She squeezed Ibai into a quilted pramsuit and put him in the buggy, opened out the hood, then grabbed her coat and left the house. Ros, who was heading back to the bakery, went with her. Amaia still had the impression that her sister was more anxious than usual. Throughout lunch she had avoided Amaia's gaze, maintaining her smile, which faded as soon as she forgot herself. They parted on the bridge, and Amaia stood watching Ros until she disappeared from view.

She crossed the bridge and walked up Calle Jaime Urrutia,

deserted in the rain, apart from a few people beneath the *gorapes*, the arcades where warm air and music would spill from a couple of bars when their doors were open. Slowing down, she studied Ibai's little face, which at first looked startled by the judder of wheels over the cobbles, but then he started to relax, staring up at her, barely able to keep his eyes open before he fell asleep. Amaia stroked his smooth cheek with the back of her hand to check if he was warm enough, and tucked him in. She walked at a leisurely pace, which was unusual for her; she was surprised how pleasant it felt to move in that way, aware of the sound of her boots on the cobbles, lulled by the natural sway of her body.

Passing through the main square, she paused in front of Arizkunenea Palace, observing the remnants of the old headstones displayed in the courtyard. Damp from the recent rain, they looked more solid, as if the wet had restored them to their original size.

She carried on until she reached the town hall, where, glancing about to make sure no one was watching, she ran her hand over the *botil harri*, the stone that symbolised Elizondo's history and gave strength to those who touched it. Despite having no time for superstition, she found the gesture reassuring. Turning back to the square, she walked past the Lamia fountain, and went to look at the stretch of the River Baztán where the backs of the houses were reflected in the smooth surface, like a parallel world trapped beneath the waters, deceptively calm in that oasis. A few stragglers leaving the Santxotena restaurant after a late lunch were leaning over the railing taking photographs. Amaia crossed the street and entered the restaurant. The female owner gave her a friendly hello; this was James's favourite place to eat, and they would often go there for dinner. She reserved a table for two, smiling, secretly contented, as the woman bent over the buggy and declared how handsome Ibai was. She knew how clichéd it was, yet she couldn't help feeling motherly pride and awe at the perfect features of her little king of the river, her water baby.

She left the restaurant, and carried on along the right-hand pavement, pausing as she approached the funeral parlour. She was uneasy about passing there with Ibai, just as she would have been nervous about taking him to a hospital waiting room or to a sick person's house. Despite having to deal with the most horrific end of life scenarios on a daily basis, she felt she was putting her son at risk, and knew instinctively that she had to protect her son at all costs from even the slightest brush with death. Lowering the pram off the pavement, she crossed back over the street, where she continued walking parallel with the river. As she passed the funeral parlour on the other side, she couldn't help glancing at the death notices, posted daily on a board in the main entrance. She remembered when she was young asking her aunt about them whenever they paused there.

'Why do you always stop to look at it?'

'To see who has died.'

'Why do you want to know who has died?'

Now, from the opposite pavement, her eyes were fixed on the noticeboard, even though she couldn't read from that distance. Her phone buzzed in her coat pocket, making her start.

'Jonan.'

'Hi, chief, I've found something. This morning we came across various blogs about the *agotes*. Most of them simply regurgitate information copied and pasted from other websites. The general tone of the discussions is one of indignation at the past injustices they suffered, but nothing that suggests any current hatred or fanaticism. The one exception is a blog called "The Hour of the Dog"; it lists the same injustices as the others, but unlike them, it extends the consequences to the present day. It's written as a diary, the narrator an *agote* boy who tells of the humiliations to which his people

137

are subjected, as if he were living in the seventeenth century. Some of the descriptions are brilliant, but here's the interesting part: I traced the IP address of the blogger – who calls himself Juan Agote – and it's registered to someone in Arizkun called—'

'Beñat Zaldúa,' said Amaia. 'I knew it!'

'It's virtually impossible these days to know whether a surname was originally *agote* – aside from the name Agote itself – but it turns out that Zaldúa was one of the most common *agote* surnames a few hundred years ago. Shall we bring him in for questioning?'

'No. Call him and ask him to come to the station tomorrow morning at a reasonable hour. He's a minor, so tell him to come with his father.'

After she hung up, she checked the time on her mobile, calculated that James would be awake, before tapping in the number. He picked up instantly:

'I was about to call,' he said. 'Where are you?'

'Ibai and I have just been to Santxotena to reserve a table.'

'You and Ibai have very good taste in restaurants.'

'Ros has agreed to babysit tonight, so I wondered if you'd like to have dinner with me.'

James chuckled. 'With pleasure. Besides, there's something I want to talk to you about, and I think that would be the ideal setting.'

'I'm on tenterhooks,' she laughed.

'Well, you'll have to wait until tonight.'

Ibai had taken a while to fall asleep; as usual he was colicky after his late afternoon feed, which he seemed to have more difficulty digesting. It was dark outside when they left the house and it had started raining again, but they decided to walk to the restaurant anyway. They opened an umbrella and James put his arm around her. Clasping her tight, he could feel her shiver beneath the thin coat she had chosen to wear.

138

'I wouldn't be at all surprised if you had nothing on under that coat.'

'That's something you'll have to find out for yourself,' she replied coquettishly.

The Santxotena was pleasantly cosy with its raspberry walls and understated rustic elegance, starting with the windows outside, which like a fairy-tale cottage had painted wooden shutters, and a profusion of perennial flowers in earthenware pots. They were given a table with a partial view of the kitchen, where the muffled sound of voices and the smells of fine cooking reached them.

Beneath her coat, Amaia was wearing a black dress she hadn't put on since before Ibai was born. She knew she looked good in it and that James loved it; wearing the dress again made her feel good. What would Judge Markina make of her dolled up like that? She pushed the thought from her mind and reproached herself for having allowed herself to entertain it.

James smiled when he saw her.

'You look gorgeous, Amaia.'

She sat down after noticing that James's wasn't the only head she had turned. The waitress took their order. Asparagus with creamed spinach for them both, followed by hake in lobster sauce for James, who always had that dish there, and for her grilled monkfish with clams. James raised his wine glass, looking disapprovingly at hers filled with water.

'It's a shame you can't even have one drink because you're breastfeeding.'

She ignored his remark and sipped her water.

'So, what is it you wanted to tell me? I'm all ears.'

'Oh, yeah,' he said, with a surge of excitement. 'I wanted to talk to you about an idea that's been going round in my head for a while. Since you got pregnant we've been visiting Elizondo more often, and now that we've had the baby, I imagine we'll be coming here all the time. You know how

139

much I love Baztán, being with your family, which is why I think this is the right moment for us to start considering getting a house here, in Elizondo.'

Amaia's eyes opened wide with surprise.

'Well, you got one thing right at least: I never expected this . . . Are you suggesting we move here?'

'No, of course I'm not, Amaia. I love our house and I love living in Pamplona: it's ideal both for your work and for my sculpture studio. Besides, you know how much that house on Mercaderes means to me.'

She nodded, reassured.

'No, I'm talking about having a second home here, a house of our own.'

'We can stay at my aunt's whenever we want. She's like a mother to me, her house is my home.'

'I appreciate that, Amaia, I know how important that house is, and always will be, to you, but one thing doesn't rule out the other. If we had our own place here we could arrange it to suit Ibai's needs, give him his own room, have all his things handy, instead of having to lug everything back and forth from Pamplona. Besides, when he gets bigger he'll need somewhere for his toys . . .'

'I don't know, James, I'm not sure I want that.'

'I've spoken to Engrasi and she thinks it's a good idea.'

'That really does surprise me,' she said, putting her fork down on the table.

'In fact,' he said with a grin, 'she gave me the idea when she told me about *Juanitaenea*.'

'My grandmother's house,' whispered Amaia, completely astonished.

'Yes.'

'But, James, that house has been standing empty for years, ever since my grandmother died. I was only five then. It must be falling apart,' she protested.

'No, it's not. Your aunt assured me that, although it'll need to be completely refurbished, the basic structure, the roof and chimneys are all in perfect condition. Over the years, your aunt has tried to keep up the basic maintenance of the building.'

Enchanted, Amaia's mind filled with images of rooms she remembered as enormous, the fireplace she could stand up in as a child; she could almost feel the smoothness of the heavy, polished furniture on her fingertips, the maroon satin counterpane on her grandmother's bed.

'I think it would be good for Ibai to spend part of his childhood here, especially in a house that belonged to his family.'

Amaia didn't know what to say. She had always felt safe in her aunt's house, yet she had unresolved issues in Elizondo. It was true that after several months of coming back there, Baztán had lost many of the dark associations from her past. Although that was partly because she had opened up to James about what had happened to her when she was nine years old, he knew that her main reason for returning was somehow to preserve the bond she had formed with the lord of the forest, a bond that lived on in the DVD she kept in her safe, which she hadn't looked at since she watched it for the first time with the bear experts in a room at Hotel Baztán. Occasionally, when she opened her safe to lock up her firearm, she would run her fingers over the disk, the image of that creature's amber eyes appearing before her, clear as day. And by simply conjuring up that memory, any shred of doubt or fear vanished as if by magic. She smiled absent-mindedly.

'Amaia, we don't think about these things until we have children. You know how happy I am in Pamplona, that I've never wanted to go back to the States except to visit. But now that we have Ibai, I realise that, if I did live there, I'd want him to find his roots, to know where his family came from, and that if I could bring him closer to that reality, I would.'

141

Amaia gazed at him, in raptures.

'I had no idea you felt that way, James. You've never mentioned it to me before, but if that's what you want, we can visit the States when Ibai is a bit older.'

'We will, Amaia, only I don't want to live there. Like I said, I want to go on living in Pamplona, but we're so lucky to be fifty kilometres away from where you were born, though anyone would think it was another planet . . . Besides,' he said, smiling, 'a farmhouse, Amaia . . . You know I adore the architecture here in Baztán. I'd love to own a house here; restoring and decorating it would be a wonderful adventure. Say yes,' he implored.

She gazed at him, at once moved and delighted by his enthusiasm.

'At least tell me you'll come and see it. Engrasi promised she'd come with us tomorrow.'

'Tomorrow? You're a right pair of schemers,' she said, pretending to be annoyed.

'Can we go?' he pleaded.

She nodded, grinning. 'Schemer!'

He leant across the table and kissed her on the mouth.

Leaving the restaurant, they discovered that the fine drizzle that had been falling over Elizondo since lunchtime appeared to have set in, with no sign of any reprieve. Amaia inhaled the moist air, remembering how much she had detested this rain when she was a child, how she longed for clear blue summer skies, which always seemed so fleeting and remote in Baztán. She had come to detest the rain so intensely that she recalled spending whole afternoons staring at it through the window, her breath misting up the glass, which she would wipe clean with the sleeve of her jumper pulled up over her fist as she dreamed of fleeing, getting out of there.

'It's freezing!' declared James. 'Let's go home.'

Amaia was shivering beneath her coat, but instead of

heading for the side streets, she came to a halt as though answering a call, before setting off in the opposite direction.

'Wait here,' she said.

'Where are you off to now?' said James, chasing after her with the umbrella in a vain attempt to shield her.

'I won't be long, I just want to look at something,' she said, coming to a halt in front of the noticeboard at the Baztán funeral parlour, which was closed and completely in darkness.

She stepped aside so that the light from the streetlamps illuminated the death notices that had caught her attention from afar that afternoon. Now she knew why: Lucía Aguirre's daughters had chosen the same photograph for their mother's death notice as the one Amaia remembered presiding in her hallway. In it she appeared cheerful and confident, wearing the same striped jersey she'd had on when she died. Doubtless one of those favourite pieces of clothing that you feel suits you, makes you look pretty, that you'd wear for a studio photograph or to look nice for a man. A bright, colourful pullover, not something you'd expect to wear when you die, or as a shroud for your ghost to appear in.

Although there was no mistaking who she was from the photograph, Amaia read the details through twice: Lucía Aguirre, aged fifty-two, her daughters Marta and María, her grandchildren and other family members, even the church she belonged to in Pamplona. So, why was Lucía Aguirre's death notice posted in a village in Baztán?

She fumbled in her coat pocket for her mobile. She knew one of the daughters' numbers was stored on her phone, though she never remembered which. She checked the time, saw that it was late, but pressed the call button anyway.

'Inspector Salazar?' replied the youthful voice of one of the sisters, who had clearly saved her number too.

'Good evening, Marta.' She took a gamble. 'Sorry to call you so late, but I wanted to ask you a question.'

'That's OK, I was watching TV. Go ahead.'

143

'I'm in Elizondo. I've just seen your mother's death notice in the window of the Baztán funeral parlour, and I'm wondering why.'

'My mother lived in Pamplona from when she was a child, but she was actually born in Baztán. I think she was two when my grandparents moved to the city. My grandfather died when she was young and my grandmother is in a care home. My mother had an aunt who also lived in Pamplona, but she died eight years ago. We have no other relatives in Baztán, but it seemed the right thing to do. I remember, when her aunt died, my mother arranged the funeral and she placed a death notice in Baztán; you know, it's a village tradition, in case anybody remembers the family.'

'Thanks, Marta, give your sister my condolences. Sorry for bothering you.'

'Please don't apologise, you've been so good to us.'

10

Spring 1980
Juan watched the sticky dough being churned by the kneading hook. They had purchased the machine only a couple of months before and, as Rosario had forecast, production had increased to the point where they were able to supply many more customers than previously. Juan was recalling the old days. The time when his wife was first carrying Flora, then Rosaura. How like a fool he had wanted a boy, to carry on the Salazar name, he supposed: Engrasi was his only sibling, and if he didn't have a male heir the surname would be lost. He hadn't minded so much when Flora came along, but when Rosaura was born he felt disappointed, though of course he tried not to let his wife see. A male child, a folly that had cast such a shadow over him that even his own mother had warned him.

'You'd better put on a brave face, unless you want your wife to take the girls back home to San Sebastián. You should be celebrating, not sulking; a woman is worth as much as a man, sometimes more.'

Tucked away in a drawer in the bakery, he had kept the list of girls' and boys' names he and Rosario made during her first two pregnancies. He checked the dough once more,

145

then went over to the drawer, took out the list and spread it on the table. The four lines where the piece of paper had remained folded all those years were visible, as were the creases and tears it suffered when his wife crumpled it up before throwing it in his face and running out of the bakery.

What a fool he was. Why had he been so insistent about choosing a silly name?

'We need to start thinking of names for the baby.'

'It's too soon,' she had snapped, changing the subject. 'Have you made up the order for the Azkunes yet?'

'Too soon? But you're five months pregnant! The baby must be big as my hand by now, and it's high time we started thinking about what we're going to call it. Come on, Rosario, you choose, look at the list and tell me which one you like,' he had insisted, holding the piece of paper up in front of her.

She had wheeled round and snatched the list out of his hand, leaving him dumbstruck. Then she leant forward as though reading, and without looking up, shot him a sidelong glance, before murmuring:

'A name, a name. Do you know what this is?'

He couldn't speak.

'A list of the dead.'

'Rosario . . .'

'A list of the dead, only the dead don't need names, the dead don't need anything,' she said under her breath, gazing at him through the strands of hair that had come loose from her bun.

'Rosario, what are you saying? You're scaring me.'

'Don't be scared,' she said, raising her head, her voice returning to normal, 'I'm only playing.'

He watched her, trying to swallow the fear choking him, which tasted of bile . . .

She screwed the piece of paper up into a ball and threw it in his face before walking out of the bakery.

'Put it back where it was,' she said, 'there are boys' names too. And believe me, this had better be a boy, because if it's a little bitch she won't need a name.'

11

She lay down next to James, convinced she wouldn't sleep that night, her head spinning with the fresh information. Three apparently unrelated murders perpetrated by three clumsy killers in three distinct places, all involving an identical amputation. In each case the severed limb had vanished from the scene, all three culprits had committed suicide in prison or in custody, leaving the same message written on the wall of their cell, or, in Medina's case, in a note addressed and delivered to her in person. Although, the way in which Quiralte had demanded Amaia's presence in exchange for revealing the whereabouts of his victim's body could also be considered a form of personal delivery. And now, discovering that Lucía Aguirre was born in Baztán had opened a new door, which could be the link between the three crimes. Her next step would be to find out where the victim in Logroño came from. What was she called? She couldn't remember her name being on the report Padua gave her. She looked again at the clock: it was nearly half past one. At two, she calculated, Ibai would wake up for his feed. She would get up then and write down all the things she needed to check. She started making a mental list and as she did so, fell asleep.

She was close to the river, listening to the incessant

splish-splash as the *lamias* tapped their webbed feet on the water's surface, although she couldn't see them. Lucía Aguirre, ashen-faced, left arm clasped about her waist, was gazing at the stump hanging by her side, severed at the elbow. There was no wind this time, and the splashes, like rain pounding on water, stopped, as Lucía Aguirre's terrified eyes met hers. She began once more to chant her refrain, only this time Amaia was able to hear her voice, dry and rasping from the sand blocking her throat, and make out the words: not trap or rat, but '*tarttalo*'.

Her baby's soft cries were enough to bring her out of sleep. She looked at the time and was surprised to see it was four o'clock.

'Well, my champion, you're holding out longer and longer. When will you sleep right through the night, I wonder?' She sighed as she picked him up.

After he'd finished feeding, she changed him and put him back in his cot.

'James,' she whispered.

'Yes?'

'I'm going to work. Ibai has had his feed, he should sleep through until morning.'

James murmured something and clumsily blew her a kiss.

The heating at the police station was turned down low at night, and when she entered the office she was glad she'd put on a thick woollen sweater under the Puffa jacket James had insisted she wear. She switched on the computer and fetched a coffee from the machine out in the corridor while going over her mental to-do list. She sat at her desk and started to look through the notes Padua had given her on the Logroño case. Exactly as she had thought, there was no mention of the victim's identity, which was designated with the initials I.L.O.

She trawled the online periodicals library of the main newspapers from La Rioja and found several references to the crime and its perpetrator, Luis Cantero, but nothing about the victim. She discovered an article about the trial, which mentioned Izaskun L.O., then finally another about the sentence for the murder of I. López Ormazábal.

Izaskun López Ormazábal.

Daughter of Alfonso and Victoria.

Born in Berroeta, Navarre on 28 August 1969. Deceased . . .

Amaia shuddered as she reread the woman's personal details. Berroeta was a tiny village of no more than a hundred inhabitants, some seven miles from Elizondo. So this woman was also born in the Baztán Valley. The force of the discovery made her slightly dizzy. She sighed, releasing the pressure that had been building up over the past few hours, then glanced about the deserted office, wishing she could share this break-through, and her unease, with someone. Far from feeling relieved at confirming her suspicions, she was aware that the abyss she had been groping for had been there all along, only now it had taken on a life of its own and was clamouring from the very earth of Baztán, mixed with the blood of its victims. It wouldn't stop until she had uncovered the truth. She knew that wouldn't be easy, but she wouldn't give up, even if she had to descend into hell itself and confront this devil who was playing games, taunting her by writing on walls the name of a fiend that devoured shepherds, virgins, and lambs: the flesh of innocents.

As though in answer to her prayers, Etxaide walked into the office holding a coffee in each hand.

'The desk sergeant told me you were here.'

'Hi, Jonan, what time is it?' she asked, glancing at her watch.

'Just gone six,' he replied, offering her one of the paper cups.

'What are you doing here so early?'

'I couldn't sleep. At the guesthouse where I'm staying there's a group of about twenty guys on a stag weekend,' he said, as if that explained everything. 'And you?'

Amaia smiled and for the next twenty minutes brought Jonan up to speed with her discoveries.

'And you think there might be others?'

She paused before replying.

'I have a feeling there are.'

'We could do a search for victims of male violence who have suffered amputations,' he suggested, opening his laptop.

'Too general,' she objected. 'Amputation could be extended to include cuts or stab wounds, which, sadly, are typical in crimes of this nature. Besides, I'm sure that in the majority of cases where a severed limb is missing, the information would be classified.'

'How about victims who were born or lived in Baztán?'

'I've already checked; the victim's place of birth is deemed irrelevant in most instances. It usually only appears on the death certificate.'

'We could do a search along those lines; there must be a special entry for violent deaths in the register of births and deaths,' he said, typing information on his laptop while Amaia sipped her fresh coffee and attempted to warm her hands on the paper cup. *I must remember to bring my own mug*, she thought, trying to peer into the darkness outside, only to encounter her own reflection in the glass, projected on to the blackness of the night still enveloping Baztán.

'Funeral parlours,' she said suddenly.

'What?' Jonan turned towards her expectantly.

'Lucía Aguirre's family placed a death notice in the Baztán funeral parlour. I wouldn't be surprised if other victims' families had done the same, assuming they were from the valley. They may also have celebrated a Mass for the dead, or possibly buried them in their village, even though they weren't living there when they died.'

'When do you think they open?' Jonan asked, checking the time.

'I doubt before nine, although most have a twenty-four-hour

emergency number you can call,' she replied, gazing once more towards the window, where a faint, distant glow announced the first light of dawn. 'I have a few things to do this morning, but if I can I'll visit the funeral parlours with you – there are two in Elizondo, I think. See if you can find any in the other villages, but don't call them – I prefer to speak to them face-to-face. Who knows, we may be able to refresh their memory.'

Amaia climbed into the car without taking off her jacket and drove through the deserted streets with the windows down so that she could enjoy the riotous dawn chorus. When she came to the Txokoto neighbourhood, she turned to go into the rear entrance of the bakery. It was closed at that hour, so she stopped the car with the headlights pointing at the wall. Someone had sprayed in thick letters 'TREACHEROUS WHORE'. She sat for a while, staring at the graffiti, which made less sense the more she looked at it. She reversed and drove home.

Bumping into Ros in the hallway, where she was on her way out, Amaia said goodbye to her without mentioning the graffiti. As she entered the silence of the house where everyone was sleeping, she noticed that, unlike in the other rooms, which were centrally heated, the temperature in the living room had dropped several degrees during the night. She knelt by the hearth to begin the ritual of lighting the fire, which she always found calming. She did it mechanically, repeating the ceremony she had learned when she was a little girl, which had always brought her a mysterious feeling of peace. When the flames began to lick the bigger logs, she stood up and glanced at her watch, working out the time difference with Louisiana. She took out her mobile and searched for Agent Dupree's number in her address book. She felt her heart miss a beat as she punched in the number, as a voice inside her screamed at her to hang up, not to make this call, just as Agent Dupree's soft drawl reached her from somewhere in New Orleans.

'Good evening, Inspector Salazar, or should I say good morning?'

Amaia sighed before replying.

'Hi, Aloisius. It's getting light here,' she said, struggling to control the tremor that passed through her entire body, despite the fire blazing in the hearth.

'How are you, Inspector?' His voice sounded as warm and understanding as she remembered.

'Confused – a lot going on at once, too much,' she confessed.

It was no good trying to deceive Dupree, besides, the whole purpose of those late-night calls was to be honest. Otherwise, what would be the point?

'I'm investigating a case in Baztán. Just a small matter I'm obliged to look into, more than anything because of my superiors' political allegiances. But I discovered today that another case I've been working on might also be connected to the Baztán Valley. I can't explain why yet, but I have a feeling that this is one of those cases, that the murderer is trying somehow to establish a connection with me. Just like in similar cases I studied at Quantico, the modus operandi fits a Ripper type, someone who contacts the police, only this one does it in a subtle way, suggesting a more complex personality.' She paused to order her thoughts.

'How much more complex?'

'I hardly dare think about it in those terms yet. What we know so far is that the murderers are all petty criminals – shoplifters, thieves, con men – all with a history of violence towards women. They were close to the females they killed, who had links to the valley: one of them lived here, the others were born in Baztán . . .' She paused again, unsure how to continue. 'I know this sounds crazy, Dupree, but I can feel in my bones that there's more to this,' she explained. 'The problem is, I don't know where to start.'

'Yes you do, Inspector Salazar, you start . . .'

'At the beginning,' she finished his sentence in a tone that betrayed her annoyance.

'And where did this begin?'

153

'With Johana Márquez's murder,' she replied.

'No,' he said abruptly.

'Hers is the first case I know of that involved an amputation. There could be earlier ones, but . . . her stepfather – her murderer – left me a note, which is what triggered this investigation.'

'But where did it begin?' Dupree repeated in a hushed voice.

A shiver ran down her spine, as she all but felt the thorns on the gorse bushes snagging her anorak as she made her way along the narrow path to the goddess-genie's cave. The jangle of gold bracelets, the long flaxen hair down to her waist, her half-smile, regal or witchlike, Mari's voice as she said: 'I saw a man enter one of those caves carrying a package, which he didn't have when he came out.'

And the enigmatic reply to her question: 'Did you see his face?'

'All I saw was one eye.'

At the other end of the phone, Aloisius gave a sigh that sounded distant, watery.

'See how you knew? Now you must go back to Baztán.'

His remark took her by surprise.

'But I've been here for two days, Aloisius.'

'No, Inspector Salazar, you still haven't gone back.'

She hung up, continuing to stare at the message on the screen for an instant.

'You shouldn't be doing that.'

The voice of Engrasi, who had stopped halfway down the staircase and was watching her, gave Amaia such a start that the phone flew out of her hand and skittered under one of the winged armchairs beside the fire.

'Oh, Auntie, you gave me a fright,' she said, bending down and fumbling beneath the chair.

The old woman came down the rest of the stairs, still contemplating her solemnly.

'And what you're doing, doesn't that frighten you?'

154

Amaia straightened up, phone in hand and waited for her heart to stop racing before she replied.

'I know what I'm doing, Auntie.'

'Do you?' she snorted. 'Do you honestly know what you're doing?'

'I need answers,' she protested.

'I can help you,' said Engrasi, walking over to the sideboard and retrieving a small bundle wrapped in black silk, which contained her tarot cards.

'First, I'd need to know which questions to ask, Auntie. You taught me that yourself. Only, I have no idea. Talking to him helps me figure that out – don't forget he's one of the FBI's foremost experts in behavioural disorders and criminal psychology. I value his opinion.'

'You're playing with things you don't understand, my dear,' she said reprovingly.

'I trust him.'

'For God's sake, Amaia! Don't you see how unnatural your relationship is?'

Amaia was about to reply, but stopped when she saw James, dressed to go out, descending the stairs, Ibai in his arms.

Her aunt shot her a final disapproving look, put the cards back in their place and went into the kitchen to make breakfast.

12

Juanitaenea stood behind the Hostal Trinkete on a flat area of dark earth surrounded by allotments. The nearest dwellings were about three hundred metres away and formed a cluster that contrasted with the solitary stone building, darkened by age, lichen, and the recent rains that seemed to have penetrated its walls, turning them a biscuit colour.

The carved wooden eaves overhung by more than a metre and a half, keeping the damp off the upper storey of the house, which appeared lighter. The main door was on the first floor, at the top of a flight of precariously narrow, uneven steps with no handrail, which seemed to emerge straight out of the wall. At ground level there were two rounded arches, their doors replaced with rough boards, which flanked another large square entrance that had retained its original iron doors. Although rusty, they still showed the beautiful metalwork forged by a local craftsman in the old days, when what mattered was precision and the satisfaction of a job well done. Behind the house stood a cluster of old oaks and beeches, as well as a weeping willow, which Amaia recalled as being majestic even in her childhood. The land was accessible from the front of the house, bordered on one side by a large vegetable garden of about a quarter of an acre, which looked established and well tended.

'For years a local fellow has looked after the garden,' said Engrasi. 'He brings me a few vegetables, and at least he keeps it tidy, unlike the rest of the place,' she added, encompassing with a sweep of her hand a pile of wooden planks, plastic buckets and the unidentifiable remains of what looked like old furniture lying outside the front of the house.

James's enthusiasm dimmed when he saw the door at the top of the strange stairway.

'Do we have to go up there to get in?' he asked, eyeing it suspiciously.

'There are some stairs up to the first floor inside the stable,' explained Engrasi, handing him a key and pointing towards one of the archways, secured with a padlock and chain.

The old door resisted slightly as James pushed it open. Engrasi flicked a switch and somewhere above them a dusty bulb cast a feeble orange glow that was lost among the rafters.

'It's a bit dark in here, which is why I wanted us to come early in the day,' she said, walking over to the closed windows, their wooden shutters covered in dust and cobwebs. 'James, perhaps you could help me open one of these.'

The copper hinges seemed to be stuck, but yielded after a few attempts, opening inwards as the morning light streamed in, tracing a perfect ray of floating dust amid the gloom.

James turned around, incredulous, as he contemplated his surroundings.

'Wow! It's enormous! And so high,' he said, gazing in awe at the rafters spanning the ceiling.

Engrasi grinned as she looked at Amaia:

'Come over here,' she said, pointing towards the dark wooden staircase that branched elegantly into two as it rose to the floor above.

James looked surprised. 'It's amazing to find a staircase like this in a stable.'

'Not really,' said Amaia. 'For hundreds of years, the stable

157

was the most important part of a house. This staircase was the equivalent of having a door to your garage.'

'Be careful going up. I'm not sure how safe it is,' said Engrasi.

The first floor comprised four huge rooms, a kitchen, and a bathroom that had been stripped bare, except for a heavy, clawfoot bathtub, which Amaia remembered well. The small windows were set deep into the thick walls and fitted with slatted wooden shutters. All four rooms were empty, except the old kitchen, where only the hearth remained. Twice the size of those in the other rooms, it was made from the same stone as the outside walls and blackened from years of use.

'I don't know why, but I was hoping the furniture would still be here,' said Amaia.

Engrasi nodded, smiling. 'There were some good pieces, mostly hand-crafted. Your father inherited them, along with the bakery. I got the house, the land and a substantial sum of money. As the son, he took more of an interest in the bakery, while I pursued my studies and then went to Paris. I only came back two years before your grandmother died. The day after the will was read, your mother got a removal van to take everything away.'

Amaia nodded. She had no memory of Juanita's furniture at her parents' house.

'She probably sold them,' she murmured.

'Yes, I think so too.'

She could hear James moving excitedly from room to room, like a child at a fairground.

'Amaia, have you seen this?' he said, opening a window that overlooked the precarious steps at the front of the house.

'I expect it was designed for when there was heavy snow-fall or flood, although I don't remember ever using it. We should probably seal it off, or remove it,' Engrasi suggested.

'No way,' said James, closing the window and making his way over to the narrow staircase leading to the attic.

Amaia followed him, carrying Ibai in the baby sling, humming to him as he kicked contentedly, apparently infected with his father's enthusiasm.

Despite the sloping ceiling, the attic was roomy. A couple of circular skylights in the roof let in the winter sun, illuminating the open room. At first glance, she thought it was Ibai's cot standing in the centre.

'Auntie,' she called, walking over to it.

'I'm sorry, dear, too many stairs for my poor old knees,' Engrasi said as she reached the attic.

Amaia moved aside so that she could see the dark wooden cot. Engrasi gazed at it, dumbstruck while James examined it from close up.

'It's the same. Identical, if it weren't for the new coat of varnish I gave ours.'

'Auntie, where did you get the one that was in your house?' asked Amaia.

'My mother gave it to me when I returned from Paris and bought my house. She used to keep it out on the patio under a tarpaulin, and I remember asking her if I could use it as a log basket. I thought it looked pretty with those carvings, but I don't remember there being two. They must have belonged to you and your sisters and Juanita brought them here when you outgrew them.'

Running her fingers over the dusty wood, Amaia felt a shooting pain in her arm, like an electric shock. She leapt backwards, causing Ibai to burst into tears, alarmed by her cry.

'Are you OK, Amaia?' James said, concerned, moving towards her.

'Yes . . .' she replied, rubbing her hand, which felt numb.

'What happened?'

'I don't know, a splinter must have pricked me or something.'

'Let me take a look,' he said.

After examining her hand thoroughly, James declared with a grin:

'I can't see anything. Maybe you pulled a muscle when you stretched your arm out.'

'I suppose,' she said, unconvinced.

Her aunt frowned as she watched them from the staircase. It was an expression Amaia knew well.

'I'm fine, Auntie,' she said, trying to sound reassuring. 'Honestly. What a beautiful attic.'

'The house is fantastic, Amaia, better than I imagined,' James said, glancing about him with childlike glee.

She nodded indulgently. As soon as she agreed to visit the house, she knew that James would fall in love with it. The house she had stayed in thousands of times as a child but which she remembered as a series of disparate images, like old photographs, her grandmother always in the foreground, the house like a backdrop, a stage upon which her *Amatxi* Juanita's life had unfolded. Descending to the floor below, she could hear James telling her aunt about all the things they could do to it.

Amaia went from room to room, opening all the shutters, letting the hazy sun light up the antique wallpaper. Leaning on the broad embrasure, she scanned the horizon until she recognised the towers of the church of Santiago. They rose above the rooftops, still slick from the overnight rain and kept shiny by the damp from the River Baztán, which seeped into tiles and bones like a gift from the sea; the feeble sunlight that warmed her as it glanced off the windows could not dry out those rooftops in an entire day. Ibai, calm once more, screwed up his eyes, pressing his head against her chest as he felt the heat from the sun. Amaia kissed the top of his head, breathing in the smell from his downy blond hair.

'What do you think, my love? What should I say to Auntie when she asks? Would you like to live in *Amatxi* Juanita's house?'

She looked at her son, who in that very instant, just before falling asleep, smiled.

'I was about to ask you the same question,' said James, who stood gazing at her tenderly from the doorway. 'What did Ibai say?'

She turned to look at him.

'He said: yes.'

James walked around *Juanitaenea* a few more times before he was ready to leave.

'I'm going to call Manolo Azpiroz immediately. He's an architect friend of mine who lives in Pamplona. He'd love to see this place,' he explained to Engrasi as he locked the padlock on the improvised door.

'Keep it,' she said, when he made to hand her back the key, 'you'll need it if you're going to show your architect friend round. Besides, as far as I'm concerned, the house is yours. At some point we can arrange to go to the notary and I'll sign over the deeds.'

James grinned and showed Amaia the key.

'Look, my love, the key to our new house.'

Amaia shook her head, pretending to frown at his enthusiasm, then stepped back a few paces to admire the façade. Above the door, *Juanitaenea* was carved in stone beneath the chequered Baztán coat of arms. Sensing a movement behind her, she wheeled round in time to glimpse a wrinkled face, trying in vain to crouch behind the plant supports in the vegetable patch. Engrasi drew level with Amaia, addressing the man in a loud voice:

'Esteban, this is my niece and nephew.'

The man straightened up and shot them a faintly hostile look. He raised a stubby-fingered hand and silently resumed his work.

'He clearly doesn't like us.'

'Pay no attention to him. He's been working the land here

for twenty years, though he's retired now. When I called him yesterday to tell him you were going to be the new owners, I sensed he wasn't very happy about it. I expect he's worried he won't be able to go on tending the garden.'

'And you told him that yesterday, even before we came to see the house?' Amaia asked, amused.

Engrasi shrugged and gave a mischievous smile.

'I have my sources.'

James flung his arms around the old lady.

'You're a wonderful woman, you know. But you can tell him from me I've no wish to get rid of him. There's plenty of land for us to make a garden round the house. Besides, I love the idea of having an allotment, only from now on he'll have to bring us some vegetables too.'

'I'll have a word with him,' said Engrasi. 'He's a good man, if a little set in his ways, but once he knows he can carry on tending the garden, he'll change his tune.'

'I'm not so sure . . .' said Amaia, turning once more to look at the man, who was spying on them, half-obscured by the bushes bordering the vegetable patch.

The wind blew in soft gusts, driving away the lingering mist, as patches of blue began to show through the grey clouds. It wouldn't rain again for a few hours. She zipped up her Puffa jacket, covering Ibai and clasping him to her chest. Then her phone vibrated in her pocket. She checked the screen and answered.

'Hi, Iriarte.'

'Chief, Beñat Zaldúa just arrived with his father.'

Amaia looked up again at the sky. 'Good, go ahead with the interview.'

'I assumed you were going to do that,' he faltered.

'Stand in for me, will you, please? I have something important to do.'

Iriarte didn't reply.

162

'You'll do a great job,' she added.

Amaia could tell Iriarte was grinning when he replied:

'As you wish.'

'One more thing: any news from Forensics on the bones found in the church?'

'No, not yet.'

As soon as she had hung up, she called Jonan's mobile.

'Jonan, you'll need to visit the funeral parlours on your own, I'll be running late – there's something I need to do.'

The autumn leaves had turned to a brown and yellow pulp, which was treacherously slippery where the ground sloped, making it impossible to drive along the track. She pulled over and walked with difficulty until she reached the edge of the thick-canopied forest. As she penetrated it she could feel the ground become harder and drier. The wind that had buffeted her on the track was scarcely perceptible, revealing its force only at the swaying treetops, through which sunlight twinkled like stars on a wintry night. The murmur of the stream flowing downhill guided her. She crossed some stepping stones, although she could easily have jumped over the narrow channel on to dry rocks. Checking the map Padua had given her, she made her way up through the undergrowth until she reached a large boulder behind which stood the cave. The path was still relatively clear of vegetation after the *Guardia Civil* had been here three months earlier, when the skeletal remains of at least a dozen individuals were discovered in the cave. A sudden thought occurred to her, and she took out her mobile, sighing with frustration when she saw she had no signal.

'Nature protects us,' she whispered.

The mouth was wide enough for her to enter without stooping. She slipped a powerful LED torch out of her pocket and, obeying her instincts, also drew her Glock. Clasping the torch in one hand and the gun in the other, she went into the cave, which bent to the right in a slight S-shape before opening out on to an oblong space of about sixty square metres, before tapering towards the far end like a funnel. The height of the cave roof was irregular: as much as four metres at its highest, while at its lowest point Amaia was obliged to walk hunched over. The air was cold and dry, possibly a few degrees cooler than outside, and had an earthy smell, as well as something sweeter that reminded her of organic compost. She scanned the walls and the floor, but they were clean, no remains of any kind, although the ground looked turned over in places. Near the mouth of the cave, where the earth was more moist, Amaia discovered a few old footprints, but nothing more. She shone the powerful beam over the walls one last time before stepping out of the cave. As she put away her gun and flashlight a shiver ran down her spine. Walking back to the large boulder, she clambered up on to it and was able to make out the spot where Mari had glimpsed the stranger. She descended as far as the stream, which she followed round the hill until she came to the point where she, Ros and James had walked up it that day. Amaia remembered it as being steeper, but recognised the grassy glade where Ros had sat down to rest. The path looked clear from there, seeming to beckon her, as if someone had passed through only recently. She climbed the small incline, increasingly nervous and tense with each step, as if a thousand eyes were watching her and someone was trying to suppress a giggle.

When she reached the top she was relieved to find nobody there. She approached the large flat rock and was surprised to find a mound of pebbles, of varying shapes and sizes. Cursing, she returned to the path, picked up an oblong stone and placed it next to the others as she scanned the view above the treetops. All was quiet. After a while, she glanced about her, suddenly self-conscious, and started back the way she came. For a moment she was tempted to look back, but she could hear Rosaura's voice echoing in her mind: 'You must leave the way you came, and once you have turned around you must never look back.' Making her way along the path, she wondered what she had hoped to find there, whether this was what Dupree had been referring to. Reaching the stepping stones, she glimpsed something. At first she thought it was a young girl, but when she looked again she realised that the moss-covered stones and the sunlight glinting through the trees had tricked her. She stepped on to the little bridge . . . and there she was. A young woman of about twenty, sitting a few metres from the bridge on one of the slippery rocks next to the stream, so close to the water it seemed impossible for her to have reached there without getting wet. Although she had on a fur-lined jacket, she was wearing a skimpy dress, revealing her long legs, which, despite the cold, she was dangling in the stream. The vision was beautiful yet disturbing, and without knowing why, Amaia lifted her hand to her Glock. The girl looked up, gave a charming smile, and waved to her.

'Good afternoon,' she said in a sing-song voice.

'Good afternoon,' replied Amaia, feeling slightly ridiculous. This was simply a rambler who had stopped to dip her feet in the stream.

That's right, all alone, on a freezing cold day, dipping her feet in a stream, she mocked herself. Clasping the butt of her gun, she slid it out of its holster.

'Did you come to leave an offering?' asked the girl.

'What?' she whispered, startled.

'You know, an offering for the lady.'

Amaia didn't reply straight away. She watched the young woman, who sat staring at her as she made a parting in her flowing hair with a tiny comb, apparently unconcerned at Amaia's presence.

'The lady prefers you to bring the stone from home.'

Amaia swallowed hard, wetting her lips before speaking.

'A-Actually, I didn't come here for that. I-I'm looking for something.'

The young woman didn't pay her much attention. She went

on combing her hair, with an exasperating care and precision that after a while became hypnotic.

A bead of cold sweat trickling down the back of Amaia's neck brought her back to reality, as did her awareness that the light was fading behind the hills. Although it couldn't have been later than three or four o'clock, she wondered how long she had been standing there watching the girl. All of a sudden a clap of thunder echoed in the distance, as the wind began to lash the treetops.

'It's coming . . .'

Her voice sounded so close that Amaia gave a start, lost her balance, and fell forward on to her knees. Alarmed, she aimed her gun at where the voice had come from, right beside her.

'But you haven't found what you were looking for.'

The young woman was now less than two metres away from where Amaia knelt, smiling as she sat on the edge of the little bridge, her feet caressing the surface of the water with a slow splash. She looked scornfully at the pistol Amaia was clutching in both hands.

'You won't need that. To see, you need light.'

Amaia continued to stare at her while the idea formed in her head. *I need light*, she thought.

'A new light,' added the girl. Without looking back, she ran barefoot towards a small pile of what seemed to be her belongings.

Disobeying the order reverberating in her head, Amaia leant forward to follow the girl's movements beyond the flimsy side of the bridge, but could no longer see her. It was as if the girl had never been there.

'Damn!' she whispered, slightly out of breath, gazing about her, still brandishing her gun. She looked up at the sky realising that within an hour it would be dark. She wasn't wearing her watch, and the clock on her phone flickered, the numbers dancing meaninglessly on the screen. She replaced her gun in its holster and, phone in hand, broke into a run until she reached the edge of the forest where the signal bar told her she could call.

'Hi, chief, I've been trying to get hold of you. I made some headway at the funeral parlour on women originally from Baztán who met violent deaths. They told me a few other interesting things too.'

Amaia let him talk while she caught her breath.

'Tell me about it later, Jonan, I'm on the dirt track, on the right-hand bend where we spoke to the forest rangers, do you remember?'

Interpreting his hesitation as a 'no', Amaia continued:

'OK, I'll drive back on to the road so that you can see me. I need you to bring your field kit, a blue lamp and some Luminol spray.'

She hung up and dialled again.

'Padua, it's Salazar,' she said, without preamble. 'I have a question. When they found the bones in the Arri Zahar cave, did they process the scene?'

'Yes, the remains were collected, labelled, photographed, and processed, however, with no DNA for comparison purposes the results were inconclusive, except, as you know, in the case of Johana Márquez.'

'I wasn't referring to the remains so much as the scene itself.'

'There wasn't one, or if there was, it was a secondary scene. The bones were scattered around the cave in what looked like a random manner. In fact, because of the teeth marks and the positioning of the bones, we initially thought this was the work of animals, until Forensics revealed that the bite marks were human and that all the bones were women's arm bones. Of course the cave was searched and photographed, but nothing was found to suggest that it was the primary crime scene. Soil samples were taken to rule out any concealed graves or the presence of cadaverine, which would have proved that a body had decomposed in there.'

They had been thorough, thought Amaia, but not as thorough as her.

'One more thing, Lieutenant. Do you know whether the woman murdered in Logroño had any relatives? What happened to her body?'

'I see that you listened to me,' he said, pleased.

'Yes, although I'm beginning to wish I hadn't,' she replied, half-joking.

'I've no idea, but I'll ask the officers I was in touch with in Logroño and see what they can tell me. I'll call you back as soon as I know anything.'

Glancing at his watch, Deputy Inspector Zabalza continued to stare out of the big windows in the police station, and saw an estate car moving along the approach road after passing the fence. The driver performed a couple of erratic manoeuvres before reaching the small ramp to the car park, where the vehicle stalled. After a few attempts to start the engine, the car finally rolled into one of the visitors' spaces. No sooner had it stopped than the passenger door swung open and a skinny youth dressed in jeans and a red-and-black padded jacket clambered out. On the driver's side, a man in his mid-forties, with the same build as the boy only taller, struggled out. As the two figures made their way over to the main entrance, Zabalza noticed that the distance between them remained unchanged, as if they were separated by an invisible, insurmountable barrier. He frowned as he remembered a lesson learned long ago, that it was not distance that separated parents and children. Here, accompanied by his father, was Beñat Zaldúa, the only suspect they had in the case so far, yet the star cop had better things to do than attend the interview. Losing sight of them after they vanished beneath the front of the building, he eyed the telephone, waiting for it to ring.

'Deputy Inspector Zabalza, Señor Zaldúa and his son are here. They say they have an appointment with you.'

'I'll be down in a minute.'

Seen from close up, the boy was extraordinarily handsome. His dark hair, contrasting with his pale skin, tumbled over his brow, partially covering his eyes and highlighting the bruise on his cheekbone. He stood, hands in pockets, staring along the corridor. The father extended a clammy palm, and Zabalza caught an unmistakable whiff of alcohol as he mumbled a greeting.

'Follow me, please.' Zabalza opened a door and ushered them into a room. 'Wait here a moment,' he said, noticing that the boy winced when he patted him on the shoulder.

Almost beside himself, Zabalza leapt up the stairs instead of waiting for the lift, and burst into Iriarte's office without knocking.

'Beñat Zaldúa and his father are downstairs. The father stinks of alcohol – he could barely park the car, while the boy has a bruise on his face, and at least one other on his shoulder; when I brushed against him he practically passed out.'

Iriarte looked at Zabalza without saying a word. He closed the lid of his laptop, reached for the gun lying on his desk and tucked it into his waistband.

'Good morning,' he said, sitting down at the table and addressing himself exclusively to the boy. 'I'm Inspector Iriarte – I think you've met my colleague. As I mentioned yesterday on the phone, we'd like to ask you a few questions concerning your blog about the *agotes* . . .'

He waited for a response, but the boy remained impassive, head lowered. When Iriarte realised he wasn't going to reply, he nodded.

'Your name is Beñat . . . Beñat Zaldúa, isn't that an *agote* surname?'

The boy raised his head defiantly, while the father muttered an objection.

'Yes, and I'm proud of it,' said Beñat.

'That's only natural, we should be proud, whatever our surname,' Iriarte replied calmly. The boy relaxed a little. 'And is that what you write about on your blog: your pride at being an *agote*?'

'That crap he writes every day has got him into trouble. He's just wasting his time.'

'Let your son do the talking,' Iriarte commanded.

'He's a minor,' the father snorted, 'and he'll talk when I say so.'

The boy hunched over in his chair until his fringe hung down over his eyes.

Zabalza could see his jaw trembling.

'If you say so,' replied Iriarte, pretending to give in. 'Let's change the subject. How about you tell me what happened to your eye?'

Without raising his head, the boy flashed a look of hatred at his father before replying:

'I walked into a door.'

'I see. And what about your shoulder? Was that a door too?'

'I fell down the stairs.'

'Beñat, I want you to stand up, take off your jacket and lift up your T-shirt.'

The father leapt to his feet, stumbling as he tripped himself up on the chair legs.

'You've no right – he's a minor. I'm taking him with me right now,' he declared, clasping a hand on his son's shoulder so hard that the boy cried out in pain.

Zabalza pounced on the father, twisting his wrist and pushing him over to the wall, where he stood motionless.

'No, you aren't,' he hissed. 'I'll tell you what's going to happen. I have reason to believe from your behaviour and from the smell of you, that you've been drinking, and yet we have CCTV footage of you arriving at the station by car. So, I'm now going to give you a blood alcohol test. If you refuse, I will arrest you. Furthermore, if you insist on exercising your right not to allow us to interview your son, we will notify social services, because, as you pointed out, he is a minor. They will take him to a medical centre where a forensic doctor will give your son a thorough examination in order to establish whether he has been mistreated – and the boy needn't say a word. What do you say to that?'

Accepting defeat, the man simply asked:

'How am I supposed to get home without a car?'

Iriarte waited for a few moments after the father and Zabalza had left the room, then sent out for a can of Coke, which he put down in front of the boy. He let him take a sip before going on.

'Like everyone else in Arizkun, I expect you're aware of what has been happening in the church.'

The boy nodded.

'As an expert on the subject of the *agotes*, what do you make of it?'

The boy looked surprised. He straightened in his chair, shook his fringe out of his face and gave a shrug.

'I don't know . . .'

'Clearly, someone is trying to draw attention to the history of the *agotes*.'

'To the injustices suffered by the *agotes*,' the boy corrected him.

'Yes, the injustices,' Iriarte conceded. 'That was a terrible time for the whole of society, where injustice was rampant . . . But it was a long time ago.'

'That doesn't make it any less unjust,' Beñat said confidently. 'Don't you see? The problem is that we never learn from history. News stops being news after a few days, sometimes

171

even a few hours, and soon everything is relegated to the past. But we forget that, by failing to take injustices seriously because they happened in the past, we're ensuring they'll be repeated again and again.'

Iriarte studied him, impressed by the clarity and passion with which he expressed his arguments. He had browsed Zaldúa's blog, and his articulateness betrayed a logical, intelligent mind. He wondered how militant the boy was, to what extent his pain and anger could be used as a battering ram against society's most established institutions, crying out for the justice he himself needed – for Beñat Zaldúa was the victim of the cruellest injustice: his father's hatred, his mother's death, the loneliness of a brilliant mind.

And while he listened to him narrate the history of the *agotes* in Arizkun, he decided that Beñat Zaldúa might be in the grip of a burning passion but deep down he was just a scared kid in search of love, affection, and understanding. And, most importantly of all – for this ruled him out as a suspect – he was alone; so alone, it was pitiful to watch him defending these lofty ideas with that bruised and battered body.

Beñat spoke continuously for twenty minutes and Iriarte listened, glancing every now and then at Zabalza, who had re-entered the room and was standing by the door, as though afraid of interrupting. When Beñat fell silent, Iriarte realised he had scarcely taken any notes while the boy was talking, instead drawing a series of doodles on the pad, something he often did when reflecting.

Zabalza walked across the room and stopped in front of the boy.

'Does your father beat you?' he asked, perhaps moved by the boy's zealous outpourings that seemed to have built a bridge between the three of them, one that disappeared when the question was posed.

Like a flower shrivelling in the cold, the boy clammed up again.

'If he does, we can help you,' said Iriarte. 'Do you have any relatives, any uncles or cousins?'

'I have a cousin in Pamplona.'

'Do you think you could stay with him?'

The boy shrugged.

'Beñat,' Iriarte went on, 'despite what Deputy Inspector Zabalza told your father, the truth is we can only help you if you acknowledge the abuse.'

'Thanks,' he said in a hushed voice, 'but I fell.'

Zabalza gave vent to his frustration with a loud sigh, which earned him a look of reproach from Iriarte.

'OK, Beñat, you fell, but you should still see a doctor.'

'I already made an appointment for tomorrow at my local surgery.'

Iriarte rose to his feet.

'All right, Beñat, it's been a pleasure meeting you,' he said, extending his hand.

The boy shook his hand hesitantly.

'If you ever change your mind, call and ask for me or for Deputy Inspector Zabalza. I'm going to check up on your father. You can wait for him here. He's in no fit state to drive, so DI Zabalza will give you both a lift home.'

Iriarte entered the waiting room where Beñat's father was sitting sideways on a chair, head propped against the wall, sleeping it off. He roused him roughly.

'We've finished speaking with your son, who has been extremely helpful.'

The man looked at him in astonishment as he stood up.

'Is that it?'

'Yes,' said Iriarte, then instantly thought, *No, that isn't it.* Blocking the man's path, he added, 'Your son is highly intelligent, and he's a good lad. If I find out that you've so much as laid a finger on him again, you'll have me to contend with.'

'I don't know what he's told you, he's a liar—'

'Did you hear what I said?' Iriarte said firmly.

173

The man bowed his head; they usually did. Men who beat their wives and kids seldom squared up to anyone bigger than them. He stepped around Iriarte and left the room. After he'd gone, the inspector reflected that he felt no better, and knew it was because his threats wouldn't be enough.

Zabalza drove in silence to Arizkun, aware only of his two passengers breathing, accompanying him like two tense strangers, or two enemies. When they arrived at the entrance to a shack just outside the village, the father climbed out of the car and walked towards it without a backward glance, but his son stayed behind for a few moments. Zabalza thought he might want to tell him something, so he waited, but the boy said nothing. He simply sat staring at the house, reluctant to get out of the car.

Zabalza switched the engine off, turned the interior lights on and swivelled round so he could see the boy's face.

'When I was your age, I had problems with my father too.'

Beñat looked at him as if he didn't know what he was talking about.

Zabalza sighed. 'He beat the living daylights out of me.'

'Because you were gay?'

Zabalza gasped, startled by the boy's astuteness. 'Let's just say my father didn't accept the way I was.'

'That isn't the case with me. I'm not gay.'

'That's not the point. It doesn't matter what their reasons are, they see you as different and that's why they beat you.'

The lad smiled bitterly. 'I know what you're going to say: that you fought back, stood up to him, and that eventually everything sorted itself out.'

'On the contrary, I didn't fight back, I didn't stand up for myself, and my father still doesn't accept me,' he said. *And neither do I*, he thought.

'So what's the moral of the story? Why are you telling me this?'

'I'm telling you this because some battles are lost before

174

they begin, because sometimes it's better to save yourself for the big fight. It's brave and admirable to fight for what you believe in, for justice everywhere, but you have to learn to discriminate, because when you're confronted with intolerance, fanaticism or stupidity, often the best thing is to walk away, to save your energy for a more deserving cause.'

'I'm seventeen,' said the boy, as if this were a disease or a sentence.

'Grin and bear it, then get out of there as soon as you can. Leave home and live your own life.'

'Is that what you did?'

'That's exactly what I didn't do.'

13

The sky remained relatively bright above the canopy of trees, although the light dimmed significantly as soon as they entered the forest. They walked briskly, each carrying a metal case, lighting their way with one of the powerful flashlights from the kit. After crossing the stone bridge, they made their way up the hill towards the large boulder.

'It's behind there,' said Amaia, directing the beam towards the cave mouth.

The entire process took less than fifteen minutes: the preliminary photographs, followed by a coating of the miraculous substance that had revolutionised forensic science: Luminol, which reacted to the iron in haemoglobin, enabling the detection of hidden traces of blood visible under ultraviolet light; as simple a phenomenon as chemiluminescence, which occurred in fireflies and some marine organisms. They donned protective orange glasses, permitting them to switch off their torches and turn on the 'new light'.

Amaia felt her back clench. The sensation was both unpleasant and yet euphoric, as she realised she had discovered the end of the thread she needed to pull. Stepping back a few paces, she told Jonan where to shine the UV lamp to make it visible, as she took a series of photographs of the message some wild beast had written in blood on the cave wall: '*Tarttalo*'.

Deputy Inspector Etxaide walked silently beside her as they returned to where the cars were parked. Darkness was descending beneath the treetops, and the wind swaying the branches produced a terrible din of creaks and groans. Every now and then lightning flashed beyond the hills, illuminating the sky, as though announcing the return of the spirit of the mountaintops. Despite the commotion, Amaia could almost hear her deputy thinking, as with every step he cast meaningful glances at her, whilst keeping his questions to himself.

'Speak up, Jonan, or you'll burst.'

'Johana Márquez was killed thirteen months ago a few kilometres from here, and the remains of her severed arm appeared in this cave, where someone has written "*Tarttalo*" – the same message Quiralte scrawled on his cell wall before following Medina to hell.'

'That's not all, Jonan,' she said, coming to a halt. 'A prisoner in Logroño jail who murdered his wife left the same message before killing himself. All three women had an arm amputated. None of the limbs has been found, except for Johana's, which was among the bones the *Guardia Civil* discovered in the cave,' she said, setting off again.

Jonan remained silent a few moments, seemingly digesting the information, then asked:

'Do you think those three men were acting together?'

'No, I don't.'

'And do you think they somehow brought the amputated arms out here?'

'Someone did, but it wasn't them, though I don't believe they carried out the amputations either. We're talking about violent men, drunks, the kind of guys who allow their basest instincts to take over with no thought for the consequences.'

'So are you talking about a third party who was involved in all the crimes, a kind of accomplice?'

'No, Jonan, not an accomplice, more like an instigator, someone who exercises enough control over these men to induce them to commit murder and then suicide, someone who takes a trophy from each of these killings, signing his name in every case: *Tarttalo*.'

Jonan stopped in his tracks and Amaia turned to look at him.

'We were all wrong! How could I have been so stupid, when it was obvious . . .'

Amaia waited. Jonan Etxaide, with his double degree in anthropology and archaeology, was no average cop; he didn't think the way other officers did, and she'd come to respect his opinion.

'Trophies, boss, you said it yourself. Trophies are something you keep as a symbol of victory, pride – they're the prisoners you take. That's why I couldn't understand why they'd been tossed into a remote cave, as if cast aside. It doesn't fit – unless these are the *tarttalo*'s trophies. Chief, according to legend, the *tarttalo* devoured his victims and left their bones at the mouth of his cave, both as a mark of his cruelty and as a warning to anyone who might dare venture near his lair. The bones weren't cast aside or abandoned; they were carefully placed to convey a message.'

'But what's even more striking, Jonan, is that our *tarttalo* fits the description in ways we never imagined. All the bones had straight, parallel score marks on them, identified as teeth marks. Human teeth.'

Jonan's eyes opened wide with surprise. 'A cannibal?'

She nodded. 'Forensics compared them with the bite marks of Johana's stepfather and of Víctor, just to make sure, but they didn't match.'

'How many bodies did the bones they found belong to?'

'About a dozen.'

'And the only match was Johana Márquez?'

'Hers were the most recent.'

178

'What did they do with the others?' asked Jonan.

'They were processed, but since they had no DNA to compare them with . . .'

'That's why you sent me in search of women from Baztán who were victims of male violence.'

'The three we have so far were either originally from here or lived here from an early age, like Johana.'

'How is it possible that no one associated the discovery of those arm bones with murdered women missing a limb?'

'The killers voluntarily confessed to their crimes, and although it's true that at least two of them denied any knowledge of the amputations, who was going to believe them? No one cross-referenced the data – that won't get done until a special crime division is set up to gather and collate all police information, until we no longer have to negotiate with rival forces.' Amaia sighed. 'You've seen for yourself how difficult it is to get to the bottom of a case like this; crimes of domestic violence have few repercussions. They're quickly closed and archived, especially if the culprit confesses and then kills himself. That makes it an open-and-shut case, and the shame the victim's relatives feel only helps to keep it hushed up.'

'I've found two more women born in the valley who were murdered by their partners. I've got their names and the addresses where they were living when it happened – one in Bilbao, the other in Burgos. That's what I was going to tell you when you called me earlier at the station. Death notices were posted for both of them at funeral parlours in the valley.'

'Any mention of severed limbs?'

'No . . .'

'And their assailants?'

'Both deceased: one took his own life at the crime scene, just before the police arrived. The other fled, only to be found hours later hanging from a tree in a nearby orchard.'

'We need to locate some relatives, urgently.'

'I'll get on to it as soon as we're back at the station.'

179

'And, Jonan, not a word to anyone. This investigation has been authorised, but we need to keep it quiet. As far as anyone else is concerned, we're investigating the desecration of the church.'

'I appreciate you confiding in me.'

'Aside from the two victims, you mentioned earlier that you'd come across something else at the funeral parlours.'

'Yes, in all the excitement, I nearly forgot. The man who owns the Baztandarra funeral parlour told me that a few weeks ago a woman came in, dragging another woman by the arm, yelling at her and thrusting her forward. She asked to see some caskets, and when he pointed to the display, she hauled her companion over and said something about how she might as well choose a coffin now, given she'll be dead soon. According to the undertaker, the other woman was petrified. She kept crying and repeating that she didn't want to die.'

'That's bizarre,' said Amaia. 'And he doesn't know these women?'

'So he claims,' Jonan said, looking dubious.

'This must be the only place in the world where everybody knows everybody else's business, but no one is prepared to talk about it,' Amaia said with a shrug.

She took out her mobile, checking the coverage as well as the time, puzzling at how early it was despite the scant light, and recalling how the numbers had vanished from the screen while she was talking to the young woman down by the stream.

'Let's go,' she said, setting off again. 'There's a call I have to make.'

But she didn't have time; no sooner had they reached their cars than her phone rang. It was Padua.

'I'm sorry, chief, the woman in Logroño didn't have any relatives, so her husband's relatives took care of her remains – she was cremated.'

'There are no parents, siblings, children?'

'No, she didn't have kids, but she did have a close friend. If you want to talk to her, I can get her number for you.'

'That won't be necessary. I wasn't thinking about talking to anyone so much as comparing DNA.'

She thanked him, then hung up. She paused to watch the storm still rumbling beyond the mountains, each lightning flash picking out the craggy contours against an otherwise cloudless sky.

'It's coming . . .' The young girl's voice echoed in her head. A shiver ran down her spine as she climbed into her car.

Lit up in the early February night, the police station resembled a phantom ship that had veered off course and washed up there by accident. She parked next to Jonan's car. As they entered the building they met Zabalza on his way out, accompanied by two members of the public. Beñat Zaldúa and his father, she assumed. Zabalza nodded a greeting to her, but walked on, avoiding her gaze.

Amaia left Jonan working at his desk and made her way to Iriarte's office.

'I just saw Zabalza leaving with the boy and his father. What came of it?'

'Nothing,' said Iriarte, shaking his head. 'It's a very sad case. The boy is clever – extremely intelligent, in fact. Unhappy after the death of his mother, he has an alcoholic father who beats him. He had bruising on his face and body, but when we asked he insisted he fell down the stairs. His blog is a refuge, as well as a way of expressing his social concerns. He's an angry teenager, like many, except that he has every reason to be one. He gave me a potted history of the *agotes* and their life in the valley that left me dumbfounded. In my opinion, his outrage on their behalf is just a means of venting his frustration; I don't believe he had anything to do with the desecrations. I honestly can't imagine him splitting a font in two with an axe. He's . . . how should I put it? Delicate.'

181

Amaia recalled the many profiles she had studied of killers who looked as if they wouldn't say boo to a goose. Then she contemplated Iriarte and decided to trust his judgement; you didn't reach the rank of detective inspector without having a good eye, and anyway, it had been her decision to delegate to him.

'Okay, we'll rule the boy out. Where do you suggest we look next?'

'To be honest, there isn't much to go on. Forensics haven't got back to us yet about the *mairu-beso*, and there have been no further incidents since we stationed a round-the-clock patrol car opposite the church.'

'I would interview all the catechists, one at a time, in their homes. The priest said he never had a problem with anyone, but the women might remember something he has forgotten, or which for some reason he prefers not to mention. And take Zabalza with you. I've noticed that women of a certain age seem to like him,' she said with a grin. 'If he can get them to talk, they might tell him something, besides giving him coffee and biscuits.'

Taking the scenic route, Amaia drove to the market square then crossed the river at Giltxaurdi. She was proceeding slowly, edging between the parked cars, when to her alarm three boys on bicycles shot out in front of her. They turned right and disappeared behind the bakery. To avoid blocking the road, she parked up on the pavement following them on foot, an unlit torch in her hand. From a distance she could hear their laughter, and it seemed that they too had torches. She approached, hugging the wall until she drew level, then switched on her torch, aiming the powerful beam at them, as she identified herself.

'Police. What are you doing here?'

One of the boys gave such a start that he lost his balance and fell, bicycle and all, on to the others. As they struggled to stay upright, one of them shaded his eyes with his hand to get a look at her.

'We're not doing anything,' he stammered.

'Really? In that case, why are you here? This is the back entrance to a bakery, you've no business being here.'

The two other boys straightened their bikes and replied:

'We weren't doing any harm, we just came to look.'

'At what?'

'At the graffiti.'

'Did you do this?'

'No, we didn't, honestly.'

'Are you lying?'

'No, it's the truth.'

'But you know who did.'

The three boys exchanged glances but remained silent.

'OK. This is what I'm going to do: call a patrol car and arrest you on suspicion of vandalism, then get in touch with your parents. Perhaps that will refresh your memories.'

'It's an old woman,' one of the boys blurted out.

'Yeah, an old woman,' the other two repeated.

'She comes every night and writes rude words. You know – whore, bitch, things like that.'

'Yeah, every night. I reckon she must be nuts,' one declared.

'Yes, a nutty old graffitist,' said the first boy.

This tickled the other two, who burst out laughing.

14

She had read somewhere that you should never return to the place where you were once happy, because if you do it will start to elude you. She supposed that whoever wrote this was right; real or otherwise, places viewed through the rose-tinted perspective of memory could turn out to be dangerously real, so disappointing they could cause our dreams to go up in smoke. For Amaia it was that house, which appeared to have a life of its own, enveloping her within its walls and giving her warmth. She knew it was her aunt's presence, visible or invisible, that gave the place its soul, even though in her dreams it was always empty, and she was always a child. She would use the key hidden in the entrance and rush inside, in the grip of rage and fear. But it was only when she crossed the threshold and sensed the thousand welcoming presences embracing her in a seemingly womb-like peace that the child who had to stay awake all night so that her mother wouldn't devour her could finally relax in front of the fire and fall asleep.

Now, as she entered her aunt's house and slipped off her coat, the merry laughter of the 'Golden Girls' reached her from the living room. Gathered round the beautiful hexagonal poker table, they appeared to have no interest in the cards, which lay strewn over the green baize; instead they were busy pulling faces and cooing over Ibai, who was being passed around to his visible delight as well as that of the old ladies.

'Amaia, for heaven's sake! He's the prettiest baby in the world!' exclaimed Miren when she saw her.

Amaia chuckled at the extravagant praise the old women lavished on Ibai, smothering him with kisses and caresses.

'You're going to spoil him with all this attention,' she said, pretending to be annoyed.

'Oh, for goodness' sake, woman, let us enjoy him. He's an absolute darling,' said another of the old women, leaning over the baby, who was beaming with joy.

James came across to give her a kiss and apologise. Gesturing towards the old biddies, he told her, 'I'm sorry, darling, there was nothing I could do. I was outnumbered. They were armed with knitting needles.'

His declaration set them all rummaging in their handbags, from which they produced tiny hand-knitted cardigans, hats and bootees for the infant.

Amaia scooped up Ibai, admiring the exquisite clothes the old ladies had knitted for her son. Cradling him, she became aware of him struggling in her arms. He instantly started to cry, demanding to be fed.

She withdrew to the bedroom, stretched out on the bed and placed Ibai next to her to breastfeed him. James followed and lay down alongside her, his arm round her back.

'What a glutton!' he exclaimed. 'He can't possibly be hungry, I only fed him an hour ago, but as soon as he gets a whiff of you . . .'

'Poor little thing, he misses me. I miss him too,' she whispered, caressing him.

'Manolo Azpiroz was here this afternoon.'

'Who?' she asked dreamily, gazing down at her son.

'Manolo, my architect friend. I showed him *Juanitaenea* and he loves it. He's full of ideas about how to restore the house while preserving its character. He's coming back in a few days to measure up and get on with the project. I'm so excited—'

'I'm really glad, darling,' she said, leaning over and kissing him on the lips.

He remained pensive.

'Amaia, I went to the bakery today to look for your sister. When we got there Ernesto told me she'd left for her house. As it's nearby and it was a sunny afternoon, I walked there via the back streets . . .'

Amaia lifted Ibai to burp him, and sat up on the bed so that she could look at James.

'Ros was cleaning paint off her front door. When I asked, she said it must have been some kids messing around. I pretended not to notice, but it wasn't graffiti, Amaia, it was abuse. Although she'd scrubbed most of it off, the word was still legible.'

'What did it say?'

'Murderer.'

When they came down to dinner, the smell of baking fish filled the house. Ros was helping Engrasi set the table. Amaia placed Ibai in the baby rocker so he would be near them while they were eating. She tucked into the baked mackerel with potatoes, a dish so simple and delicious it never ceased to amaze her. She reflected that it was small wonder she was famished: she'd barely had time to grab a bite all day. After dinner, while the others were clearing the table, she put Ibai to bed, returning to the dining room in time to catch Ros before she went upstairs.

'Rosaura, would you do a reading for me?'

Engrasi, who was carrying some cups, instantly paused, ears pricked.

Ros looked away evasively.

'Oh, Amaia, I'm dreadfully tired this evening, why don't

you ask Auntie? She's been longing to do one, haven't you, Auntie?' she said, walking out into the kitchen.

Engrasi exchanged knowing glances with Amaia, then waved a hand at her, before directing her reply towards the kitchen:

'Of course, dear, you go on up to bed.'

When Ros and James had gone, the two of them sat down facing one another. Engrasi began the slow ritual of unfolding the silk cloth from around the cards, then shuffling them slowly between her pale, bony fingers.

'I'm glad you've finally decided to do this, dear. For weeks now, whenever I pick up the cards, I can feel their energy flowing towards you.'

Amaia gave a forced smile. She had only asked Ros because it was the perfect excuse to discuss what was going on at the bakery.

'That's why I was surprised when you asked Ros, although I'm sure you have your reasons.'

'Ros has a problem.'

The old lady chuckled half-heartedly.

'Amaia, you know that I love all three of you. I'd do anything for you, but I think it's high time you realised that Ros isn't merely older than you, she's an adult, and her personality and her way of being are naturally problematic. She's one of those people who suffer as if they were bearing an invisible cross – but woe betide anyone who tries to lighten her load. By all means, offer your help; but don't interfere, because she'll take that as an insult.'

Amaia thought it over, nodding.

'That sounds like good advice.'

'Which you won't take . . .' said Engrasi.

She placed the cards in front of her niece and waited for her to cut the pack. Then she took both piles, shuffled them again, spread them out in front of Amaia and watched as she picked the cards.

187

Amaia let her finger hover above each one without touching it, as if she were about to leave a fingerprint, then waited for her aunt to slide the card away before choosing another. When she had chosen twelve, her aunt arranged them in a circle like a clock dial, or the cardinal points on a compass. As she turned the cards over, her face changed from an expression of surprise to one of deepest reverence.

'Oh, my child! How you've grown, what a woman you have turned into,' she declared, pointing to the empress, which was the dominant card. 'You've always been strong – you had to be to endure the terrible ordeals you went through – but since last year there's a new side to you,' she said, pointing to a different card, 'a door you opened in despair, behind which something extraordinary awaited you, something that changed your way of seeing.'

Amaia couldn't help smiling as she travelled back in time and space to those amber eyes gazing at her through the thick forest.

'Things don't happen without a reason, Amaia; this wasn't an accident or coincidence.' Engrasi touched one of the cards, then withdrew her finger as if she had received an electric shock. She looked up in surprise. 'I never knew that, it was never revealed to me.'

Amaia's interest quickened, and she peered intently at the colourful designs on the cards.

'The curse that hung over you was there before you were born.'

'But—'

'Don't interrupt,' snapped Engrasi. 'I knew you had always been different, that knowledge of death marks people for ever, but in different ways. It can turn them into an unhappy shadow of what they might have been, or, as in your case, imbue them with tremendous strength, extraordinary ability and insight. I believe you were born that way; I think *Amatxi* Juanita knew this, as did your father, and your mother. And the first time I met you, when I returned from Paris, I knew it too. The little girl with the eyes of a fighter, who moved around her mother as if she were ready to hit the ground at any moment, keeping a safe distance, avoiding her mother's touch and gaze, holding her breath when she felt she was being scrutinised. The little girl who stayed awake so as not to be devoured.

'Amaia, you've changed – and that's good, because it was inevitable, but it is also dangerous. Powerful forces are looming over you, pulling you in all directions. Here he is,' she said, pointing to a card. 'The guardian who watches over you, whose love for you is pure, who will never leave your side, because his aim is to protect you. And here,' she said, showing the next card, 'the powerful priestess who forces you into battle, who demands extraordinary respect and devotion. She admires you, and will use you as a battering ram against her enemies, for you are no more than a weapon to her, a soldier sent to fight evil, to assist her in her age-old struggle to re-establish harmony. A harmony disrupted by a monstrous act that led to the awakening of beasts, of powers that had lain dormant for centuries in the depths of the valley, which you must now help to vanquish.'

'But is this priestess good?' asked Amaia, smiling at her aunt. Whatever form it took, Engrasi's love was absolute and genuine.

'She is neither good nor evil; she is a force of nature, a perfect balance, she can be as cruel and ruthless as Mother Earth herself.'

Amaia gazed intently at the cards and, moving anticlockwise, pointed at one.

'You said that the balance was destroyed by a monstrous act. Dupree told me to search for the original act, what unleashed the evil.'

'Oh, Dupree!' exclaimed Engrasi, aghast. 'Why do you persist with him, Amaia? That man could do you untold harm. I mean it.'

'He would never harm me.'

'Perhaps not the Dupree you knew, but how can you be sure that he's on your side after what happened?'

'Because I know him, Auntie. And I don't care how much his circumstances may have changed. He's still the best criminologist I've ever known, an honest cop through and through. His impartiality got him into his current situation – that and nothing else. It's not my business to judge him, because he doesn't judge me, he has always backed me up. He was and continues to be the best mentor any cop could wish for. I refuse to analyse his situation, which I know nothing about. All I know is that he always answers my calls.'

Engrasi's face remained solemn as she gazed at her in silence. She pursed her lips and said:

'Just promise me you won't get caught up in that investigation under any circumstances.'

'In an FBI case on the other side of the world? I don't see how I could.'

'Don't get caught up under any circumstances,' she repeated.

'I won't . . . Unless he asks me to.'

'If he's as good a friend as you say, he won't.'

Amaia contemplated the cards in silence, picked out one and slid it across the table, gathering the others into a pile.

'You forget that he speaks to me, he responds to my needs whenever I call. Don't you think that in doing so he's putting me in a privileged position?'

'I hardly see it as a privilege, more like a curse.'

'Either way, it's the same curse that supposedly singled me out before I was born,' said Amaia, pointing at the cards. 'The same curse that fills my dreams with dead people who lean over my bed, like guardians of the forest or goddesses of thunder,' she said irritably, raising her voice slightly. 'Auntie, all this is a waste of time,' she sighed, suddenly weary.

Engrasi covered her mouth, both hands clasped over her lips as she looked with growing alarm at her niece.

190

'No, no, no, hush, Amaia. You mustn't believe . . .'

Amaia paused before finishing the old saying, uttered down the centuries by thousands of people from Baztán:

'. . . they exist, you mustn't deny their existence.'

They sat in silence for a few moments, catching their breath, while Engrasi looked at the cards in disarray.

'We haven't finished yet,' she said, pointing at the pack.

'I'm afraid I must go, Auntie. There's something I need to do.'

'But—' Engrasi protested.

'We'll carry on, I promise,' said Amaia, standing up and putting on her coat. She leaned over and gave her aunt a kiss. 'Now go to bed, I don't want to find you here when I get back.'

But Engrasi was still sitting there when Amaia left the house.

She noticed at once how the damp from the river, together with the mist that had rolled down the hillsides as night fell, clung to her black wool coat in thousands of microscopic droplets, giving it a grey sheen. She walked down the empty street towards the bridge, paused for a few seconds, checking the time on her phone as she glanced at the dark river where the weir echoed in the silence of the night. The Txokoto and Trinkete taverns were closed at this hour, and there were no lights inside. She slipped between the houses, hugging the walls until she reached the main door of the bakery. She paused on the corner to listen, and when she was satisfied, made her way round the back to the unlit car park, where she concealed herself behind some rubbish bins. Checking her torch and her mobile once more, she instinctively felt for her holstered gun, and smiled.

She waited the best part of half an hour before hearing the crunch of footsteps approaching on the gravel. A single, rather small figure, clad in black from head to foot, strode towards the back door of the bakery. Amaia waited for the sound of plastic beads rattling inside the spray can, as the intruder shook the canister and the hiss of gas announcing the imminent graffiti. A couple of sprays, more shaking, another hiss . . . Amaia stepped out from behind the bins, training both her torch and her phone camera on the artist.

'Stop, police,' she said, opting for the classic approach as she turned on her torch and clicked the camera button several times.

The woman let out a little shriek, dropped the spray can and took to her heels.

Amaia didn't bother giving chase. Not only had she recognised the woman, she'd taken a couple of good snapshots of her: white hair lit up like a halo by the powerful beam, can in hand, a coarse insult painted in the background, a comical look of surprise on her face. She stooped to pick up the spray can and put it in a bag before setting off for the nocturnal artist's house.

Rosaura's mother-in-law opened the door. She'd had time to put on a floral housecoat over her outdoor clothes, but was still out of breath after sprinting home. Amaia didn't think she had seen her, although of course she had heard her voice when she announced herself. The woman was no fool; if she had any doubts about who had caught her in the act, they must have vanished when she saw Amaia in the doorway. Even so, she tried to brazen it out.

'What are you doing here? You and your family aren't welcome in this house, especially not at this time of night,' she said, pretending to be offended, while making a show of looking at the clock.

'Oh, I didn't come here to see you. I came to see Freddy.'

'Well, he doesn't want to see you,' she said, growing more confident.

From within, Amaia heard a hoarse voice she barely recognised.

'Is that you, Amaia?'

'Yes, Freddy, I dropped by to see you,' she said, raising her voice from the doorway.

'Let her in, *Ama*.'

'I don't think that's a good idea,' the woman replied, unsure of herself once more.

'*Ama*, I said let her in.' His voice sounded weary.

The woman said nothing, but stood her ground, blocking the entrance as she gazed at Amaia defiantly.

Amaia put her hand on the woman's shoulder, pushing her backwards while at the same time holding on to her to prevent her falling over. She advanced towards the sitting room. The furniture had been rearranged to accommodate Freddy's wheelchair between two armchairs in front of the TV, which was on but with the volume turned down.

His posture in the chair scarcely betrayed the fact that he was paralysed from the neck down. But the athletic physique of which he had always been so proud had given way to a withered body that was little more than a skeleton wrapped in flesh, accentuated by his bulky clothes. His face was still handsome, though; perhaps more so than ever. He seemed to radiate a melancholy calm, which, together with a pallor that was belied only by his bloodshot eyes, gave him an air of kindliness and self-assurance that he had lacked before.

'Hello, Amaia,' he said, smiling.

'Hello, Freddy.'

'Are you on your own?' he said, glancing towards the front door. 'I thought perhaps . . . Ros . . .'

'No, Freddy, I came alone. I need to talk to you.'

He appeared not to be listening.

'How is Ros? She never comes to visit. I'd love it if she did . . . But I understand that she doesn't want to see me. It's normal.'

Still propped up in the doorway glaring at Amaia, Freddy's mother cut in angrily:

'Normal! There's nothing normal about it, unless you're cold-blooded – which she is.'

193

Amaia paid her no attention. She manoeuvred one of the armchairs until it was facing the wheelchair and sat down opposite her former brother-in-law.

'She's fine, Freddy, but perhaps you ought to explain to your mother why it's normal that Ros doesn't want to see you.'

'He doesn't need to explain anything,' the woman snapped. 'I know what her problem is: she daren't show her face around here after what she did to my poor boy. And I can tell you another thing: it's just as well. Because if she showed up here, I swear to God I wouldn't be accountable for my actions.'

Amaia continued to ignore her.

'Freddy, I think you need to have a talk with your mother.'

He swallowed hard before replying:

'Amaia, this is between Ros and me, I don't think my mother—'

'I said that Ros was fine, but that's not entirely true. She's been having a slight problem lately,' she said, holding up in front of his eyes her mobile showing the image of his mother in flagrante delicto.

He looked genuinely surprised.

'What's this?'

'It's your mother, twenty minutes ago, spraying abuse on the bakery door. This is what she has been up to the past few months: harassing Ros, threatening her, writing "murderous whore" both there and on her front door at home.'

'*Ama?*'

His mother remained silent, staring at the floor with a sneer.

'*Ama!*' Freddy bellowed. 'What's all this about?'

His mother's breath was coming in short gasps. Suddenly she rushed towards him and flung her arms around his legs.

'What did you expect? I did what I had to do. What any mother would do. Every time I see her in the street I want to kill her because of all the suffering she caused you.'

194

'She didn't do anything, *Ama*, it was me.'

'But she's to blame, for being heartless. She abandoned you – the pain drove you out of your wits, my poor boy,' she said, crying with rage as she clung to his lifeless limbs. 'Look at you!' she declared, raising her head. 'Look at what that bitch has done to you!'

Freddy wept silently.

'Tell her, Freddy,' Amaia insisted. 'Tell her why you were a suspect in the Anne Arbizu murder, tell her why Ros walked out and why you tried to take your own life.'

Freddy's mother shook her head.

'I know why.'

'No, you don't.'

Freddy wept as he contemplated his mother.

'The time has come, Freddy. Your silence is causing other people a lot of suffering and, given the family tendency to act without thinking, I wouldn't be surprised if your mother ended up doing some real harm. You owe it to her, but more than anything you owe it to Ros.'

Freddy stopped crying, his face regaining the air of serenity she'd observed earlier.

'You're right, I owe it to Ros.'

'You don't owe that bitch anything!' his mother hissed.

'Don't insult her, *Ama*, she doesn't deserve it. Ros loved me, she looked after me, she was faithful. When she left it was because she found out I was seeing another woman.'

'That's a lie,' replied his mother, determined not to concede defeat. 'What woman?'

'Anne Arbizu.' He whispered her name, and despite the months that had passed, Amaia could see he was still grieving.

His mother gaped in disbelief.

'I was infatuated with her like a child. I thought only of myself. Ros suspected something was going on. Finally, she got fed up and left. The day I found out about Anne's murder, I couldn't bear it, and . . . well, you know what I did.'

195

His mother rose to her feet, and said to him, simply:

'You should have told me, son.' Then she straightened her clothes and walked out to the kitchen, drying her tears.

Amaia remained sitting opposite him, gazing after Freddy's mother with concern.

'Don't worry about her,' he said calmly. 'She'll get over it. She has always forgiven me, and this won't be an exception. I just feel sorry for Ros, I hope she doesn't think . . . well, that I had anything to do with it.'

'I doubt she thinks that . . .'

'I hurt her a lot through my thoughtlessness and stupidity, but also knowingly. You see, Amaia, I was so crazy about Anne, I couldn't see straight. I was happy with Ros, I truly loved her, but that girl Anne . . . things with Anne were different. She got under my skin. I couldn't help myself. Once she chose you, there was no way you could resist her power.'

Amaia looked at him in astonishment, while he seemed to drink in the words from the air, mesmerised.

'She chose me. She pulled my strings, worked me like a puppet. I'm sure she led Víctor on, but also that she was close to your sister.'

'Ros insisted she only knew her by sight,' said Amaia, puzzled.

'I mean Flora, not Ros. One day, I went to fetch something from the bakery and saw them together. Anne was coming out of the back entrance, they exchanged a few words and embraced each other warmly. The following Sunday, Ros and I were having an aperitif at a bar under the arcades when Flora stopped by to say hello on her way back from church. When Anne walked past, I pretended not to see her. Ros didn't suspect anything, but Flora snubbed her too, which seemed strange after I'd seen them together. I asked Anne about it the next time I saw her, but she insisted I was mistaken and got quite annoyed, so I dropped the subject. After all, what did I care.'

'Are you sure about this, Freddy?'

'Yes, positive.'

Amaia sat thinking.

'Sometimes she comes to see me,' he said softly.

'Who does?'

'Anne. Once at the hospital and twice since I've been here.'

Amaia looked at him, not knowing what to say.

'If I had the use of my limbs, I'd take my own life. Did you know that witches and suicides find no rest when they die?'

While Freddy was talking, she had felt her mobile vibrate but decided to ignore it. As she left the house, she saw there were two missed called from Jonan. She dialled his number and waited for him to pick up.

'Chief, I've found two relatives of the murdered women: a sister and an aunt, one in Bilbao, the other in Burgos, and both of them have agreed to see you.'

She looked at her watch and saw it was past midnight.

'It's a bit late to call now . . . Call them first thing tomorrow and tell them I'm on my way. Text me their addresses.'

'Don't you want me to go with you, chief?' asked Jonan, a little disappointed.

After a moment's reflection she decided that this was something she had to deal with on her own.

'I'll use the opportunity to visit my sister Flora in Zarautz on family business. You stay here and rest. You've been glued to your computer for days. Things in Arizkun seem to have calmed down, so why not take the day off and we'll talk when I get back.'

As she approached her aunt's house, she made out a figure lurking in the shadow between two streetlamps. Instinctively she moved her hand to her gun. The man took a step forward, emerging from the gloom: Fermín Montes, clearly the worse for drink. He waited for her to draw level.

'Amaia—'

'You've got a nerve coming here,' she snapped. 'This is my home – do you understand? My home. You have no right.'

'I just want to talk to you,' he explained.

'Then make an appointment to see me in my office. Sit down in front of me and say whatever you have to say, but don't hang around waiting for me at the police station or outside my house. Remember, I'm in the middle of an investigation, and you're suspended.'

'Make an appointment? But I thought we were friends—'

'That rings a bell,' she said ironically. 'Didn't I say that? And what was your reply? Ah, yes: "Think again."'

'The assessment is this week.'

'Judging from your behaviour, you don't seem too concerned about it.'

'What are you planning to tell them?'

Amaia turned towards him, taken aback at his brazenness.

'You don't get it, do you, Montes?'

'What are you planning to tell them?' he repeated.

She contemplated his ashen face: the puffy bags that had formed under his eyes, the unfamiliar wrinkles around his mouth, which wore a grimace of angry contempt.

'What am I planning to tell them? That you practically blew your brains out last year.'

'Come on, Salazar, you know that's not true,' Montes protested.

'Make an appointment,' she said, taking out her key and walking up to the front door. 'This conversation is over.'

He stood staring at her, pursing his lips, then said:

'I don't see the use in making an appointment. According to what I hear, you spend more time away from the station than inside it, leaving others to do your work for you. Isn't that so, Salazar?'

She wheeled round, grinning at him, her smile vanishing abruptly as she retorted:

'Detective Inspector Salazar to you. And remember to use that name when you ask for an appointment.'

Montes stiffened for an instant, as Amaia noticed his face flush in the dim light. She waited for him to answer back, but instead he turned on his heel and walked away.

She took off her boots before going upstairs, grateful as always for the little lamp they now habitually left on in the bedroom. She paused to watch Ibai, who was fast asleep, arms outstretched, hands splayed like starfish pointing north and south, his gentle pulse, barely perceptible in the artery on his pale neck. James stirred slightly when he sensed her presence, embracing her and drawing her to him. He smiled, eyes still closed.

'Your feet are freezing,' he whispered, wrapping his own around them.

'Not just my feet . . .'

'Where else?' he asked groggily.

'Here,' she said, guiding his hand to her breasts.

James opened his eyes, suddenly wide-awake, raising himself on one elbow as he continued to caress her.

'Anywhere else?'

She nodded, pretending to pout.

'Where?' asked James, gallantly, rolling on top of her. 'Here?' he said, kissing her neck.

She shook her head.

'Here?' he said, moving down her chest and brushing her skin softly with his lips.

She shook her head again.

'Give me a clue,' he asked, grinning. 'Further down?'

She nodded, pretending to be bashful.

He slid beneath the duvet, kissing her belly until he reached her sex.

'I think I've found the place you mean,' he said, kissing her there too. Then he poked his head out from under the duvet, feigning indignation.

'Hey . . . you've been fooling me,' he said, 'this place isn't cold at all – in fact, it's burning hot.'

She smiled mischievously and pushed his head beneath the covers again.

'Back to work, slave.'

He obeyed.

She could hear the baby crying as if from a long way off, in a different room. She opened her eyes, got out of bed, and went to find him. The wooden floors heated by the fireplaces warmed the soles of her feet. Shafts of light spilling through the windows traced motes of dust hanging in the air, which swirled as she passed through them.

She began to climb the stairs, listening to the distant crying, though the sound no longer made her want to hurry; instead she was drawn by the need to satisfy the curiosity of a nine-year-old. She looked down at her hands sliding up the banister, at her small feet, peeping out from beneath the embroidered white nightdress *Amatxi* Juanita had made for her, and at the lace waistband threaded with a pale pink ribbon she had chosen from among the many her grandmother had shown her. A rhythmical sound accompanied Ibai's sobs – tick-tock, like breaking waves, or the mechanism of a clock. Tick-tock, as the sobs gradually began to subside before ceasing completely. And then she heard someone calling:

'Amaia.' The voice sounded sweet and a long way off, like the baby's cries.

She continued her ascent fearlessly: after all, she was in *Amatxi* Juanita's house, nothing bad could happen to her there.

'Amaia,' the voice called again.

'I'm coming,' she replied, struck by the similarity of the two voices, the one calling out and the one that answered.

As she reached the landing, she paused to listen. Amid the stillness in the house she could hear the logs crackling in the hearths, the creak of floorboards beneath her weight, and the rhythmical tick-tock, which seemed to be coming from upstairs.

'Amaia,' the sad little girl's voice called.

Extending her small hand until she was touching the banister rail, she climbed the remaining steps. The tick-tock grew louder and louder. One step at a time, as though in rhythm with the tapping sounds, until she came to the top. Then Ibai started to cry again and she realised the noise was coming from the cradle, which stood in the centre of the spacious room. It was rocking back and forth, as though an invisible hand were pushing it violently until it reached the wooden rail that acted as a brake. Tick-tock, tick-tock. She ran towards it, arms outstretched as if to halt the rocking motion. Then she saw her. A little girl sitting in a corner of the attic in her nightdress, golden locks tumbling over her shoulders. She was shedding silent tears that were as thick and dark as engine oil; they spilled into her lap, soaking her nightdress, staining it black. Amaia felt a searing pain in her chest as she realised that the little girl was her, terrified and alone. She wanted to tell her not to cry any more, that everything would be all right, but her voice stuck in her throat as the girl raised the stump of her severed arm, signalling the cradle where Ibai was now screaming frenziedly.

'Don't let *Ama* eat him too, like she did me.'

Amaia turned towards the cradle, seized the baby and fled downstairs, even as she heard the little girl repeat her warning:

'Don't let *Ama* eat him too, like she did me.'

She rushed down the stairs, clutching Ibai to her breast. Other wretched looking children were waiting for her lined up on either side of the staircase to form a corridor. They wept silently, gazing at her mournfully as they held their amputated stumps aloft. She screamed, and her scream penetrated her sleep, dragging her sweating and trembling from her trance, arms clasped to her chest as if she were still carrying her son, the little girl's voice calling out to her from the underworld.

James was asleep, but Ibai was moving restlessly in his cot. She picked him up, shreds of her nightmare still lingering in her mind as she tentatively switched on the bedside light to try to rid herself of the images once and for all. She glanced at the clock; it was almost dawn. She laid the baby next to her on the bed and offered him her breast. He looked up at her, smiling so hard that more than once he lost suction on the nipple, then after a few minutes he started to cry for more. She changed him over to the other breast, but soon realised it wouldn't be enough. She sighed, gazing wistfully down at her son, then went down to the kitchen to prepare a bottle for him. Nature was taking its course; she was no longer producing enough milk to feed Ibai; her body was simply adapting. She hardly ever breastfed him nowadays – who was she trying to fool? Not nature, for sure. She went back up to the room, where James was awake and taking care of Ibai. He looked at Amaia in surprise as she took the baby in her arms and gave him the bottle, tears streaming down her face.

15

Zarautz was the place where she wanted to live as a child. The avenue bordered by shady trees, the elegant houses on the seafront promenade, the charming old quarter with its shops and bars, people milling in the street even when it was raining, the smell of the rough, untamed sea, spraying the air with droplets of water. And the light, which by the sea is as different to the light in a mountain valley as blue eyes are to brown. She wasn't so sure about this any more, because although up until recently she was convinced that she hated where she came from and would never to go back to Elizondo, during the past twelve months the tables had turned; nothing of what she had once taken for granted, none of her certainties, remained the same. Her roots were calling her, calling back those who were born there, on the bend in the River Baztán. She had heard the call, but still had the strength to resist it. What she couldn't ignore was the call of the dead. She knew, she understood, that there was a pact stronger than her, a power that compelled her to confront time and again those who wanted to tarnish the valley's reputation. But that was where her convictions ended.

Thick white cumulus clouds floated in the sky above a sea that wasn't quite blue, breaking on the shore in perfect white waves that resounded rhythmically amid the quiet, luminous winter morning of Zarautz. A small band of surfers carrying their boards walked towards the sea – a long way off, as the tide was out – to join the large group already in the water. Two magnificent horses trotted past her on the compacted sand. She raised her eyes towards the windows of the houses on the promenade, reflecting how wonderful it must be to wake up every morning with a view over the Bay of Biscay, to have the money for that. A glimpse at the prices in a local estate agent showed that nothing had changed since one hundred and fifty years ago when the first businessmen from the Basque Country and Madrid began erecting their magnificent villas along that piece of coastline: the place remained the preserve of the wealthy. She located the building she was looking for and followed the path around to the side, where the entrance overlooked the garden. A liveried doorman announced her arrival and told her which floor to go to. As she stepped out of the lift, an open door greeted her. Her sister's voice rang out from inside, mingling with the strains of soft music.

'Come in, Amaia, help yourself to coffee – I'm just finishing getting dressed.'

If Flora's aim was to impress her, she succeeded. Even from the doorway, which opened on to a vast living room, you could see the sea. The orange-tinted picture windows extended the whole length of the apartment and from floor to ceiling: the effect was breathtaking. Amaia paused in the centre of the room, overwhelmed by the beauty and the light. This was a luxury worth paying for.

Flora entered the room and smiled when she saw her.

'Amazing, isn't it? That's how I felt the first time I walked in here. Afterwards, they showed me a few other places, but I couldn't get this image out of my head all night. The next day I bought it.'

Amaia managed to tear her eyes away from the view to

look at her sister, who had stopped at a discreet distance and seemed reluctant to come any nearer.

'You look fantastic, Flora,' she said, sincerely.

Her sister had on a red dress and was caked in make-up, yet she carried it off with grace and elegance.

She twirled around so that Amaia could see her outfit from the back.

'I won't kiss you, because I've got my TV face on. We're filming in an hour and a half.'

Of course that's the reason, thought Amaia.

Freed from the requirement to show affection, Flora clattered across the room in her heels, leaving an invisible trail of expensive perfume as she brushed past Amaia.

'Things are obviously going well for you, Flora. You have a beautiful home,' said Amaia, casting her eye over the sumptuous décor, which she had only just noticed, 'and you look fantastic.'

Flora came back, carrying a tray with two coffees.

'I can't say the same for you – you're dreadfully thin. I thought all first-time mothers got fat, you could do with putting on a few kilos.'

Amaia smiled. 'Being a mother is exhausting, Flora, but it's worth the effort.' It was a throwaway remark, but Amaia noticed her sister wince. 'How's the programme going?' She changed the subject.

Flora's face lit up. 'Well, so far we've broadcast forty programmes on local TV, and even before episode ten was aired we started receiving offers from the national channels. We signed a deal last week to begin broadcasting as of this spring. They've bought two seasons in advance, which means I'll be filming two or three programmes a day. It's hard work, but extremely rewarding.'

'Ros is doing really well too, at the bakery. She's even managed to increase sales.'

'Has she now,' Flora said disdainfully. 'Ros is simply reaping the rewards of all my hard work. Or do you suppose these things happen overnight?'

'No. I'm just telling you that she's doing fine.'

'Well, it was about time Ros woke up.'

Amaia stayed silent for over a minute while she enjoyed her coffee admiring the peculiar mouse-shaped coastline of Guetaria, sensing Flora's growing tension as she sat opposite her. Her sister had finished her coffee, and was tugging continuously at the hem of her impeccable dress.

'To what do I owe the honour of your visit?' she said at last.

Amaia set down her cup on the tray and looked straight at her sister.

'An investigation,' she said.

Flora's smile faded slightly.

'Tell me about Anne Arbizu,' said Amaia, still scanning her sister's face.

Flora's apparent calm was betrayed by a slight tremor of her jaw. Amaia thought she would refuse, but once more her sister surprised her.

'What do you want to know?'

'Why didn't you tell me you and she were friends?'

'You never asked, little sister, besides, there's nothing strange about it. I've lived all my life in Elizondo, I know practically everyone, at least by sight. In fact, I used to know all the women there, except for that Dominican girl, what was her name?'

'But you didn't just know Anne Arbizu by sight, you were friends.'

Flora remained silent while she tried to gauge how much her sister knew. Amaia put her out of her misery.

'Someone told me they saw her coming out of the back of the bakery.'

'She could have gone there to see one of the employees, couldn't she?'

'No, Flora, she went to see you. You said a fond goodbye in the doorway.'

Flora rose to her feet and walked over to the window so that Amaia could not see her face.

'I don't see why this is relevant, assuming it's even true.'

Amaia also rose to her feet, but remained where she was.

'Flora, Anne Arbizu died a violent death; Anne Arbizu was having an affair with your brother-in-law, Freddy; Anne Arbizu was the cause of all Ros's suffering; Anne Arbizu was on friendly enough terms with you that the pair of you hugged and kisssed each other goodbye. Anne Arbizu was drowned in the river by your estranged husband. And you, Flora, you killed the man you were married to for twenty years – and, regardless of your statement and your bluster, I don't believe you acted in self-defence, because I know for a fact that Víctor did what he did because he was incapable of confronting you. He would rather have dropped dead than threaten you.'

Flora gritted her teeth and continued to stare out of the window, stubbornly silent.

'I know you, Flora. I know what you thought of the victims, the just deserts of common sluts. I remember word for word your defence of the guardian of virtue who punished those brazen little whores. You didn't give a damn about them. I don't believe you put a stop to Víctor because he was leaving a trail of murdered girls in the valley. It was because he killed Anne. That was his mistake.'

Flora turned around very slowly, every gesture betraying the effort she was making to control herself.

'Don't talk nonsense. I said all that to provoke him. I suspected him, I knew the man – as you said, we were married for twenty years – and he responded by threatening me. You were there, you saw how he screamed at me and told me he was going to kill me.'

Amaia burst out laughing. 'You've got to be joking, Flora!

It isn't true. If Víctor was the way he was, it was because he was in your power. He adored, worshipped, and respected you – you alone. And yes, you're right, I was there, but that's not how I remember it. I heard the first shot, which I'm sure must have taken him down, and when I arrived I saw you fire a second shot . . . Now I think that what I actually saw was you giving him the coup de grâce.'

'You can't prove anything,' Flora shouted angrily, turning back towards the window.

Amaia smiled. 'You're right, I can't, but what I can prove is that Anne Arbizu was far more complex and sinister than her angelic appearance suggested. Bordering on psychopathic, she was a schemer who wielded control over everyone she met. I want to know what kind of relationship you had with her, what influence she had over you, whether you loved her enough to avenge her death.'

Pressing her head to the glass, Flora remained motionless for a few moments, before letting out a guttural wail, flattening her hands against the window to hold herself up. When she turned round, her face was streaked with tears, spoiling her careful make-up. She lurched over to the sofa, sinking down on to it as she wept. Her sobs came from deep inside her, in choking gasps so despairing it seemed they might never stop. Overcome with grief and bitterness, she abandoned herself to tears in a way that moved Amaia. She realised this was the first time she had seen her eldest sister cry; even when they were small, Amaia had never seen Flora shed a single tear. And she wondered whether she might not be mistaken. People like Flora go through life wearing a steel carapace that makes them appear impervious, yet beneath that tough exterior there is still flesh and blood, a heart. Yes, perhaps she was mistaken, perhaps Flora's grief was a result of having been forced to shoot Víctor, a man she had once loved, in her own way.

'Flora . . . forgive me.'

Flora raised her head and Amaia saw her ashen face; there

was no sign of pity or grief in her eyes, only anger and resentment. When she spoke, her voice was cold and deliberate, her tone incongruous and threatening in a way that made Amaia shudder.

'Stop poking your nose into this, Amaia Salazar, stop pursuing Anne Arbizu, forget about her. You're out of your depth here, sister, you haven't a clue what you're getting yourself into, or what you're talking about. Your methods of detection will get you nowhere in this case. I suggest you drop it now, while you still can.'

She stood up and headed towards the bathroom.

'Are you satisfied now?' she said, then added: 'Close the door on your way out.'

As she made her way to the door, Amaia noticed a photograph of Ibai gazing at her from a beautiful antique silver frame. She paused to look at it, and, reaching for the door handle, she reflected that her sister was the strangest person she knew.

Zuriñe Zabaleta lived in Calle Alameda Mazarredo in Bilbao, from where she had a perfect view of the Guggenheim museum. The black-and-white marble entrance announced a building in the French style, with meticulous details that were repeated inside: French doors reaching up to the ceiling, cornices, and wood panelling. Amaia recognised works by well-known artists. In one corner a sculpture by James Wexford that brought a smile to her face that didn't escape the owner, who came out to greet her, saying:

'Oh, that's a work by an American sculptor. Original, don't you think?'

'Magnificent,' she replied, instantly gaining the woman's approval.

She was dressed in sombre colours, in what were obviously expensive clothes that made her look older than she was. She led Amaia over to a circle of armchairs, arranged to offer the best view of the Guggenheim, its surfaces gleaming with their strange muted shine. She invited Amaia to take a seat.

'The officer I spoke to yesterday told me you wanted to ask me a few questions about my sister's murder.' The woman spoke in an educated, reserved tone, but Amaia noticed a slight catch in her voice when she mentioned the crime. 'I never imagined that after all this time . . .'

'Your family originally came from Baztán, didn't they?'

'My mother was from Ziga; my father's family were well-known businessmen in Neguri. My mother used to summer in Getxo, which is where they met.'

'But your sister was born in Baztán, wasn't she?'

'Things were different then. My mother wanted to go back home to have her baby. She always spoke of it as a terrible ordeal: imagine having your first child at home. She gave birth to me here, in the hospital.'

'I'd like you to tell me about the relationship between your sister and your brother-in-law.'

'My brother-in-law was an executive at Telefónica. A rather dull man, I always thought, but my sister fell in love with him and they got married. They lived in Deusto, in a very nice area.'

'Did your sister work?'

'My parents died when I was nineteen, not long after Edurne got married. They left us a number of properties, as well as a trust fund, which enabled us both to live the way we wanted. In Edurne's case, she was president of Unicef in the Basque Country.'

'There were no previous complaints of abuse, but it's possible you witnessed something . . .'

'Never. As I said, he was a rather tedious fellow, a bore who talked only about his work. They had no children, so they used to go out a lot – trips to the theatre, the opera, dinner with other couples, occasionally with my husband and me. They were one of those couples who seem to stay together out of inertia, neither of them willing to take the first step . . . But I never had the slightest inkling that he might do anything like that. Except . . . a few months before it happened, my sister told me he had started going out more, arriving home late, and a couple of times she had caught him lying about where he had been. My sister suspected he was seeing another woman, although she had no proof. In any event, she wasn't prepared to put up with that. Naturally, I asked her whether he had ever hit her. She said he hadn't, but that when she pestered him too much with her questions, he would occasionally vent his anger on the furniture or hurl whatever happened to be in his hand at the time. One day, while we were having coffee, she suddenly started talking about divorce, more as a possible course of action she was contemplating than a decision she had taken. Naturally, I supported her, told her I'd stand by her if that's what she decided to do. That was the last time I saw her alive. The next time was in the morgue, her face so disfigured we had to hold the vigil with a closed casket.' She paused for a moment as she conjured the image. 'The pathologist said she died as a result of her injuries; he beat her to death. Can you imagine how brutal someone would have to be to beat a woman to death?'

Amaia gazed at her in silence.

'After he killed her, he wrecked the entire apartment. He smashed up the furniture, tore all my sister's clothes to shreds, then made a botched attempt to set the place alight. During his rampage, he broke nearly all his fingers and a few toes. As much of the blood came from him as from my sister; and when he'd finished, he leapt from the eighth-floor window. He died before the ambulance arrived.'

'Did the neighbours hear anything?'

'It was an exclusive building, like this one; each apartment took up a whole floor. It seems that at that time there was no one living on the floor above or the one below.'

Amaia paused before posing the crucial question:

'Did he amputate one of her limbs?'

'The pathologist told us that was done later, after she was dead. It makes no sense,' she groaned. 'Why did he have to do that?'

She closed her eyes for a few seconds, then went on:

'They never found it, despite searching the entire place with sniffer dogs. And they were sure he hadn't left the building; there was a doorman who swore he never left his post, and would have seen him leaving and then re-entering, covered in blood. Besides, the building had CCTV, and the footage corroborated the doorman's statement. Although there was a blind spot where he could have slipped past, they found none of his prints in the entrance, or in the lift or on the stairs – so he couldn't have gone that way either, given that his prints were all over the apartment, and his shoes were soaked in blood.'

She sighed, leaning back against a cushion. She looked exhausted, but went on:

'I don't know where a worm like him got his courage from; not in a million years would I have imagined that spineless creature having the guts to do what he did.'

'Just a couple more things, and I'll leave you in peace.'

'Of course.'

'Did he leave a note, a message?'

'He left the same message a dozen times over, scrawled in his own blood on the walls.'

'*Tarttalo*,' said Amaia.

The woman nodded.

Amaia leant forward in her chair, drawing closer to the woman.

'You must understand that this interview is part of an ongoing investigation. I can't tell you any more, but I think that with your help we might be able to locate the missing remains of your sister.'

The woman smiled in an effort to suppress the grimace of

212

pain contorting her face. Amaia handed her a plastic tube containing a cotton bud.

'Rub the inside of your cheek with this, that should do the trick.'

The satnav informed her that Entrambasaguas was in Burgos: forty-three kilometres or fifty minutes by car from Bilbao while Google had an entry giving the number of inhabitants as thirty-seven. She sighed; these tiny villages made her feel claustrophobic, though she didn't know why. Abuse and domestic violence were not associated with rural life any more than they were with other social groupings or places, and yet she always felt assailed by childhood memories of feeling trapped in the place where she was born. It was absurd; things would have been no different had she lived in a big city – they certainly weren't for Edurne in Bilbao, forever twinned with that other woman from Entrambasaguas, with whom she had never exchanged a word.

Amaia focused on the road ahead, which was becoming more difficult to negotiate as she advanced, first with continuous sleet, which gave way to heavy snow when she crossed the bridge and entered Entrambasaguas. She slowed as she reached the tiny main square, trying to get her bearings, surprised by the Christmassy image of the old stone public laundry that was still in remarkably good condition standing at the centre, next to a horse trough and a single jet fountain.

'Water galore!' she declared as she drove off in search of the house.

Surrounded by a large field, the house was quite well-lit, and more like a chalet with its hipped roof and stairs leading up to the entrance flanked by enormous pots containing ornamental shrubs. The snowfall enhanced the Christmas-postcard effect that had captivated her at the public laundry. She parked her car at the edge of the field and walked up a path of reddish stone slabs that were rapidly disappearing beneath the snow.

The woman who opened the door could have been the same age as her aunt, but any resemblance to her ended there. She was tall, almost the same height as Amaia, though rather stout; even so she led Amaia sure-footedly into the living room, where a lively fire was burning in the grate.

'We both knew he'd kill her in the end,' she said evenly.

Amaia felt herself relax; it was rare when interviewing a victim's relatives not to be exposed to outbursts of emotion. In most cases, she chose to maintain a professional distance that inspired confidence without establishing an emotional bond. It was best to get straight to the point, as she had in Bilbao, asking direct, concise questions and avoiding wherever possible any reference to the more grisly aspects of the case: bodies, blood, gashes, wounds – anything conjuring up graphic images that might make the relatives suffer or lose their nerve, and possibly hinder the investigation. But, every now and then, she was fortunate enough to come across a witness like this. In her experience, they were often lonely people who had close ties to the victim, and plenty of time to think. All she had to do was let them talk. The woman handed her a cup of tea before continuing.

'He was a bad man; a wolf in sheep's clothing, until the day he wed my niece. From then on he showed his true colours. He was jealous and possessive, he never allowed her to work outside the house, even though she'd been to secretarial college and had a job as a clerk at a store in Burgos before she married. Gradually, he forced her to break off all relations with friends and neighbours. And he only agreed to me seeing her because that way he could keep an eye on her and, well, I was the girl's only living relative, apart from a great-aunt who lived in Navarre but who died two years ago. He didn't beat her, but he made her dress like a country bumpkin. He wouldn't let her wear heels or make-up, or even go to the hairdresser; she wore her hair in a long braid until the day she died. She wasn't allowed anywhere on her own, so I had to accompany her to the shops, the chemist or the doctor's. The poor girl's health was never good. She was diabetic, you see. I tried for years to persuade her to leave him, but I knew she was right when she said that if she did he wouldn't give up until he'd found her and killed her.'

She paused, staring at the hearth.

'And so all I could do was to stay by her side, do my best to prevent the worst. Not a day goes by without me wishing I'd insisted. There are groups that help women escape . . . I saw a programme about it the other day . . .'

A tear rolled down her cheek, which she hurriedly wiped away with the back of her hand as she gestured towards a framed photograph on a side table. A pale woman with dark rings under her eyes smiled cheerfully at the camera, holding the forelegs of a small dog and pretending to dance with it.

'That's María, with the little dog . . . It all started with the dog, you see. The mongrel showed up here in late summer. She was overjoyed – I suppose because they had no children, and it was an affectionate creature. Her husband said nothing, but I had never seen her so contented, and of course, he wouldn't allow that. He let her become attached to the dog, then after three or four months he hanged it from that tree at the entrance to the house. She screamed so much when she saw it I thought she'd go mad with grief. He sat down at the table and demanded his dinner, but instead she went to the kitchen drawer and fetched a knife. He yelled at her, but from the way she glared at him he knew he'd gone too far. She went outside and cut the little dog down, cradled it in her arms and wept until she was exhausted. Then she went to the garage to fetch a shovel, dug a hole beneath the tree and buried the animal there. By the time she had finished, her hands were covered in blisters. He sat, stern-faced, without saying a word.

215

She walked in, flung the rope on the table and went to bed, where she stayed for two days. After that María lost all her enthusiasm; she became sullen, pensive. She would look straight through him as if he wasn't there. He was as surly as ever, but he didn't dare look her in the eye. I was convinced then that she would leave him, and I urged her to come to stay with me. I even offered her money to go somewhere else. But she was oddly calm and told me she didn't want to put me in any danger by moving to my house, and that if anyone should leave it was him. This house was hers; her father bought it for her when she became engaged, and it was in her name.

'Not long afterwards, I dropped by one morning and, even though I knew she was very frail, I was surprised to find that she wasn't up . . . I had the key so I let myself in. The house was in order, and I made straight for the bedroom. At first I thought she was asleep on her back, but she wasn't asleep, she was dead. They said he had suffocated her with a pillow. She had no other injuries, apart from the missing arm, which we didn't discover until the police pulled back the covers.'

Amaia listened with bated breath as the woman went on.

'They said he did it after she died, you see, but why? He cut off her hair too. I didn't even notice that when I went in, but when they moved the body I saw a bald patch on the nape of her neck,' she said, fingering the back of her own head.

'They found him two kilometres from here, hanging from a tree in an orchard his parents owned. Ironic, don't you think, hanging from a tree, just like the little dog?'

She fell silent, smiling bitterly as she gazed at the photograph. Amaia glanced around her.

'Did she leave you this house?'

The woman nodded.

'And I imagine you've kept her things . . .'

'Exactly as she left them.'

'Perhaps you still have a toothbrush or hairbrush of hers?'

'That's for the DNA, isn't it? I watch those forensic series on TV. I thought you might ask. I have something I think you could use.'

She picked up a wooden box from the table and handed it to Amaia.

Opening the box, Amaia couldn't stop her mind travelling back to the day when her mother sat her down on a stool in the kitchen and sheared her hair off after threading it in a long braid. She automatically raised her hand to her head, then realised what she was doing and lowered it. She tried to regain her composure. At the bottom of the box, curled up like a tiny sleeping animal, lay a braid of chestnut hair. Amaia closed the lid again so as not to have to look at it.

'I'm afraid it won't be of any use. We can only extract DNA from a hair follicle, not from cut hair.'

This wasn't strictly true: there were advanced techniques capable of extracting DNA from cut hair, but they were costly and complicated and a follicle was easier.

'Take a closer look,' replied the woman. 'Part of the hair has been cut but, like I said, she had a bald patch above the nape of her neck where some of her hair was pulled out by the roots. He left it at the foot of the tree he hanged himself from, along with a note.'

Amaia opened the box again and looked uneasily at the hair.

'He left a note?' she asked, her eyes fixed on the thick braid.

'Yes, but the police took it away. It said something absurd, nonsensical. I don't remember what exactly, except that it was a single word, rather like the name of a cake.'

'*Tarttalo.*'

'Yes, that's right, *Tarttalo.*'

It was snowing heavily when she set off from Entrambasaguas. She stopped briefly next to the stone laundry in the square to set the satnav for Elizondo. With two hundred kilometres to cover, she concentrated on the task of driving through snow, casting sidelong glances at the bag containing the two DNA samples: the capsule with the sample of Edurne Zabaleta's sister's saliva, and María Abásolo's braid. She needed to establish the link as soon as possible: if they could show a definite connection between the victims and the bones found in the cave, they would at least have proof that *he* existed. The mere thought of a murderer powerful and manipulative enough to convince someone (whether or not that someone was violent or reckless) to carry out a crime to order was extraordinary. And yet it wasn't that uncommon. During the past few years, the FBI had been treating instigation to murder as a priority in a country where, unlike Spain, accessories to murder and those instigating others to kill were handed down sentences as harsh as those given to the perpetrators themselves. The role played by the instigator gained in relevance when it was proven that this type of killer had the capacity to make people from all walks of life conform to his master plan, like loyal slaves. There were several widely publicised cases of pseudo-religious sect leaders who instigate their followers to commit mass suicide, and the power and control they had over people was horrifying.

Her mobile rang, interrupting her musings. She switched the phone to hands-free and answered Dr San Martín's call.

'Good afternoon, Inspector. Is this a good time?'

'I'm driving, but it's OK, I can talk.'

'We have the results of the tests on the bones found at the desecration site in Arizkun. I'd like to discuss them with you.'

'Please, go ahead.'

'Not over the phone. It's best you come to Pamplona. I'm meeting the Commissioner at seven in his office, can you make it there by then?'

Amaia glanced at the clock on the mobile screen.

'Maybe by seven thirty, I'm driving through snow.'

Amaia hung up, irritated at the prospect of having to stop off in Pamplona on the way home. She'd been away all day, but she could guess what the meeting would be about. Those silly desecrations had everyone rattled: the Mayor, the Archbishop, the Vatican envoy, and of course the Commissioner, who had to listen to all of them, including her, even though she had no idea what she was going to say to him. Following up clues in the village had led nowhere, and there had been no further desecrations since the church was put under surveillance. She was sure the culprits belonged to a group of young would-be satanists, who had been discouraged by the police presence; the matter could be easily resolved if the church installed CCTV or hired private security. If they were hoping she would provide someone for them to crucify, they were in for a disappointment.

She parked outside the police station and stretched her arms and legs, feeling numb and slightly dizzy after driving so attentively through the snowstorm. She went up to the first floor, unannounced, and knocked on the door of her boss's office.

'Come in, Salazar. How are you?'

'Fine, thanks.'

San Martín, who was installed on one of the conference chairs, rose and shook her hand.

'Take a seat,' the Commissioner said, sitting down himself.

Various files and forensic reports spread out on the table showed they had already started discussing the matter. Amaia went over in her mind the points she planned to set out in her own report, while she waited for the Commissioner to speak.

'Inspector, I summoned you here because the desecration case has taken an unexpected and surprising turn in light of the DNA tests on the bones found at the church in Arizkun. You'll have noticed they took a bit longer than usual. That's because when Dr San Martín informed me of the results, I asked him to rerun the tests, which have now been repeated a total of three times.'

Amaia felt suddenly confused. The meeting wasn't going at all the way she had expected. Her eyes glided over the file containing the results; she was burning with curiosity to know what they were. But she kept calm, listened and waited to see where this was all leading.

San Martín fidgeted slightly in his seat, before addressing her.

'Salazar, I want you to know that I oversaw and double-checked the second and third analyses, and I can guarantee that the results are genuine.'

Amaia was starting to feel uncomfortable.

'I don't doubt your professionalism, Doctor,' she said hurriedly.

San Martín looked at the Commissioner, who in turn glanced at Amaia before nodding to give him the go-ahead.

'The bones were in good condition, despite being charred at one end, but this didn't impede the analysis. We concluded that they belonged to a nine-month-old male foetus or a newborn baby, and are approximately one hundred and fifty years old, give or take five years.'

'That fits quite well with Deputy Inspector Etxaide's theory about this being a *mairu-beso*, a baby's arm.'

'As I said, the interior of the bone was in fairly good condition, enabling us to carry out routine DNA tests as part of the analyses. As you know, we automatically run all unknown DNA through the CODIS database.' The doctor gave a sigh. 'And here's the surprising part. It came up with a match.'

'But you just told me the bones belonged to a one-hundred-and-fifty-year-old newborn. How could his DNA possibly be in CODIS?'

'It couldn't, but that of someone related to him could. What we found was a twenty-five per cent match with your DNA.'

Amaia gazed at the Commissioner, stupefied.

'It's true,' he said. 'The doctor informed me immediately,

and I told him to repeat the whole process, with the utmost discretion. The first tests had been carried out by Nasertic, our usual laboratory, but in light of the results, we decided to use Zaragoza and San Sebastián, both of whom came up with identical results.'

'Meaning . . .'

'Meaning that the bones from the desecration at the church at Arizkun belonged to one of your relatives. Your ancestor four or five times removed.'

Amaia opened the files containing the reports and read them closely. The forensic pathologists from Zaragoza and San Sebastián who had signed them were both authorities in their field.

Her thoughts raced as she assimilated the facts, a torrent of ideas jostling for position, while Dr San Martín and the Commissioner carried on talking. The only voice she could hear clearly was the one in her head assuring her: *There's no such thing as coincidence, things don't just happen.*

The choice of victim is never random, where did it begin? She all but heard Dupree's voice.

'I need to make a call,' she said, interrupting San Martín.

The Commissioner looked at her, clearly surprised. She held his gaze, resolutely.

'We'll carry on this conversation, but I need to make a call first.'

The Commissioner nodded his approval, and she rose, reaching for her phone as she went out into the corridor. Etxaide picked up immediately.

'Hi, chief, how did it go?'

'Fine, Jonan. I want to ask you a question. If you need more time to research the answer, that's fine, just say so, but we need to be certain.'

'Certainly,' he said solemnly.

'It's about the *mairu-beso*. You told me they were arm bones belonging to children who died before being baptised.

221

Are there any references to the use of adult arms? Male or female?'

'I don't need to look that up to tell you it's impossible. The *mairu-beso*'s mystico-magical properties derive from a precise set of stipulations. Firstly, they must be unbaptised. This doesn't rule out adults, but would have been extremely unlikely at a time when baptism was a religious as well as a social and cultural obligation, a sign of belonging to a group. Anyone who wasn't a Christian was either a Jew or a Muslim. In fact, the word *mairu* comes from the pejorative *Moor* used to designate Muslims, and is synonymous with non-Christian. Secondly, there's the question of age: the bones had to come from either a miscarried or aborted foetus, or a baby that had died during childbirth or immediately after being born. The Church had strict rules about this; they refused to baptise the sick or dying, and, because of the high infant mortality rates, babies were often baptised in a hurry, to spare them from the ignominy of being buried at a crossroads or outside the cemetery walls, along with suicides and murderers. Another reason why they couldn't belong to adults: it was believed that a newborn's soul was in transit, hovering between two worlds, and that this was what awakened the *mairu-beso*'s magical properties. Desecrating the babies' bodies and using their arm, but under normal circumstances, also imbued them with magic powers. The spirits of unbaptised children could not go to heaven or hell, or return to the limbo they had escaped from, so they remained as protectors of their parents' home. There are documented cases of families keeping their dead baby's cradle or laying a place for them at the table, even leaving food out for them. Subsequent children weren't dressed in their dead siblings' clothes or named after them, for fear they might reclaim their things, along with the life of the new brother or sister. At the same time, if treated with respect, the *mairu* – the spirit of the dead child was a blessing that brought joy to the household, even played with its siblings.

It was thought that from birth up until the age of two these children had the power to see the *mairu* while they were in transit. That would explain the playful chatter and smiles babies seem to direct at people no one else can see.'

Amaia gave a deep sigh. 'My God . . .'

'The appearance of child spirits among different cultures is more widespread than we imagine. In Japan, for example, they are known as *zashiki warashi*, or sitting room spirits, and are thought to bring joy to the houses they inhabit . . . I hope I've been helpful,' said Deputy Inspector Etxaide.

'You're always helpful, Jonan. It's just that I had an idea, which . . . well, I can't tell you about it right now. I'll call you in half an hour.'

She hung up and went back into the Commissioner's office, where the two men broke off their conversation.

'Sit down,' said the Commissioner. 'Doctor, explain to her what you just told me . . .'

'Yes, I was telling the Commissioner that there are a couple of things we should bear in mind. You come from an area with relatively few inhabitants. I don't know what the population was a hundred and fifty years ago, but I'm sure it would have been quite low, given that social mobility was more restricted than it is today. What I'm trying to say is that in such a small community it's natural that partial genetic matches should occur, because different families were, and still are, more likely to be related.'

Amaia reflected, then shook her head.

'I don't believe in coincidences,' she replied unequivocally.

The Commissioner agreed. 'Nor do I.'

'He left it there for me as a provocation. He knew we'd find the match. This is his way of sending me a message.'

'Christ Almighty, Salazar!' the Commissioner exclaimed. 'I hate to see you involved like this; being provoked by a criminal is always a challenge. So what do you make of all this?'

Amaia took a few moments to gather her thoughts before replying:

'As I said, I don't believe any of it is a coincidence. I think the desecrations in the church at Arizkun were orchestrated with the sole purpose of sending me a message. If I hadn't been assigned to the case, it was inevitable that I would be after the discovery of the DNA match. He's attracting my attention because I head the murder squad, but also because I led the investigation into the *basajaun* case. The publicity I got from that case roused his interest. He thinks he's terribly clever and wants to engage in a kind of duel or a game of cat and mouse with someone he sees as his equal. There are plenty of documented examples of criminals who have communicated in various ways with police chiefs, or who decided which officer would lead an investigation by consistently addressing them, as occurred in the Ripper case. I'll need more time to assimilate this fresh information and develop a profile.'

The Commissioner nodded. 'I'll inform the Baztán police chief and Inspector Iriarte. We'll open a parallel inquiry to try to find the grave or graves your relative's bones were taken from.'

'Don't bother – it's a *mairu-beso*, the arm of an unbaptised child. In those days children who died without being baptised weren't buried in cemeteries.'

She waited until she left the police station before making another call. Glancing at her watch, she saw it was nearly eight o'clock. She missed James and Ibai; she'd been on the move all day and still had about an hour's drive ahead of her to get to Elizondo. It had stopped snowing, and the evening chill invigorated her, made her shiver, helped to clear her head, to compartmentalise what she had just heard in the Commissioner's office and devise a strategy. She paused beside her car, tapped in Lieutenant Padua's number at *Guardia Civil* headquarters, and explained to him what she needed.

'I've obtained DNA samples from two victims of cases

224

identical to those of Johana Márquez, Lucía Aguirre and the woman in Logroño. I need access to the bones found in the cave in order to compare them.'

'You realise that unless the samples were collected by a forensic science technician they'll be inadmissible in court.'

'I'm not worried about that, this is an unofficial investigation and if necessary I can get more samples: I've located two close relatives. What I need is to be able to compare the two I have with the bones found in the cave. A match would establish a pattern, and that enables me to obtain an exhumation order. So far, the amputations have been attributed to the husbands. Unless I can establish a link between the victims and the bones from Baztán cave, I have nothing.'

'Inspector, you know I want to help – after all, I got you into this – but you don't need me to remind you about rivalries between police forces; they won't release the information without a court order.'

Amaia hung up and stood staring at her phone, as if debating whether to dial or fling it through the air.

'Damn!' she declared, then tapped in Judge Markina's mobile number.

Markina's polite, manly voice answered at the other end.

'Good evening, Inspector,' he said.

Hearing him speak, she was surprised to find herself thinking about his mouth, the sculptured line of his moist, full lips. Overwhelmed with embarrassment, she felt a sudden, adolescent impulse to hang up.

'Good evening,' she managed to reply.

Markina remained silent, but Amaia was aware of his breathing at the other end of the line, and couldn't help imagining how warm it would feel on her skin. Despite the intense cold, she blushed to the roots of her hair.

'Your honour, the investigation of the case I told you about is going in the direction I had expected. I've obtained DNA from the relatives of two more victims, which I need to compare with the bones found in Baztán, currently being held by the *Guardia Civil*.'

'Are you in Pamplona?'

'Yes.'

'Good. I'll meet you in half an hour at Restaurante Europa.'

'Your honour,' she protested. 'I thought I made it very clear when we last met what my motives were for being interested in this case.'

He seemed upset when he replied:

'You certainly did, Inspector. I've just got back from a trip, and I plan to have dinner at the Europa. That's the earliest I can see you, but, if you prefer, you can come to my office tomorrow morning from eight o'clock onwards. Call my secretary and arrange it with her.'

All of a sudden she felt foolish and pompous.

'No, no, I'm sorry, I'll be there in half an hour.'

She hung up, cursing her clumsiness.

He must think I'm an idiot, she thought as she climbed into her car.

Before driving off, she made another call to Deputy Inspector Etxaide, informing him about her trip to Bilbao and Burgos, as well as the meeting with the Commissioner. After all, she owed him that much.

The entrance to the bar at the Europa was through the building next door to the restaurant. Despite the afternoon snowfall, which had now melted, a few patrons stood chatting outside, resting their glasses on a couple of high tables flanking the entrance.

No sooner had she crossed the threshold, than she spotted Markina sitting alone at the far end of the bar. He would have been difficult to miss. His grey suit and white shirt, worn without a tie, gave him a serious air, belied by his dark locks tumbling over his brow. He sat on his bar stool with the casual elegance of a model in a fashion magazine.

A lively group of women of a certain age were casting appreciative glances and comments in Markina's direction, while he sat impassively browsing a well-thumbed newspaper. His lips sketched a smile when he saw Amaia walk in, causing at least half the women to turn towards the object of his interest and look daggers at her.

'Care for a glass of wine?' he asked by way of a greeting, pointing to his own glass and gesturing to the waiter.

'No, I think I'll have a Coca-Cola,' she replied.

'It's too cold for Coca-Cola. Have some wine. This one's excellent, a Rioja.'

'Very well,' she acquiesced.

While the waiter was pouring her wine, she wondered why she wasn't more firm with Markina, why she always ended up accepting his invitations. He offered Amaia his seat, then went over to the group of women, who were standing up and content to let him take a stool. He placed it beside Amaia's, turning his back on the women, who continued to keep him in their sights.

Markina gazed at Amaia for five long seconds before looking away, embarrassed.

'I hope you feel more at ease in here than at the restaurant the other day.'

She didn't reply. Now it was her turn to lower her eyes, feeling ashamed and absurdly unfair.

'So you've been to Bilbao?' he asked, recovering his professional tone.

'Yes, also to a tiny village in Burgos with a population of forty. Both victims died two, and two and a half years ago respectively, both at the hands of their husbands, who took their own lives after committing the crime. Both were born in Baztán, but brought up somewhere else, and in both cases their forearms were amputated and the limbs were never found.'

Markina listened attentively, taking small sips from his

glass. It was all Amaia could do to avert her eyes from his mouth and the way he moistened his lips with his tongue.

'. . . And in both cases the same signature, "*Tarttalo*", was scrawled in blood on the walls or in a suicide note. Just the one word.'

'What do you require to move the investigation forward?'

'It's essential we establish the link I suspect exists between them. In order to do that I'll need access to the bone samples discovered by the *Guardia Civil* in the cave in Baztán. If there's a match, we could open an official investigation and ask to carry out a reconstruction using the original bones, or a second autopsy, which would give us one hundred per cent certainty.'

'Are you talking about exhuming the bodies?' he asked.

She knew he wouldn't like the idea – no judge ever did. They usually came up against an absolute refusal from the relatives, because of all the disagreeable implications. And so, when a judge agreed to an exhumation order, he or she did so only as a last resort. On occasion, a refusal would hamper the task of the investigating officers, who'd have to content themselves with DNA samples, which could not be used to establish an unquestionable match. And as every lawyer in the world knew, if reasonable doubt could be shown, his or her client walked free.

'Only if there's a match between the bones and our five victims.'

She emphasised the word 'our' in an effort to make him feel part of the investigation. If he was even half as honest as he was rumoured to be in judicial circles, he would feel duty-bound to dispense justice for those victims, and that was what mattered most.

'Did you yourself collect the samples you have?'

'Yes.'

'Did you follow the procedures?'

'Yes, to the letter. But in any event, that won't be a problem. The victims' relatives gave the samples voluntarily and signed a document to that effect.'

'I don't want to cause a stir before we have something more concrete. It's no secret that in courtrooms discretion is notable for its absence.'

Amaia smiled. He had repeated the 'we'; she was sure he would give his authorisation.

'I assure you, I'm being extremely careful; only one of the most trustworthy members of my team knows about this, and I plan to have the tests carried out at an independent laboratory.'

Markina mulled this over, absentmindedly stroking the line of his chin in a gesture Amaia found both virile and incredibly sensual.

'I'll process the court order first thing,' he said. 'Carry on as you are – you're doing a great job. And it's important you keep me informed every step of the way, if I'm to back you up as you progress . . . and . . .'

He paused, giving her that special look of his.

'Have dinner with me, please,' he whispered.

She gazed at him in astonishment, because her training in behavioural profiling, body language and determining whether someone was lying or not, was telling her that this wasn't an examining magistrate but a man in love.

At that very moment her mobile rang. Fishing it out of her bag, she was puzzled to see Flora's name on the screen; Flora never called her, not even at Christmas or on her birthday; she preferred to send cards, as stiff and polite as she was.

Amaia looked uneasily at Markina, who was eagerly awaiting her reply.

'Excuse me, I need to take this,' she said, standing up and walking outside, unable to hear above the clamour of the crowded bar. 'Flora?'

'Amaia, the clinic just called – it's *Ama*. It seems there's been a serious incident.'

Amaia said nothing.

'Are you there?

'Yes.'

'The director told me she had a fit and injured one of the orderlies.'

'Why are you calling me, Flora?'

'Oh, believe me, I wouldn't be if those idiots hadn't rung the local police.'

'They called the police? How serious was the attack?' she asked, even as she was assailed by images she thought had been banished for ever.

'I don't know, Amaia,' said Flora in the tone she adopted when people were trying her patience. 'All they told me was that the police had arrived, and that we should get there as soon as possible. I'm leaving straight away, but it'll take me at least two hours.'

Amaia sighed, defeated.

'All right, I'm on my way. Tell them I'll be there in about half an hour.'

She went back into the bar, weaving through the crowd until she reached Markina.

'Your honour,' she said, drawing near to make herself heard, 'I have to go, something urgent has cropped up.'

Suddenly she felt they were too close, and took a step back, taking her coat from the stool.

'I'll go with you.'

'There's no need, my car is parked right outside,' she said.

But he was already on his feet moving towards the door. She followed him, and as they walked out she noticed the group of women watching her. She lowered her head, and, quickening her pace, drew level with Markina.

'Where's your car?'

'Right here, on the main road,' she replied.

With a faint smile, he took her coat from her and held it up so she could put it on.

'I'll only be taking it off again to drive.'

He draped it over her shoulders, allowing his hands to linger perhaps a moment longer than necessary. He didn't say a word until they reached her car. Amaia opened the door, flung her coat on the passenger seat and got in.

'Goodbye, your honour, thank you for everything. I'll keep you informed.'

He leant over the open door and said:

'If you hadn't got the call, would you have said yes?'

She took two seconds to reply. 'No.'

'Good night, Inspector Salazar,' he said, pushing the door closed.

Turning the key in the ignition, she looked round as she drove off towards the motorway. Markina had gone, leaving her feeling strangely empty.

16

The Santa María de las Nieves psychiatric clinic was situated outside of town on a bare, treeless hill. Surrounded by towering walls, its prison-like appearance was in no way diminished by the ornamental shrubs, wrought-iron gates, guards' cabin, fenced car park, and CCTV cameras. A building that seemed designed to house a priceless treasure, but merely contained within its walls the disturbed minds of its patients.

A patrol car at the entrance signalled the police presence. Amaia lowered her window enough to show her badge. The officer saluted her uneasily and she smiled and said good evening.

'Who's in charge?'

'Inspector Ayegui, Inspector.'

She was in luck. She didn't know many officers from the Estella force, within whose jurisdiction the clinic fell, but she had run into Ayegui several years back and he was a good cop, slightly old school, but fair; he did things by the book.

This was the first time she had visited Santa María de las Nieves. The court order had been clear: her mother must be detained in a high-security psychiatric hospital. Flora had

232

organised everything, and Amaia had to admit that the institution was exactly what she would have expected from Flora; it bore no resemblance to her preconceived ideas about what a high-security psychiatric hospital might look like. She assumed it was the best that money could buy. After crossing the threshold, which she reached through a formal garden, she found herself in a spacious hallway similar to a hotel lobby, except that instead of a receptionist there was a male nurse in a white uniform. She approached the desk and was about to introduce herself when a uniformed officer came running down a side corridor.

'Detective Inspector Salazar?'

She nodded.

'Come with me, please.'

She could see as soon as she entered that Inspector Ayegui had taken over the luxurious office. He was sitting at the desk speaking on the telephone. Behind him, a middle-aged man with an air of dejection was leaning against the mantelpiece above the fireplace, a look of deep despair on his face; the ousted director, she assumed. Seeing her walk in, he approached her anxiously, introducing himself.

'Señorita Salazar, I regret that we've been forced to meet under these circumstances,' he said, shaking her hand with a firmness she hadn't expected.

'Inspector Salazar,' she corrected, 'from the Navarre force.'

The look of irritation he gave Inspector Ayegui and the tension that seemed to run right through his body were apparent to her.

After their greeting he shrank back, his eagerness to explain apparently reduced to mere intent. He stayed silent, glancing at her and wringing his hands in what was clearly a defensive gesture.

Inspector Ayegui hung up the telephone and stepped out from behind the desk.

'Come with me, Inspector,' he said, placing a friendly hand on her arm and leading her out into the corridor, remembering to close the door behind him as the director looked on, visibly relieved. 'How are you, Inspector?' he greeted her. 'I imagine the director is in a state of shock. I find myself having to deal with psychiatrists more often than I would wish. They always strike me as a bit unbalanced,' he said, grinning.

Ayegui guided her back to reception and over to the lift, talking as they went.

'According to the director, the incident took place at around seven o'clock this evening. The patient had been watching TV, and after having dinner in her room, while the orderly was helping her into bed, your mother pulled a sharp object from underneath her pillow and stabbed the man in the stomach, causing massive internal bleeding. The staff here wear alarm bracelets, like the ones battered women use to alert the police in case of an attack, so his colleagues appeared within seconds and administered emergency first aid. Fortunately for him shrinks are also medical doctors. He's in bad shape, but he'll live.'

Amaia gazed at him evenly as the lift rose to the second floor.

'This way,' he said, gesturing at the broad, brightly lit corridor.

Two uniformed police officers were talking outside what looked like an ordinary room, except for the red and white security tape limiting access. When they were a few yards away, Inspector Ayegui pulled up.

'The patient has been immobilised, sedated and taken to a secure area. We'll give the director ten minutes to recover and then he can explain to you all about the treatment she's been receiving, and the medical implications of her actions,' he said, in an apologetic tone. 'The room is still being processed so we can't go in there yet. What I can tell you is that despite the carpeted corridors and besuited doctors, this is a high-security hospital, and the weapon she used wasn't the homemade variety you find in prisons. This was brought in from the outside: somebody gave it to her, and when you give a weapon to a dangerous mental patient it's for a reason.'

Amaia looked at the open door as though drawn towards the void.

'What sort of object is it?'

'We're not sure yet, a kind of pointed spike, a bit like an ice pick or an awl, but with a short, sharp blade.' He gestured to one of the officers on the door. 'Bring me the weapon used in the attack.'

The officer returned instantly with an evidence case, from which he removed a bag containing what at first glance looked like a small knife. Amaia took a photo of it with her mobile, but the flash reflecting off the plastic blurred the image.

'Could you take it out, please?' she asked.

The officer looked at his superior, who nodded. Opening the zip, he held it up in his gloved hand, while Amaia took pictures, paying special attention to the handle, which was yellowed and cracked with age. She sent off the image, accompanied by a brief message, and waited a few moments for her mobile to ring. She placed it on loudspeaker so that Ayegui could hear.

'I know exactly what this is,' Dr San Martín's voice rang out at the other end, 'I've seen lots of them. A cardiologist friend of mine collects them. It's an old scalpel, probably eighteenth-century European. The carved handle is made of ivory, which they later stopped using because it's too porous. Judging from the bloodstains, I'm assuming it's been used as a weapon. As for the blade, I can't see it properly, the metal is too tarnished.'

She thanked San Martín and hung up.

'If it is a scalpel, then maybe there was no need to bring it in; it could come from here,' suggested Ayegui.

'Inspector,' an officer addressed her from the lift, 'your family is here.'

'Go ahead,' Ayegui nodded, 'I'll join you in a few minutes.'

Rosaura had just entered the director's office. Flora followed, escorted by an elegant gentleman who made the introductions.

'I asked Father Sarasola to accompany me, both as a family friend and in his professional capacity as a psychiatrist.'

'Dr Sarasola and I are acquainted,' said the director, shaking his hand and looking at him nervously.

Amaia said nothing, she waited until the introductions were over and the priest approached her.

'Inspector Salazar.'

Disguising her surprise, Amaia shook his hand, waiting until everyone was sitting down before addressing the director.

'How has the patient been over the past few days?'

'In good spirits. Her rehabilitation is going well, she has less difficulty walking, although on the communication front we haven't made much progress and she barely speaks. In this type of illness, physical and mental deterioration can take different routes.'

'Are you saying that you've noticed a marked physical improvement?'

'Our advanced rehabilitation technique, combining massage, exercise, and electro-stimulation is obtaining excellent results,' he declared proudly. 'She has more mobility and only uses her walking frame as a safeguard now. She has also gained weight and muscle mass, she's stronger.' His expression clouded slightly. 'Well, she succeeded in knocking over Gabriel, the orderly she attacked, who is no weakling.'

Inspector Ayegui entered the room without bothering to knock or introduce himself:

'What medication was the patient taking?' he demanded, abruptly.

'I'm afraid I can't reveal that, it would be a breach of doctor–patient confidentiality,' the director replied, looking askance at Sarasola. The priest, as was his custom, stood gazing out of the window, seemingly oblivious to what was going on in the room.

'I think I can safely say, under the circumstances, that patient confidentiality is suspended, but it makes no difference – I already know the answers' Ayegui said smirking. 'They wouldn't happen to be white, red and yellow capsules, little blue tablets and some pink ones, like these?' he said, unfurling his fingers and showing the assortment of pills to the director, who gazed at them in disbelief.

'How? Where . . .?'

'While searching her room for any other possible weapons, we noticed one of the hollow bed legs has been tampered with. The plastic plug on the end is loose and the frame is stuffed with pills identical to these.'

'That's impossible!' exclaimed the director. 'Rosario is seriously ill. Without her medication, she would never have been able to make such great strides towards normality these past few months,' he said, gazing at Flora and Ros, as though hoping to gain more sympathy from them. 'Her treatment has been closely monitored. This hospital is renowned for its progressive approach towards caring for the mentally ill. We constantly follow their progress, relapses, assessing any variations in behaviour. Every change in medication or therapy is decided by a panel of nine experts, including myself. Stopping Rosario's medication would be dangerous, and couldn't have gone undetected. Yet, as I said before, Rosario has been calm, cheerful and cooperative; her appetite is improving, she has gained weight and she's sleeping well. It's out of the question,' he declared emphatically, 'that a patient with her symptoms could improve like that

237

without medication, or if for some reason her medication was interrupted. My colleague here,' he said, gesturing towards Sarasola, 'will tell you that achieving a chemical balance is essential in such treatments, that discontinuing a patient's medication completely or partially, even taking away a single pill, have a destabilising effect.'

'Well, judging by the amount stuffed inside the bed frame, this patient hasn't been taking hers for months. A few are discoloured, possibly from saliva; she must have pretended to swallow them and then spat them out,' said Ayegui.

'I tell you that's imposs—'

'Which would also explain her attack on the orderly.'

'You don't understand. It's impossible for Rosario *not* to be on medication, she can't pretend to be normal,' the director explained. 'Besides, only yesterday one of her doctors gave her a therapeutic evaluation.' He sighed as he opened a drawer and lifted out a thick file.

'I insist on a paper copy of all reports,' he explained. 'We can't risk being exposed to a computer virus that could destroy such vulnerable patients' medical records.' He put the file on the table. 'You can't take this with you, but by all means have a look, although it might be a bit mystifying to the uninitiated. Perhaps the good doctor . . .' his voice trailed off, as he sat down forlornly in his expensive chair.

Amaia drew nearer to the desk, leant over and showed the director the image on her mobile.

'Our expert tells us that the weapon she used is an antique scalpel, possibly from a collection. Do you keep anything like that here?'

The director glanced at the image uneasily.

'Certainly not.'

'Apparently some doctors like to collect them. Is it possible one of the doctors here might keep similar items in his or her office . . .'

'Not that I'm aware of, but I doubt it; we follow a strict security regime here. We aren't even allowed to carry a ball-point in our lab coat pocket. Anything that could be used as a weapon is forbidden – sharp or heavy objects, lace-up shoes, belts – and the rule applies to patients and staff alike, including doctors. Naturally we keep medical implements, but only in the surgery, safely locked up in a cabinet. And besides, they're state of the art, nothing like that.'

'So, if it couldn't come from inside the clinic then it must have been brought from the outside,' she said, looking at him sceptically.

'That's impossible,' he protested. 'You've seen our security system, visitors have to pass through a metal detector, and leave their bags at the entrance. Patients in the blue zone aren't allowed visitors, the others only receive those we authorise. In Rosario's case, no one but your siblings. All visitors without exception are subject to the same security checks. They are told that they have to inform the staff before bringing in any objects, food or reading material. Visitors remain at all times in the patient's room, they aren't permitted to wander into the corridors, or to have any contact with other patients, which would anyhow be impossible as they spend most of the time in their rooms, and are confined there during visiting hours. Not that you'd be aware of that, because you've never been to see your mother,' he added, snidely. 'But your siblings can confirm everything I've just said.'

'Sisters,' corrected Amaia.

'What?' the director replied, bewildered.

'That's the second time you've used the word siblings. I only have two sisters,' she said, waving her hand towards them.

The director turned pale.

'Surely you're not serious . . . Your brother often comes here to visit your mother,' he said, looking to Amaia's sisters for confirmation.

239

'We don't have a brother,' Rosaura assured the astonished doctor, whose face contorted into a grimace.

'Doctor,' Amaia shouted, rousing him and forcing him to look her in the eye. 'How often did he visit her?'

'I'm not sure, I'd need to look at the register, but I'd say at least every couple of weeks . . .'

'Why wasn't I told about this?' Flora cut in.

'It comes under doctor–patient confidentiality. Our patients are only allowed to see visitors they themselves request, to avoid any well-intentioned but unwelcome visitors possibly doing more harm than good.'

'You mean to say that she asked to see this visitor herself?'

The director checked on his computer.

'Yes, she has four people on her list: Flora, Rosaura, Javier and Amaia Salazar.'

'I'm on her list,' Amaia murmured in disbelief.

'There is no Javier Salazar, there never has been, we don't have a brother!' roared Flora. 'How could you have allowed this impostor to worm his way in here? It's outrageous!'

'You forget that Rosario asked to see him.'

Amaia glanced at Inspector Ayegui, who shook his head, walked over to the desk and stood beside her.

'When did this individual last visit the patient?'

The director swallowed hard; from his twisted features he seemed to be fighting off a wave of nausea.

'This morning,' he replied, shamefaced.

An indignant murmur came from everyone in the room. The director staggered to his feet, spreading his hands before him as he urged calm.

'He went through all the security gates, identified himself, left his ID card, filled in the form, which is compulsory at every visit. We aren't the police, but we run routine checks. Our security system is excellent.'

'Hardly,' Amaia parried.

Ayegui pointed an accusatory finger at the director. 'You'd

better give us all the CCTV footage where this individual shows up, as well as the forms he filled in. With any luck, we might be able to retrieve a fingerprint.'

A uniformed police officer came into the room. He whispered something in Ayegui's ear, who nodded.

'Come with me, Inspector Salazar,' he said, making to leave, but not without first turning to address the director:

'Get me that information, now.'

'Certainly,' the director replied, lifting the receiver, relieved to escape Flora's reproachful gaze.

The whiteness of the room was disturbed only by the bloodstain on the floor, which seemed to follow the outline of the orderly's haunches. The forensic team, clad in hooded white jumpsuits and over-shoes, appeared to merge with the room, until one of them wheeled round and came over to them.

'Pleased to meet you again, Inspector,' she said.

Amaia recognised one of the pathologists who had helped recover Lucía Aguirre's remains.

'I'm sorry,' she said, racking her brains for the woman's name. 'I didn't recognise you in your overalls.'

'Just like the CSIs in the movies, right?' she chuckled. 'Good-looking, hair worn loose at the crime scene.'

'What have you got?' Ayegui prodded her.

'Something rather interesting,' she said, turning towards the room. 'There were a few bloody fingerprints on the bedframe, suggesting it was pulled out. When we moved it we found some writing hidden behind the bedhead. Come and have a look,' she said, beckoning them in, 'we've finished processing the scene.'

Voices started to echo in Amaia's head, from a place in her mind she only visited in dreams. Her palms suddenly felt sweaty; her heart started pounding, her breath quickened, and yet she knew she mustn't let the others notice. The voices of the *lamia* grew clearer as they cried in unison: 'Catch him, catch him, catch the rat.'

She walked around the bed and looked: gleaming in the bright hospital light illuminating the wall behind the bedhead, she recognised her mother's neat handwriting. She had written one word in the orderly's blood: '*TARTTALO*'.

Amaia closed her eyes and gave an audible sigh. When she opened them again, the voices had stopped, but the message was still there.

17

The security room at Santa María de las Nieves wouldn't have looked out of place in a prison. There were screens that monitored the inside, corridors, lifts, all the communal areas, a few of the rooms, the nurses' stations, as well as the offices. The head of security was a man of about fifty, who gave them a tour of the entire system with what seemed like a proprietorial satisfaction.

'Do any of the patients' rooms have cameras?' asked Ayegui.

'No,' the director's voice rang out behind him. 'Patients considered a low security risk have the right to privacy in their own rooms. There are spyholes in the doors to enable us to keep an eye on them. Only patients in the blue zone are filmed twenty-four hours a day, but they are all locked in their rooms, except when in treatment or therapy, or in the garden. In Rosario's case, she was always on her own.'

Amaia glanced at the screens, which registered very little activity.

'It's late,' explained the director. 'Most of the patients are asleep, or confined to their beds.'

The head of security pointed to one of the screens. 'I've found all the tapes with the visitor on them. It was easy, I checked the date and time in the register. Unfortunately, with

243

the exception of recordings of patients kept for psychiatric assessments, tapes are automatically wiped after forty days. Unless there's an incident, that is, although there hasn't been a single one involving visitors or intruders in the twelve years I've worked here. Of course where the patients are concerned it's different,' the man said, lowering his voice so the director couldn't hear him. 'You wouldn't believe what some of them get up to.'

Amaia nodded as a shiver ran down her spine. Yes, she could imagine.

'We'll start with the oldest ones, in case you see anything of interest before they get wiped.'

'Let me make it quite clear that you aren't to wipe any of the recordings in which this guy shows up,' said Ayegui.

The security guard glanced at the director, who was propped up against the wall, as though about to collapse.

'Naturally,' he murmured.

Ayegui answered a brief call, and after he had hung up, he explained:

'It's been confirmed that the ID card he used is a fake. That doesn't surprise me, it's relatively easy to find gangs who will provide anything for a price, from fake ID cards to a whole new identity.'

From the room's shadowy recesses, the director heaved a weary sigh. 'Let's see those images.'

The CCTV cameras were clearly positioned to cover as much of the hospital as possible. The cameras at the entrances were designed to make sure no one got out; they weren't concerned about security breaches involving people intent on gaining entry – who in their right mind would want to enter a place with a sign that said 'High-Security Psychiatric Hospital'? On the screen, a youngish man, no older than forty, slim, wearing jeans, a roll-neck sweater, glasses, a cap and a goatee, could be seen entering, passing through the metal detector at the main security door, handing over his ID card

244

and being escorted to Rosario's room by an orderly. A total of three visits were recorded, in which he wore identical clothes and avoided looking up at the cameras, except for that morning, when at the last security gate before the exit he had removed his cap for a few brief seconds.

'He seems to be showing us his face deliberately,' said Ayegui.

'I'm afraid it won't be much use,' the guard said. 'This camera monitors the car park so it's placed high up. The image is fully enlarged, but you can't see much.'

'We have more resources,' said Ayegui, 'we'll see what can be done.' He turned towards the director: 'Will I need a court order to take this lot away?'

'No, of course not,' he said dejectedly.

Flora stood waiting in the middle of the spacious office. As soon as they walked back in she confronted the director.

'Where's my mother now?' she asked.

'Oh, you needn't worry about Rosario. She's fine. We've sedated her and she's sleeping. We've put her in the high-security unit; obviously she can't have any visitors until we've reassessed her and resumed her treatment.'

Flora appeared satisfied. She straightened her jacket and gave a faint smile, before looking the director in the eye. Amaia knew she was about to pounce.

'Dr Franz, prepare for my mother's immediate transferral. After this incident, she won't be staying in this institution any longer than necessary, and you can be sure that as soon as this investigation is over I will demand to know who is responsible. I intend to sue both you and Santa María de las Nieves.'

The director's face flushed. 'Please, you can't . . .' he stammered. 'It's a mistake to move her now, she could suffer a serious relapse.'

'Really? More serious than not taking her medication for weeks? More serious than receiving visits from strangers who supply her with weapons? I doubt that, Doctor.'

'What happened is extremely regrettable, but you have to understand that we are the victims of a deception. We thought the man was your brother; the police admitted he was using fake ID. She requested his visits and seemed happy when he came. Why should we suspect anything?'

'Are you telling me that you let yourselves be dictated to by a mentally disturbed woman?' retorted Flora. 'And how do you explain the fact that she wasn't taking her medication?'

'That I can't explain,' the director confessed. 'It's medically impossible for Rosario to have been in control of herself . . . unless, that is . . .' The director appeared to contemplate something, before ruling it out as absurd and resuming his entreaties. 'For God's sake, don't move her. This will be a devastating blow for the hospital,' he said, with a slight tremor.

Amaia felt sorry for the beleaguered man, who looked as if he was on the verge of suffering a stroke. She glanced at her sisters, then turned towards the others.

'Could you leave us alone for a few moments?'

'Certainly,' replied both Dr Franz and Inspector Ayegui, heading towards the door.

'Family only,' Amaia said, addressing Father Sarasola, who hadn't moved from his position over by the window.

When they had all left the room, Amaia sat down with her sisters.

'I agree we should move her, Flora.'

Flora looked surprised, as if she'd been expecting her sister to oppose her.

'But first I want you to tell me how you know Father Sarasola – although I think I can imagine – and what he's doing here.'

'He got in touch with me about three months ago,' said Flora. 'Father Sarasola is a medical doctor, an expert in psychiatry, one of the best in the world, I believe. He told me he was acquainted with *Ama*'s case because it had been cited in various international symposiums on psychiatry. He said he was extremely interested in her progress, that he had some novel ideas about her treatment. He offered to move her to his Opus Dei clinic in Pamplona and to provide free care. Needless to say, the fees there are astronomical, but that wasn't enough to persuade me. I was intrigued, but it also occurred to me that this might be an opportunity for *Ama* to benefit from new methods, new therapies, even though she seemed so happy here, which for me has always been the most important consideration. Now, of course, her safety has to come first; it seems anyone can get in here, and she wasn't even taking her medication. You tell me.'

Ros nodded. 'I agree, and let's not forget that poor man she nearly killed . . .'

'Yes, that too,' conceded Flora.

Amaia stood up. 'All right, but before I accept her transfer, I want to talk to Father Sarasola.'

Father Sarasola didn't seem in the least surprised by her request, and said as much while she was closing the door to the office Dr Franz had provided for them to talk in.

'Inspector Salazar, I knew things wouldn't be as straightforward with you as with your sisters. I've been looking forward to this encounter.'

'And why is that?' she asked.

'Because explanations aren't good enough for you, you want the truth.'

'So, make me happy by telling me the truth. Why do you want to treat my mother?'

'I could talk for hours about the clinical interest of a case like hers, but that wouldn't be the whole story. I think she needs to be moved to keep her from the evil that came looking for her.'

Amaia's mouth opened wide in astonishment. 'I see you're a man of your word.'

'I believe it is vital that she be removed from his path and kept in isolation to prevent him from carrying out his mission.'

Amaia said nothing, waiting for him to continue.

'We've been interested in your mother for some time. She presents a distinctive pattern of behaviour that occurs only in certain cases, the type of case that interests us because of a subtle nuance.'

'And what might that be?'

'The nuance that differentiates your mother's case from other cases of mental illness is evil.'

'Evil,' Amaia repeated.

'The Catholic Church has been trying for centuries to discover the causes of evil. In recent years, psychiatry has made great leaps and bounds in the field of behavioural disorders, yet there is a group of illnesses where little progress has been made since the first cases were documented in the Middle Ages. The fact that evil people exist is nothing new. I don't mean mad or mentally deranged, but cruel and heartless, people who derive pleasure from causing their fellow men to suffer. Evil governs these people and their actions; the mental illnesses that afflict them aren't the usual, simple illnesses, they are the perfect breeding ground for evil. It is evil that makes them mad, not the other way round.'

Amaia shook her head as if rousing herself from a reverie. Dr Sarasola was putting into words a belief she had always held without daring to give it a name, without daring to use the word that fell so easily from his lips. Ever since she had been a very small child, she had known that Rosario wasn't quite right in the head, but she also knew that her mother had enough control over it to keep her distance from the no-man's land that separated them. She only strayed into it at night, when she leant over Amaia's bed, mad enough to threaten to eat her, evil enough to enjoy her fear, lucid enough to do it when no one could see her.

'I disagree,' she lied, keen to see how far Sarasola would

go. 'I know that human beings are capable of many things. Yes, some men commit horrific acts, but as for evil . . . It may be their upbringing, lack of love, mental illness, drugs, bad company . . . but I refuse to believe that such individuals are guided by exterior forces of evil. It's my understanding that in the Church you speak of free will; so surely it all comes down to human nature, else how do you explain goodness?'

'It's true that human beings are free to decide, but there's a boundary, a limit, a point where someone takes the plunge and abandons themselves to pure evil. I'm not talking about a man who commits an act of violence in the heat of the moment. When he calms down and realises what he has done, he is wracked with grief and remorse. I'm talking about abnormal cruelty, someone who commits an atrocious act – like the man who arrived home in the middle of the night, smashed his wife's head in with a hammer and then did the same to his year-old twins and his three-month-old baby while they slept in their cots. Or the woman who strangled her four children to death with the cable from her phone charger. She killed them one by one – it took her more than an hour to carry out her crimes . . . And, yes, admittedly she was on drugs, but I've met hundreds of drug addicts who pester their mother for money and then feel terrible remorse afterwards, but they have never, they would never, commit such monstrous acts. I won't deny that in some circumstances and situations drug abuse is like a rising tide that eventually breaks through the floodgates, but what enters through those cracks is another matter, just as what we allow to enter is another matter. I don't believe I need to say more; for you this is familiar territory.'

Amaia looked at him in alarm. She felt utterly exposed in a way she had only previously experienced with Dupree, who also knew a thing or two about evil and the nuances of abnormal behaviour.

'Evil exists and is at work in the world. You know how to

identify it as well as I do. Yes, people are confused about the issue, but a great deal of this confusion is the result of their having strayed from God's path and the Church.'

Amaia frowned.

'Don't look at me like that. A hundred years ago, any man or woman could identify the seven deadly sins and recite the Lord's Prayer. Those sins are the ones that condemn the sinner, destroying his soul and his body. Pride, greed, envy, wrath, lust, gluttony, sloth: seven sins that exist in today's world no less than they did a hundred years ago, but you would be hard-pressed to find more than a handful of people who can name them. I am a psychiatrist, but I confess that modern psychiatry, Freud with his psychoanalysis and all that nonsense, has confused people, cast them adrift, convinced them that all their problems are the result of not having received enough motherly love when they were young – as if that justified everything. And because they cannot identify evil, they label any kind of aberration as insanity: 'He must be crazy to do a thing like that.' Countless times I've heard people setting themselves up as an authority on psychiatry, pronouncing their self-justifying diagnosis. But evil exists, it is out there, and you know as well as I do that your mother isn't simply mentally ill.'

Amaia gazed at him, weighing up this man so fluent in arguments she herself did not dare put into words, yet whom she instinctively mistrusted. She had to make a decision – and she had to do it now.

'What do you suggest?'

'We will treat both her mental illness and her soul. Our team is made up of the world's foremost experts.'

'You don't intend to exorcise her, do you?'

Father Sarasola chuckled. 'I doubt that would do any good; your mother isn't possessed. She's wicked, her soul is as black as night.'

Amaia's heart skipped a beat and she felt her chest tighten

as the years of suppressed anguish broke free, hearing the priest articulate what she had known for as long as she was able to think.

'Do you think evil is what drove her mad?'

'No, I think she dabbled in things she shouldn't have. Now she's paying the price.'

Amaia weighed the consequences of what she was about to say. 'The man who has been coming to see her might have been instigating others to take their own lives.'

'I don't think that's your mother's care. Her work isn't yet done.'

Amaia's head was spinning from this man's extraordinary powers of perception: he could read her mind like a book.

'She mustn't receive any visitors, she mustn't see anyone, not even my sisters?'

'Those are our rules. Given the circumstances, I think that is best for everyone.'

Amaia recognised the young technician who was slipping off her overalls outside the door to the room.

'Hello again,' she said, approaching. 'Are you done?'

'Hello, Inspector. Yes, we've collected everything we can: prints, photos, samples . . . We're done.'

Amaia peered inside the doorway and contemplated the trail left behind by the forensic team. Now in the centre of the room, the bedframe partially hid the bloodstain on the floor. The bedding was neatly piled on a leather chair that stood out from the white walls, having clearly been brought in from an office. There were no curtains, and the table and chair beneath the window were bolted to the wall and floor. On the opposite wall were two closed doors. The foam pillow had a long gash in it where the scalpel had been concealed. Every surface that could have been touched was covered in the greasy black powder used to lift fingerprints.

'What's behind those doors?' she asked the young woman.

251

'A wardrobe and a toilet – just the bowl, no lid – and a basin that works with a foot pedal. We've been over them. The wardrobe is only opened to take out clean clothes; it doesn't hold many – the patients wear a hospital smock, gown and slippers.'

Amaia rummaged in her bag for some plastic gloves, which she slipped on, surveying the room from the doorway as though an invisible barrier prevented her from crossing the threshold.

'You don't happen to have a spare pair of overalls, do you?'

'Oh, yes, of course,' the young woman said, bending over her sports bag and taking out a fresh pair. 'But there's no need, the room has been processed, you're free to go in.'

Amaia knew there was no longer any risk of her contaminating the scene, but she took them all the same.

'I don't want to get dirty,' she explained, tearing at the plastic packaging.

The young woman flashed her colleague a puzzled glance.

'We're off now. Is there anything else you need?'

'No, thank you.'

When the lift doors had closed, Amaia donned the overshoes, pulled up the hood and adjusted it. Then she took a paper tissue out of her bag, left it where the forensic team had kept their equipment, then waited at length in the doorway, still unable to cross the threshold. She swallowed hard before stepping inside the room, covering her nose and mouth with the handkerchief.

The first thing she noticed was the stench of the wretched orderly's blood, mixed with a subtler odour of faeces and digestive fluids. She felt briefly glad of these smells, for they masked that other one. But the further she penetrated into the room, the more it condensed, finally pervading the space with the dizzying scent of fear. No memories are as precise, vivid and evocative as those conjured through smells. They are so inextricable from the sensations experienced with them, that it's astonishing how much a few hints can make us remember.

A shudder went through Amaia's body as she smelled her. She held back the tears filling her eyes with deep breaths. Memories survive because an olfactory neuron's axons always plug into the same bulb, the same archive, in order to preserve a smell. 'Your killer's odour should occupy a place of honour in your memory,' she said to herself, half hysterical, almost enraged. She struggled to control the panic closing in on her, blurring the edges of her vision until she was practically in darkness, like the protagonist of a sinister play trembling in the glare of a powerful spotlight while everyone else melts away into the shadows.

No, she told herself. No! And she shut her eyes tight so as not to see the black wave threatening to engulf her, to cast her into a familiar abyss.

She heard the little girl's voice clearly. Ourfatherwhoart-inheavenhallowedbethyname . . . The girl was so afraid, so small . . .

'I'm no longer a little girl,' she whispered, raising her hand instinctively to her holster. She felt the smoothness of the Glock beneath the antiseptic overalls, as light filled the room once more. She stood motionless, taking a few moments to steady herself. When she opened her eyes again she saw only a crime scene that had been processed by Forensics. She went to the tiny bathroom and checked the wardrobe. She ran her fingers over the bars of the bedframe and felt the cold metal through her gloves. Approaching the chair that was a fixture of the room, she contemplated it as if it bore a mark that was invisible yet palpable. She considered sitting on it, but ruled that out. She removed the folded bedclothes from the office chair and laid them on the bed, holding them as far away from her as she could. She was still clasping the tissue over her nose and mouth, determined not to breathe in her mother's scent, not to let the smell of fear invade her once more. With one hand, she dragged the chair over to the wall, where the blood still shone beneath the glare of the fluorescent strip light.

She sat down and observed the word that screamed out from the wall as it would have done in a museum, a macabre museum of horrors where at the behest of a devilish benefactor the artists exhibited their creations, all of which shared a central theme, a theme dedicated to her. A theme that, with this latest work, established an undeniable link between a group of seemingly unrelated killers, a monstrous instigator who amputated and collected women's arms, and . . . her mother. She laughed at this last thought, so loud that the sound echoed around the room and startled her. It wasn't really laughter, but rather a hysterical, guttural howl, which, she reflected, suited the environment. Was this the work of a madman?

'Even mad people have a behavioural profile.' She could hear the voice of her instructor at Quantico. And yet she didn't believe this person was mad: how could he be if he was manipulating the behaviour of so many people? Of all the different types of killer recorded at the FBI's Behavioural Analysisis Unit, the instigator was by far the most mysterious, the most unusual, the one about which they knew the least.

The control over his own needs, the ruthless control he exercised over his followers, was godlike. And that was his game: to let himself be worshipped and served like a deity, benevolent towards his adepts, yet at the same time so cruel and unforgiving that no one dared provoke his wrath. Letting himself be loved, taking as if he were giving, enslaving as if he were liberating, controlling from the shadows and exercising an invisible omnipotence over his creatures. The challenge for a police profiler was to analyse the way he chose his followers, how he managed to beguile and influence them to the point of creating in them the need to serve him.

She had no doubt that they were dealing with an extremely

patient individual. She knew through Padua that some of the bones in the cave dated back several years, to when his activities started, back to his first victim, his first servant. Four years had gone by since Zuriñe Zabaleta was murdered in Bilbao; three since Izaskun López, the woman in Logroño, died; two and a half since María Abásolo's husband killed her after he killed her dog; just over a year since the Johana Márquez case; and roughly six months since that of Lucía Aguirre, counting from the time she was reported missing until Amaia's maternity leave ended and Quiralte told her where the body was buried. In each case, the women had been killed by their husbands or partners, who either committed suicide immediately afterwards or while in prison, leaving behind the same message. In each case, the victim's right arm had been severed at the elbow after death, with a precision that didn't tally with the rest of the killers' modus operandi. None of the severed limbs had been located, except in the case of Johana Márquez, whose DNA had been successfully compared and matched with bones found at the time of her murder in the Arri Zahar cave. It had so far proved impossible to carry out the same procedure with the other victims. Spain's DNA database was still in its infancy. Limited to members of the armed forces and security services, medical personnel, a few criminals and a handful of victims, it was of little use. That's why they used CODIS – the Combined DNA Index System – which had yielded excellent results, enabling them to compare DNA collected from past crimes and to catch killers who had remained at large for years, as in the famous case of Tony King. But once again, rivalries between the different forces complicated matters.

She needed the results of the DNA tests; if she could prove that the bones in the cave belonged to these women, her path would be clear. Things had speeded up since they were able to have the tests done by Nasertic, a laboratory in Navarre, instead of sending them off to Zaragoza or San Sebastián; even so, for tests like these, which weren't marked urgent, it might be at least a fortnight before they got the results.

Amaia unzipped her overalls and reached for her mobile, checked the time, looked for a number in her address book, dialled it and, without taking her eyes off the wall, waited.

'Good evening, Inspector, still working?' A woman with a thick Russian accent answered.

'As are you, it would seem,' retorted Amaia.

True to her notions of efficiency, Dr Takchenko wasted no time on polite chitchat.

'You know I'm a night owl. What can I do for you, Inspector?'

'You'll be receiving some DNA samples tomorrow, taken from bones processed by the *Guardia Civil*. I want you to compare them with two samples – one of saliva, the other of hair – to see if there's a match.'

'How many DNA samples do you want me to compare them with?'

'Twelve.'

'Come in the evening; the tests will take all night. The saliva will be easier, but extracting DNA from the hair will be time-consuming.' She ended the call.

Amaia sat motionless for a while longer, silently contemplating the word daubed on the wall. She was concentrating on a kind of primeval space into which she would plunge, emptying her mind of all thought, before allowing the facts and questions to sweep over her like a storm of ideas. It was instinct and perception, not logic, that took the first step towards discovering what the killer was trying to say. *Tarttalo*. Signing himself as the monstrous, mythological Cyclops spoke of his inhuman, cruel, cannibalistic nature, audacious enough to display the bones that betrayed his crimes at the mouth of his cave; except that this *tarttalo* also needed to sign the crimes of others to show who was the true instigator of their acts. This signature was the climax of his control over his servants; it didn't matter how many different hands penned it, for there was only one author. Pointing her mobile at the wall, she took a photo and sent it to Deputy Inspector Etxaide. Ten seconds later he called. The sound of Jonan's voice came as a relief and made her smile.

'Where on earth are you?' he asked when she picked up.

'At the hospital where my mother is interned. Earlier this evening she attacked an orderly with a sharp weapon brought in by the suspect, who posed as her son. We found out he has visited her several times in the past few months.'

'Is she all right? I mean, she isn't . . .'

'No, she's fine, Jonan. I've managed to obtain a court order from the examining magistrate instructing the *Guardia Civil* to hand over the bone samples from the Arri Zahar cave. I've just spoken to Dr Takchenko, she will have the results early tomorrow morning. Be prepared.'

Jonan remained silent for a few moments.

'Chief, this changes everything. Now your mother is involved, the case has turned into a personal provocation, a challenge directed at you. The only other examples that spring to mind are Jack the Ripper, who addressed his letters to the detective investigating his crimes, and serial killers like Ted Bundy or the Zodiac Killer, who sent letters to a few newspapers. This guy is more subtle and at the same time more direct; the fact that he got so close to your mother is a clear sign of his arrogance. He poses as your brother and becomes your equal. He's challenging you.'

Amaia thought about it. Yes, this was a clear provocation. She made a mental list of the events that had brought her to this conclusion: a copycat killer who appeared while she was investigating the *basajaun* case; the note addressed to her found on Jasón Medina when he died; Quiralte's insistence that only she interrogate him, to the point of waiting until

257

her maternity leave was over to reveal the whereabouts of Lucía Aguirre's body, before taking his own life; the way Lieutenant Padua had insisted on bringing her in on the case . . . Events orchestrated from the shadows with the sole purpose of catching her attention. And now Rosario; getting close to her had been his boldest move . . . and yet something didn't feel right.

'I need time to think,' she said.

'Will you tell the Commissioner?'

'Not until we have the test results. As soon as we have a match, I'll inform him and we'll open the investigation officially. For the moment, this incident is a private matter: a mental patient attacks an orderly and scrawls some gibberish on the wall. The images we have of the suspect aren't good, I'm not sure they'll give us much. The fact that he managed to get in here only shows up the poor security at the hospital.'

'What about Markina?'

'Markina . . .' The mere thought of having to tell him about this was abhorrent to her, but she knew she couldn't avoid it – after all, he was the one signing the court orders.

'We'll wait until tomorrow, when the order for the samples comes into effect.'

Registering the weariness in her voice, Jonan asked, 'Where is the hospital, chief? Shall I come and pick you up?'

'Thanks, Jonan, that won't be necessary. I came by car. I'm finished here now. I'll see you tomorrow morning at the police station.'

As she made her way to the door, Amaia glanced about her one last time. The sinister power of her mother's absent presence became palpable again. Crossing the threshold, she gave a start when she saw the sorry figure of Dr Franz waiting for her.

His face was ashen, the same shade as his elegant suit. His crumpled tie and shirt collar twisted about his neck gave him an even more forlorn air, and yet his voice had the calm, objective tone of someone who is thinking straight.

'You don't think this adds up either, do you?'

Amaia could tell from his body language that he had more to say and waited for him to go on.

'I can't get the thought out of my head, ever since the incident happened – or rather, since I discovered the context in which it happened. Naturally, the focus has been the assault on the orderly, and the fact that an individual posing as her son gave your mother a weapon. But there's a more significant aspect to all this, one which I find deeply puzzling: notably that your mother hasn't been taking her medication for weeks.'

Amaia gazed at him, not daring to move, despite her overwhelming desire to tear off the technician's white overalls she was still wearing, which reeked of fear.

'Your mother was diagnosed with schizophrenia many years ago. Her violent episodes and her obsession towards you during her most acute phase clearly point to such a diagnosis. All the psychiatrists who have treated her here concur, as do those at the hospital where a previous attack on a nurse led to her being sectioned, as did her GP. Schizophrenia and Alzheimer's, or senile dementia; with a complex patient like Rosario, who suffers so many mood swings, it's difficult to establish where the symptoms of one illness end and those of the other begin. And then this happens . . . From a medical point of view, it is unremarkable: patients like her are extremely violent when they don't take their drugs. What I can't get out of my head is how Rosario was able to behave so calmly for so long without being medicated. Even with the strongest will in the world, a violent schizophrenic cannot possibly feign normality. How could she imitate the serenity provided by the drugs?'

Amaia studied the doctor's expression, in which genuine bewilderment vied with a creeping suspicion.

'I saw the bag they took away containing about four

months' worth of drugs. Clearly she had carried on taking the muscle relaxants, tranquilisers, sleeping pills, as well as a few tablets for other conditions, but not the anti-psychotic drugs.'

'Perhaps, as Inspector Ayegui pointed out, the fact that she wasn't taking them explains the assault,' said Amaia.

He let out a bitter laugh. 'You have no idea!' he said, his smile twisting into a grimace. 'Your mother has been officially diagnosed completely insane, a violent schizophrenic who can only be controlled with medication. Without the drugs, her rage is like that of an avenging demon. And that's how we found her when we went to the nurse's aid, in a deranged frenzy, licking the blood from her hands as she watched the man possibly bleed to death.'

Blood-smeared hands with which she had scrawled on the wall, hiding it behind the bed before they arrived, thought Amaia.

'I'm not sure what you're driving at. On the one hand, you acknowledge she wasn't taking her medication – for which the hospital is entirely to blame – and on the other you say that, without medication, she becomes violent. Why then are you so surprised?'

'What puzzles me is that she ought to have lost control within days of stopping the drugs, yet she managed to control her rage. I don't understand how . . . unless she was pretending.'

'You just told me that even with the strongest will in the world it's impossible for this type of patient to feign normality.'

'I'm not talking about feigning sanity,' said Dr Franz, 'but rather the exact opposite – feigning insanity.'

Amaia tore off the white overalls, the overshoes and lastly the gloves, then threw them inside the room. She grabbed her bag, brushing past the director as she made her way to the lift.

'Transferring her from here is a mistake,' his voice rang out behind her, 'and will severely damage the hospital's reputation.'

Amaia stepped into the lift. When she turned, she saw the director's abject features had resolved into an expression of fierce determination.

'I won't give up until I find out what really happened here,' she heard him say before the doors closed on him.

18

It was five in the morning by the time she arrived in Elizondo. The sky was so dark it looked as if dawn might never break; there was no sign of moon or stars, and she imagined a thick layer of black cloud absorbing all trace of light while taking the edge off the cold. The tyres juddered over the cobbles on the bridge, while the rushing waters of the Txokoto weir welcomed her with their eternal chant. She lowered the window slightly to breathe in the damp rising from the river, barely distinguishable in the gloom, like a smudge of black silk.

She parked outside the arched entrance to her aunt's house, groping for the keyhole. The journey back to Baztán had been a long one, dominated by an emptiness that impeded the flow of her thoughts. It seemed like days rather than hours since she had left the house; the fatigue and tension had caught up with her, in the form of a terrible fragility that had nothing to do with sleepiness. No sooner had she crossed the threshold than she felt comforted by the aroma of logs, furniture wax, flowers, even the sweet smell of butter and biscuits that Ibai gave off. She had to stop herself from running upstairs and taking him in her arms; there was something she had to do first. She walked through to the back of the house and into the garage, which Engrasi used as a woodshed, utility room, and pantry. She entered the tiny bathroom, took off all her clothes and placed them in a bin bag, turned on the shower and stood under the jet of water as she scrubbed her body with a piece of soap she had found in the sink. When she had finished, she dried herself vigorously with a small towel, which she also deposited in the bin bag, before returning, naked, to the hallway, where she put on her aunt's thick wool housecoat. Then she opened the front door, walked barefoot across the freezing ground towards the dustbin and, after tying a knot in the bag, flung it inside. Walking back into the house, she found James sitting on the stairs.

'What on earth are you doing?' he asked with a grin, amused by her outfit.

She locked the door before replying somewhat guiltily: 'I went to throw something in the bin.'

'You're barefoot and it's two degrees centigrade out there,' he said, rising and spreading his arms in a gesture that was like a ritual between them.

She walked up to him until their bodies were touching, breathing in his warm odour as she held him close. She raised her head and James kissed her.

'Oh, James, it was horrible,' she said, unable to avoid putting on the babyish voice she used only with him.

'It's over now, sweetheart. You're home, I'll take care of you.'

Amaia hugged him even more tightly.

'I wasn't expecting it, James. I never thought I'd have to confront this again.'

'Ros told me all about it when she got back. I'm really sorry, Amaia, I know how hard this must be, especially for you.'

'There's a lot more, James. Stuff I can't tell you about. Everything is—'

He cupped her face in his hands, raising her head so he could kiss her again.

'Let's go to bed, Amaia. You're cold and tired,' he said, running his fingers through her damp hair.

Like a sleepwalker, she allowed him to guide her up the stairs, then she climbed naked between the warm sheets, clinging to her husband's body. The smell of his skin, his strong arms and his eternally mischievous boy's smile were always enough to stir her desire. They made love noiselessly, with a deep, intense vigour the kind of love-making people engage in after funerals, or following the death of a friend, affirming life in the face of grief; a passionate, magnificent healing sort of love-making that seeks to erase the sordidness of the world.

She woke with the impression of having slept only a few minutes, but saw from the clock that nearly an hour had passed: she wasn't even aware she had been asleep. She heard James's steady breathing and sat up, leaning over him to peer at the baby. He was fast asleep on his back, mouth ajar, arms folded and his tiny hands splayed out, palms upturned. She donned James's pyjamas, which had been discarded on the floor, pulling the covers over him before tiptoeing out of the room.

The embers in the grate were cold. She stirred them to make a hollow for a new batch of logs, which she stacked like building blocks, thinking as she worked. The fire took instantly, sparked by the nest of kindling she had placed at the centre. She moved back as she felt the heat on her face, sitting in one of the wing-back chairs in front of the hearth. She felt for her mobile in her pyjama pocket and checked the clock, calculating the time difference between there and New Orleans as she looked up the number in her address book.

Aloisius Dupree. *Your relationship is unhealthy*: she was irritated as she recalled her aunt Engrasi's words. Besides being her friend, Dupree was the best cop she had ever known: intuitive, smart, savvy . . . God knows, she needed help. There was nothing normal about whatever it was she was confronting, nor was she exactly what people would call a normal cop. The list of extraordinary things that had happened to her in the past year seemed to be piling up. She knew she could get to the bottom of this case, but she needed help, someone to guide her along the paths she had to take, which were full of twists and turns.

Please, I beg you not to call him again.

'Damn it, Auntie,' she muttered, slipping the phone back inside the pyjamas.

As though drawn by a tune she alone could hear, Amaia stood up and walked over to the sideboard, her gaze fixed on the black silk bundle sitting behind one of the glass doors. She went upstairs to the first floor, barely brushing her aunt's bedroom door. The old lady's voice rang out from the darkness:

'I'll be down in a minute.'

By the time Engrasi arrived, Amaia had picked up the bundle and was unfastening the cloth. As she clasped the cards, they felt warm, like a living thing; she paused, struggling with the doubts this action always roused in her. She shuffled the deck, hardly glancing at the cards as she went over the evidence in her mind, the lines of investigation, the still sketchy theories.

'What do I need to know?' asked Amaia, passing the cards to her aunt, who had sat down opposite her and was watching in silence.

'Shuffle them,' Engrasi instructed her.

The sensations of the present brought back memories of the past. The silky feel of the cards sliding between her chubby little fingers, the peculiar smell they gave off when she moved them, shuffled them, the instinctive way she chose them, the ceremony with which she turned each card over – something her aunt had taught her, which she repeated with great solemnity – knowing even before she did so what would be on the other side. Then that instant when the mystery resolved in a flash, as the path she should follow became clear in her mind, as she established the relationships between the cards. Simplifying her method, the way she had as a child, she took from the top of the pack. While Engrasi arranged the cards in the form of a cross, Amaia yielded to the tyranny of her memory of all those past occasions. One by one she turned the cards, gripped by a deepening sense of unease as she recognised each card she had chosen, as if no time had elapsed since the day Ros read them for her a year earlier.

The chance that the same sequence should be repeated, card for card, was remote, but that they should also spell out that gloomy message was terrifying. And while her astonished aunt rotated the cards and a fresh figure appeared before Amaia's eyes, Ros's tremulous voice reached her like a dark echo from the past.

'*You've opened a different door . . . Ask a question,*' Ros commanded.

'*What is it that I ought to know?*'

'*Give me three cards.*'

Amaia had given them to her.

Her sister had placed them where her aunt was placing them now, and the colourful pictures on the Tarot of Marseilles were duplicated before her eyes, as though copied from the year before.

'*What you ought to know is that there's another element in the game – infinitely more dangerous. He's your enemy, he's coming for you and your family. He's already arrived on the scene, and he will continue trying to attract your attention until you join his game.*'

'But, what does he want from me, from my family?'

She turned over the card; on the table the Grim Reaper stared back at her through empty sockets.

'*He wants your bones,*' said Ros from the past.

'He wants your bones,' said Engrasi.

Amaia glared at her aunt. Trembling with rage, she picked

266

up the cards and, without thinking, hurled them across the room. They flew as one over the wing-back chair and hit the mantelpiece above the fireplace with a dull thud, then scattered on the hearth.

Amaia remained silent, assimilating what had just happened. From where she sat, she could see that some of the cards had landed face up, their bright colours drawing her gaze like a magnet, even as she had a sense of rising anger and revulsion, and cursed her own stupidity for having fallen into the old trap of trying to keep one step ahead of fate.

Engrasi's wise words had become ingrained in her, forming part of a litany that would echo in her head forever:

'The cards are a door, and doors should never be opened just for the sake of it, or left open behind us. Doors can't harm us, Amaia, only what comes through them. Remember to close them after the reading is over. What you need to know will be revealed to you, what remains hidden belongs to the realm of the hidden.'

Engrasi sat watching her quietly. Meeting her gaze, Amaia could have sworn her aunt was afraid.

'Forgive me, Auntie, I'll pick them up,' she said, avoiding Engrasi's startled eyes.

She knelt in the hearth gathering the cards into a bundle once more. Her aunt handed her the strip of silk as she sat down to count them in front of the fire: fifty-six minor and twenty-two major arcanas, yet she counted only twenty-one. She leaned over to one side to look for the missing card, and saw it had landed upright inside the hearth. The flames had shrunk, so there was no danger of the card catching alight. She took the tongs from the wall and picked it up by a corner, lifted it out of the hearth and set it face down on the floor. Replacing the tongs, she reached for the card to put it with the others. The pain leapt up her arm like an electric shock, toppling her backwards, so that she ended up sitting on the floor, propped up against the chair. She was sure this was a heart attack. The shooting pain that caused her arm to go limp, as if all the tendons had suddenly snapped, the spasm in her chest, the thought forming in her mind, despite or perhaps because of her panic: *I'm going to die.*

A doctor had once told her: 'You know it's a heart attack because you think you're dying.'

Doing her best not to cry out, Amaia became aware of her aunt stooping over her, sobbing, murmuring words she could barely make out, and of something else, as she looked in bewilderment at the place where the pain was coming from: the tips of her thumb and forefinger. She stared at the card she was still clutching, her fingers curled up in self-defence. Controlling an impulse to snatch at it, she used her free hand to tug it gently, leaving a piece of skin stuck to the shiny surface of the card, like an indelible print. The pain ceased at once, as she glanced uneasily at the card, which had fallen face down between her legs, hardly daring to touch it again. It seemed incredible that a piece of card could retain enough heat to cause a burn like that. When a while later she took her hand out from under the cold running tap, the skin on her fingers seemed intact. All that remained of the pain was a slight tingling sensation, like when cold hands are warmed too quickly.

Engrasi insisted on drying her niece's hands, inspecting her fingers closely. 'What do you think just happened, Amaia?'

'I'm not sure.'

'I've never seen anything like it, except the other day at *Juanitaenea* when you touched the cradle in the attic.'

Amaia recalled the episode, the way her arm had gone slack as if the tendons had snapped. Suddenly she smiled.

'I know what this is!' she exclaimed, relieved. 'I've been getting shoulder pain and the physio told me it was probably tendonitis from carrying Ibai. Also, I've been going to the shooting gallery a lot to prepare for a target practice test. That's what this is, Auntie. The last time I went, the instructor told me my shoulder must be wrecked. At the time it was only a tingling sensation, but clearly the swelling has worsened with all the effort.'

Engrasi looked unconvinced.

'If you say so . . .'

19

There was no mark on her finger when she woke up later that morning, but she felt too angry to drive and so decided on a brisk walk to the police station after putting on a warm hat and turning up the collar of her coat. A strong southerly wind was blowing that day, which would eventually sweep the rain clouds from the valley. Buffeted like a rag doll, she was obliged to lean forward. She resented having to concentrate solely on staying upright and was reminded of a passage from Dante's *Inferno* where sinners were doomed to walk into the wind for eternity. A sudden gust lifted the hem of her coat, adding to her exasperation. The idea that this monster had the nerve to involve Rosario was a personal affront, which, after she had recovered from the initial shock of having to deal with her mother again, infuriated her in a way that alarmed her. It wasn't good for a police officer to become this emotionally involved; if she couldn't control her anger at this provocation, she would lose her judgement and be unfit to lead the investigation. Knowing this made her even more furious. She quickened her pace to a slow trot, hoping the exertion might calm her down.

It was nearly nine o'clock when she arrived at the police station; despite the brief lie-in, her night without sleep had left dark circles under her eyes. Ibai had woken up grizzling. After a failed attempt to breastfeed him, James had calmed him with a bottle, leaving her feeling angry and inadequate, which in turn had upset the baby. He understood, he understood everything, damn it. She was a useless mother, incapable of fulfilling her son's most basic needs. And she was a useless cop, a cop monsters played hide-and-seek with.

She recognised Montes's voice even before she reached Inspector Iriarte's office, instantly recalling their conversation outside her house. She said good morning without stopping or glancing inside the office, from where a chorus of greetings rang out. The last thing she needed right now was for Montes to have done what she said and requested a formal interview with her.

She entered the conference room, which she was using as an office, closing the door behind her. Deputy Inspector Etxaide walked in as she was taking off her coat.

'Good morning, chief.'

Amaia noticed him staring at her intently, perhaps scrutinising the dark rings under her eyes and debating whether to obey his natural impulse and make a personal remark, or get straight down to work. Etxaide was a brilliant detective; she was aware that some people thought he wasn't imposing or tough enough, that his humane side was more in evidence than his cop side, but so far as she was concerned those 'defects' were infinitely preferable to Zabalza's coldness or Montes's cockiness. She gave a sheepish smile, as if to explain her appearance, and Etxaide chose to get straight down to business.

'It seems Markina had an early start. Lieutenant Padua called an hour ago to say the court order has arrived and the samples will be with us this morning.'

'Excellent,' she said, jotting something down.

'Also, you had a call from the Estella force: they can't do anything with the CCTV footage from the car park at Santa

María de las Nieves. They've enlarged the images as much as possible, but they're too blurred to be of any use. This is what they sent,' he said, placing a series of grey-and-black smudges on the desk.

She looked at them, frowning. After checking her watch, she calculated the time in Virginia: four in the morning, possibly later.

Jonan appeared to hesitate, then blurted, 'About what happened at the clinic yesterday—'

'It was nothing more than an isolated incident, which has little bearing on our investigation, Jonan. So until we have the DNA test results and can start putting things in context, building a profile, let's treat it as such, shall we?'

Jonan didn't seem entirely satisfied with her suggestion, but nodded all the same.

'I want you to go home now and get some rest.' He made as if to protest, but she held up her hand. 'You can do anything I need you to do from there. By all means, keep searching for similarities with other crimes of domestic violence, but try to get a few hours' sleep. We'll leave for Huesca in the evening; the bear doctors are going to help us fast-track this. I'll pick you up at seven in Pamplona, and I'll bring the samples. I suspect this is going to be an all-nighter.'

'It'll be good to see them again,' said Jonan, grinning as he moved towards the door. Grasping the handle, he turned, as if he'd remembered something.

'Chief, there was an email in my inbox this morning . . .' he hesitated.

'Yes?'

'A really strange one, which I think must be for you although it was sent to me.'

'Who's it from?'

'Well, that's the strange part. It's from . . . Best if I just show it to you,' he said, walking back to his computer and bringing up his inbox on the screen.

'The Golden Comb,' Jonan read out loud. 'It's not exactly anonymous, but comes from one of those weird addresses. The sign-off is this symbol, which looks like a mermaid to me.'

'That's a *lamia*,' Amaia said, studying the tiny icon at the foot of the page.

Jonan looked at her open-mouthed.

'Sorry, chief, did you say *lamia*? I thought I was the mythology specialist.'

'Well, it can't be a mermaid – it has webbed feet, not a fish tail – so obviously it's a *lamia*.'

'I don't think it's that obvious. Most people would have mistaken it for a mermaid. Besides, you're the one who usually pokes fun at me for making those sorts of observations.'

She grinned, remaining silent as she read the message.

Jonan went on:

'Either they got the wrong address, or it's some sort of joke, otherwise I don't see that it makes much sense.'

Amaia printed it out and placed the sheet of paper on the desk.

'If you receive any others, forward them to me.'

She waited for him to leave before rereading the message.

A stone you must bring from home
is the offering the lady demands
an offering to the storm to obtain absolution
and to fulfil the destiny marked out for you from birth.

She glanced uneasily at the phone, silently rehearsing what she would say, until she hit on a tone that was sufficiently distant and professional to enable her to explain everything.

'Good morning, Inmaculada, Inspector Salazar here; I'd like to speak to the judge.'

There followed a brief silence in which Amaia thought she heard the woman sigh, before replying obsequiously:

'I'm afraid he's extremely busy this morning, but if you'd like to leave a message I'll make sure he gets it.'

'Yes, of course, by all means,' replied Amaia, imitating the secretary's tone. 'Now put me through to the judge, Inmaculada, or else I'll be forced to go there in person, in which case I might just have to stick my weapon up your backside.'

Amaia grinned mischievously as she heard Inmaculada flinch, imagining the startled look on her face. Instead of a response, there was a ringing tone followed by Markina's voice on the far end of the line.

'Inspector?'

'Good morning, your honour.'

'Good morning. I hope the emergency last night proved to be a false alarm.'

'I beg your pardon?'

'Last night, the emergency that made you rush off.'

'That's precisely what I wanted to talk to you about.'

She spent the next quarter of an hour recounting the incident as impartially as possible. Markina listened attentively without interrupting, so that after she had finished she wasn't sure he was still there.

'This changes everything,' said Markina.

'I don't agree,' she protested. 'Yes, it adds another dimension to the case, but as far as the investigation is concerned, nothing has changed. Until we have confirmation that the bones found in the cave belong to the victims of these crimes, everything else, including the signatures, are fortuitous.'

'Inspector, the mere fact that the killer has made contact with you is cause for concern.'

'You forget that I'm a homicide detective, your honour; killers are my stock in trade. While it's rare for a felon to contact the investigating officer, there are plenty of documented precedents,' she said, thinking on her feet. 'This is simply one example of the arrogant behaviour these individuals display.'

274

'I think that initiating contact with your mother displays something more than mere arrogance. It is intimidation.'

Markina was right, but Amaia wasn't going to admit it.

'I certainly have never come across a case like this,' he added.

'Perhaps there are no cases with direct parallels, but it isn't unusual for criminals to leave clues or hidden messages, especially in cases involving multiple homicide or serial killers.'

'Do you think we're dealing with a serial killer?'

'I know we are.'

He remained silent for a few moments. 'How do you feel?'

'What do you mean?'

'I mean, how do you feel in yourself?'

'If you're asking me whether I can distance myself from the case, the answer is yes.'

'What I'm asking, Inspector, is how this makes you feel personally.'

'Well, that's a personal question, your honour, and unless you have reason to believe that the way it affects me might influence the investigation, you have no right to ask.'

As soon as she opened her mouth she regretted her tone: the last thing she needed was to lose Markina's trust and backing. When he spoke, his voice was cooler but unruffled.

'When and where are the tests being carried out?'

'At an independent laboratory in Huesca. The molecular biologist there worked with us on another case. Her findings were extremely helpful. She has agreed to run the tests tonight, so my deputy and I are taking the samples there. We should have the results first thing tomorrow morning.'

'Good, I'm going with you,' he said.

'Oh, that won't be necessary, your honour, we'll be up all night and—'

'Inspector. If the results turn out as we anticipate, then as from tomorrow we'll be opening the investigation. I'm sure

275

you of all people can appreciate the significance and repercussions that will have.'

She bit her tongue as they said goodbye until the evening. She wasn't happy about this; there were several reasons why she didn't want Markina tracking her.

After she hung up, she reflected that the conversation hadn't gone the way she intended. Markina unsettled her. Admitting that didn't make her feel any better, but at least they were taking another step towards solving the case. For the time being she would simply have to try to keep her distance from him.

'Don't be such a drama queen!' she berated herself out loud. And yet her inner voice continued to urge keeping her distance.

She went back to the email with the *lamia* symbol, then spent the next hour drawing diagrams on the whiteboard and filling in the boxes with names.

Stepping back to the centre of the room, she studied it with a critical eye. A gentle tapping at the door interrupted her musings:

'Am I disturbing you, chief?'

'No, Iriarte, come in, take a seat.'

He did so, positioning his chair so that it faced the board. Amaia turned to block his view, walked forward a few paces, placed her finger on the bottom of the board, and flipped it so that he couldn't see what she'd written.

'Any news on the Arizkun front?' she asked, returning to her desk and sitting down opposite him. Iriarte's bewilderment at her decision to hide the chart didn't escape her.

'No, all quiet. No further incidents, but no progress either.'

'Well, in one sense that's what we expected. We know the Church wanted a head on a pole but, as I've tried to explain, the majority of culprits in these desecration cases are never found. Taking a few security measures is enough of a deterrent.'

'Apparently,' Iriarte replied, his mind elsewhere.

276

'Is Inspector Montes still here?'

'No, he left.'

She was surprised. Much as she preferred not having to talk to him, she'd hoped he would finally give in and defer to her.

'That's what I wanted to talk to you about.'

'About Montes?'

'As you know, Montes's hearing takes place this Friday in Pamplona, where a tribunal will decide whether or not he remains suspended. Now that you're in charge, your opinion will carry a lot of weight.'

Amaia stayed silent for a few moments, then replied irritably, 'Yes, Inspector Iriarte, I'm well aware of that. Now, are you going to tell me what this is about?'

He took a deep breath, exhaling slowly before he answered:

'What it's about is that I will be testifying in favour of Montes's reinstatement.'

'You're fully entitled to your own opinion.'

'Oh, for God's sake, chief! Don't you think the guy has been punished enough?'

'Punished? This isn't about punishment, Inspector, it's a disciplinary measure. Have you forgotten what he did? What he was about to do?'

'No, I haven't forgotten. I've gone over what happened that day a thousand times, and I believe it was the result of an accumulation of circumstances. Montes had recently been through a painful divorce, he was drinking too much, he wasn't focused, and his frustrated relationship with . . . Well, you know who, the realisation that she had been using him . . . it was all too much for him.'

'I don't think I need remind you that, as police officers, we are expected to work under extreme pressure. We can't allow our personal lives to affect the way we do our job. Of course we're only human, and sometimes it's unavoidable, but there's a line we must never cross – and he crossed it.'

'I know he did,' admitted Iriarte. 'But that was a year ago. Things have changed since then. He's focused. He's been in therapy, he's stopped drinking.'

'If you say so.'

'Well, he drinks less – and you can't deny that he's a good officer. The team isn't the same without him.'

'I'm perfectly aware of that. Why do you think I haven't looked for a replacement? However, I don't think he's ready to come back yet. I'm not sure he can be trusted. And in a homicide unit, where our lives are on the line and the outcome of an investigation depends on teamwork, trust is crucial.'

'Trust is a two-way street,' Iriarte retorted.

'What are you implying?'

'You can't demand trust from people if you don't show faith in them,' he said, gesturing towards the whiteboard she had concealed from him.

She stood up.

'Firstly, I'm not keeping information from you. What's on that board concerns a case I am working on in a private capacity, which hasn't been officially opened yet. In the event that happens, I will inform the team and assign to the investigation those officers I consider most suitable. I must decide whether this information is relevant to the case we're currently working on, or whether combining the two cases would jeopardise both investigations. However, if you want to question my ability to make such decisions, feel free to take your complaints to the Commissioner.'

He gazed down at his hands.

'I have nothing to say to the Commissioner. I'm not calling your abilities into question. I find it hurtful that you trust some and not others, that's all.'

'I trust those whom I can trust. How am I supposed to do that with people who go around saying that I leave others to do the work while I go off gallivanting all day? Montes wouldn't have taunted me with that accusation if what happened within these walls stayed within these walls.'

'Chief, you know perfectly well that Montes has his own opinions and his own way of expressing them. He doesn't need others to give him ideas. Yes, it's true that he's a bit touchy, but that's only normal under the circumstances, but I can assure you that as far as I'm concerned, regardless of any sympathy I may have for Montes, not a word of what we say in here goes beyond that door.'

She gave him a hard stare. 'Montes may have changed in lots of ways, but not enough, in my opinion.'

'What about that?' said Iriarte, nodding at the board.

'What is it you want, Inspector?'

'I want you to trust me and tell me what's on that whiteboard.'

She stared him in the eye for a few seconds, then walked over to the board, gently pushed the bottom corner until it swivelled round, and for the next hour she placed her trust in Iriarte.

She went into the house, smiling when she heard the familiar tinkle of plates and glasses. Her aunt was setting the table: that meant she was on time.

'Oh, look what the cat dragged in!' exclaimed her aunt. 'Ros, lay another place.'

'I have a bone to pick with you,' her sister said, coming out of the kitchen. 'Something very strange happened to me this morning,' she went on, staring straight at Amaia, causing both Engrasi and James to stop what they were doing. 'I arrived at the bakery to discover a team of decorators from Pamplona painting the walls and doors.'

'And?' Amaia encouraged her.

'And then they went round to my house and did exactly the same. And when I demanded to know who was behind it, they told me that they had been hired and paid anonymously.'

279

'Excellent!' said Amaia.

'Is that all you've got to say?'

'Er . . . I don't know . . . Did they do a good job?'

Ros looked at her, grinning and shaking her head.

'It's funny . . .'

'What's funny?'

'For years we all thought Flora was the big sister, and – even funnier – that you were the baby.'

'I *am* the baby, you're both older than me,' said Amaia.

'Thank you,' said Ros, planting a kiss on her cheek.

'I have no idea what you're talking about, but you're welcome.'

They ate and chatted animatedly, except for Engrasi, who was quieter and more pensive than usual. After they'd finished, while Amaia played with Ibai, her aunt sat down beside her.

'So you're driving to Huesca this evening?'

'Yes.'

'And before you've even set off, you know the result,' she said.

Amaia gazed at her solemnly.

'How's your shoulder?' asked her aunt.

'It's fine,' she replied warily.

'I'm scared, Amaia. All your life I've been scared for you, for obvious reasons, as well as those that weren't so obvious. I can remember as if it were yesterday when you came in here, aged nine, and read the cards as if you'd been doing it all your life. A terrible evil hung over you then. Because of that, together with the injury and humiliation you had recently suffered, the doors opened in a way they rarely do. In fact, I've only seen it happen once since – when Víctor . . . But . . . There's something in you, Amaia, which attracts the cruellest forces. You have a terrifying instinct for tracking down evil, and as for your job . . . Well, I suppose that was inevitable.'

'Are you telling me that I'm cursed?' Amaia grinned, but with less conviction than she would have liked.

'Quite the reverse, my angel . . . Quite the reverse. People who have had near-death experiences sometimes possess the same traits, but what marks you out is something different. I've always known you were special, but how special, in what way? Be careful, Amaia. There are as many powers attacking you as there are defending you.'

Amaia stood up to embrace her aunt, feeling how frail she was now. She kissed her head, her soft white hair.

'Don't worry about me, Auntie, I'll be careful,' she said, smiling. 'Besides, I have a gun, and I'm a crack shot . . .'

'Stop talking nonsense!' Engrasi scolded her, wriggling free and drying the tears rolling down her cheeks with the back of her hand.

A wintry sun finally emerged once the blustery wind had swept the clouds away. Lulled by the buggy wheels juddering over Elizondo's cobbled streets, Ibai was fast asleep as they went for a stroll, taking advantage of the afternoon light. Amaia listened as an excited James brought her up-to-date with his plans for *Juanitaenea*. When they were approaching home, he came to a halt, and she stopped beside him.

'Amaia, is everything OK?'

'Of course.'

'Only, I heard you talking to your aunt . . .'

'Oh, James, you know what she's like. She's elderly and very sensitive. She worries, but you shouldn't. I wouldn't be able to do my job if I thought both of you were worrying.'

He resumed walking, although from his demeanour she could tell he wasn't convinced. He stopped again.

'What about us?'

Amaia swallowed hard and moistened her lips, ill at ease. 'What do you mean?'

'Are things OK between us?'

She looked him in the eye, summoning all the conviction she could muster.

'Yes.'

'Good,' he said, relaxing. They moved off again.

'I'm afraid I'll be away tonight too.'

'I understand, it's your job.'

'I'm going with Jonan.' She reflected, then added: 'Judge Markina will be accompanying us to oversee and assess the tests. This is huge: if we get the results we're anticipating, we could uncover one of the worst cases in the criminal history of this country.'

James gazed at her quizzically, and she knew instantly it was because she was saying too much: she never explained her work in any detail, and this fell into the category of 'things she couldn't discuss'. She also knew why she was doing it. She had felt the need to be at least partially honest by mentioning Markina, while at the same time minimising his importance by swamping James with more information than she would ordinarily have offered. Watching him walk along with the buggy, she felt suddenly ashamed. She sighed loudly, to attract his attention.

'What's up?'

'Nothing,' she lied. 'I just remembered I have to make an urgent call to the States. You go on ahead,' she told him. 'There's still time for me to bath Ibai before I leave.'

She took out her mobile, searched for the number and, sitting on the low wall by the river, made the call. A man's voice at the other end answered in English.

'Good morning,' she said, though it was dark in Elizondo. 'Is that Agent Johnson? My name is Amaia Salazar, from the Navarre police in Spain. Inspector Dupree gave me your number. I was hoping you might be able to help me.'

Johnson paused before replying:

'Oh, yes, I remember: you were here two years ago, right? I hope you'll come visit us in the next exchange. So, Dupree gave you my number, you said?'

'Yes, he told me if I needed help, you were the one to call.'

'If that's what Dupree told you, then consider me at your service. How can I be of assistance?'

'I have some very poor quality images of a suspect's face. We've done everything we can, but all we come up with are grey splodges. I understand that you work with a new system of image restoration and face recognition, which could be our only chance.'

'Send them over. I'll do what I can,' Johnson replied.

She wrote down his email address and ended the call.

20

It was eight o'clock by the time she parked in front of Deputy Inspector Etxaide's building. She made a missed call and waited, noting how lively the street was compared to Elizondo, where only stragglers on their way home could be seen at that hour.

She felt homesick for Pamplona. The lights, the people, her house in the old quarter, but James seemed delighted to be in Baztán, even more so since they had decided to take over *Juanitaenea*. She knew he loved Elizondo and that house, but although she felt more and more at home there, she wasn't entirely sure it would ever give her the same feeling of freedom that she enjoyed in Pamplona. She wondered whether she hadn't been rash in agreeing to take over the house.

She slid over to the passenger seat when she saw Jonan walk out of the main door; she had lots to think about, and Jonan loved driving. He tossed his thick Puffa jacket on to the back seat and turned on the engine.

'To Aínsa, right?'

'Yes, but first we're stopping off at the petrol station on the way out of Pamplona. Judge Markina is meeting us there. He insisted on accompanying us to make sure the correct procedures are followed.'

Jonan said nothing, but the look of bewilderment he tried to conceal in his usual polite way didn't escape her. He remained silent until they reached the petrol station; no sooner had they parked and stepped out of the car than a pair of headlights flashed at them from another vehicle.

Markina climbed out and came towards them; in his jeans and thick, blue pullover, he looked little more than thirty. Amaia noticed that Jonan was watching her reaction.

'Good evening, Inspector Salazar,' said Markina, extending his hand.

She shook the tips of his fingers, avoiding looking him in the eye.

'Your honour, this is my partner, Detective Deputy Inspector Etxaide.'

The judge greeted him in the same manner.

'We could all go in my car, if you prefer.'

Amaia saw Jonan cast an approving glance at the judge's BMW, but she shook her head.

'I go everywhere in my own car, in case I get a call,' she explained. 'I can't risk having to depend on others to drive me.'

'I understand,' said Markina, 'but if Deputy Inspector Etxaide takes your car, you can accompany me in mine.'

Amaia looked uneasily at Jonan and back at Markina.

'It's just that . . . my deputy and I have work to catch up on. We thought we'd use the journey to get through some of it. You know how it is.'

Markina looked her straight in the eye, and she knew that he knew she was lying.

'I was hoping you might fill me in on how the investigation is going. If, as you're expecting, the results are positive, I'll need to be up to speed to open the case.'

Amaia nodded, lowering her head.

'All right.' She gave in, reluctantly. 'Jonan, we'll follow you.'

She climbed into Markina's car, realising how awkward she

felt as she waited for him to fasten his seat belt. Sitting in that confined space with him made her feel absurdly self-conscious. She concealed her unease by checking the messages on her phone, even rereading some of them, determined to appear indifferent to his closeness, to the way his fingers gripped the steering wheel, the effortless way he changed gears, the brief, penetrating glances he gave her, as though seeing her for the first time. She sensed from the way he leant back in his seat and the faint smile playing on his lips that he was enjoying the journey. They drove in silence for an hour. At first she felt relieved at not having to talk, until she registered that the lack of conversation between them created a level of intimacy that alarmed her.

'I thought you wanted us to talk about the case,' she reminded him.

He glanced at her, before concentrating again on the road.

'I was lying,' he confessed. 'I just wanted to be with you.'

'But . . .' she protested uneasily.

'You needn't talk if you don't feel like it, just let me enjoy your company.'

They sat in silence for the rest of the journey. Markina drove with a languid elegance, casting sidelong glances at her that were brief enough not to intimidate her, though sufficiently intense to do exactly that. Amaia's mounting irritation forced her to go over the progress of the investigation in her head, as she tried hopelessly to see something beyond the sides of the road, in the darkness of the night. The streets in Aínsa seemed lively, doubtless because the weekend was approaching; despite the outside thermometers showing two degrees below zero, no sooner had they crossed the bridge than they saw clusters of people outside the bars and the few shops that had remained open to cater for the many tourists. Jonan took a road that sloped steeply upwards, curving around the hill where Aínsa's medieval castle stood. Markina followed, staring in awe at the houses clinging to the side of the hill as if defying the law of gravity.

'I've never been here before, I must say it's impressive.'

'Just wait until we get to the top,' she said.

Aínsa is a time tunnel, and despite the parked cars and the lights from the restaurants, the sensation of travelling back into the past when reaching the square takes everyone's breath away. Markina was no exception; as he followed Jonan to the place where they parked, the smile never left his face.

'It's incredible,' he said.

Amaia looked at him, amused. She was reminded of her own impressions when she had first visited the town. At 580 metres above sea level, the plunging temperature combined with the damp atmosphere from the confluence of the rivers Cinca and Ara had caused a layer of frost to form on the cobblestones and they gleamed like mother-of-pearl beneath the romantic haze of the streetlamps.

Jonan came up, whirling his arms to get warm.

'And I thought it was cold in Elizondo!' He grinned.

Amaia buttoned up her coat and took a woollen hat out of her pocket.

Only Markina seemed unaffected by the cold. He stepped out of the car, and without putting on his coat, glanced about in awe.

'This place is amazing . . .'

Jonan took the briefcase containing the samples out of the boot, and he and Amaia made their way towards the fortress where both the Nature Interpretation Centre and the laboratory run by the two doctors from the Institute for the Study of Pyrenean Plantigrades were situated. Markina quickened his pace until he caught up with them in the doorway. Amaia noticed his surprise when, after passing through the spacious rooms where wounded birds were convalescing, they arrived at the modest door of the laboratory. Dr González came out to greet them, beaming as he embraced Jonan and shook Amaia's hand. Dr Takchenko, a few steps behind, welcomed them graciously.

'Good evening, Inspector, it's good to see you.'

Amaia smiled at her habitual reserve.

'Dr González, Dr Takchenko, I'd like you to meet Judge Markina.'

Dr González shook his hand, while Dr Takchenko walked over, raising one eyebrow and gazing at Amaia.

'I hope my being here won't inconvenience you,' Markina said, by way of a greeting. 'The results of these tests could lead to the opening of an important criminal investigation. We need to take every precaution to ensure that the evidence is handled correctly.'

Dr Takchenko shook his hand and studied him from close up, then turned on her heel, calling over her shoulder:

'Come on, come on, the samples.'

The small group followed her through the three rooms that made up the laboratory. In the last of these, Dr Takchenko installed herself behind a counter, indicating the surface with a wave of her hand. Jonan placed the briefcase on top, opening it while Dr Takchenko pulled on a pair of gloves.

'Now let me see,' she said, bending over to peruse the samples. Good, saliva . . .' She picked up the tube containing the swab.

'We need to deproteinise the saliva sample,' she said, addressing Judge Markina. 'That'll take all night; afterwards we add phenol-chloroform to extract the DNA, followed by precipitation, drying, and precipitation in water. The sample will be ready for testing tomorrow morning. The DNA thermo-cycler takes between three and eight hours, plus another two hours in the agar jelly before electrophoresis will enable us to see the results. I reckon that will be around midday.'

Amaia sighed.

'You think that's a long time? Well, the hair will take longer,' Dr Takchenko announced. 'The probability of extracting DNA from saliva is ninety-nine per cent, but with hair that goes down to sixty-six.' She picked up María Abásolo's braid and scrutinised it. 'You're lucky: this is a good sample.'

Amaia shuddered as once more she saw the whitish ends of the hairs where they'd been pulled out by the roots.

'And these are the bones?' asked Dr Takchenko. 'Good Lord, how many did you say there were?'

'Twelve.'

'Like I said, midday tomorrow. I'll get started immediately. Give me hand will you, doctor?' she said to her husband.

'Of course,' he replied dutifully, then turned to their visitors. 'Make yourselves at home. You can leave your coats in the office and . . . well, there are plenty of stools in the lab, help yourselves.'

Amaia glanced at her watch and spoke to Deputy Inspector Etxaide.

'It's past ten o'clock, you head off and have dinner, then I'll go when you come back.'

'Anyone else coming?' asked Jonan.

'We've eaten,' replied Dr González. 'We'll make coffee when you get back.'

'I'll go with you, Jonan. If you don't mind, that is,' said Markina, addressing Amaia.

She shook her head, as the two men made their way towards the exit.

Amaia sat down on a stool and for the next half-hour watched the comings and goings of the two scientists. They barely exchanged a word, absorbed in their task, taking care to verify techniques and check procedures.

'I suppose you can't tell me what this is all about . . .' Dr Takchenko asked.

'I don't see why not. We're trying to establish a link between the two samples and the bones that were processed by the *Guardia Civil*. If there's a match, we're looking at a series of crimes that have taken place over a number of years, which encompass the entire northern area. Needless to say, this information is confidential.'

The scientists nodded in unison.

'Naturally,' said Dr Takchenko. 'Is this related to the bones discovered in the Baztán cave?'

'Yes, it is.'

'We were sent pictures of those remains at the time. From the way they were arranged, we immediately ruled out the involvement of predators: no animal leaves the bones of its prey in a pile like that. They looked . . . as if they had been arranged for effect.'

'I think you're right,' Amaia said pensively.

They fell silent once more, absorbed in their task, going over the list of procedures again and again, until finally the first phase was completed.

'Now we must wait,' Dr Takchenko announced.

Dr Gonzalez peeled off his gloves and threw them into a waste container, gazing at Amaia with an expression she knew well of someone debating whether to speak his mind.

'I've given this a lot of thought, you know? My wife and I have talked about it and we agree. What's happening in your valley is appalling.'

'In *my* valley?' Amaia smiled with a mixture of confusion and denial.

'You know what I'm referring to: you were born there, you belong in some way. It's one of the most beautiful places I've ever seen, a place where you can sense the communion between man and nature, a place that provides plenty of reasons for rediscovering a kind of faith.' As he said these last words, he looked straight at Amaia, who knew instinctively what he was talking about. She nodded. '. . . And yet, perhaps for that very reason, something obscene seems to be lurking there, something vile and wicked.'

'There are places,' Dr Takchenko broke in, 'where such things occur, as if they were mirrors or doors between two worlds, or perhaps enhancers of energy. It's as though the universe has to compensate for so much perfection. I know places like that; Jerusalem is a good example of what I mean. Could it be that something has upset the balance in the valley, which is why such terrible and wonderful things are happening there now? It doesn't seem like a coincidence.'

Amaia mulled over the doctors' words. No, she didn't believe in coincidences. The crimes committed against the girls on the banks of the River Baztán possessed the same degree of obscenity and sacrilege as a desecration. She reflected on recent events in Arizkun and on the history of the valley, the difficulties faced by the early settlers, their harsh lives, their battle with disease, plagues, ruined harvests, a hostile climate . . . And then there was witchcraft; and the Inquisition, which had interrogated hundreds of terrified inhabitants, many of whom chose to incriminate themselves in exchange for clemency. And she thought about that other Salazar, the Inquisitor, who for many years had travelled all over Baztán, making his home amongst the inhabitants to try to determine whether or not evil resided in the valley. An inquisitor who had resolved on his own initiative to unravel the mystery of that place, who had obtained, without coercion or torture, more than a thousand voluntary confessions from people who admitted to practising witchcraft, along with three thousand from those who accused their neighbours of engaging in evil deeds. Inquisitor Salazar was something of a modern-day detective, a brilliant man with an open mind. After gathering a year's worth of material, he returned to Logroño, where he explained to the members of the Holy Office that he had found no evidence to support the existence of witches in Baztán, that what was happening there was quite different in nature. The shrewd Inquisitor Salazar had understood – and here Dr González was right – Baztán was the gateway to marvels: both wonderful and terrible.

Yes, perhaps it was one of those places that the universe cannot leave in peace.

Half an hour later, Jonan came back to join them, contented and with a glow to his cheeks.

'It seems his honour is something of a *gourmet*. He found an excellent restaurant on the square, and insisted on paying the bill. He's waiting for you there. It's the second building on the right as you leave the fortress.'

Amaia took her coat and walked out into the cold Aínsa night. The north wind stung her face as she crossed the path in front of the fortress. She pulled the sleeves of her jumper down over her hands, regretting having left her gloves behind. She could see more cars, no doubt attracted by the many bars whose doors were open on to the square. She located the restaurant and weaved her way between the parked vehicles, cursing the flat soles of her boots as she slipped on the icy cobblestones. From the small, rather crowded bar at the front, she could see into the cosy restaurant, which was arranged around a central fireplace. Markina gestured to her from a table near the hearth.

'I thought you'd like to sit here,' he said as she approached. 'It's warm by the fire.'

Markina was right. As she took her seat the warmth, mixed with the aroma of cooking, made her suddenly feel hungry. She ordered an entrecote with mushrooms, and was surprised when he asked for the same.

'I thought you had dinner with Deputy Inspector Etxaide.'

'You give me so few opportunities to dine with you, surely

you don't imagine I would pass up on this one, even though it isn't as I would wish it to be. Will you have some wine?' he said, holding an excellent vintage poised above her glass.

'I'm afraid not, I'm officially on duty.'

'Of course,' he conceded.

Amaia gobbled her food, relieved that Markina barely spoke during the meal, although several times she caught him looking at her, with that serene, oddly melancholy expression that belied the faint smile on his lips.

When they left, it felt even colder outside after the warmth of the fire. Amaia adjusted her coat and hat, pulling the sleeves of her jumper over her hands as before.

'Don't you have any gloves?' asked Markina, beside her.

'I left them behind.'

'Here, take mine, they'll be too big, but at least . . .'

Amaia gave a sigh, finally losing her patience. She turned towards him.

'Stop doing that,' she snapped.

'Stop doing what?' he replied, bewildered.

'Whatever it is you're doing. Giving me those looks, waiting to have dinner with me, fussing over me. Stop it.'

He stepped out in front of her. His gaze focused on a remote corner of the square for two seconds before looking straight at her. All trace of a smile had vanished from his face.

'You can't ask me that. Well, you can, but I'm unable to do what you ask. I can't deny what I feel. I won't, because I'm doing nothing wrong. I'll stop looking at you, I won't fuss over you, if it bothers you, but that won't change how I feel.'

Amaia closed her eyes for an instant, casting about for arguments to use against him. She found one.

'You do realise that I'm married?' she said, realising how feeble an excuse it was.

'I know,' he said calmly.

'And that doesn't matter to you?'

Leaning forward, he seized Amaia's hands and pressed his gloves onto them.

'Only as much as it matters to you.'

Dr Takchenko had placed the bone samples provided by the *Guardia Civil* in the tiny Eppendorf tubes, ranged inside the thermo-cycler.

'Well, at least this is nearly done. Another hour in here, then they have to stand for two hours.'

'I thought the *Guardia Civil* had carried out DNA tests on the bones,' said Markina.

'They did. Their report is attached. But because of the quantity of samples, we decided to repeat the procedure to be on the safe side.'

Markina nodded, then went to join Jonan and Dr González, who were calling him over to have coffee at the far end of the laboratory.

'He's a handsome man,' said Dr Takchenko when he was out of earshot.

Amaia looked at her in surprise.

'Extremely handsome,' the doctor added.

Amaia turned to glance at Markina, then nodded at Dr Takchenko.

'And something of a temptation. Am I mistaken, Inspector?'

Slightly unnerved, Amaia went on the defensive. 'Why do you say that?'

'It's obvious you're attracted to him.'

Amaia opened her mouth as if to deny it, but this time she found no arguments. Anxiously, she wondered whether something in her manner had betrayed her unease.

The doctor gazed at her benevolently and smiled.

'Oh, for goodness' sake! It's no big deal, Inspector. Don't torment yourself, we all feel tempted at one time or another.'

Amaia frowned.

'And when temptation looks that good in jeans, it's normal to have doubts,' Dr Takchenko added mischievously.

'That's what worries me,' confessed Amaia. 'The mere fact of doubting is enough to make me question things.'

'But it's normal to have doubts.'

'I thought it wasn't. I love my husband. I'm happy with him. I don't want to be with another man.'

'Don't be silly, Inspector!' Dr Takchenko chuckled, breaking off her work to give Amaia an impish smile. 'I, too, love my husband, but I wouldn't say no to a roll in the hay with your judge – possibly two.'

Amaia's eyes opened wide with surprise at this sally from the habitually reserved doctor.

'Good heavens, Doctor!' she exclaimed, feigning shock. 'Clearly, working with bears has brought out your wild side. A roll in the hay? I would say at least a couple of days in bed.'

They both laughed, causing the men to turn their heads and stare at them from the depths of the laboratory.

'I see you've been giving it some thought,' whispered the doctor, without taking her eyes off the men.

Amaia climbed down from her stool and moved closer to the counter that separated them.

'Maybe I have, but thinking and doing aren't the same thing. That isn't what I want.'

'Are you sure?'

'Absolutely, only he's not making it easy.'

'Mitjail Kotch,' said the doctor.

'Who?'

'He was my classmate at the Faculty of Medicine. Then we worked at the same institute for three years. He was one of those men who believe that, if you want a woman, you'll have her. Every day, both in the faculty and later on at work, he would make advances, invite me out, bring me flowers or give me suggestive looks.'

'And?'

'Mitjail Kotch didn't make things easy for me, but not once did I consider the possibility of going to bed with him.'

'So, you think that the mere fact of considering means something's not right? Admitting he's attractive means you're willing to deceive your husband?' Amaia said, gesturing towards the group of men.

'Oh, my God! Everything is so black and white with you! You sound like a Russian. That's temptation, Inspector, we're neither blind nor invisible.'

Amaia gave her a questioning look.

'When we decide that we love someone so much we renounce all others, it doesn't make us blind or invisible; we continue to see and be seen. There's no merit in being faithful when we aren't tempted by what we see, or when no one is tempted by us. The true test arises when we meet someone we would fall in love with if we were single, a person who makes the grade, whom we like and are attracted to, who would be perfect if we hadn't chosen another perfect person. That's being faithful, Inspector. And don't worry – you're doing just fine.'

The early hours dragged by, bringing with them an even greater chill. They drank another round of coffee, after which Dr González dug out a pack of cards and the three men became absorbed in playing a silent game. Dr Takchenko preferred to immerse herself in a thick technical manual, which seemed to entertain her, while Amaia went over the case in her head as she contemplated the thermo-cycler, purring on its metal counter like a contented feline. Her instinct told her that those samples contained the very essence of life stolen by the most diabolical pairing she had ever encountered: the cold, powerful mind of the instigator, and the brute subservience that blindly obeyed. As the purring came to a halt, the machine gave a high-pitched whine that made Amaia jump, just as Jonan received a text message and her own phone started to ring. They glanced at one another in alarm, and then she answered Inspector Iriarte's call.

'Chief, there's been another attack on the church at Arizkun.'

Amaia stood up and walked to the far end of the laboratory.

'Talk me through it,' she whispered.

'Someone drove a forklift into the wall and made a great hole, then . . .' he paused.

'Have they left any remains?'

'Yes . . . Another tiny arm . . . This one's a bit different, though, there's no sign of charring . . .'

Amaia could sense Iriarte's emotion from the way he said 'tiny arm'. He was a father himself, and his kids' arms probably weren't much bigger.

'All right, Inspector, set the wheels in motion: inform San Martín, and seal off the area. Don't touch anything until I arrive – which will be in about two hours. I'll leave right away and will call you from the car.'

She grabbed her coat and made her way over to the door, where Jonan was waiting for her.

'Something's come up and I need to leave,' she said to the others. 'Jonan, I want you to stay here, this is very important. Thanks for everything, Dr González, Dr Takchenko. Your honour, I'll call you tomorrow.'

Markina picked up his coat and followed her in silence. He said nothing as they passed through the room containing the huge birdcages, or when they crossed the parade ground inside the fortress.

Before reaching the car, Amaia pressed her key fob. Markina restrained her with a gesture.

'Amaia . . .'

She took a deep breath, exhaling slowly.

'Inspector Salazar,' she retorted, trying to keep her patience.

'Very well, as you wish, Inspector Salazar,' he conceded

reluctantly. Leaning over, he gave her a peck on the cheek: 'Drive carefully, Inspector,' he whispered. 'You mean a lot to me.'

She stepped back, her heart thumping even as she shook her head.

'You mustn't do that, you mustn't do that,' she said, climbing into her car and turning the key in the ignition.

21

As she drove, Amaia tried to curb the impulse to accelerate, focusing what little concentration she had left after her encounter with Markina on not veering off the road on a bend. The surface was coated with a film of white frost and patches of black ice, making night-driving both arduous and hazardous. The locals, who were used to this, avoided taking to the roads at night. Even in the schools, classes would start mid-morning to avoid students having to travel the treacherous mountain passes in the dark. Just before she reached the turning on to the motorway, she pulled up at the side of the road and called Iriarte.

'What happened?' she asked as soon as he picked up.

'At around three this morning, neighbours were woken by the sound of the Bobcat crashing into the church wall. They looked out of their windows but didn't see anyone. We arrived to find a hole in the wall. Inside, on the altar—'

'The bones,' Amaia cut in.

'Yes, the bones.'

'Knocking down the church wall can't have been easy.'

'They chose the spot where the old doorway the *agotes* were forced to use had once been. It was bricked up. The Bobcat forks went through it like butter.'

'What about the patrol car that was supposed to be guarding the church?'

'Fifteen minutes earlier, they received an emergency call about a fire at the Ursua mansion. Since they were closest, naturally they were sent there.'

'A fire?'

'Really it was nothing much, a bit of petrol on the main door, which went up like a tinderbox. The patrol car officers doused the flames with the extinguishers from their vehicle.'

'Doesn't the Ursua mansion also play a role in *agote* history?'

'Yes, the theory goes that the squire of Ursua brought the *agotes* in as workers and slaves.'

She hung up, fumbled beneath her seat for the portable siren she rarely used, lowered the car window and fixed it to the roof. As she joined the motorway, she activated the siren and accelerated, recapturing a sensation of speed she hadn't experienced since her time at the academy. She kept at 180 kmph for a while, overtaking the few cars that were on the road at that time of the morning. Meanwhile, her thoughts turned to Iriarte, one of the most honest cops she knew. His appearance was impeccable and his reports were meticulous, if a little on the pedestrian side. He almost never lost his head or made inappropriate comments. Being so rooted in Elizondo was both his strength and his weakness. She recalled seeing him lose control for an instant when they discovered the lifeless body of a young girl from the village, and when he'd said 'tiny arm' earlier . . . All of a sudden, she found herself thinking about Ibai. She glanced once more at the speedometer, which showed a hundred and ninety, and instinctively lifted her foot off the accelerator. 'Being a parent isn't easy,' Iriarte had told her once, but it wasn't so much that as the terrible responsibility it brought with it. To what extent did being a parent influence her actions? She had always been careful – she had to be, she was a cop for God's sake! But the responsibility she felt towards her son – never to abandon him, never to leave her child without a mother – would that restrict her life, her job, determine how fast she drove? Another thought came to her, an image of the tiny bones left on the church altar, bones belonging to her family, bones that contained the same essence as hers and those of her son, bones that were her roots and her legacy.

'The *Ama* will be careful,' she whispered as she accelerated and the car flew along the motorway towards Pamplona.

At six in the morning, there was no sign of dawn breaking in the skies above Arizkun. The church was lit up. A pair of patrol cars crawled around the perimeter, bordered by a parapet wall designed to prevent vehicles from driving right up to the door.

The forklift, a miniature Bobcat, was sticking out of the wall, its prongs embedded in the brickwork and covered in black debris. The jagged hole it had made measured about a metre high and the same width. Before entering, Amaia circled the church, inspecting the fence surrounding the tiny back garden and the narrow pathway behind.

Iriarte and Zabalza followed in her wake, carrying torches.

'We've checked the outside,' Zabalza observed.

'Well, we're checking it again,' she replied curtly.

Dr Martín was waiting for them inside.

'Greetings, Salazar,' he said, his eyes meeting hers and then shifting to the small bundle on the altar, protected with foil. She walked up to it and uncovered the bones.

Amaia was conscious that Iriarte and San Martín were both looking at her, not at the bones. She did her best to remain impassive as she examined them thoroughly.

'They look different to the previous ones, don't they, Doctor?'

'Indeed: there's no sign of charring and the joints are intact. But above all they're much whiter. That's because they've been inside a tightly sealed coffin with low levels of humidity rather than in direct contact with the soil. See how perfectly preserved the knuckle joints are.'

Amaia paused to contemplate those bones that might be related to her, before covering them again, perhaps a little too carefully, protectively almost. She turned to San Martín to pose the question that had remained unspoken between them since she arrived.

'Do you suppose . . .?'

'There's no way of telling, Inspector. What I *can* say is that they weren't taken from the same place. That's easy to see from the condition they're in. I'll analyse them myself. Within twenty-four hours, possibly sooner, we'll have the answer.'

She nodded, then turned and went over to where the fork-lift had demolished part of the wall. The damage looked worse from the inside. She could see the metal forks poking out from amid the rubble.

'So, this is where the old door used by the *agotes* was.'

'Yes,' Zabalza's voice rang out behind her, 'that's what the priest tells us.'

'Come to think of it, where is he?'

'We sent him and the chaplain home. They were rather distressed.'

'You did the right thing. I imagine this has been dusted for fingerprints,' she said, examining the truck.

'Yes.'

'Where did it come from?'

'From a soft drinks warehouse nearby. It's used for shifting pallets.'

She checked the time, then walked over to Iriarte, Zabalza trailing her.

'We'll meet back at the police station. I want to go over everything we've got on the desecrations. And bring in the boy who has the blog, I want to talk to him.'

'Now?' Zabalza made no effort to conceal his astonishment.

302

'Yes, now. Do you have a problem with that, Inspector?'

'The lad has already been questioned. We decided he wasn't involved.'

'In light of these latest developments, I consider it necessary to question him again. I have reason to believe that whoever is responsible for this has links with the valley. Also, I think that there is more than one person involved. I don't believe the boy could have done these things on his own – breaking down the wall, placing the bones on the altar. he had an accomplice,' she explained, making her way to the door.

'Possibly, but the boy isn't involved,' Zabalza insisted.

She stopped in her tracks, staring straight at him. Iriarte also turned to look at the deputy inspector.

'Do you have a better theory, Inspector?' Amaia asked. 'What makes you so sure?'

There was a tell-tale catch in his voice when he replied: 'I just know.'

Iriarte cautioned him, 'I think you might be getting ahead of yourself here, Zabalza.'

'No,' Amaia cut in, 'let him explain. If he has a theory, I want to hear it. That's why we work as a team, to see things from other points of view.'

Zabalza nervously ran a hand over his face, then checked himself. As if afraid his hands would betray him, he clasped his fingers tightly together, then changed his mind and thrust them into the pockets of his ski jacket.

'The lad is a victim. His father has been beating the living daylights out of him ever since his mother died. He's a clever kid, he does well at school. His passion for history and the origins of his people are what keep him from going mad in that house. I've spoken to him; he may be extremely bright, but his self-esteem is seriously low. Believe me, he doesn't possess the confidence needed to carry out something like this. He's dominated by his father and is in a lot of pain.'

Amaia reflected before responding:

'Teenagers have an extraordinary capacity for rage. The fact that he is, or appears to be, dominated by his father could be feeding a controlled rage that occasionally erupts in these attempts to draw attention to himself. What's more, if you weren't so emotionally involved, you'd see that these desecrations have his name written all over them.'

'What?' replied Zabalza, taken aback, removing his hands from his pockets and gazing at her, then at Iriarte. 'What are you saying?'

'I'm saying that you seem to identify with this boy and that is colouring your judgement.'

Zabalza's face turned bright pink as if it were glowing from inside. His lower lip began to quiver.

'How dare you! Big shot *Agent* Salazar!' he roared.

'Be careful what you say,' Iriarte warned him.

'He doesn't scare me,' she said, stepping forward until she stood nose to nose with Zabalza. 'You don't scare me, but I think you ought to treat me with the same courtesy as I extend to you, despite the fact that you're disloyal, that it was you who gave Montes the lab report that got him into all that trouble, that you're a blabbermouth who places himself and his colleagues at risk by discussing investigations with people outside of work, and finally that you're incapable of recognising when you've overstepped the mark.'

Zabalza's eyes were flashing, his face pinched with anger, but he held her gaze defiantly. She lowered her voice and addressed him again.

'If you disagree with my theories, you are at liberty to form your own, but don't ever talk to me like that again. Identifying with a victim is an expression of our humanity – something many people assume cops don't have. Our humanity is what gives us understanding and helps us gain information from people who aren't willing to volunteer it. We should never relinquish that humanity, but it's vital that we distance ourselves so as not to become personally involved. So, I'll say it again: I have the distinct impression that you identify with the victim. Am I mistaken?'

Zabalza lowered his eyes, even so there was still a trace of defiance in his reply: 'I don't see the need to drag him out of bed, it's six in the morning, he's a minor.'

'If we wait any longer, we'll be dragging him out of school – isn't that worse?'

'He won't be going to school, not with those bruises all over his face.'

Amaia was silent for a few seconds, then she said, 'All right, nine o'clock at the station.'

Zabalza muttered something under his breath and walked out of the church.

Barely ten minutes after she started to read the reports about the desecrations, Amaia's eyes began smarting as if she had grit in them. She spun round in her chair, gazing outside to give them a rest. Dawn was breaking, but the fine rain lashing against the windows made it difficult to see very far. Staying up all night, followed by the drive through the darkness, was starting to take its toll. She didn't feel sleepy, but her eyes were another matter. She turned back to the screen and opened her mail inbox. She had two new messages. The first was a grovelling email from Dr Franz, expressing concern over the tremendous harm the patient might suffer, as well as the harm that would be done to his reputation. This time he aired his theory about a conspiracy to undermine him, even going so far as to question Dr Sarasola's motives for transferring Rosario. He also reiterated his team's suspicions about Rosario's ability to control herself whilst unmedicated. Amaia pressed the delete button.

The second was a forwarded message from Jonan. She opened it with interest. 'The lady awaits your offering.' She was about to delete it, but finally dragged and dropped it into a new folder she named 'Lady'.

Iriarte came into the room, struggling to push open the door while carrying a mug in each hand. He handed one to her. She read the words on the mug with surprise: *Zorionak, Aita: Happy Birthday, Dad.*

'Very cute,' she said with a grin.

'They're the only ones I've got, but they're better than paper.'

'Thanks, what a difference,' she said, cradling the mug in her hands.

'Zabalza is on his way here with the kid and his father.'

She nodded.

'He's an OK guy – Zabalza, I mean. I've been working with him for years now and he's proven himself as a good cop.'

Amaia gazed at Iriarte, listening as she sipped her coffee.

'It's true he's been going through a bad patch, I guess it's to do with his private life – not that I'm defending the way he spoke to you this morning, but—'

'Inspector Iriarte,' she interrupted. 'Are you sure you aren't in the wrong job? This is the second time in less than forty-eight hours that you've presented me with a defence plea on behalf of a colleague. You'd be great in a work tribunal.'

'I didn't mean to upset you.'

'You haven't upset me, but let these guys fight their own battles. The tussle between me and Zabalza isn't over yet. A few people have difficulty accepting it, but in this team, the alpha male is a woman.'

Iriarte's mobile rang and he rushed to take the call.

'It's Zabalza, he's downstairs with the boy and his father.'

'Where are they?'

'In an office on the ground floor.'

'Tell him to take them into one of the interview rooms. I want a uniformed officer to stand guard inside the room without speaking to them.'

306

Iriarte relayed the information and hung up.

'Shall we go?' he said, setting his mug down on the table.

'Not yet,' she replied. 'I think I'll have another coffee first.'

Three-quarters of an hour later, Amaia walked into the interview room, ignoring the angry glares of Zabalza, who was waiting outside. The atmosphere inside the room reeked of sweat and tension. The lengthy wait and the presence of an armed guard had produced the desired effect.

'Good morning, I'm Detective Inspector Salazar of the Navarre police murder squad,' she said, flashing her badge, and sitting down opposite them.

'Hey,' began the father, 'you've got a nerve, dragging us here so early, then making us wait for an hour. It's a disgrace!'

Amaia noticed the sleep in the man's eyes; a whitish trail of dried saliva stretching from his mouth to his left ear.

'Shut up,' she snapped. 'I've summoned your son here because he's the prime suspect in a serious crime,' she said, fixing her eyes on the boy, who sat up straight and glanced at this father. 'Believe me, having to wait an hour is the least of his worries, because if he refuses to cooperate, he's going to spend a lot longer than that in far worse places than this. And if you wish to discuss what constitutes a disgrace, you and I can have a talk afterwards. I now intend to question your son. You can remain silent or call a lawyer, but don't interrupt me again.'

She looked at the boy. Zabalza was right: he had a nasty-looking bruise on his cheek, together with a couple more on his chin, which were turning yellow. He sat stiffly, his clothes hanging loosely from his skinny frame.

'Beñat. Beñat Zaldúa, is that correct?'

As the boy nodded, a strand of hair tumbled on to his forehead. Amaia studied him. He was nervous, biting his lower lip, arms folded in a defensive posture; from time to time he ran his hand over his mouth, as though wiping his lips.

Yes, he was on the defensive, but the truth weighed on him; his folded arms were an attempt to stifle the words that were struggling to come out, to alleviate his burden. He wanted to talk, but he was afraid. It was her job to resolve that contradiction.

'Beñat, although you're a minor, you are old enough to be held accountable for your actions. I am willing to put in a good word with the judge to ensure that he is lenient with you, in light of your circumstances,' she said, casting a brief glance at the father. 'I want to help you, and provided you're honest with me I will. But if you lie to me, or hide anything from me, I'll abandon you to your fate – and it won't be a pleasant one.' She let her words sink in, before adding: 'Will you let me help you, Beñat?'

He nodded vigorously.

The interrogation was more like a frantic confession, as the boy explained how he had been contacted via his blog by a man; how he was sure at first that he'd met someone who believed in and defended the same ideas; how, with each fresh attack on the church, things had gradually started to get out of hand, especially when he learned about the human bones left on the altar. That had nothing to do with his beliefs. He gave a description of the man, whom he had only met face to face during the desecrations: he called himself 'Agote', and half the fingers on his right hand were missing. When he had finished unburdening himself, he gave such a loud sigh that Amaia couldn't help smiling.

'Much better now, right?'

Amaia left the room and spoke to Zabalza, who was waiting beside the door.

'Put out an APB with the description of this guy with the missing fingers.'

Zabalza nodded, lowering his head. Iriarte went up to her.

'Your husband called. He says to call him back straight away, it's urgent.'

She gave a start. James had never left a message at the police station before; it had to be something really important for him not to be able to wait until she took her phone off silent after the interrogation. She leapt up the stairs, and went into the meeting room she was using as an office.

'James?'

'Amaia, Jonan told me you were back in Elizondo.'

'Yes, I haven't had time to call. What's wrong?'

'I think you need to come home.'

'Is it Ibai? Has something happened to him?'

'No, Ibai is fine, we're all fine, don't worry, just come straight home.'

'Oh, for God's sake, James, tell me now, I'm going out of my mind here!'

'My architect friend, Manolo Azpiroz, arrived this morning. I gave him the keys so that he could go on ahead to *Juanitaenea* while I was getting Ibai ready. He called me soon afterwards to say he didn't think it was a good idea to start on the garden, because everything would get ruined with all the building work. I assured him we hadn't done anything to the garden, and he told me that in various places around the house the earth has been disturbed, turned over, as if ready for planting. Amaia, I'm at the house now and Manolo is right. There are holes everywhere. I can see something inside . . .'

'What is it?'

'It looks like bones . . .'

She grabbed her field kit and took the stairs without waiting for the lift. In the passageway on the ground floor, Iriarte and Zabalza were talking in hushed tones; from their gestures she guessed they were arguing.

'Inspector Iriarte, will you come with me, please.'

A minute later, Iriarte had fetched his coat and walked out with her, no questions asked. They drove the short distance from the police station to *Juanitaenea*, Amaia's head buzzing

309

with reproaches. Why hadn't she thought of this before? No grave, no charnel house. The unbaptised children of Baztán were not buried at crossroads, or outside the churchyard; they had a place of their own. They were buried in the *itxusuria*, the corridor of souls, the strip of ground where water dripped from the eaves, marking a line between the inside and outside of the house. Why had she been so blind? Her family had always lived in Baztán. Why hadn't it occurred to her that, like so many others, they had buried their children in the *itxusuria*?

James was standing next to Ibai's buggy, waiting for her at the edge of the kitchen garden. His unusually serious manner betrayed a hint of resentment, bordering on indignation, which surprised Amaia. Her James, with his wholesome, laid-back attitude to life, felt aggrieved when the ugly side of things took him off guard. Amaia planted a kiss on the sleeping Ibai's hand, then stood to one side to talk to James.

'It's . . . It's . . . Well, I don't know whether it's gruesome or shocking. I don't even know if they're human – they could be someone's pets.'

Amaia gazed at him tenderly. 'I'll deal with this, James. Take the baby home, and don't say a word to Ros or my aunt until we know more.'

She leant forward and gave him a kiss, before turning towards Iriarte, who was waiting for her on the path up to the house, holding an umbrella.

They walked over to the doors leading to the stable, leaving her field kit on the rickety outside staircase. She pulled on a pair of gloves and handed another pair to Iriarte. The drizzle of the last few hours had softened the earth, which stuck to her boots, hampering her movement; she remembered how she had slipped on the cobbles in Aínsa, and resolved to throw them away as soon as she got home. She circled the house perimeter, observing the mounds of earth, which were clearly visible. Pausing at the one nearest to her, she alerted Iriarte

310

to a partial shoeprint, the edges of which were starting to dissolve in the rain. Iriarte stooped, shielding the mound with his umbrella so that he could photograph the print, having first placed a ruler next to it. They moved on to the next mound, which had a hole in it, as if a giant seed had sprouted through the surface, dislodging the soil. They took a photo, then Amaia set to work. Using her fingers as a trowel, she pushed aside the clods, the black Baztán soil staining her gloves, until she came upon a skull no bigger than a small apple. A few metres away, another hole, hurriedly filled in, was empty, and at the far corner of the house, where the eaves had left their mark on the ground, was the mound James had mentioned. Protruding from the mud were some blackened bones, which could have been mistaken for roots. Amaia stood up to allow Iriarte to photograph the site, casting her eye towards the rear of the house, where she could see at least nine excavations in that section alone, plus a few more on the other side.

The line of the eaves marked the spot. The slow drip-drip of water for over two hundred years had left a channel in the ground that the desecrator only had to follow. She rummaged in her pocket for the key James had given her, removed the padlock from the door into the stable and called Iriarte. He entered, shaking the water off his clothes.

'Is this your grandmother's house?'

'Yes, it's been in my family for generations.'

He glanced around.

'Inspector, I want to talk about what's outside,' she said.

Iriarte nodded solemnly.

'I think you know what this is. An *itxusuria* – the traditional family burial plot in Baztán. The infants buried here are members of my family. This was their mothers' way of honouring them, allowing them to remain at home, as sentinels who guarded the house. If we call San Martín, he'll come here with his team and dig up all the little ones. As you are from Baztán yourself, I think you'll understand what I'm about to ask you. This is my family graveyard. I want to preserve it. A discovery like this would turn the place into a media circus. Besides, I suspect that whoever desecrated the church at Arizkun – and I don't mean that poor kid – also plundered these graves. The publicity might scare him off. What do you think?'

'I wouldn't let anyone dig up my family graveyard.'

She nodded, overcome with emotion, unable to speak. Walking to the door, she pulled her hood up over her head again.

'Now, let's carry on.'

She resumed where they had left off, finding three more skeletons in two of the mounds. The bones were broken and badly decayed, their shape barely distinguishable. Poking out of a third were the shreds of what looked like a piece of dirty sacking. Seeing the remains of the cot blanket made her shudder. She knelt on the moist earth, pushing aside layers of soil until she revealed the loving bundle made by a mother for her baby. A piece of oilcloth covered the grave, but it was the blanket that broke Amaia's heart, because it so clearly revealed the pain of a mother laying her baby to rest in the earth, still trying to protect it, to keep it warm. She felt the coldness of the rain soaking through her jeans. Her eyes brimmed with tears that fell on to the bones of the beloved infant, perhaps on the same spot where, years before, the tears of its mother, her great-grandmother, had fallen.

Or was it her great-great-grandmother? A young woman, racked by grief, who, at nightfall, had laid her infant in the ground and covered it with a blanket. Amaia peeled the fabric away where it had been torn, and the tiny bones, astonishingly intact, cried out from their miniature tomb, revealing the work of the desecrator. She covered the skeleton with the blanket and closed the bundle, scattering soil on top.

Iriarte, who had remained silently by her side, trying in

vain to shelter her with the umbrella, proffered his arm to help her up. She accepted. They went back to the side of the house, where Amaia looked once more at the traces of the disturbed graves. The rain would help flatten them out again. As she gazed at those insignificant mounds of earth, she could feel the grief of generations weighing on her shoulders, the tears women in her family had shed over that strip of ground, kept as a corridor of souls. Betrayed by her imagination, she saw herself forced to lay Ibai in the mud, even as the breath left her body. She turned pale, the strength draining out of her.

'Are you OK, chief?'

'Yes,' she said, walking on as she composed herself. 'I'm sorry,' she murmured.

Iriarte put the briefcase in the boot, then opened the passenger door for her. For a moment, Amaia contemplated walking back to her aunt's house as Calle Braulio Iriarte was on the other side of the Trinkete, but her trousers were wet and muddy, her limbs beginning to ache as if she was ill, so she climbed into the car. She thought she glimpsed a face hiding among the trellises, and recognised the hostile gaze of the man who looked after the kitchen garden.

Turning the corner, they saw Fermín Montes standing outside Bar Txokoto smoking, barely sheltered from the rain beneath the eaves. Iriarte raised his hand slightly as Montes waved, then drove on up the street to Engrasi's house.

Before getting out of the car, Amaia turned to Iriarte.

'Do I have your word?'

'Yes.'

She looked straight at him, stony-faced, and nodded.

No sooner had she stepped out of the car than Fermín, who had followed them at a trot, approached the open door holding up an umbrella.

'Inspector Salazar, I'd like a word with you.'

Amaia gazed at him, as if he were an apparition, suddenly exhausted.

'Not now, Montes.'

'Why not? We can talk in the bar if you prefer.'

'Not now . . .' she repeated, stooping to pick her things up off the seat.

'How long are you going to keep avoiding me?'

'Make an appointment,' she said, without looking at him.

'Why are you doing this to me?' he protested. 'I don't understand.'

Iriarte got out of the car, walked around to the other side, stepping between them.

'Not now, Inspector Montes,' he said firmly. '*Not . . . now*,' he repeated, addressing him slowly, like a child.

Montes nodded grudgingly.

Amaia walked towards the front door, leaving the two men face-to-face in the rain.

She dragged herself into the house, feeling physically ill. The change from the damp air outside to the dry, fragrant heat radiating from the hearth, made her shiver uncontrollably. Alarmed by her appearance, James handed the baby to Engrasi.

'Amaia, you look awful! Are you sick?'

'Just tired,' she replied, sitting on the stairs to remove her muddy boots.

James stooped to kiss her brow, then recoiled.

'Tired my eye, you're burning up!'

'Get out of those wet clothes and take a hot shower,' her aunt ordered, laying Ibai in his cradle. 'I'll be up in ten minutes to see you.'

'Ibai,' whispered Amaia, extending a hand towards the boy.

'You'd better not touch him until we know what's wrong with you. You don't want to infect him.'

James helped her out of her damp clothes and into the shower. Feeling the hot water on her skin, Amaia knew what was wrong with her. Her body was reacting to the fact that she hadn't breastfed Ibai properly for days. Her breasts were swollen and tender. Stepping out of the shower, she took a couple of anti-inflammatories, then rummaged in her bag for the box containing two tablets she had put off taking, which would prevent her from ever breastfeeding her son again. She placed them on her tongue and swallowed them, together with her distress at feeling she was a failed mother. Devastated and bewildered, she sat on the bed and didn't even notice falling asleep. James returned with the bottle of water she no longer needed, and, seeing her like that, naked and sleeping, utterly exhausted, he wondered whether coming back to Baztán had been such a good idea. He spread the duvet over her, lay down beside her, gently draping his arm over her feverish body, feeling like a stowaway on a cruise ship.

22

It was four thirty in the afternoon when James woke her by planting gentle kisses on her head. She grinned as she smelled the aroma of coffee he always brought with him to the bed.

'Wake up, Sleeping Beauty, your fever has gone. How are you feeling?'

She thought about it. Her lips were dry and felt like cardboard, her hair clung to her scalp as if it were wet, and her legs still tingled slightly, but otherwise she felt fine. She smiled, silently giving thanks for what had been a dreamless sleep that brought no memories.

'I'm fine; I told you, I was just tired.'

James gazed at her quizzically but said nothing. He knew she hated him telling her to take care, rest more, get more sleep. He sighed, holding out her coffee.

'Jonan called.'

'What? Why didn't you wake me up?'

'That's what I'm doing! He said he'd call back in ten minutes.'

Amaia sat up in bed, propping herself against the wooden bedhead, which, despite the plumped-up pillows, dug into her spine. She took the coffee and sipped at it while with her free hand she looked up Jonan's number.

'Chief, I'm passing you over to Dr Takchenko,' he said when he picked up.

'Inspector Salazar, we've found matches between the hair and saliva and bone samples number six and eleven respectively from the *Guardia Civil*. With sample six the match is one hundred per cent, so I can confirm that the hair and the bone belonged to one and the same person. In the case of sample eleven, the number of matching alleles suggests that the bone and the saliva belonged to two siblings. I hope we have been of some assistance,' she said, handing the phone back to Jonan before Amaia had a chance to reply.

'Chief, you heard it. We have a match. Markina is on the phone to the Commissioner as we speak. I'm driving back to Pamplona with him. I imagine the Commissioner will call you as soon as he hangs up.'

'Good work, Jonan. I'll see you in Pamplona . . .' she said, as she heard the beep of an incoming call.

'Sir?'

'Inspector, Judge Markina just called to inform me about your findings. We've arranged to meet at the police station in Pamplona in about two and a half hours.'

'I'll be there.'

'Inspector . . . could you possibly come a little earlier? There's something I'd like to discuss with you.'

'Of course, I'll be there in an hour.'

She went over the information they had so far, assuming that the Commissioner wanted her to bring him up to speed before Markina officially announced his intention of opening the case. The test results cast everything in a fresh light: two more women murdered by their husbands in apparently unconnected crimes of domestic violence; both had suffered identical amputations and their bones had turned up in a cave in Arri Zahar. Both aggressors had taken their own lives after killing their respective partners, which was not uncommon. The severed limbs had been removed from the crime scenes, and a few of the bones presented bite marks, as in the case of Johana Márquez. The victims' bones had also been piled up at the entrance to a cave, imitating a mythical monster, whose name the culprit used openly, signing his crimes in the blood of his victims, sacrificed for him by his followers. '*Tarttalo*' screamed out from the walls obscenely, brazenly. His audacity had attained new heights with the messages he sent to the police via an emissary like Medina, or when he forced Quiralte to wait until her maternity leave was over before revealing the whereabouts of Lucía Aguirre's body. And finally, in an even more daring and provocative gesture, he had approached her mother. The thought of the two of them together made her shudder. Did they talk? She wasn't sure how capable Rosario was of intelligible speech; apparently capable enough to approve a list of visitors, or to request that person in particular. On reflection, Amaia realised the visitor must have known Rosario prior to her internment at Santa María de las Nieves, because since the court ordered her confinement there seven years ago, her only contact had been with the medical staff and her fellow patients.

They could practically rule out an employee, or former employee, because the visitor's disguise wasn't designed to prevent him from being recognised by those who knew him, merely to make it difficult to identify him. No, this had to be someone outside the hospital. Someone who knew Rosario. But from when? From before she became ill and was sent to one mental institution after another? From way back? In Baztán? The choice of cave suggested knowledge of the area, although any one of hundreds of hikers who tramped through those woods every summer could have chanced across it, or been guided there by the dozens of signposted trails that featured on the various websites covering the valley, even in Baztán Town Hall.

And yet, something about the staging, the signature of the crimes, together with the choice of name suggested an unwholesome connection to the valley. At first, like Padua, she had thought that associating himself with a mythological creature by calling himself 'Tarttalo' was simply a way of drawing attention to his activities in the wake of the *basajaun* case. She would never understand what made journalists give killers these absurd names, which in the *basajaun* case couldn't have been more arbitrary. Then it occurred to her that the same might be said about the way the police labelled their cases. And yet *basajaun* wasn't just arbitrary, it was inaccurate. An image of the forest came to her, so vividly and intensely that the serene, majestic presence of its guardian felt almost palpable. She smiled, the way she always did when evoking that image, which never failed to bring her a feeling of peace.

After greeting a few familiar faces at the entrance, she went straight up to the Commissioner's office and waited for a uniformed officer to announce her arrival. Like the last time, her chief was accompanied by Dr San Martín. His presence set alarm bells ringing in her head. She greeted her superior, shook the doctor's hand and took the seat the Commissioner indicated.

'Inspector, we're waiting for Judge Markina to arrive to confirm what we already know: that tests show the bones found in the Baztán cave belong to two female victims of violent crimes bearing the same signature.' The Commissioner put on a pair of glasses, leant forward, and read out loud: 'TARTTALO. The judge informed me over the telephone that he intends to open the case. Congratulations, you've done an excellent job, especially considering the difficulty of investigating cold cases without ruffling feathers.'

He paused. Amaia thought: *But* . . . She knew when a pause preceded a 'but', yet try as she might she couldn't imagine what might follow. The Commissioner himself had just said that Markina was opening the case, she was in charge of the murder squad, no one could take her off the investigation, and the evidence they had was more than enough – overwhelming, in fact. The families demanded justice, *but* . . .

'Inspector . . .' The Commissioner hesitated. 'There's something else, something unrelated to this particular case.'

'Unrelated?' She waited, impatient for him to get to the point.

San Martín cleared his throat, then suddenly she understood.

'Is this connected with the bones found at the desecration site in Arizkun?'

'Yes,' said San Martín.

'Do they also belong to my family?' she asked, as images of the tiny holes in the disturbed earth flashed through her mind.

'Inspector, before I go on, let me make it clear that, due to the circumstances surrounding the first set of bones, I myself carried out the tests on these ones and, needless to say, I followed strict procedures.'

'Do they belong to a relative of mine?' she asked, trying to hurry him along.

San Martín glanced at the Commissioner before continuing:

'Inspector, are you familiar with the percentages of DNA which establish our genetic links to a family, that is to say whether a relative is once, twice or thrice removed?'

Amaia shrugged. 'I think so: we share fifty per cent of our parents' alleles, twenty-five per cent of our grandparents' and so on . . .'

'That's right,' replied San Martín. 'Each human being's genes are unique. Although the DNA of our immediate relatives is genetically very close, a whole array of things define us as individuals.'

Amaia sighed: *where was all this leading?*

'Salazar, the results of the DNA tests I carried out on the bones found in Arizkun yesterday show a one hundred per cent match with your own.'

She sat gaping at him.

320

'But that's impossible.' Her mind was racing. 'I couldn't have contaminated the samples – I never touched them.'

'I'm not talking about transferred DNA, Salazar, I'm talking about the actual bone matter.'

'There must be some mistake. Someone has messed up.'

'I told you: I myself carried out the tests. And in the light of the results, I repeated the procedure and obtained the same result. It's your DNA.'

'But . . .' Amaia smiled, incredulous. 'Obviously it can't be my arm,' she said, laughing uneasily.

'Do you know whether you had another sister?'

'I have two, neither of whom are missing a limb. And besides, you just told me that each individual is unique, they may look like me, but they couldn't be me.'

'Unless they were your identical twin.'

Amaia made to answer, then paused. Eventually, she said very slowly:

'I don't have a twin.'

As she spoke, she saw everything around her dissolve into a thick oily blackness that seeped down the walls and swallowed up the light, covering every surface and dripping from her eyes into her hands, which lay open on her lap. A little girl who wept.

A little girl who wept tears heavy with fear, lifting her arm severed from the shoulder as she cried out: 'Don't let *Ama* eat you!' The identical cradle in *Juanitaenea*, rocked by the little one-armed girl, the little girl who never stopped crying.

A thousand images flashed through her mind, recalled from dreams. In them, the little girl, who she had always assumed was her, stood silently beside her, identical as a reflection in the dark mirror of a nightmare. A more melancholy version of her, because underneath the grey veil of pain, Amaia had the will to survive: her rebellion against her fate shone like a winter moon in the deep blue pools of her eyes. Not that other little girl. The only light that shone in her eyes was from

321

her endless tears, so black that they spilled about her like a beguiling pool of jet. Her silent passivity exuded a despair and acceptance of her fate that she cut a tragic figure, although at times she wept so intensely it seemed she was incapable of bearing it any longer. Once, the little girl sobbed with gasping breaths that arose from the depths of her being, while in her lap lay Amaia's Glock, her police firearm, the thing that made her feel safe. The girl pressed the gun to her own head, as though dying were a kind of release. 'Don't do it!' Amaia had shouted at the little girl she thought was her, even as the phantom she carried in her bones raised the stub of her amputated arm, showing it to her: 'I can't let *Ama* eat me.'

She became aware again of the office, of the presence of the two men looking at her. For an instant she was worried they had noticed her disquiet, that all those thoughts swirling about in her head had been reflected in her face. She swiftly picked up the thread of what San Martín was explaining, as he pointed with his pen to a chart on the table.

'There's no possibility of error. At the Commissioner's request, everything has been tested twice, and they've been sent to Nasertic again. We'll have the results back from there tomorrow, but that's a mere formality; I can assure you their findings won't be any different.'

'Inspector, the fact that you were unaware you had a twin sister who died when you were born isn't necessarily significant; your parents could have been so upset by her death that they decided not to speak about her, or perhaps they didn't wish to traumatise you by telling you that your twin had died. Moreover, until 1979 burial registries were handwritten, there was no obligation by law to register the deaths of unborn children – in the majority of cases, they were recorded as 'abortive babies', with no reference to the sex or estimated age of the foetus. In some parishes, they got around the obstacle of a baby being unbaptised by performing a secret burial, and offering a generous tip to the gravedigger. It's clear that whoever is doing this is acquainted with you and your family; he gets his knowledge first-hand. As the doctor told you, the condition of the bones suggests they have never been in contact with the earth and must have been kept in a dry, sealed environment. You need to tell us in which graveyard or graveyards your relatives are buried, so that we can look into this.'

Amaia listened, stunned. She thought for a moment, then nodded slowly.

A uniformed officer announced Judge Markina's arrival. As if they had taken an unspoken decision, the Commissioner and San Martín gathered up the reports on the table before ushering him in. The meeting lasted less than fifteen minutes. Markina notified them of the test results, which naturally had to be repeated through the official channels, and revealed his intention to open an investigation. He praised the discretion and care shown by the Commissioner and by a silent Amaia, who simply nodded in response. When the meeting was over, she hurried away, thankful that Markina hadn't given her one of his looks. Jonan was waiting for her in the corridor and started to talk excitedly when he saw her.

'Chief, isn't it amazing? We did it, they're going to reopen the case . . .'

She nodded a couple of times, distractedly, and he sensed her anxiety.

'Did everything go OK in there?'

'Yes, fine. This is about something else.'

He remained silent for a few moments before asking, 'Do you want to tell me about it?'

When they had reached the car, she turned to look at him. She had tremendous respect for Jonan; he genuinely cared about her beyond their police work together. She gave a faint smile that remained on her lips without spreading to her eyes.

'I need to think first, Jonan, then I'll tell you.'

He nodded. 'Shall I take you home? We needn't talk if you don't want to, but I think it's unwise for you to drive; it's been snowing and the road is bad at the Belate pass.'

'Thanks, Jonan, but I think you should go home; you've missed a lot of sleep too. I'll be careful, the drive will do me good.'

As she left the car park, she could see Jonan standing where she had left him.

Piles of snow bordered the road as far as the Belate tunnel. On the other side, there was only darkness and the clatter of grit hitting the undercarriage. She was haunted by images of the disturbed mounds of soil surrounding *Juanitaenea*, the rotting blanket, the cradle in the attic – identical to Ibai's – the whiteness of the bones carrying her DNA, proof that they hadn't been in the earth. How could a person's traces be obliterated? How could she have heard no mention of her? San Martín had spoken of a newborn. Had she died at birth? Did the arm prove that she was dead? Could it have been amputated after she was born, because of some disease? Might she still be alive? Finding herself in Calle Santiago, Amaia realised she had been driving in a trance, on automatic pilot. She slowed as she rolled through the empty streets down to the bridge, stopping at Muniartea to listen to the roaring water at the weir. It had been raining all day and a lingering dampness, reminiscent of a Baztán tomb, seeped inside the car. She felt a sudden uncontrollable rage towards that accursed place: the water, the river, the medieval cobblestones, the centuries of suffering it had been built on. She parked, for the first time scarcely aware of the welcome the house seemed to offer as she crossed its threshold, enveloping her in its warm embrace.

Everyone had gone to bed. She took her laptop and became immersed in typing on the keyboard. For several minutes, she looked up various databases and registers until, finally, exasperated, she closed the screen and went upstairs. Realising how noisy her boots were, she crept back down, slipped them off and climbed the stairs in her stockinged feet. She paused outside her aunt's bedroom before knocking. Engrasi's soft voice responded from within.

'Auntie, could you come downstairs? I need to talk to you.'

'Of course, my dear,' she replied anxiously. 'I'll be right down.'

Amaia also paused outside Ros's door, but decided that her sister couldn't know any more than she did.

While she was waiting for her aunt to appear, Amaia stood in the centre of the living room gazing into the hearth, as though a fire were burning there which only she could see. For once she didn't have the heart to light it.

She waited until her aunt was sitting down before turning to address her.

'Auntie, what do you remember from around the time when I was born?'

'I remember a great deal, though little about Elizondo. I lived in Paris then. I had next to no contact with anyone from here. You were four by the time I returned.'

'But didn't *Amatxi* Juanita tell you about things that had happened while you were away?'

'Of course, she told me lots of things, mainly village gossip, filling me in on who had married who, who had children, or who had died.'

'How many sisters do I have, Auntie?'

Engrasi gave a shrug as if to say this was obvious. 'Two: Flora and Ros.'

'Did *Amatxi* Juanita tell you about me being born with another little girl?'

'A twin?'

'An identical twin.'

'No, she never told me anything of the sort. What makes you think that?'

Amaia didn't reply but continued with her questions.

325

'Nothing about my mother having had a miscarriage, a still-born baby?'

'I've no idea, Amaia, but it wouldn't surprise me. Miscarriages were considered taboo in those days, and women would avoid talking about them, pretend they hadn't happened.'

'Do you remember the cradle identical to Ibai's in Juanita's attic? That little girl existed, Auntie. She either died at birth or was miscarried.'

'Amaia, I don't know where you got this from—'

'I have irrefutable proof, Auntie, I can't explain, because it falls into the category of things I'm not allowed to discuss, but I know she existed, that she was born at the same time as me, that she was my identical twin, and that something happened to her.'

Her aunt looked doubtful.

'I don't know, Amaia. I'm sure that, if you'd had a sister, even one that was stillborn, I would have known about it, your grandmother would have known – especially if she died at birth, because there'd have to be a death certificate or a funeral.'

'That's the first thing I checked. There isn't one.'

'Well, you were born in your parents' house, as were your sisters. That was the norm in those days; hardly any women gave birth in hospital. The village doctor assisted at the births. You must remember him, Dr Manuel Hidalgo, he's dead now. His sister used to help him. She was a nurse, quite a bit younger. As far as I know, she still lives in the valley. I saw her a couple of months ago in the church, celebrating the anniversary of the choir. She had a good singing voice when she was young.'

'Do you remember her name?'

'Yes, Fina. Fina Hidalgo.'

Amaia let out a sigh, and it was as if with that gesture what had been sustaining her gave way. She slumped, exhausted, into the sofa next to her aunt.

'I've always dreamt about her, Auntie, from when I was small. I still do. I thought she was me, but now I know she was my sister, the little girl I was born with. They say identical twins are like the same person, joined by a special bond that enables them to see and feel the same things. All my life I have been experiencing her pain, Auntie.'

'Oh, Amaia,' exclaimed Engrasi, clasping her frail, wrinkled hands over her mouth, then holding them out towards Amaia, who curled up and nestled her head in her aunt's lap.

'She speaks to me, Auntie, she speaks to me in dreams and tells me terrible things.'

Engrasi stroked her niece's silken locks, as she had so often done when she was a child. Soon afterwards, she realised that Amaia had fallen asleep, yet she carried on running her fingers through her hair, feeling the tiny dent in her head and the outline of the hidden scar, which she could have found blindfolded.

'What have they done to you? What have they done to you, my child?'

Grief and rage choked her voice once again, as her hands trembled and her eyes misted a little more.

23

23 June 1980

A storm was raging over Elizondo. Lit by a candle, Juan knelt and prayed on the bathroom floor. He realised this wasn't the most suitable place to address God from, but he was an old-fashioned man and felt ashamed lest anyone should see him in that state. Humiliated, terrified, his eyes red from crying.

About nine o'clock that evening Rosario had asked him to take the two girls over to his mother's house. They had marvelled at the bonfires the older boys had started lighting in the streets for the Saint John's celebrations. She had called Dr Hidalgo herself. Three hours had gone by since then. They had only come out of the room to ask for candles when the light had faded. That was an hour ago. Juan could no longer endure the ominous silence that had descended over the house after his wife's dreadful screams. Exiled to the bathroom, he had finally given way, his fingers intertwined as he prayed to God with all his heart that everything would be all right. Rosario had been behaving very oddly, refusing to go to the hospital, despite Dr Hidalgo's insistence, or to be given an ultrasound, even though she was carrying twins. She had decided to give birth at home, as with her other pregnancies, and had forbidden her husband to tell his family that she was expecting a double birth.

He heard muttering on the far side of the door, then Dr Hidalgo's voice accompanied by gentle knocking.

'Juan, are you in there?'

He rose swiftly, glimpsed his bloodshot eyes in the mirror, his face distorted in the shadows cast by the candle flame.

'Yes, I'm coming,' he said, turning on the tap and splashing his face with water. He emerged still holding the towel. 'Is Rosario all right?'

'Yes, don't worry, she's fine and so are the babies. Two strong, healthy little girls, Juan. Congratulations,' he said, thrusting out a hand that reeked of disinfectant.

Juan seized it in his, smiling.

'Can I see them?'

'Wait a while, my sister is washing her and getting her ready. You can go through presently.'

'Two more daughters, it seems I only know how to make girls.' Juan was grinning from ear to ear. 'Let me offer you a drink,' he proposed.

Dr Hidalgo smiled.

'Just one, I have to attend two other women who are about to give birth. I'm hoping they don't decide to go into labour tonight; the moon may move the tides, but the storm moves the river . . .'

Juan fetched two glasses and poured a shot of whisky into each.

When Fina Hidalgo poked her head round the living room door, Juan made to put down his glass.

'There's no hurry, finish your drink and give her a few minutes. She isn't going anywhere, she's exhausted.'

But Juan drained his glass and hurried towards the corridor.

'Wait,' she said, barring his way. 'I said she isn't ready yet, she wanted to put on a fresh nightdress, give her a few minutes.'

But Juan didn't want to wait. What was this old maid

talking about? He'd seen his wife naked hundreds of times; how did Fina Hidalgo imagine she had got pregnant in the first place?

He brushed past her, but she grabbed his arm, detaining him.

'Give her a few minutes,' she implored.

Juan's smile vanished, as Dr Hidalgo approached.

'What's got into you, Fina? Let the man go to his wife.'

A warm, pungent smell of blood and sweat mixed with the sharp aroma of disinfectant pervaded the bedroom. Rosario was standing, in a clean nightdress, leaning over the twins. Juan smiled uneasily as he glimpsed the expression on his wife's face when she saw him. She was holding one of the tiny silk cushions that usually adorned her bed and pressing it over one of the babies' faces.

'For God's sake, Rosario! What are you doing?' he cried, pushing her sharply away from the cradle and knocking her over.

Rosario was a strong woman, but weakened after being in labour. She lay powerless on the bed, staring at him solemnly, without making a sound or uttering a word.

No sooner had Juan removed the cushion from his daughter's face than the child started to sob.

'Oh, my God, oh, my God!' he wailed in despair.

Dr Hidalgo took the baby from him, examined her nose, put his fingers into her mouth to make sure nothing was blocking her throat. The baby was screaming her lungs out, screwing her face up angrily.

'She's all right, Juan, she's all right, the baby is all right.'

But Juan seemed not to hear him. He was staring at his daughter, shaking his head. Dr Hidalgo cupped Juan's face, forcing him to look him in the eye.

'She's all right, Juan – listen to her cry, she's all right, there's nothing wrong with her. When a newborn cries like that, it means everything is fine.'

330

Finally, Juan seemed to hear him. His face relaxed an instant, but then, wriggling free of the doctor, he turned towards the second cradle. The other little girl wasn't crying. She lay inert, fists half-clenched either side of her head, eyes closed. Juan reached out his hand towards her, but even before he touched her he knew she was dead.

24

With the intense cold that morning came a thick, low-lying fog, heavy with moisture. The bright sunlight that had been missing the previous few days seemed to illuminate it from inside, making it glitter, as if the fog contained tiny splinters of glass. Amaia drove slowly along the motorway, guided by the white line she could barely glimpse through her side window. Her eyes smarted from the strain, making her angry as well as frustrated. She had woken in the early hours from a dream plagued with voices; people speaking an incomprehensible dialogue, which reached her from the darkness like a radio badly tuned into a broadcast from the netherworld. Messages and words merged with muffled entreaties, cries and demands. When she awoke she was unable to shake off a feeling of hopelessness and confusion. She had come to on the sofa where she had fallen asleep. Her aunt had drawn a blanket over her, and placed a cushion under her head. She had dragged herself upstairs to their room, where Ibai was splayed out on the bed, leaving James on the edge of the mattress.

'You sleep like your father,' she had whispered, lying down beside the boy for a few minutes.

Ibai's delightful calm when he slept grounded her, restored

her confidence, filled her with a sense that everything would be all right. Utterly still, he slept with the peace of the just, trustingly, arms outstretched like windmills' sails, his lips slightly parted, so still that several times she had to draw near to hear him breathe. As she'd leaned in to inhale the sweet fragrance of his skin, the child had awoken, as though answering her call. The perfect smile that appeared on her son's face was instantly infectious, but the magic didn't last, the baby started clamouring to be fed, groping with tiny fists at her breasts that could no longer suckle him. She had passed him to James, who had taken him downstairs while she berated herself once more for being a lousy mother.

She entered the meeting room and saw that Jonan hadn't arrived yet. Switching on her computer, she found two emails flagged for her attention. The now habitual message from Dr Franz, and one from the Golden Comb forwarded by Jonan. She opened it.

'The lady awaits your offering.'

'Well, the lady can go on waiting,' she said, pressing delete.

Dr Franz's email appeared to be an extended version of all the previous ones, except for one section that caught her interest. 'Maybe you should look into how Dr Sarasola came to know so much about your mother's case, details of her treatment, in particular her behaviour, which is subject to doctor–patient confidentiality. This seems all the more "curious" given that he has never treated her – and I know that because I have checked.'

She reread the message twice, but this time she didn't delete it. She was convinced that Tarttalo had known her mother prior to her confinement at Santa María de las Nieves. She considered the possibility that Sarasola and her mother's visitor were one and the same, but ruled it out; Dr Franz knew Sarasola too well to be duped by a pair of dark glasses and

333

a fake beard. Besides, his height and build didn't match the figure glimpsed in the images. Even so, she couldn't get the idea out of her head.

She got up and made her way to the general office. Zabalza was working, half-obscured behind his computer screen, and didn't notice her presence until she was standing right next to him.

'Good morning, Inspector.'

'Morning, chief.'

Amaia noticed that he lowered his voice when he said the word chief, so that it was inaudible.

'I have a job for you. Write down this name: Rosario Iturzaeta Belarrain. I want you to search the following hospital registers: Virgen del Camino, Comarcal de Irún, Clínica Santa María de las Nieves and Hospital Universitario. I need a list of all the people who treated her in those hospitals, or interacted with her, or visited her in the casualty department.'

Zabalza finished taking notes and looked up. 'That's a lot of information.'

'I know. Once you have compiled it, I want you to cross-check the lists, and tell me if anyone's name appears more than once.'

'That'll take days,' he protested.

'Then you'd better get started straight away.'

She turned on her heels and left the office, grinning to herself as she felt Zabalza's eyes burning a hole in her back.

'Ah, one more thing,' she said, turning suddenly, stifling a laugh as Zabalza lowered his gaze like a naughty schoolboy. 'I need you to find an address for a Fina Hidalgo. I'm not sure whether that's short for Rufina or Josefina; all I know is that she lives in the valley. Look in the town hall register. It's urgent.'

He nodded without looking up.

'Did you get all that?' she asked mockingly.

334

'Yes,' he muttered.

'I beg your pardon?'

'Yes, I got it, chief.'

She smiled noticing once more how the word stuck in his craw.

On her way out, she bumped into Jonan, who was chatting to Iriarte in the corridor.

Fina Hidalgo lived in a fine stone house in the centre of Irurita, the second largest town in Baztán. It had two floors, one of which featured a bay window, much in fashion at the close of the eighteenth century. But what most distinguished it was the astonishing garden. A weeping willow stood on either side of a red slate pathway bordered with primroses and enormous, perfectly trimmed lavender bushes. What caught the eye was the riot of colours, from pale green to darkest crimson, highlighted by the red cyclamens adorning the windows. Millions of tiny water droplets beaded the inside of a spacious conservatory adjoining the house. A woman greeted her from the doorway.

'Hello, come this way, I'm sure you won't want to miss this,' she said, walking back inside the conservatory.

Despite the abundance of plants and the overpowering humidity, the place was pleasant, and an aroma of menthol permeated the air, which was warmer than outside.

'One is a slave to one's habits,' the woman said, leaning over to pluck some new shoots from a few of the shrubs. She did so using a fingernail, which looked suitably dirty and stained green with the chlorophyll oozing from the plant. Then she tossed the shoots into an empty flowerpot.

Amaia observed her. She was dressed in wellies with a paisley pattern, jodhpurs, and a pink blouse. Her hair was a faded red colour, possibly natural; she wore it in a ponytail fastened with a slide. When at last the woman raised her eyes to speak, Amaia noticed a smudge of pale red on her lips. She was still very beautiful – about sixty-five, Amaia thought. Zabalza had informed her that Fina Hidalgo had recently retired, and by the look of her garden, this was her main hobby.

'I've been expecting you. Your colleague said you would come. I'll just finish doing this, then we'll go in and have some tea. If I don't remove these shoots, they suck up all the plant's energy,' she said, tutting under her breath.

The interior of the house was no less exuberant than the garden. Markedly Victorian in influence, the profusion of mostly porcelain ornaments was at once impressive and overwhelming. Fina Hidalgo served their tea in an exquisite cup and saucer, before sitting down opposite her.

'My brother died some years ago. He bought this house, but thankfully he allowed me to decorate it to my taste. The greenhouse was his idea. To begin with, I wasn't so keen, but gardening is like a drug, once you start . . .'

'I understand that you worked as his assistant.'

'The fact is I had no choice. My brother was a good man, but somewhat old-fashioned. He was twenty years my senior. I was a late and unexpected addition to the family. My parents, poor things, died soon after each other, when I was fourteen. They made my brother promise always to take care of me. As if we women weren't able to take care of ourselves! I'm sure they meant well, but he took them literally. That's why I studied nursing – note that I say nursing and not medicine – and became his assistant.'

'I see,' said Amaia.

'I carried on working with him until his retirement, when finally I was able to work outside the valley, in hospitals, with other doctors. I'm retired myself now and, surprise, surprise, I've discovered that this is where I want to be!'

Amaia smiled in empathy. 'Did you assist your brother with childbirths?'

'Of course. I also have a diploma in midwifery.'

'The birth I'm interested in took place in June 1980.'

'Oh, then it must be in the files. Come with me,' she said, getting up.

'You have medical files here?'

'Yes, my brother ran two surgeries: one in Elizondo, the other here. Most country doctors did. When he retired, he closed the surgery in Elizondo, and moved everything here.'

They entered a study that resembled a smoking room in an English gentlemen's club: a magnificent pipe collection occupied an entire wall, competing with another, adorned with stethoscopes and ear-trumpets. She recalled what San Martín had said about doctors often collecting items pertaining to their profession.

'Did you say 1980?'

'That's right.'

Fina jotted down the date on a scrap of paper. 'And the patient's name?'

'Rosario Iturzaeta.'

She looked up, surprised. 'I remember her, she had a nervous disorder, what we'd now call a neurotic.'

Without knowing quite why, Amaia felt ill at ease.

'Her medical records don't interest me. I only want information about the births. Will I need a court order?'

'Not as far as I'm concerned. My brother's dead, as is your patient, probably. You're a police officer, you won't have a problem getting one, so why waste time?' she said with a shrug.

'Thank you.'

Fina Hidalgo smiled before bending over the files. Once more Amaia found herself thinking that she must have been a great beauty.

'Here it is,' she said, holding up a thick file. 'She has a long history. Now, let's see. Yes, here we are . . . The first child was born in 1973, a natural birth with no complications, an apparently healthy girl named Flora. The second was in 1975, also a natural birth with no complications, an apparently

337

healthy girl named Rosaura. The third was in 1980, a natural birth, twins, no complications, two apparently healthy girls, no names given.'

The casual way in which the woman announced that she had a twin sister set Amaia's pulse racing. She snatched the yellowing page from her hands.

'Apparently healthy? What if one of these two girls was sick or died? Wouldn't that be in the file?'

'No. In those days, home births were quite primitive; babies weren't weighed or measured, they were given the Apgar test and a routine check-up. "Apparently healthy" is just an expression. A heart defect, for example, would have gone undetected, unless the child presented with obvious symptoms at birth.'

'What if one of these babies underwent surgery, if, say, she had a limb amputated?'

'All but the most minor surgery would have been performed in hospital.'

'What if one of them died?'

'If she died here in the valley there's sure to be a death certificate somewhere. My brother signed all the death certificates in those days, unless a patient died at a hospital in Pamplona.'

'Could you look for it, please?'

'Of course, although it might be more difficult because the babies have no names.'

Amaia reread the report, and verified that both girls' names were indeed missing. She remembered how she had struggled to choose a name for Ibai before he was born. Was this something she and her mother had in common?

Fina Hidalgo opened a different cupboard and retrieved another box of files with the relevant dates on it.

'Did she die in the same year?'

'Yes, we think she died shortly after she was born.'

The woman then plucked a page from among the others.

'Here it is: baby newly born to parents Juan Salazar and Rosario Iturzaeta. Cause of death – oh my goodness! It says here: "cot death".'

Amaia looked at her, questioningly.

'Cot death is the old name for Sudden Infant Death Syndrome, or SIDS, as it is now known,' said the woman, passing the document to Amaia. 'It probably means the child had problems.'

'You mean that she was sick?'

'Well, not sick necessarily; some conditions only become apparent a few hours after a baby is born.'

'I don't understand.'

'Certain disabilities, for instance, or birth defects. The majority of babies are born with misshapen heads. Their faces are squashed from being in the birth canal. They may even appear to have a slight squint. But it's only after a few hours that other things become noticeable.'

'OK . . .' Amaia said slowly. 'But there's no reason why those things should be fatal . . .'

The woman stood gazing at Amaia, one hand on either side of the box, her mouth curved into a smile.

'So, you're one of them,' she said.

The hairs on the back of Amaia's neck stood on end. She had an instant feeling of revulsion, comparable to discovering that a beautiful pot of geraniums is infested with maggots.

'One of what?' she asked, knowing that she wouldn't like the answer.

'One of those people who make a big fuss over things they know nothing about. Although, I'm sure you'd have no objection to aborting a foetus if it had brain damage.'

'A newborn and a foetus aren't the same thing.'

'Really? As a midwife, I've seen thousands of newborns

and hundreds of aborted foetuses. I make no distinction between them.'

'Well, there is one, based on the fact that a newborn is independent of its mother, as stated by the law.'

'Yes, the law,' she said, running a hand through her hair. 'The law is an ass. Do you know what it means for a couple with three or four children to have to cope with another baby, especially one that's disabled?'

'Wait a minute, are you telling me that you and your brother . . . killed newborns with birth defects?'

'Oh, not my brother. He was like you: a naïve, lily-livered moralist. But I have no problem admitting it – those offences have a statute of limitation. The families mostly did it themselves; I only helped occasionally when they couldn't bring themselves to destroy the fruit of their womb, or some such nonsense. But they'd deny it as much as I. Officially they were "cot deaths". Furthermore, the doctor who signed their death certificates, a man with a spotless reputation, is dead.'

'Offences?' Amaia said angrily. 'Is that what you call them? In my book, it's murder.'

'Oh, for God's sake!' exclaimed the woman, her air of exasperation quickly turning to disdain. 'You're joking, aren't you?'

Amaia studied her at length. With her pink blouse and wellies, this charming elderly lady who had spent her life growing azaleas and bringing children into the world was a remorseless sociopath. A surge of anger displaced her previous unease. She went over in her mind the legal possibilities of arresting the woman, before realising Fina Hidalgo was right: there was no way of proving any crime that fell outside the statute of limitations. With a simple denial, even the most average lawyer could get her off any charge.

'I'll take this certificate with me,' Amaia said, fixing her with a cold stare.

The woman shrugged. 'Take whatever you like. I'm always happy to cooperate with the police.'

Amaia made her own way out through the garden, welcoming the fresh air, which helped dispel the oppressiveness of the house. As she strode towards the entrance, she heard the woman's voice behind her, speaking in a mocking tone:

'Wouldn't you like to take a bunch of flowers with you, Inspector?'

Amaia wheeled around and looked straight at her, and without quite knowing why, she said:

'Go alone!'

The smile froze on the woman's face. She started to tremble as though suddenly exposed to an icy wind. She tried to muster another smile, but her mouth twisted into a snarl, revealing her teeth and gums, as all trace of her beauty vanished.

Amaia quickened her pace in time with her pounding heart. She climbed into the car and kept driving until she had left the town. Only then did she realise that she was still clutching the yellowing document in her hand, crushed against the wheel.

'Go alone,' she repeated, incredulous.

It was an invocation; a kind of charm used against witches, which she hadn't heard for almost thirty years. A vivid memory flashed into her mind of *Amatxi* Juanita telling her: 'When you know you're in the presence of a witch, cross your fingers like this' – and she would poke her thumb between her index and middle fingers – 'and if she asks you something, reply "Go alone". That is the witches' curse: they are always alone. They can never rest, not even after they are dead.' The freshness of that memory, consigned to oblivion all those years, made her smile, as did her own bewilderment at having uttered it, the fact that this awful woman had made her remember it. She pulled over to the side of the road and called the Baztán Town Hall to enquire about the gravedigger's office, then drove to the cemetery in Elizondo.

The office was a cement cubicle, invisible from a distance amid the porticoed mausoleums at the top of the cemetery, which reminded her of the ones in New Orleans. Inside stood a small desk and chair surrounded by ropes, brooms, buckets, bits of scaffolding, struts, dowels, shovels, and a small cart. In one corner was a pair of lockable metal filing cabinets, and, incongruous in these surroundings, a wall calendar showing a cat curled up in a basket. An elderly man in a boilersuit sat hunched over the desk; he straightened up when he heard her approach. Amaia noticed a radio on the desk and next to it a couple of loose batteries.

'Ah, hello, you're the one who called about the files.'
She nodded.
'If they date back to 1980 and before, then they're here,' he said, getting up and tapping the metal cabinet with his finger. 'Anything after that is being computerised, but that takes a long time . . .' He shrugged. His expression said it all.

The man fished out a ledger with the relevant date and placed it on the desk. Gingerly, he unfolded the death certificate Amaia had handed to him and, using his finger as a guide, scanned the handwritten list of names in the book.

'There's no record of it in here,' he said, raising his head.
'Could the fact that she had no name complicate matters?'
'The date and cause of death should be enough. It isn't here.'
'Could it be in a different ledger?'
'There's one for each year, but they never get filled,' he said, flicking through the empty pages at the back of the book. 'Are you sure she was buried in this cemetery?'
'Where else? The family is from Elizondo.'

342

'Yes, but if one of the grandparents was from another village, the child might have been buried there . . .'

Amaia left the office, folding the certificate. She slipped it into her inside coat pocket, then made her way towards Juanita's grave. She saw the tiny metal crosses, one bearing her grandmother's name. To the left of it was that of her grandfather, whom she had never known, and behind that, her father's, which for years she had avoided looking at. It was strange how she remembered every detail about the day her aunt called to tell her that her father had died. She had sensed it seconds before the telephone rang, and during that instant all the coldness, all the silence separating father and daughter engulfed her like a timeless sentence, for time had run out. She cast a sidelong glance at the name inscribed on the cross, and felt a stab of pain as the old question resurged: Why did he let it happen?

She took a step back, surveying the grassy surface of the ground, which showed no signs of having been disturbed. She walked to the top, passing close to the grave of Ainhoa Elizasu – the girl whose murder had brought her back to Baztán to investigate the worst case of her career. She could see that someone had left flowers there, as well as a rag doll. Further on, towards the end of the row, she found the old family vault where her great-grandparents were interred, alongside uncles and aunts who had died before she was born. The iron rings adorning it had left rusty marks and years of rain had formed an orange trail. The heavy tombstone was intact.

She turned and set off in the direction of the central pathway. As she reached the intersection, she caught sight of Flora standing motionless in front of Anne Arbizu's grave, head tilted slightly. Surprised, she called out to her:

'Flora!'

Her sister looked round; as she did so, Amaia could see she had tears in her eyes.

343

'Hello, Amaia, what are you doing here?'

'Just taking a stroll,' she fibbed, advancing until she drew level with her sister.

'Me too,' said Flora, avoiding her gaze as she stepped towards the path, Amaia following her.

The two sisters walked for several metres without speaking or looking at one another.

'Flora, do you know if there's another family vault or tomb in this or any other cemetery, besides that of our great-grandparents and the graves down here?'

'No, and if you ask me, it's shameful having the great-grandparents up there while Granny, Granddad, and *Aita* languish down here. Dotted about the cemetery like beggars.'

'I never understood why our parents didn't purchase their own vault. It's the kind of thing *Ama* would have thought about. It's strange she doesn't mind the prospect of being buried alongside *Amatxi* Juanita.'

'That's where you're wrong: she had *Aita* buried next to *Amatxi* because that's what he wanted, but *Ama* never felt she belonged here. She's made provisions to be buried in her family vault at the Polloe Cemetery in San Sebastián.'

Amaia stopped in her tracks. 'Are you sure about that?'

'Yes. I have a handwritten letter from her, dating back years, giving instructions about her funeral and burial.'

Amaia thought for a few moments, before asking:

'Flora, you were seven when I was born, what are your memories from that time?'

'What a question! How do you expect me to remember anything?'

'I don't know; you weren't that young, you must have *some* memories.'

Flora thought it over.

'I remember Ros and me feeding you. Dad used to let us. He would prepare the bottles, place you in our arms while

344

we sat on the sofa, while we took turns. I guess we thought it was fun.'

'What about *Ama*?'

'Well, she was suffering with her nerves around that time – she's had such a hard time, the poor dear.'

'Yes,' replied Amaia coldly.

Flora rounded on her suddenly.

'Look, if you want to talk, we'll talk, but if you're going to be like that, then I'm leaving,' she said, marching towards the exit.

'Flora, wait.'

'No, I won't wait.'

'I need to know what happened during that time.'

Without turning around, Flora raised her arm in a farewell gesture before disappearing through the cemetery gates.

Amaia gave a sigh. Making her way back to Anne Arbizu's grave, she picked up the small shiny object she thought she had glimpsed. A walnut. Amaia knew that her sister had been holding it in her hand moments before she had called out to her. A walnut. She replaced it and left the same way as Flora had. Just then, her mobile rang. She gazed at the screen, taken aback. It was Flora.

'Mum had a friend called Elena Ochoa. She lives in the whitewashed house next to the market. I have no idea whether she'll want to talk to you; she and *Ama* haven't spoken for years, not since they fell out. She probably knows more about that time than anyone. I just hope you'll show some respect, and refrain from bad-mouthing our mother so that I won't have cause to regret making this call.'

She hung up without waiting for a reply.

'I know who you are,' said the woman when she saw Amaia. 'Your mother and I were friends, but that was many years ago. Won't you come in?' she said, standing aside to let Amaia through.

An enormous sideboard made it difficult to navigate the narrow hallway. Amaia waited for her to show the way.

'In the kitchen,' she said softly.

Amaia entered the first door on the left, then waited for Elena, who followed and invited her to sit down on a chair leaning against the wall.

'Would you like a coffee? I was about to make some.'

Amaia accepted, though she didn't really want one. Despite making every effort to appear friendly, the woman was clearly uncomfortable. Her gestures betrayed a kind of controlled nervousness that made her seem terribly volatile and fragile. She placed the coffees on a tray, carried them over to the kitchen table and sat down at one end. Some of the sugar she spooned into her cup spilled on the tablecloth.

'Oh, for heaven's sake!' she cried, somewhat overdramatically.

Amaia pretended to concentrate on her coffee, waiting for her to sit down again after she'd wiped the table.

'It's delicious,' she said.

'Yes,' Elena replied offhandedly, then raised her eyes and looked straight at her. 'You're Amaia, aren't you? The youngest.'

Amaia nodded.

'By the time you were born, your mother and I had drifted apart. It upset me because I was very fond of her.' She paused. 'I loved her; it hurt me deeply when our friendship ended. I had no women friends, and when your mother moved here we became inseparable. We did everything together. We went for walks, took care of our little girls – I have a daughter too, the same age as your eldest sister. We went out shopping, to the park, but most of all we talked. It's good to have someone to talk to.'

Amaia nodded, encouraging her to continue.

'So when we drifted apart . . . well, it made me very sad. I thought that over time she would change her mind, and . . . But of course she never did.'

She raised her cup, as if to hide her face.

'What made two such good friends fall out?'

'The only thing that can come between two women,' she said, looking at her and nodding. 'A man.'

Amaia tried to trace as far back as she could the pattern of her mother's behaviour. Had she really been so blind? Had her prejudice as a daughter prevented her from seeing that her mother was a woman with needs? Had Rosario lost her mind because of a man, because in a society as conservative and insular as that of Baztán, she didn't feel free to run away with him?'

'My mother had a lover?'

The woman's eyes opened wide with surprise.

'Oh, no, of course not. Whatever gave you that idea? No, it wasn't that sort of relationship . . .'

Amaia spread both her hands, asking for an explanation.

'The group was supposed to be about emotional and corporal expression – the kind of nonsense people were into in the seventies, you know: relaxation, the tantras, yoga, meditation. We used to meet at a farmhouse. The man who ran the courses was extremely attractive, elegantly dressed, a smooth-talker. He was a psychologist or something, I'm not sure if he had any proper credentials. It was fun to begin with. We talked about UFO sightings, abductions, astral travelling and that sort of rubbish. Then gradually we stopped talking about those subjects and the focus shifted to sorcery, magic, occult symbols, and the history of witchcraft in the valley. I wasn't very interested in that kind of thing, but your mother was fascinated. I must confess, they did have a certain appeal. She loved the secret meetings, belonging to a clandestine society . . .'

Lowering her gaze, she fell silent. Amaia waited until it became clear Elena's mind had drifted far away.

'Elena,' she said softly. The woman raised her head and smiled weakly. 'What happened? What made you leave the group?'

'The sacrifices.'

'Sacrifices?'

'Cockerels, cats, lambs . . .'

'They killed animals?'

'No, they sacrificed them, using different methods. They collected the blood in wooden bowls, storing it in glass bottles with some component that prevented it from clotting. The blood took on an absurd significance. But I didn't want to be part of that, it felt wrong . . . Look, I grew up on a farm, we killed chickens and rabbits, we even slaughtered pigs – but not like that. Then we met the other group. Our teacher, as we called him, told us about other groups like ours, all over Navarre; he would often visit them and stay away for days. One day he proudly announced that a group from Lesaka was coming to meet us. They were supposed to help us to complete our training so we could advance to the next level. A dozen men and women arrived; they kept going on about *the sacrifice*, as if it were something special. Because we had already sacrificed small animals – God forgive me – all this talk made me nervous, so I asked them outright. One of the men gazed at me, with a look of ecstasy. "A cat or a lamb is *a* sacrifice, but *the sacrifice* has to be human," he said. I'm no scaredy-cat. I'd heard my grandparents tell stories about witches who sacrificed children and ate their flesh, but I thought those were old wives' tales. Then, a few weeks later, our teacher arrived with a big smile on his face and told us that the group from Lesaka had carried out *the sacrifice*. I thought he was just saying that to build up his mystique; I mean, I didn't really believe it. Even so, I scoured the newspapers for stories of murdered or missing children. I found nothing, but I felt uneasy. I spoke to your mother about it, said I thought we should leave the group, but she flew into a rage. She said I didn't understand the importance of what we were doing, the powers we were tapping into. Well, it was then that I realised they had brainwashed her. She accused me of being a traitor, and we fell out. I never met with the group again, but for months afterwards I received reminders from them.'

'Reminders?'

'Things other people wouldn't have noticed, but I knew perfectly well what they were.'

'What kind of things?'

'Things . . . Drops of blood outside my house, a box containing herbs entwined with animal fur. One day my daughter came home carrying some walnuts; she said a woman in the street had given them to her.'

'Walnuts? What do they signify?' asked Amaia, recalling the one Flora had placed on Anne Arbizu's grave.

'The walnut is a symbol of the witch's power. The witch concentrates her power inside its tiny brain. If a child is given one and eats it, that child will fall seriously ill.'

Amaia noticed that the woman was wringing her hands in her lap, suddenly agitated.

'Why do you suppose they sent you these "reminders"?'

'To remind me not to talk about the group.'

'Did my mother go on attending those meetings?'

'I'm sure she did, although of course I didn't see her there myself. But the fact that she never spoke to me again is proof enough.'

'Could you give me a list of all the people who took part?'

'No,' she said calmly. 'I won't do that.'

'Do you know if the group still exists?'

'No.'

'Can you give me the address of the place where they met?'

'You haven't been listening. If I do that, something terrible will happen to my family.'

Studying Elena's face, Amaia came to the conclusion that she truly believed this.

'All right, Elena, don't worry. You've been a great help,' she said, rising to her feet and instantly sensing the woman's relief. 'Just one more thing . . .'

The woman stiffened again as she waited to hear the question.

'Did your group ever contemplate carrying out a human sacrifice?'

The woman crossed herself.

'Please, leave,' she said, literally propelling Amaia down the corridor. 'Leave.' She opened the door, all but pushing her out of the house.

25

It was nearly lunchtime. She drove back slowly to her aunt's house, grateful for the timid rays of sun filtering through the clouds, creating a fug inside the car.

'Amaia's back.' She heard her sister's voice as she walked through the door.

She sat on the stairs to take off her boots and went in stockinged feet to greet James. He was standing in the centre of the living room holding Ibai over one shoulder and rocking him, as if they were dancing. Amaia walked over and kissed the sleeping child.

'You're a great dancer, James, you've managed to bore your son to sleep!'

He laughed. 'That's because this is a slow dance. Just wait until you see us do the salsa, samba, or even tango.'

Engrasi emerged from the kitchen carrying a loaf of bread. She nodded. 'I can vouch for that, you've got a couple of great dancers here.'

Suddenly remembering something, Amaia followed her aunt back into the kitchen.

'Auntie, you know the guy who tends the kitchen garden at *Juanitaenea* – Esteban? You told me you were going to talk to him about staying on to look after it.'

351

'I did. He was relieved.'

'Well, when he saw me the other day, he hid behind the bushes and gave me dirty looks. It was the day I came home with that fever, so I forgot to mention it. But, to be honest, he doesn't seem that friendly.'

'I'm afraid I can't do anything about that, my child. He's a surly fellow, prickly. He wasn't like that before, but life hasn't been kind to him. His wife suffered from terrible depression and barely left the house. He came home from work one day and found her dead. It seems she killed herself in front of their son, who was ten or eleven at the time. Apparently the boy was very close to his mother, and he took it badly. Esteban sent him to a college – in Switzerland, I believe. He sacrificed a lot to give him a good education, but once the boy had left he never came back. To begin with, Esteban talked about him all the time, about how gifted he was, how he had gone to the States, how well he was doing. Then gradually he stopped mentioning him. He hardly speaks at all now, except to tell me how the garden is doing. And even avoids that if he can. I think he must suffer from depression too, like a lot of people in these parts.'

James put Ibai in his cradle and they sat down to eat.

'It's wonderful, all of us eating together,' said Engrasi as they sat down.

Amaia frowned. 'You know what my job is like . . . Actually, I have to go to San Sebastián this afternoon.'

James didn't try to conceal his disappointment. 'Will you stay the night there?'

'Not if I find what I'm looking for.'

He said nothing, but remained subdued throughout the rest of the meal.

'San Sebastián . . .' Engrasi repeated thoughtfully.

'I'll be back as soon as I can.'

'My exhibition at the Guggenheim is in a few days' time. I hope you can make that.'

'Let's not get ahead of ourselves,' she retorted.

'Is that judge going with you this time too?' James asked, looking straight at her.

Engrasi and Ros both stopped eating and glanced up at her.

'No, James, he isn't, but maybe that's not such a bad idea. I'm going there to look for a baby's body in a cemetery. I'll doubtless need an exhumation order, so a judge might come in handy,' she said sarcastically.

He lowered his eyes, remorsefully, while she felt her anger rise, fully aware it was a defence against his – possibly justified? – suspicions. Her mobile buzzed on the table with an unpleasant sound like a dying insect. She answered, still glaring at James.

'Salazar,' she said abruptly.

If Iriarte sensed her irritation, he didn't let it show.

'Chief, we've had a report of shots being fired in a private house, a bungalow near Giltxaurdi.'

'Any fatalities or casualties?'

'No, a woman claims she shot at an intruder.'

Amaia was on the verge of telling him they could deal with it themselves, when he added:

'Jonan thinks you ought to come. It's a rather unusual case of domestic violence.'

In the garden surrounding the bungalow someone had pruned all the shrubs and plants to ground level, giving it the desolate air of a battleground. Amaia walked through the wire fence, then stood gazing at the patio and the paved pathway, where she could see several drops of blood.

'They aren't keen gardeners,' quipped Iriarte.

'A clear line of sight, nowhere for a prowler to lurk. Extreme, but effective,' added Jonan.

A woman with blonde hair and a purposeful manner opened the door to them.

'This way,' she said, steering them into the kitchen.

'My name is Ana Otaño, I'm the sister of the woman who fired the shots, Nuría. But before you speak to her, there are a few things I think you need to know.'

'Good, go ahead,' said Amaia, signalling to Jonan, who left the kitchen and headed for the living room.

'This is our parents' house. *Ama* died and *Aita* is in a care home. My sister has lived here since she moved back home. The guy she shot at is Antonio Garrido, her estranged husband, who has a restraining order on him. We disliked him from the start, but she seemed smitten with him. A few months after they married, he persuaded her to move to Murcia on the pretext of work. She started calling less and less, and when we did speak she always sounded strange.

'Gradually he succeeded in making her cut all ties with the family. After that, we heard nothing from her for two years. All that time he had been keeping her imprisoned in his house, chained up like an animal, until one day she managed to escape and get help. She weighed forty kilos and walked with a limp because he had broken her leg and refused to take her to hospital. Her skin was shrivelled, her hair was matted and great clumps of it had been torn out. She spent four months in hospital; afterwards, I brought her here. She suffers from agoraphobia and won't go any further than the garden fence, but she's getting better. The sparkle has returned to her eyes, her hair is starting to grow back – soft as a baby's beneath that woolly hat she wears all the time. Then, a month ago, that pig was released on parole, and the first thing he did was call to tell her he was coming for her.'

She paused and sighed.

'I kept telephoning, but she wouldn't pick up, so I came round and banged on the door. Eventually I got in through a window and went round the house calling out her name, but she didn't reply. I knew she couldn't have gone out; I had difficulty even getting her to go to the doctor. I searched the house from top to bottom – and do you know where I found

354

her? Curled up inside the dryer. I still can't believe she was in there, whimpering, trying to stifle her sobs. When she saw me, she started screaming like a rat in a trap and she wet herself. Finally, I persuaded her to come out, then I bathed her, dressed her and coaxed her into the car. We both knew the day would arrive when that bastard would come for her, but I also knew that I could do nothing more for my sister. I vowed to myself that, if that guy ever crossed my path, one of us would end up in prison.

'The day I found her in the dryer, I realised that if I didn't do something, before long I would be burying my sister. All the way in the car she kept screaming: "He's going to kill me! There's nothing anyone can do, he's going to kill me!" And so I took her to the funeral parlour and I told her: "Since you've already decided you're going to die, at least pick out a coffin you like." As she stood staring at the caskets she stopped crying and said: "I don't want to die." I bundled her back in the car and drove her to the forest, where I made her do target practice until we'd used up all the ammunition. She was crying and shaking so much she would have missed a mattress at two paces. And so we returned the next day, and every day the day after that. We spent a whole month shooting up all my recycled rubbish – plastic, tin, glass containers . . . As the days went by and Nuría got better at it her attitude changed. For the first time in her life, she seemed strong – and I mean that literally, because Nuría has always been like a doll; a nervous, fragile doll that might break at any moment. I insisted that she come and live with me, but she wanted to stay here; I decided that in the end what mattered was that she felt empowered.' She heaved a sigh. 'And now, if you want, you can talk to Nuría.'

A trail of blood guided them to the living room. The door had been sprayed with blood. An officer from Forensics was stooping over some bloody remains on the floor.

Jonan walked over to Amaia, speaking in whispers so that

355

the woman sitting by the window couldn't hear. Then he slipped into her hand a blurred photocopy of the criminal record of a thirty-five-year-old man. The woman was skeletal and wore a baggy tracksuit that accentuated her painful thinness. A few blonde curls escaped from beneath her woollen hat. She had an air of fragility belied by her serene smile and her wistful expression as she watched the police process the living room.

'It seems the intruder broke in through the bedroom window, calling out her name as he made his way to the living room. She was waiting for him exactly where she is now. When he entered she pulled the trigger, hitting his right ear. That's a piece of it on the floor, and you can see the impact stain on the door. The spent cartridge is under the sofa. He bled like a pig, there's a trail from here to the fence outside. He must have a car outside.'

Amaia and Iriarte glanced around them.

'We'll notify hospitals, pharmacies and first-aid centres: the guy will have to get treated somewhere.'

'Not to mention he must be deaf in one ear.'

'What's that smell?' said Amaia, screwing up her nose.

'Faeces, chief,' replied Jonan, grinning. 'The guy shat himself – diarrhoea, to be precise. He left a trail all the way out.'

'Did you hear that, Nuría?' said Ana, sitting down beside her sister. 'The bastard was so terrified he shat himself!'

'Hello, Nuría,' said Amaia, crouching down in front of her. 'Are you feeling OK? Do you think you could answer a few questions?'

'Yes,' she replied calmly.

'Could you tell us in your own words what happened?'

'I was in here reading,' she said, pointing at the book on the table, 'when I heard a noise in the bedroom. I knew it was him.'

'How did you know?'

'Who else would smash a window to get into the house?

Ana knows about the broken latch in the bathroom. Besides, he rang me a few days ago to tell me he was coming, and he called my name after he broke in.'

'What did he say?'

'He said: "I'm here, Nuría, there's no use hiding."'

'And what did you do?'

'I tried using the phone, but it didn't work.'

Iriarte picked up the receiver, which was sitting on top of the television.

'The line's dead. He must have cut it from outside.'

'What happened next?' asked Amaia.

'I grabbed the shotgun and waited.'

'The shotgun was in here?'

'I keep it by me always. I even sleep with it.'

'Go on.'

'He appeared in the doorway and stood looking at me. He said something about sending me to the hospital and started to laugh. Then I asked him to leave. "Get out," I said, "or I'll shoot." He kept laughing as he came into the room . . . so I shot him.'

'He said he would send you to the hospital?'

'Yes, something like that.'

'How many shots did you fire?'

'One.'

'Good. Do you think you might be able to come down to the station to make a statement?'

Her sister made as if to protest, but Nuría broke in:

'Yes, I'll go.'

'You needn't come today. If you aren't feeling well, it can wait until tomorrow.'

'I feel fine.'

'Are you staying here, or will you go to your sister's house?'

'I'm staying here – this is my home.'

'We'll put a patrol car outside, but you'd be better off staying with your sister.'

'Don't worry about me. Now he knows I'm not afraid of him, he won't be back.'

Amaia looked at Iriarte and nodded.

'All right, we're done here,' she said, standing up and making her way to the front door.

'Inspector,' Nuría called her back. 'Is it true he shat himself?'

'It would seem so,' said Amaia, glancing at the stains.

The woman sat erect, holding her head up, lips parted in an expression of childlike wonder, as if she'd received a surprise birthday present.

'One last thing, Nuría. Does Antonio have any distinguishing features?'

'Oh, yes,' she said, lifting her hand, 'the tops of his index, middle and fourth fingers are missing on his right hand. He had an accident with a paper-cutter years ago at work.'

They were at the door when Nuría caught up with them.

'"I'm taking you to the hospital" – those were his exact words, I remember now. "I'm taking you to the hospital."'

'Are you sure he said "take", not "send"?'

'Yes, that's what he said, I'm positive.'

26

23 June 1980

He could not stop weeping, even though the violent sobs and breathless gasps had long since given way to a calm that radiated from the pit of his stomach, like a sinister abyss where his initial despair and horror had installed themselves.

Sitting in his living room at home – in what had been his and his wife's home up until that day – he cradled his newborn baby girl in his arms and wept inconsolably, as if someone had opened a tap releasing all the pent-up tears he never knew he had.

Pale and distraught, Dr Manuel Hidalgo sat opposite his friend, looking alternately at the baby in his arms and the tears rolling down Juan's cheeks on to the blanket the infant was wrapped in.

'What happened in there?' Juan managed to say.

'I'm to blame, Juan. I told you that Rosario was depressed, that she was unwell, but I'm her doctor, I should have insisted she give birth at the hospital.'

'What now, Manuel? What will you do now?'

'I don't know,' said the doctor, stunned.

His sister, who had remained standing by the wall, chimed in. 'The truth is, we don't really know what happened.'

Juan sat up with a jolt.

'How can you say that, Fina? You both saw what Rosario was doing when we went into the room.'

'What *you* think she was doing . . . All I saw was a woman who could have been trying to place a pillow under her baby's head.'

'Fina, the pillow was on her face, not under her head.'

'Maybe she dropped it when you pushed her.'

Juan shook his head, but it was Manuel who replied.

'Fina, what are you driving at?'

'I've examined the body. There are no signs of violence. Yes, it appears she's been asphyxiated, but it could also be a cot death. They are very common among newborns, and the majority occur within the first few hours.'

'Fina, this is no cot death,' retorted her brother.

'So, what do you want to do?' she asked, raising her voice. 'Call the police? Cause a big scandal that will be in all the newspapers? Send a sick woman, a good mother, to jail because you, my brother, made the mistake of not treating her symptoms? Is that what you'll tell the police? That you could have avoided this if you'd treated her? Have you thought about what this will do to your family and to your career?'

Dr Hidalgo closed his eyes and appeared to sink even further into the sofa.

'Is this true?' asked Juan. 'Would Rosario be normal if she took tablets?'

'I don't know, Juan, but they couldn't make her any worse.'

Juan had stopped crying.

'What are you going to do?' he asked.

The doctor stood up and went out into the kitchen. Fina had been terribly efficient. The tiny shrouded body lay on the kitchen table, a cloth over its face. Walking up to it, he thought how it reminded him of the way his mother used to let the bread rest while the yeast did its work.

He removed the cloth and examined the tiny, lifeless face.

It showed the purplish discolouring associated with asphyxia, but not enough to hide the redness on the tiny nose, the unmistakable sign of applied pressure.

He opened his case and threw a small, lined register bearing the title 'Death Certificates' on to the table. Turning the first page, he wrote in his neat script 'Cot Death', and signed it. He gazed once more at the dead baby girl's face, then wheeled round just in time to throw up in the sink.

27

'Good morning,' she said, addressing the receptionist. 'I'd like to speak to Dr Sarasola. Could you tell him I'm here, please?'

The man's face registered a look of mild surprise before he fully regained his composure.

'I'm sorry. I don't know anyone of that name working at our centre.'

Amaia made no attempt to conceal her astonishment.

'What do you mean? Dr Sarasola. Father Sarasola, in the psychiatry department.'

The receptionist shook his head.

Amaia gave Jonan a puzzled look before showing the man her badge. Then she said:

'Tell him Detective Inspector Salazar is here.'

The man picked up the phone and dialled a number, trying not to show how intimidated he was by her badge. He gave her a friendly smile as he hung up.

'Please forgive me, we have a strict privacy rule here to protect prominent figures like Father Sarasola. If everyone knew he was here, this reception would be full of people wanting to speak with him. He'll see you at once. Take the lift to the fourth floor; someone will be waiting for you there. And once again, I'm sorry for the inconvenience.'

Amaia started towards the lifts without replying. When the doors opened on the fourth floor, a young nun was waiting to guide them down the passageway to an office next to the nurses' station. She asked them to take a seat before quietly leaving the room.

'How nice to see you again, Inspector. You haven't come alone, so I assume this is a police rather than a medical matter,' he said, extending his hand to Deputy Inspector Etxaide.

'A bit of both, but let's start with the police part.'

Sarasola sat down and folded his hands.

'As I'm sure you know, there's been another desecration at the church in Arizkun. Someone created a diversion by starting a fire at an old medieval mansion nearby, perpetrating the act while the patrol car was investigating that. This time they caused damage to the façade of the building, once again leaving bones next to the altar. Prior to this, we interviewed a teenager from Arizkun who harbours resentment towards the Church, deriving from his unhealthy obsession with the *agotes* and their history. He is exceptionally bright, and still grieving for his deceased mother, which most likely explains why he has been led astray. Although we think he may be guilty of aiding and abetting, he certainly isn't the perpetrator. We haven't solved the case yet, but I believe we are close to apprehending the culprit. When we do it will be largely thanks to the young boy's cooperation.'

'I see . . .' mused Sarasola, 'a paragon of virtue. I imagine that you've arrested the little angel. The diocese will press charges against him.'

'I just told you, he has been assisting us with—'

'But isn't he the culprit?'

Amaia studied Sarasola, wondering whether the Church wanted the real culprit or simply a scapegoat.

'No, he's just a mixed-up teenager who has been manipulated by a criminal. We see no reason to press charges against him.'

Sarasola looked at her sharply, as though about to protest, but finally relented, his lips curving in a smile.

'Very well. If you disagree, we'll await developments.'

She recognised a concession, the granting of something in exchange for something else. She waited.

'And now, I imagine, comes the medical part.'

Amaia smiled: so that was it.

'Wouldn't you prefer to speak in private?' said Sarasola. Then, glancing at Jonan: 'Forgive me, but these are sensitive matters . . .'

'He can stay,' said Amaia.

'I'd prefer it if he didn't,' said Sarasola abruptly.

'I'll wait for you at the nurses' station,' Jonan said, leaving the room.

Sarasola waited until the door was closed before he spoke.

'We're very discreet regarding medical information. Bear in mind that you're her daughter, but for everyone else Rosario's treatment is subject to patient doctor–patient privilege.'

'The other day at Santa María de las Nieves, you said you were familiar with Rosario's case, yet she has never been your patient. How did you first meet her and become interested in her?'

'As I explained, we're always on the lookout for psychiatric patients who present specific characteristics. Your mother's case falls into that category.'

'The nuance of evil?'

'The nuance of evil. Cases presented at psychiatrists' congresses enable us to make advances. The patient's name is never divulged, only their age and aspects of their personal and family histories that are relevant to their illness.'

'Is that how you became acquainted with Rosario's illness?'

'Yes, as far as I can recall, I first heard about her case at a congress. It might even have been Dr Franz who first mentioned her.'

'Dr Franz from Santa María de las Nieves?'

'Don't worry, I assure you there's nothing unusual about

364

that. As I say, it's common practice and, alongside the papers we publish in specialised science journals, it enables us to exchange viewpoints and share treatment methods. It's a key part of our profession. Would you care to see her?'

Amaia gave a start. 'What?'

'Would you like to see your mother? She's perfectly calm. In fact she looks very well.'

'No,' Amaia replied.

'She won't be able to see you; she's under observation behind a two-way mirror, like the ones you use at police stations. I think that seeing her will give you an idea of her present state, it will help you to stop speculating.'

Dr Sarasola was already on his feet and making for the door. Amaia followed him, increasingly bewildered. She had no wish to see her mother, yet Sarasola was right: she needed to know to what extent Dr Franz's claims about her improvement were true, to what extent she was susceptible to being manipulated.

The room where Rosario was confined was indeed identical to the one next to the interview room at the police station. Amaia followed Sarasola as he entered and greeted the technician who was recording everything that went on in the observation room. Rosario sat with her back to them, facing the curtainless windows that let in a dazzling light, silhouetting her outline. Amaia walked in behind the doctor and approached the glass warily.

It was as if she had shouted Rosario's name, or a bolt of lightning had shot out of her and touched her mother. Like a shark sensing blood, Rosario turned slowly towards the mirror, a hideous grin spreading across her face, which Amaia glimpsed only fleetingly, for she instinctively leapt to one side, flattening herself against the wall.

'She can see me,' she said, trembling.

'No, she can't. She can neither see nor hear you; this room is completely cut off.'

'She can see me,' Amaia repeated. 'Draw the curtain.'

Sarasola observed her with a clinical interest.

'I said, draw the curtain,' she repeated, pulling out her weapon.

Sarasola walked over to the window and pressed a button, which lowered an electric blind.

Only when she heard it click did Amaia step far enough away from the wall to make sure the window was completely hidden. Then she holstered her weapon and strode out of the room. Sarasola followed, but not before turning to the technician and saying:

'Did you get all that?'

Amaia marched furiously down the hallway, Sarasola hot on her heels.

'You knew that was going to happen.'

'I didn't know what would happen,' he replied.

'But you knew something would happen, you knew she'd respond,' she said, turning her head to look at him.

This time he didn't reply.

'It was a set-up, you should have consulted me.'

'Wait, please. What just happened is terribly important, we need to discuss it.'

'Well, I'm sorry, Dr Sarasola,' she said, without slowing down, 'I'm leaving now, so it'll have to wait.'

As they reached the nurses' station, a gaggle of half a dozen doctors in white coats came towards them. They halted deferentially when they saw the priest. Gesturing towards them, Sarasola said to Amaia:

'What a lucky coincidence! You see, Inspector, this is the medical team who are looking after your mother. In fact, it is Dr Berasategui who—'

'Another time,' Amaia cut him off.

She glanced at the smiling doctors, muttering under her breath, 'If it's all the same to you,' as she brushed past, heading for the lifts.

366

Jonan got into the lift with her; she waited for the doors to close before speaking.

'Damn it, Jonan, I think bringing my mother here was a mistake. I was never entirely convinced, but now I'm having serious doubts – and it's not because I don't think she'll receive the right treatment. There's something else.'

'Sarasola?'

'I suppose. He has a certain something, but he's so arrogant . . . Then again, in some ways I know he's right.'

'When I was a boy, rumours went round that they performed exorcisms in the psychiatric department at the Opus Dei hospital. It was said that whenever a suspected case of possession was detected anywhere in the world, the Church paid to have the patient transferred here for "treatment".' Jonan wasn't smiling as he said this.

Amaia replied, equally serious:

'When Sarasola suggested transferring her here, I asked him, half in jest, whether they planned to exorcise her.' She remained thoughtful.

Jonan paused to give her time, before asking:

'And what did he say?'

'That in my mother's case, it wouldn't be necessary. He wasn't joking.'

28

The hallway smelled of furniture wax and metal polish used to clean the numerous brass trimmings from the front door to the old-fashioned lift complete with wood panelling, uphol-stered seat and ivory buttons, which they admired as they took the stairs.

The apartment had a main door as well as a tradesmen's entrance. After knocking on both, a man of about seventy poked his head through the latter, smiling.

'Are you Amaia?'

She nodded. Before she had time to say anything, the man flung his arms around her, kissing her on both cheeks.

'I'm your Uncle Ignacio, so pleased to meet you.'

The man led them down a dark hallway, which seemed all the more gloomy contrasted with the luminous room he ushered them into. Two women and another man were waiting for them.

'Amaia, this is your Aunt Angela, and this is your Aunt Miren and her husband Samuel.'

The two women stood up, rather laboriously to embrace her.

'Amaia, dear, we were delighted when you called! It's dreadful that we've never met.'

Clasping one hand each, they steered Amaia over to the sofa, then sat down either side of her.

'So you're a police officer?'

'With the Navarre police,' she replied.

'Goodness! And an inspector, no less!'

Overwhelmed, Amaia glanced at Jonan, who had sat down opposite her and was beaming contentedly. She felt strange. With the exception of *Amatxi* Juanita and Aunt Engrasi, none of her relatives had exhibited this kind of family pride in her, yet these people had only met her ten minutes ago and hadn't even known she existed until she made the call a few hours ago. Her aunts and uncle from San Sebastián, to whom Rosario had occasionally referred when reminiscing about her childhood, had been the subject of repeated questions that were inevitably met with the curt response, 'We aren't on speaking terms; it's an adult problem.'

Ignacio and Miren were twins. Angela, who was the eldest, bore a striking resemblance to Rosario, which was all the more uncanny because of how different they were; Angela possessed the same elegance Amaia had always admired in her mother, but with none of Rosario's haughtiness. She appeared relaxed and permanently smiling, though the biggest difference was in their eyes. Angela's gaze glided over the Bay of Biscay, visible in all its splendour through the living room windows, before travelling serenely over the porcelain coffee set they were drinking from, only to settle once more on Amaia, a warm smile on her lips which had none of the tension that always overshadowed Rosario's gestures. Then suddenly her face clouded.

'How is your mother? She's not . . .'

'No, she's still alive, in a special hospital. She's . . . fragile.'

'We had no idea you existed, Amaia. Your older sisters, yes – Flora and Rosaura, is that right? But we didn't know she'd had a third child. Her calls became less frequent, and she was always very cold and brusque when we called her. Then one

369

day she simply told us to leave her alone, that she had only one family now, the one she'd made with her husband in Baztán, and she wanted nothing more to do with us.'

'Yes, relationships were never my mother's strong point.'

'And yet, when she was little,' said Angela, 'she was a ray of sunshine, always cheerful, always singing. It was only later on that she started to behave strangely.'

'Was that after she went to live in Baztán?'

'No, on the contrary. To begin with, things continued to be fine between us. She would bring your sisters here in the summer, and we went there several times.'

Ignacio chimed in: 'I think it was after the little girl died.'

'You knew about that?' Amaia sat up straight.

'In a manner of speaking . . . We knew about it when it happened. But she hadn't even told us that she was expecting. She called one day to say that she'd given birth to a stillborn baby girl.'

'Stillborn?'

'Yes.'

'Do you remember the date?'

'Well, my son had just had his First Communion in May, so it must have been the summer of 1980. Yes, 1980.'

Amaia heaved a loud sigh. 'That was the year I was born.'

Her aunts and uncle looked at her, bewildered.

'I recently discovered that I had an identical twin, who, according to the death certificate, was born healthy and died shortly afterwards of Sudden Infant Death Syndrome.'

'Oh, good Lord!' Miren shuddered. 'So that little girl . . .'

'I'm not surprised,' said Angela. 'Rosario was always a bit sparing with the truth. She would only explain things when it suited her and, even then, her explanations were often fictitious.'

'Why do you think she told you about the stillborn baby, but not about her twin sister?'

'It's obvious: she had to tell us, so that she could bury her here.'

370

Amaia felt her heart miss a beat. 'She's buried here?'

'Yes, in the family vault. We all have the right to be buried there, only as co-owners we need to inform the others each time it's opened. She knew that, otherwise I doubt she'd have told us anything. As I recall, she didn't even want us to attend the funeral. We went in the end, but only because I insisted.'

'What about my father?'

'She told us he had stayed at home to look after the girls, and to oversee things at the bakery. Apparently, they couldn't afford to close even for one day.'

'The funeral was a sad affair,' said Ignacio.

'No priest, no mourners, just the three of us, Rosario, the gravedigger, and that tiny casket with the cross missing. "Why is there no cross on the coffin?" I asked. And she replied: "She doesn't need one, she wasn't baptised".'

Amaia bit her lip as she listened.

'We laid a wreath; that was the only thing that marked the grave after it was sealed. I asked Rosario what the child's name was, so that I could get the stonemason to engrave it on the tombstone, but Rosario told us the baby had no name, so there's nothing on the tombstone, but she's in there. Fortunately, it hasn't been opened since – no more deaths in the family, touch wood,' she said, reaching out to touch the table.

Amaia thought this over.

'Did any of you see the body?'

'The child's body? No, the casket was sealed. Not that we wanted to: the last thing anyone wants to see is a dead baby.'

Amaia gazed at her aunts and uncle, deep in thought.

'Besides the fact that only you and my father knew about her, my twin's existence is shrouded in mystery. Inconsistencies on her birth and death certificates, as well as the recent discovery of bones belonging to a twin of mine make her disappearance even more suspicious.'

'But, we saw her being buried.'

371

'You didn't see the . . .' Amaia was going to say 'corpse', when it occurred to her that the word had connotations that were inappropriate for a stillborn baby '. . . her body,' she said.

'Oh my God, what are you insinuating?' said Angela, horrified. 'That perhaps there was no body?'

'Not a whole one, at least.'

Her aunts and uncle fell silent, exchanging worried glances. When Angela spoke again, her voice was solemn:

'What do you propose to do now?'

'See for myself.'

'Oh, but that means . . .' Angela said, clasping a hand to her mouth, as though unable to articulate something so horrible.

'Yes.' Amaia nodded. 'I wouldn't ask your permission to do this unless I thought it was the only way we can be sure.'

Miren seized her hand. 'You don't need our permission, Amaia. As a family member, you have every right to ask for the vault to be opened.'

'I'll call the cemetery,' said Ignacio, rising to his feet. He came back a few moments later. 'We'll have to wait until the cemetery closes at eight o'clock. They don't want to open the grave with people around.'

'Of course,' murmured Amaia.

'We'll go with you,' said Angela, speaking for the others, who nodded, 'But you'll understand if we don't look inside. We're a little old for this sort of distress.'

'That won't be necessary. I'm sorry to have to put you through this; you've been very kind, and you're right, it won't be pleasant—'

'That's why we don't want to look.' Her uncle laughed. 'But we'd like to accompany you.'

'Thank you,' she replied, genuinely touched.

'Chief, can we talk?' said Jonan.

She stood up and followed him into the corridor.

372

'Even if you have no trouble opening the vault, you'll need a court order to open the coffin. Your relatives won't ask any questions, and my lips are sealed, but if we find something anomalous, we'll need to explain why we opened it.'

'Jonan, I can't tell Judge Markina about this, it's too . . . I can't tell this to any judge, I still have no proof. I'm not sure of anything. My suspicions are too awful. I just want to find out whether she's in there, to see her little coffin.'

Jonan nodded; he hadn't expected her to go by the book, not the Inspector Salazar he knew. While they were talking in the corridor, Miren's husband walked past.

'You're staying to supper,' he announced.

The Polloe Cemetery sits on a hill in the Egia neighbourhood of San Sebastián. With the ring-road tunnel underneath it, the burial ground extends over fifteen acres, contains 3,500 niches and 7,500 vaults, the majority of which are huge stone and marble structures, testifying to the city's past splendour. That of Amaia's mother's family had three sections: two lower ones flanking a central raised level surmounted by an enormous cross, which took up the entire surface. Three municipal employees were waiting for them next to the tomb, smoking and chatting. Using a hoist they had erected on the vault, they placed two thick metal bars on the ground and slid the tomb-stone on to them.

Amaia's relatives remained at the foot of the tomb, stepping back a few paces after it was opened. She and Etxaide went over to take a look. All around the outside edge a line of mud and moss had formed, showing that the vault had not been opened in years. A stale odour wafted from inside, which looked dry. Piled on a metal rack on the right-hand side were two old caskets. Nothing more.

'It's too dark in there,' said Amaia. 'I'm going to need a ladder.'

One of the cemetery workers walked over to her.

'Señora, if you want to go inside, you'll need a—'

'Yes,' she said, flashing her badge at him.

He cast his eye over it and stepped back. They installed the ladder. After pulling on a pair of gloves, Amaia went down into the vault.

'Be careful,' her aunt called from the edge.

Jonan followed her. The vault was more spacious than it had appeared from outside. Over in one corner where the ceiling was lower, they saw the casket. It was exactly as her aunt had remembered: small, white, with a mark on the lid where the cross had been before it was prised off.

Amaia came to a sudden halt, unsure of her reasons for being there. Was she really about to open the coffin of her sister, whose existence she had only just discovered? Did she really want to do this?

And then the face identical to hers flashed into her mind, cloaked in suffering and eternal sorrow, those dark, heavy, endless tears. She felt a hand on her shoulder.

'Do you want me to do it, chief?' asked Jonan.

'No,' she said, turning to look at him, thinking how well he knew her. 'I'll do it, but I need your help. Let's carry it into the light.'

As they picked up one end each, they could feel the weight of something inside. As Jonan gave a loud sigh, Amaia looked at him once again, grateful for his presence, for his support.

'Pass me the crowbar,' she said to one of the gravediggers, who was peering into the vault.

Running her fingers beneath the lid of the coffin in search of the edge, she positioned the crowbar. The nails slid out with a screech of metal against wood. Easing the end of the crowbar in a little further, she prised the lid off gently. Jonan clutched it with both hands and, before removing it, glanced at Amaia. She nodded.

What appeared to be a white towel had been wrapped around a bulky mass. Amaia gazed at it for a few seconds.

Then she took hold of one corner of the towel and lifted it, revealing the tattered remains of a plastic bag and a large amount of what looked like gravel.

Jonan stared at Amaia, openmouthed. She thrust her hand inside the casket and seized a fistful of tiny stones. As she watched the powdery grit fall slowly from her hand, she knew her search would yield nothing more.

29

24 June 1980

On that bright summer's day dawn was breaking as Juan prepared a baby bottle in the kitchen. The evening before, Dr Hidalgo's sister had brought everything he needed and shown him what to do. This was his first time: Rosario had breastfed Flora and Rosaura, but the doctor had put her on some strong medication that wasn't compatible with breastfeeding. And besides, he had told Juan that it would be best if she didn't have to touch the child. So Juan had brought her cradle into the front room; from there he could hear her crying to be fed. He cradled her in his arms, smiling tenderly as he saw how vigorously she sucked on the teat. As he leaned over to kiss her brow, his eyes strayed to the other cradle, where her baby sister's body lay, a tiny motionless bundle.

Seeing Rosario emerge from the bedroom looking so beautiful, he felt even more grief-stricken. In her pinstriped suit, with her make-up on and her hair swept back, no one would have believed that less than twelve hours ago she was giving birth.

'Rosario . . . Let me go with you,' he pleaded once more. She kept her distance from him. Standing in the centre of the room, she glanced at the girl in his arms then turned towards the window.

376

'We decided, Juan. It's best if you stay here to look after the girls and tend the bakery while I go to San Sebastián to arrange the funeral. I've called my brother and sisters. They're expecting me.'

He closed his eyes, rallying his strength. 'I have no objection to you burying her there, but do you have to take her like that?'

'We've talked about this. I don't want anyone to know about this. You must promise not to say a word to anyone, even your mother. We've had a baby girl. This is her. If anyone sees me, we can say that I took her to the hospital because she had a slight cough. And when I get back tomorrow we can say that she's better.'

Rosario glanced out of the window. 'The taxi's here.'

Juan looked out. It had come from Pamplona. As usual, Rosario had thought of everything. He turned in time to see her pick up her bag, lean over the dead baby's cradle, scoop her up and wrap her expertly in an exquisite shawl, holding her as if she were alive.

'I'll be back tomorrow,' she said, holding the bundle in her arms with what seemed like tenderness.

He watched her for a few seconds, entranced. She looked no different from the day she took their other two daughters to the church to be baptised. He lowered his eyes, and, clasping his little girl to his chest, turned away for the very first time so as not to see his wife.

30

After taking her leave of her aunts and uncle, Amaia climbed into the car. She let Jonan drive.

'All is not lost, chief.'

She sighed. 'Yes, it is.'

'On the bright side, the fact that there's no body could mean she's still alive.'

'No, Jonan, she's dead.'

'You can't know that.' She remained silent. 'Maybe she's one of those stolen babies they've been reporting on in the press. Apparently there were many cases.'

'Nobody stole my mother's baby.'

'With all due respect, she could have been the result of an extra-marital affair. Or maybe they needed money; people pay a fortune for a newborn baby.'

'A newborn baby with one arm?'

'Maybe that's why they gave her up for adoption. Maybe the arm had to be removed because she had a birth defect.'

Amaia considered the idea. Would Rosario have accepted a child with a birth defect, or would she have been ashamed to have a disabled daughter? It wasn't out of the question.

'What do you suggest?' she said.

'I think we should start with what we know. She only has

one arm, so she probably wears a prosthetic limb. Social security keeps a national register of everyone with a prosthetic limb, which includes their date of birth as well as the serial numbers of the prostheses.'

'But why the need for a death certificate if they intended to give her up for adoption?'

'It could be fake, if the doctor who signed it agreed to cooperate.'

Amaia remembered the expression on Fina Hidalgo's face when she said: 'So, you're one of them.'

'Yes, I suppose so,' she conceded.

If Jonan was right, the sole aim would have been to deceive her father. 'Oh, *Aita*, how could you have been so blind?'

Night was falling rapidly as they sped along the motorway across the Leitzaran Valley. The light was fading, merging with the darkness in a final blaze of silver that seemed to float above the treetops, stretching as far as the horizon. It was as if day were resisting night in a last show of radiance and beauty, which plunged Amaia into an even deeper melancholy.

The mobile interrupted her reverie.

'Hello, Inspector,' came Dr San Martín's cheery voice.

From his tone, she knew he had good news.

'We have the results of the metal tests . . . and . . .' he said, pausing exasperatingly for effect '. . . as I suspected, the scalpel is an antique – from the seventeenth century, to be precise. They date it from the alloys used back in those times, as well as the methods of melting and forging the metals, all of which give it a unique character. But here's the real surprise.' From his voice, Amaia could tell he was grinning. 'The scalpel and the piece of metal embedded in Lucía Aguirre's bone share the same alloy and forging methods.'

Amaia straightened in her seat, intrigued.

Knowing he had her full attention, San Martín continued:

'The only explanation for this is that they were produced at the same time. We're talking about handcrafted pieces, which suggests to me a set of medical instruments specially made for a surgeon.'

'You're saying that the metal tooth and the scalpel come from the same set of instruments?'

'That's right, señora. Now I know this, I can assume that the tooth comes from a surgical saw. Their use was widespread among surgeons before the invention of antibiotics. Back then, amputation was the most common solution to a serious infection.'

'Is that what was used to amputate Lucía's arm?'

'Probably. As I say, we won't know until I make a cast, but it seems likely. After all, why else would it be embedded in the bone?'

'Could it be the same saw that was used on Johana?'

'I'd need to make a cast—'

'But it's possible.'

'Judging from the precision with which Lucía's arm bone was severed . . . Yes, I think it's possible. As I've said, the similarities were visible to the naked eye.'

She ended the call and gazed at Jonan, who was clasping the steering wheel so tightly his knuckles gleamed white.

'OK, so this proves that the *tarttalo* and your mother's visitor are one and the same person, and that he could also be our desecrator in Arizkun, given that he left your ancestors' *mairus* there for you to find. This in turn brings us closer to someone from Elizondo who knew about the graves at your grandmother's house. And the fact that the culprit also left your sister's bones establishes beyond doubt a link to the only person who could possibly know where they were . . . Remember, her bones weren't buried in the earth. In order to find them, he needed information only your mother possessed.'

Amaia blew out her cheeks, as though unable to take all this in.

'So,' she murmured after a few seconds, 'the purpose of the desecrations was merely to attract my attention – but to what? The *tarttalo*'s crimes? What is he trying to tell us? Where does my twin sister come into all this? Was she one of the *tarttalo*'s victims?' Amaia paused, then burst out laughing. 'Is the *tarttalo* my mother?'

Jonan smiled at this suggestion.

'That's impossible, chief. Some of the bones were in that cave for over ten years – wasn't she quite ill by then, or even hospitalised? Certainly the more recent ones were placed there after she was interned. How long ago was that?'

'She wouldn't have been interned ten years ago, although she was in no fit state to take part in anything like that. But she knows who this person is.'

'That's for sure,' agreed Jonan. 'Although she might not know exactly who he is, or what he's up to.'

Amaia remained thoughtful.

'Nuría's husband, the guy with the missing fingers, is an important lead,' said Jonan.

'Yes, except that he was in prison when Johana was killed,' she replied.

'And yet he's the guy that the lad from Arizkun identified as our desecrator.'

'Oh God, I feel like my head is about to explode,' she said suddenly. 'I need to think about all this. Calmly . . .'

It was dark by the time they arrived in Elizondo.

'Drop me off here,' said Amaia, as they turned into Calle Santiago. 'I could do with some fresh air.'

Jonan pulled over and stopped the car.

Amaia got out, pausing for a few seconds beside the open door while she put on her gloves and zipped up her coat. The afternoon rain had left the ground damp, but now an occasional star flickered in the clear night sky. Once the tail-lights on Jonan's car had disappeared, the street was silent and empty.

Amaia walked at a leisurely pace, contemplating the powerful silence that hung over the Baztán night, a silence that was only possible there and which seemed at once peaceful and deafening. Its message of solitude and desolation made her long for Pamplona and their house on Calle Mercaderes: a crowded, bustling street that was hardly ever quiet, that deceived no one.

The silence in Elizondo proclaimed a peace that did not exist, an outward serenity that was raging beneath like a river of red-hot lava, keeping pace with the River Baztán, endowing the inhabitants with a telluric, thrusting energy that welled up from the depths of the underworld.

She heard strains of music and turned to look. A few couples, faithful customers, were going into the Bar Saoia. Once the bar door closed, the street returned to normal. It was cold, but the wind had dropped and the night felt pleasant. As she made her way towards Muniartea the noise of the weir broke the silence. Removing one of her gloves, she placed her hand on the icy stone, where the name of the bridge had been carved.

'Muniartea.'

She read the name out loud, as she had done countless times as a child. Her voice, scarcely louder than a whisper, was drowned out by the constant murmur of water and the gentle breeze rising off the river. She felt a sudden yearning for summer nights, when the lamps beside the weir were lit, lending it an idyllic, picture-postcard quality. On winter evenings, a thick blanket of darkness descended upon Baztán with all its might; the inhabitants barely attempted to encroach upon its territory, preferring the narrow confines of their houses. Amaia took a step back, peering into the black waters flowing beneath her feet towards a raging sea many kilometres downstream. Replacing her glove, she wandered into the Txokoto neighbourhood, where the thick house walls muffled the noise of the weir, which echoed like a memory through the entrance to Señora Nati's orchards.

The orange glow of the streetlamps barely lit the corners where they were placed, surrounding them with small circles that hardly connected with each other. Much the way Txokoto must have looked in medieval times, she reflected, when those old timber-framed houses were built, creating the earliest neighbourhoods in Elizondo. She turned left after walking past the wooden shutters that covered the windows of Mantecadas Salazar, the family bakery, at night. The deserted car park was unlit. She wished she had a torch so that she could admire the freshly painted walls, which, despite the gloom, she could see were no longer covered in graffiti. Otherwise, she had no need of light, for she could easily locate the lock in the dark, as she had so often as a child. She removed her gloves, firmly grasping the key in her coat pocket, still with a piece of cord attached by her father so she could wear it about her neck. Searching with her finger for the groove, she pushed the key in, turning it gently. She went in, flicking the switch on her right before closing the door behind her. The bakery smelled of syrup. It was a fresh, sweet aroma that brought back memories of the good times and softened the wheaty, acrid smell of flour. Closing her eyes for an instant, she thrust aside the powerful images conjured by her olfactory memory, gathering as in a nightmare. She walked back to the wall and threw all the switches. The bright lights banished the ghosts of the past to the room's shadowy dark corners. The bakery was still pleasantly warm after the last batch made that afternoon. Amaia took off her coat, which she folded, placing it carefully on one of the metal work surfaces before hoisting herself up on to it.

She knew that this was where chaos had been unleashed. On the night her mother had waited for her in the bakery, hit her over the head and left her for dead in the kneading trough, hell had opened beneath her feet. But that wasn't the beginning. She gazed uneasily at the trough, filled with flour and covered with a piece of plastic sheeting that allowed her to see the interior, smooth and white like a coffin. She pushed the thought aside once more. Her eyes searched for the essences, now ranged neatly in flasks on a metal shelf. She had gone in there to fetch her money, the money her father had given her as a birthday gift and which she'd had to hide from her mother . . . But Rosario knew everything. She could sense Amaia's presence, even when they were in different rooms; it was as if she threw an invisible rope around her, ensnaring but not subjugating her. A rope like the one she had thrown earlier that day in the hospital, like the thread that binds the spider to its prey. As far back as Amaia could remember, she had been aware of this presence as if it were an invisible yet solid division separating the two of them, a division that prevented her mother from touching her, caressing her or caring for her. It was the reason why her father and sisters were the ones who helped her get dressed or comb her hair, why her father took her to the doctor or checked her temperature when she was poorly, why Rosario never touched her or held her hand. An invisible division that at once separated and joined them like the two ends of a cable. A perfect, absolute division of space, which her mother would occasionally cross at night while the others were asleep, leaning over her bed to remind her . . . Of what? Amaia reflected, even as her eyes slid back to the kneading trough . . . To remind her that a death sentence was hanging over her, that she would never stop repeating this to her, the way condemned men are reminded not only that are they doomed, but that each new day is one less in the countdown to death. 'Sleep, little bitch, *Ama* won't eat you today.' 'But one day she will,' another faceless voice would say, 'one day she will.' Amaia had always known this. And that's why she would lie awake until she was sure that her executioner was asleep, that's why she would slip between her sisters' sheets, pleading and vowing obedience. And that night had simply been the night when the sentence was finally to be carried out.

384

'But when did it all begin, Inspector?' She heard Dupree's voice once more. 'Press rewind, Inspector.'

'If that was the sentence, when was it passed? When did she condemn me? And why?'

She knew it had always been there. Now she was beginning to think that it had started the day she was born with that other baby girl identical to her, who had cried in her dreams for as long as she could recall. Jonan was mistaken; she could understand his belief, his hope, his optimism, that refusal to accept wickedness, or think the worst, but there wouldn't be a happy ending, they wouldn't find a woman the same age as her on a list of people with prosthetic limbs. There were things of which Iriarte and Jonan were unaware, but which they were beginning to intuit. They didn't know that Rosario's threats had always grown more intense as Amaia's birthday approached. She hadn't forgotten how each year her mother's habitual coldness turned to hostility as that day loomed closer. She could sense the looks her mother gave her behind her back, gauging the resistance her quarry might offer, and the distance separating them. Looks that, even without seeing them, made the hairs on her neck stand on end, expressing the finality of the threat, which in the following days would keep her awake all night. She remembered how the imminence of the sentence hanging over her intensified, until it turned into something dark and palpable, enveloping her, suffocating her with its inevitability.

Once the anniversary of her birth had passed, the relationship between them reverted to that strange state of mutual avoidance and watchfulness, a kind of tense calm, which was the nearest she came to normality during her childhood. That date, Amaia's birthday, which should have been a celebration as it was for other children, as it was for her sisters, was the most stressful time of the year for her, a date marked in her internal calendar as doomed. One could theorise about how the death of her twin sister had made Rosario suffer,

385

traumatised her, how Amaia's birthday brought back terrible memories. But Amaia knew none of that was true, that what she saw in Rosario wasn't sorrow, or a mother's grief, but rather the determination, kept in abeyance, to carry out a plan that reached its climax around the anniversary of the birth of the identical baby girls. 'A *mairu* always belongs to a dead child.' That is its essence.

'The choice of victim is never random.'

No, she didn't believe that the little girl in her dreams was now a woman, living somewhere else with another family, another surname. Regardless of the empty coffin and the false death certificate, she didn't believe that her mother had given up her baby for adoption. If Rosario had managed to conceal the fact that she was pregnant with twins up until she gave birth, she could easily have given Amaia's sister up for adoption without any need to pretend that she was dead – after all, she had another baby to show everyone. No one but her father would have known about the twin cradles. The birth certificate proved that there had been two babies: in which case, if her sister had died of natural causes and her death certificate had been signed by a doctor, why all the pretence? The reason she went through that whole rigmarole of fake certificates and a fake burial was because there was a body, a real body, that had to be disposed of. A body missing an arm, which at least as far as they could tell from the skeleton, presented no malformation that would have justified its amputation. And if it hadn't been operated on in a hospital, then the arm must have been removed post-mortem. Either that or the bones had been taken from a grave, like the *mairus-besos* at *Juanitaenea*. All of a sudden, an image from a dream came back to her as clearly as if it was real.

A little girl who was her was curled up in a corner, raising the stump of her arm towards Amaia and whispering. Amaia ran downstairs, clutching something to her chest, while a row of small children covered in mud raised their stumps at her.

What were they saying? She couldn't remember, but sensing how important it was she screwed up her eyes in an effort to recapture the dream. The harder she tried to retain the image, the more it escaped her, like mist breaking up. She felt a throbbing pain in her temples. Without taking her eyes off the kneading trough, which seemed to have a hypnotic power over her, she reached for her coat and took out her mobile. Staring at the whiteness of the flour, she debated whether to call or not. Finally, she closed her eyes and murmured:

'To hell with it.'

She looked at the time: 00:03, that meant it was 18:03 in Louisiana. As bad a time as any. She did a number search and pressed the keypad. At first she heard no ringtone, so she took the phone away from her ear to check the screen. The message was clear: 'Agent Dupree, calling'. She raised the mobile once more, straining to hear, but as before, there was nothing, until finally she heard a crackle like a twig snapping.

'Agent Dupree?' she asked hesitantly.

'Is it night-time already in Baztán, Inspector Salazar?'

'Aloisius . . .' she murmured.

'Answer me, is it night-time?'

'Yes, it is.'

'You always call me when it's night-time.'

She said nothing. His remark sounded as peculiar as it did plausible. She had the strange impression of talking to someone she knew, of knowing for certain to whom she was talking and yet not knowing.

'What can I do for you, Salazar?'

'Aloisius . . .' she said, as though trying to convince herself, to establish contact with an elusive reality, 'there's something I need to know,' she whispered. 'I've searched for the answer, but I just get more confused. I've followed the procedure, I've gone back to the beginning, but the solution eludes me.'

The silence at the far end of the phone seemed broken only by a constant murmuring, as of flowing water. Amaia pursed her lips, trying to suppress the mental image conjured by the sound.

'Aloisius, I've found out that I had a twin sister, a baby girl born at the same time as me.'

At the other end, Agent Dupree made a sound like a blocked drain, as he seemed to take a deep breath.

'There is some evidence to suggest she may still be alive . . .'

A series of rasping coughs and splutters reached her through the phone.

'Oh, Aloisius,' she exclaimed, clasping her hand over her mouth to prevent herself from posing the question that was on her lips: 'Are you all right?' she wondered.

The wheezing at the other end of the line gave way to an ominous silence, which sounded like empty air, or perhaps just the opposite.

She waited.

'You're not asking the right question,' said Dupree, his voice recovering its usual clarity.

Amaia's lips curved as she recognised her friend. 'It isn't easy.'

'Yes, it is, that's why you called me.'

Amaia swallowed hard, her eyes wandering back to the trough.

'What I want to know is whether my sister is—'

'No,' he cut across her. Now his voice sounded as if it was coming from deep inside a dank cave.

She started to cry and went on:

'. . . whether my sister is dead,' she said, her voice cracking with emotion.

A few seconds passed before he replied. 'She's dead.'

Amaia's sobs grew louder. 'How do you know?'

'No, how do you know? Because you dream about her, because you dream about dead people, Inspector Salazar, because she has told you.'

'But how could you know?'

'You know how, Salazar.'

She held the mobile away from her face, and, wide-eyed, saw that the screen was blank. On closer inspection she realised it had switched itself off. She pressed the on button, felt the phone buzz, saw the start-up message, and the photo of Ibai filling the screen. She searched in dialled calls but found nothing, only the last call she had made to Iriarte from her car. Nor was there any trace of the call she had just made to Dupree in the register of incoming and outgoing calls.

All at once, the mobile rang. She gave a start and it slipped from her hands, skittering under the table with a clatter, as the back came off. The ringing stopped. Crouching under the table she gathered up the two bits of casing and the battery, clumsily reassembling them. As soon as she switched it back on, the mobile began to ring again. She gazed at the screen, not recognising the number, then answered.

'Dupree?'

'Inspector Salazar,' a cautious voice replied at the far end. 'This is Agent Johnson of the FBI. You called me, remember?'

'Yes, of course, Agent Johnson,' she said, doing her best to sound normal. 'I didn't recognise your number.'

'That's because I'm calling you from my private phone. We have the results of the image you sent me. It seemed like it was urgent.'

'Yes, Agent Johnson, thanks.'

'I've just sent you an email with the expert's report attached. I took a quick look. Part of the image appears to be damaged, but even so there's a marked improvement in the rest of it. Have a look and, if you need any more help, don't hesitate to call me on this number. I admire Agent Dupree, but since his disappearance, things have changed around here. To begin with they followed all the usual procedures when an agent disappears, but a few days ago the information dried up and now there's just silence. That's how it goes over here, Inspector. One day you're a hero, the next you're a bastard, based on a bunch of rumours. Aloisius Dupree is a friend of mine; not only that, he's one of the best agents I've ever known. If he acts like this, it's for a reason. I only hope he shows up so that all this can be straightened out, because over here silence is damning. In the meantime, if you need anything, call me. I'm at your disposal.'

31

When she ended the call, sure enough there was a message on her phone telling her she had incoming mail. She resisted the urge to see what the forensics expert and his new program had managed to do with the face of the visitor to the Santa María de las Nieves hospital – after all, the quality of the image would be much better on a computer. She put on her coat, but only after she had opened the bakery door did she switch off the lights and lock up. After the bright lights inside, the car park seemed darker than before. She stood still, buttoning up her coat, thrust the key in her pocket then started for home. As she walked past the door of Hostal Trinkete, she noticed a light on inside, although there were no customers and the place appeared closed; perhaps a couple of doubles were playing Basque pelota in the court. The game was still popular among the younger generation in Baztán, who seemed to be keeping up the tradition. Although some would disagree. She had once heard the *pelotari* Oskar Lasa, Lasa III, maintain that the game would never be great again because young people weren't willing to suffer. 'I've tried teaching many kids, some of whom had a lot of promise, but at the first sign of pain they start to cry like sissies. I tell them: "If it doesn't hurt, you're not doing it right."'

A culture of pain, of accepting that something would hurt, that your fingers would swell up like sausages, that this searing pain, similar to sticking your hand in the flames, would creep up your arm to your shoulder like poison, that when you hit the next ball the skin on your palm would split open, even bleed a little. And occasionally the terrific impact of the ball on your hand would rupture a vein, which would bleed inside, forming a hard, excruciatingly painful lump in your hand that required urgent surgery.

A culture of pain, of accepting that this would hurt, and yet . . . She thought about Dupree and what Johnson had told her: 'Over here, silence is damning.'

Over here too, she whispered.

She spotted the curls of smoke from his cigarette before she saw him, recognised his expensive shoes before he stepped out of the darkness, where, face hidden, he had been leaning against the wall waiting for her.

'Hello, Salazar,' said Montes.

She could tell from the glassy look in his eyes and the way he held her gaze that he'd been drinking, although he wasn't drunk.

'What are you doing here?' she replied.

'Waiting for you.'

'On my way home?' she said, glancing about them, as if to emphasise the inappropriateness of his behaviour.

'You left me no choice. You've been avoiding me for days.'

'I've been waiting for you to follow the correct procedure and make an appointment to see me in my office.'

He tilted his head slightly to one side.

'Hell, Amaia, I thought we were friends.'

She gazed at him in disbelief, a faint smile on her lips.

'This isn't happening,' she said, as she started walking towards her aunt's house.

Montes threw away his cigarette and followed until he drew level with her.

'I know what I did was wrong, but you must understand that I was going through a bad patch. I guess I didn't react well.'

'You can say that again,' she cut across him.

He stepped out in front of her, blocking her way.

'My hearing is the day after tomorrow. I want to know what you are going to tell them.'

'Make an appointment to see me in my office.' She stepped around him and carried on walking.

'You know me.'

'Do I? I thought I did, but it turns out I was wrong. I have no idea who you are.'

He wheeled round to face her. 'You're going screw me over, aren't you?'

She didn't reply.

'Yes, you are, you're going to screw me over, you fucking bitch. Just like all the other bitches in your family who can't resist the pleasure of destroying a man, putting him in a wheelchair, or blowing his brains out – what difference does it make? I wonder how long it will be before you destroy your wimp of a husband.'

Amaia stopped in her tracks and listened to the thick, black venom spewing out of Montes. She realised he was only trying to provoke her. She told herself to be careful, even as a voice inside her said: 'Yes, I know, I know what he's doing, so why not give him what he wants?'

She strode back the way she had come, until she was standing inches from Montes. She could smell the beer on his breath, and his expensive cologne, his badge of identity.

'I don't need to lift a finger, Montes. I don't have to say a single a word against you,' she said. 'Yes, you're screwed – but you did it to yourself. You flouted the rules and procedures; you abandoned an ongoing investigation, with all the disrespect that implies to your colleagues, the victims and their families. You disobeyed direct orders, compromised an inquiry by removing evidence from the police station, you drew your weapon and aimed it at a member of the public, then you tried to blow out the few brains you have left. If Iriarte hadn't stopped you, you'd be rotting away in a niche where no one would have left a single flower. So, what's changed in the past year?'

'The psychiatric assessments recommend I be reinstated.'

'And how did you manage to pull that off, Montes? Nothing's changed. You might as well have died; you've turned into a zombie, the living dead. You haven't progressed a single step since that day. You aren't in therapy, you still refuse to recognise my authority, you're still the same jerk who can't be trusted and who is only interested in justifying his actions: "Oh, I was going through a bad patch",' she said mockingly. '"Teacher hates me", "Nobody loves me".'

As she spoke, Montes's face had turned ashen, his lips set in a dark line.

'You're a cop, for Christ's sake! Have some balls, do whatever you have to do, but stop whining like a sissy. You make me sick.'

Seizing hold of her by the coat, Montes raised his free hand, fist clenched. She winced, convinced he was going to hit her, yet even so she continued to taunt him:

'Are you going to punch me, Montes? Do you want to shut me up because you can't stand hearing the truth?'

He looked straight at her and Amaia glimpsed the rage in his eyes, then suddenly he smiled, released his grip on her coat and opened his raised hand.

'No, of course not,' he said, his face contorting in an insane leer. 'I see your little game. God knows, I'd like nothing better than to smash your face in, but I'm not going to, Inspector, because you have the badge and the gun. I'd be digging my own grave. I refuse to give you that pleasure.'

She looked at him, shaking her head. 'You're in an even worse state than I thought, Montes. Is that what this is about? You still think everyone is out to get you . . .'

Amaia unzipped her coat, taking out her badge and gun as she brushed past Montes, heading down an alleyway between two houses, with no overlooking windows. In it stood a barrel, an antique bedframe any dealer would have taken, and an old plough. She laid her badge and gun on the barrel, then stood there, staring at Montes.

He came up, grinning with genuine delight this time, then paused at the entrance to the alleyway.

'Without reprisals or repercussions?' he asked.

'I give you my word – and, as you know, mine is my bond.'

Still he seemed to hesitate.

Amaia had no doubts, not any more: she was sick of this guy. A part of her she didn't recognise longed to give him a good kicking, punch his lights out. The thought made her lips curve in a smile, although Montes was at least forty kilos heavier, right then, she didn't care. She'd take a beating, for sure, but so would he. Looking straight at him, she saw the hesitation in his eyes and felt a flicker of disappointment.

'Come on, you sissy, you're not chickening out now, are you? I thought you wanted to smash my face in? Well, this is your chance, you won't get another.'

This had the desired effect. Montes stepped into the alleyway like an angry bull. In fact, recalling it later, she pictured him as a bull. Head jutting forward slightly, fists clenched, eyes narrowed, trying to look intimidating.

She waited for him until the last second, then stepped to one side and punched him in the ribs. He careened into the wall, hitting his shoulder.

'Fucking whore!' he roared.

She grinned, recalling an old joke the girls at the police academy used to repeat: 'When a jerk calls you a whore, it's because he hasn't a hope in hell of fucking you.'

His shoulder must have been smarting, but, true to his bull-like nature, he stood erect: 'I wonder what your poofter friend would think if he heard you call people sissies.'

She grinned as if to say, *Oh, now you've completely done it.*

'As a cop, Deputy Inspector Etxaide runs rings around you. Not only that, he's more courageous and honourable than you'll ever be. Sissy.'

Montes lunged at her once more – eyes wide open this time. There was less distance between them now, and his fist came at her like lightning. Although it barely glanced off her cheek, her head was thrown to one side and struck the wall. Everything went black for an instant, but the stinging pain in her cheek brought her back to reality. Montes was almost upon her, but she managed to punch him as hard as she could in the stomach, which was even more flaccid than she had expected. Then, as he doubled over clutching his belly, she raised her leg with perfect timing and kneed him in the mouth. He gaped at her in surprise, his lip split open and bloody. She pushed his shoulder until he was standing with his back against the wall. They remained like that for a few seconds, gazing at one another, catching their breath, until Montes bent his knees, then slid to the ground. Amaia did the same.

They heard voices approaching. The young *pelotistas* were leaving the Trinkete, carrying their sports' bags, discussing the match as they walked down the street. When they had gone past, Amaia reached in her coat for a packet of tissues and tossed it over to Montes. He took a few, pressing them against the cut on his lip.

'You hit like a girl,' he said, then burst into laughter.

'So do you.'

'Yes, I thought I was in better shape,' he admitted, lowering his gaze before continuing. 'Look, I know I acted like a jerk, but . . . I mean, I'm not trying to justify myself, I just want to explain.'

She nodded.

'Flora . . . Well, I suppose I was in love . . .' He appeared to think better of this. 'What the fuck! I was crazy about her. I've never met anyone like her before. And you know what the worst of it is? Even after what's happened, I think I still love her.'

Amaia sighed. Did love justify everything? She thought perhaps it did. She had come across this kind of destructive love more than once during her time as a cop. She knew it wasn't love, it was the walking dead who didn't realise they were dead and 'going through the motions'. She wondered what Lasa III would have made of this culture of pain in love, possibly the only context in which society still justified suffering.

'I like Jonan,' Montes volunteered suddenly. 'I don't know why I said what I did. I think he's a good cop, and a good person. I ran into him in a bar a couple of months ago. I was a bit . . . Well, I'd had a fair amount to drink. I started talking. He's a good listener, so I went on drinking. When we left the bar, I was clearly in no fit state to drive, so I ended up sleeping on his couch . . . I don't suppose he mentioned it to you.'

'No, of course he didn't. And then you see him at the station and can't even buy him a coffee from the machine.'

'Hell, you know what it's like, he's . . . The other guys don't feel comfortable around him either.'

'Take another look, Montes: some of those machos who do the war dance around the coffee machine would rather go with you than with me.'

His eyes opened wide. 'Iriarte?'

She burst out laughing until the tears stung her swollen cheek. When she was able to speak again, she said:

'Let's change the subject, shall we? I never said a word to you.'

Montes scrambled to his feet, offering her a hand, which she accepted. Then she retrieved her badge and gun from the barrel and put them away.

'I'd love to go on talking,' she said, 'but I have to work when I get home.'

They walked out of the alleyway towards her aunt's house. Amaia took out her keys and approached the door.

'Good night, Montes,' she said wearily.

'Chief.'

She wheeled round, taken aback. Montes was standing to attention, hand raised in a salute.

'Montes, there's no need.'

'Oh, I think there is,' he said firmly.

And she knew this was the closest she would get to receiving an apology from a man like Montes, so she accepted. Facing him, she raised her hand and returned the salute.

When she closed the door behind her, a big grin spread across her face.

She sensed her aunt's silent presence sitting in front of the fire, waiting for her the way she used to when she was a teenager. Amaia slipped out of her shoes by the door and padded into the living room, realising at once that Engrasi had fallen asleep. An intense feeling of love welled up inside her, as she leaned over to plant a kiss on her aunt's brow.

'A fine time to be coming home, young lady!'

Amaia straightened up and smiled.

'I thought you were asleep.'

'I can't sleep when I'm fretting, and as long as you're out there, that's what I do.'

'But, Auntie . . .' she tutted as she slumped into the other armchair.

'I mean it, Amaia. I know you have a difficult job, that for some reason what you have to do goes beyond what most people would consider normal, but . . . You've done it again.'

Amaia lowered her eyes.

'You're looking for trouble, Amaia Salazar.'

'He's the only one who can help me.'

'That isn't true.'

'It is, Auntie. You don't understand: I went to San Sebastián and the tomb was empty. I need to know.'

'So did he tell you something you don't already know? Think about it, Amaia,' said Engrasi, struggling to her feet. 'I'm going to bed now, but you think about that.'

After sitting for so long, her aunt was unsteady on her feet, so Amaia accompanied her upstairs to her room. When Engrasi kissed her cheek, she noticed the bruise.

'What on earth happened to you?' she asked.

'I was charged by a bull,' Amaia said, chuckling.

'Well, if you're laughing, it can't be that bad. Goodnight, my dear.'

Amaia paused. 'Auntie . . . The dead . . .'

'What?' Engrasi asked.

'Can they . . . do things?'

'The dead do what they can.'

32

Amaia went into her bedroom. The lamp cast a soft light over James, who was fast asleep.

'Hello, my love,' she whispered.

She leaned over to kiss him and to take a peek at Ibai, who was sleeping on his side, a dummy in his mouth for the first time; he had always refused it when he was breast-feeding.

James gestured towards the baby:

'He's so good; you've no idea how good he is. And, of course, for lack of a tit, he has a teat,' he said grinning. 'I'm thinking of getting a couple for myself,' he said, cupping her breasts.

'That's not such a bad idea,' she laughed, pushing his hands away, 'I still have to work for a bit.'

'For long?'

'No, not for long.'

'Then I'll stay awake.'

She grinned, grabbed her laptop and left the room.

There were at least four messages in her inbox from Dr Franz. This was starting to get tiresome, but she couldn't make up her mind whether to reply to them or delete them without even reading them. On the face of it, they seemed to typify the classic angry response to rejection, yet there was a basic logic to them that gave her food for thought. Leaving them for later, she opened Johnson's email.

It was no secret that the FBI had the best facial recognition system in the world, capable of the most precise multimodal biometric verification on both distinct and indistinct images. These advances had been adapted to new programs like Indra, which was in use at European airports, but which had the drawback of only working with actual faces or extremely well-defined images.

The US government had invested over a billion dollars in developing a system that could identify faces in the street, at a football ground or from CCTV footage. Along with Johnson's email telling her they hadn't come up with a match after feeding the image into their system was a detailed report from the expert, complete with comments and a blow-by-blow account of the process, which used layers of light. In short: they had managed to illuminate blurred areas of the face to reveal that this was in fact an elaborate disguise, making a precise reconstruction more difficult. The report also suggested that either the camera lens was damaged, or a foreign body had shown up on the exposures. Attached were two images, one which the expert had labelled 'spider', another that had been digitally processed.

Amaia opened the second file, and found herself contemplating a young Caucasian male face with regular features. The hat, beard and glasses had been digitally removed, and the vacant stare of the reconstruction offered no information. Opening the 'spider' file, she gazed at the image with surprise. Here was the face with the hat, glasses and beard, but in the centre of the forehead a dark eye with long lashes, which the expert had referred to as a 'spider'. She studied the image closely for a few seconds before forwarding the message to Jonan and to Iriarte.

The emails from Dr Franz were exactly as she had expected: a half-pleading, half-whining defence of his beloved clinic. But in the last two he also made unsubstantiated accusations against Sarasola: 'That man is hiding something, he's not what he seems, I have no proof yet.' No, of course he didn't. He had also attached various reports from other doctors at the centre, together with articles from well-known science journals, corroborating his view that it would be impossible for the patient to act normally without being on medication. After skim-reading them, Amaia concluded that she found medical jargon wearisome. She checked the time, closed her laptop and wondered whether James would be waiting for her as he had promised. She smiled as she climbed the stairs: James always kept his promises.

For the first time in days she woke serenely when James placed Ibai next to her. She spent the next few minutes kissing the child's head and hands. Then he awoke so sweetly and gave her such a smile that her heart lit up in a way she had never imagined possible. Clasping his tiny hands in hers, she remembered Iriarte's words: 'a tiny arm'. Images flashed into her mind of that little skull, its soft spot not yet closed, and the graves of the *mairu* surrounding *Juanitaenea*. 'So, you're one of them.' '*The dead do what they can.*'

James came in with Ibai's bottle and a coffee for her. He opened the shutters and stood gazing at her.

'Amaia, what happened to your face?'

She remembered the blow, feeling a sharp pain as she touched her cheek. She got out of bed, and examined her face in the mirror. It wasn't all that swollen, but a bruise stretching from her cheek to her ear would turn various shades of brown, black and yellow over the next few days. She applied a layer of make-up, which only made her face throb painfully. In the end she gave up, as Zabalza's voice echoed in her head, assuring her that Beñat Zaldúa wouldn't go to school with bruises on his face.

'Right, in that case I shan't go to school today either,' she told her reflection in the glass.

She spent the rest of the morning making calls that gave her the feeling she was getting nowhere. Nuría's husband had yet to be found. Patrol cars were stationed outside her house, as well as the church, where no further desecrations had taken place. Of course not: the *tarttalo* had her full attention now, which had been the sole aim of that piece of theatre, so there was no point in him continuing along that path.

Although she had checked her emails the night before, she did so again before speaking with Etxaide and Iriarte about the enhanced images.

Iriarte thought that either the lens or the recording was damaged, or that an actual spider might easily have crawled on to the camera outside the hospital. Jonan had suggested that the 'spider' was what it appeared to be: an eye, which the visitor had worn as a finishing touch to complete the image he wished to portray; after all, the *tarttalo* was a Cyclops. In all the other recordings from previous weeks, they had only glimpsed the top of his head, yet on that last day, he had looked up at the camera and remained like that long enough for them to capture an image of his face.

'I don't think that's a coincidence,' said Etxaide.

Neither did Amaia.

'Around midday, we're hoping to get further results that will date the surgical instruments more precisely. So far we've drawn a blank with the hospital registers of amputees, with

403

or without prosthetic arms, but we're not even halfway through . . .'

Before hanging up, Jonan told her:

'Ah, I got another of those emails, chief. I'll forward it to you.'

Seconds later it appeared in her inbox. As before, it was concise and insistent. 'The lady awaits your offering.' The image of the *lamia* appeared on the bottom right-hand corner. All at once she felt exasperated by this stupid game. She covered her face with her hands and held them there, as though somehow she might peel away her irritation. All she succeeded in doing was to chafe the skin on her cheek, which only made her more irritated. She called Jonan back.

'I know you're busy, but have you had a chance to find out anything about where these emails came from?'

'I have, as a matter of fact, although it doesn't help us much. They were sent from a free account, with no name, only an alias: servantsofthelady@hotmail.com. From the headings, you can see they are sent from a dynamic IP address; after tracking that address, connection by connection, it seems that they were sent from a free Internet access point, like the ones they have in airports or coach stations . . . It's virtually impossible to trace the sender – they have to be online. This has been done in special cases involving international terrorists, but . . . For now, I'll keep looking. Chances are, even if we do find out where they're being sent from, the person will be long gone . . .'

'OK, don't worry about it.' She hung up.

After his breakfast and early morning playtime, Ibai started to get sleepy, so James took care of him. Amaia kissed them both, said goodbye to her aunt and, grabbing her Puffa jacket, left the house. She got into the car, turned on the ignition, then suddenly remembered something and switched it off again. She climbed out of the car and went back to the house, where she stood staring at the paving until her eye alighted on two or three small rounded stones along the edges that looked loose. She picked one of them up, slipped it into her pocket and got back into the car.

As she headed out of Elizondo she tried to concentrate on driving, but once she was on the main road she exhaled, emptying her lungs, aware how tense she was. Her knuckles shone white as she gripped the wheel and her hands felt clammy, despite the winter cold, which seemed to go on forever in Baztán. She wiped them one at a time on her trouser legs. Damn it! She felt afraid, and she hated it. Usually she welcomed fear – it was what kept police officers alive, alert and cautious. But the fear she was feeling wasn't the sort that quickened your pulse when you apprehended an armed suspect; it was that other fear, that old, familiar fear that smelled of sweat and urine, that age-old fear in her soul, which for the past year she had been able to keep at bay, but which was now reclaiming its territory. The territory of fear. She had been there before, and knew she couldn't defeat it, that the only way to stay sane was to confront her fear, time after time. She felt a deep sadness, both for herself and for the other little girl, as she realised that the chink of light she had discovered was once more closing up. Her anger rose, like a powerful tide. Why should she endure this? She wouldn't: perhaps in the past, when they were mere children, the forces of the universe had conspired against them, making them live in fear all those years, but she was no longer a child and she refused to play that game, to allow them to carry on manipulating her.

She drove for a few miles along what seemed like quite a good country road, until she came across a herd of *pottoks*, semi-wild horses that grazed freely around Baztán. She pulled over to the side and waited. The habitually skittish *pottoks* remained blocking the road, so she sat for a while watching them. A small mare approached, sniffing inquisitively at

405

Amaia's proffered hand. Realising that the *pottoks* had no intention of moving, Amaia opened the boot of her car, took out the pair of wellingtons that she kept in there for emergencies, and grabbed a torch. She set off down the first part of the slope, descending sideways to avoid slipping in the tall, wet grass. Further down, it thinned out on both sides of the riverbank, as if it had been mown. She followed the river, which flowed silently along that stretch, until she reached a cement bridge with a rusty handrail that she avoided touching. On the far side, she passed through a crude fence, doubtless erected to prevent animals from straying, making sure it was properly closed behind her. She crossed the open pasture towards a large farmhouse that looked abandoned but not derelict; it was carefully boarded up with timber planks nailed to the window frames. As she approached, she caught the unmistakable scent of sheep and saw the tiny dark droppings, which explained the perfectly cropped grass in the meadow. After circling the house, she started to get her bearings; if she walked ahead a few metres, she would reach the edge of the forest, near where she had pulled over in her car on the previous occasion. Checking her phone coverage, she saw that the signal grew weaker the closer she came to the wooded area. Her pulse started to race, pounding in her ears with a swift whistling sound. Whoosh, whoosh, whoosh. She took a deep breath to try to calm herself, instinctively quickening her pace, her eyes fixed on a tiny patch of light at the end of the path that indicated the way out of the forest. She headed towards it, struggling to suppress her childish urge to break into a run, together with the paranoid impression that someone was following her. Raising her hand to her holster, she heard herself say ironically: *That's right, babe, a gun. What use will that be?*

When she was eleven, like all kids her age, she and her friends used to dare one another to go into the graveyard at night.

It was a stupid game, consisting of retrieving various objects placed on tombs at the top end of the cemetery. When it grew dark, they would draw lots to see who would go in and fetch them. The rules stipulated that they must walk all the way there and back, without hurrying, while the others waited by the railings. Often, just as they were approaching the exit, some joker would shout: 'Look out, behind you!' It was enough to make even the pluckiest among them break into a run, as if the devil himself were on their heels. Total panic. She recalled how the others would fall about laughing while keeping an eye on the path, just in case something other than their screams was making their friend flee . . . And next time, even though they all knew the kids would cry out, they still ran. Just in case.

She reached the end of the path and came out into a clearing, currently occupied by a flock of sheep, that stretched as far as the magical stream where the young woman had waylaid her. As the flock fanned out ahead of her approach, she advanced through the gap in their ranks. In the distance she could see the shepherd sitting on a rock. She waved at him, prompting him to wave back. Reassured by his presence, she crossed the bridge, which was little more than a promontory over the stream. A shiver ran down her spine as she did so. She carried on until she reached the patch of ferns bordering the slope, then started to climb, leaning on the ancient rocks that formed a natural stairway. Pausing at the rugged stretch of level ground where James and Ros had waited for her on a previous visit, she noticed that the pathway that continued upwards looked clearer, as if someone had been there before her. Even so, there were plenty of brambles and thistles to scratch passers-by.

Plunging her hands into her pockets, she set off up the path. Her impression that someone had been this way recently grew as the path widened out with each step until she reached her destination. She was faintly surprised, but mostly relieved, to find no one there. She spent a few seconds re-familiarising herself with the place. The mouth of the cave, like a twisted smile hewn from the rock, gaped in front of her; the magnificent 'lady' rock standing three metres high with its voluptuous curves overlooking the valley; and on the table rock, more than a dozen tiny stones, arranged like pieces on a primitive draughtboard. She went over and studied them.

They weren't stones taken from the path; someone had brought them here as an offering to the lady. Amaia shook her head in disbelief, then realised that she was doing exactly the same. She fumbled for the stone she had taken from outside her aunt's house and clasped it in her hand, tentatively: *'a stone, you must bring from home'*, *'the lady prefers you to bring one from home'*.

She wondered how many people in the valley were receiving those messages. Were they being passed on like those chain letters you were supposed to forward in the hope they would bring you a fortune, or at least free you from a curse?

Amaia had no intention of forwarding anything, but leaving a stone could do no harm. She glanced about her, half-expecting to discover a spy-camera concealed among the branches, or half a dozen *paparazzi* poised to take shots that would be accompanied by the caption: *Gullible Detective Inspector resorts to magic rituals!* She clasped the stone in her hand, then noticed a blob of cement and scratched at it with her nail, trying without success to remove it. She set it down, completing one of the rows, then turned around to face the cave, walking in a straight line until she reached the entrance. Taking out her torch, she leaned forward and shone it inside. She caught the sweet scent of flowers, yet she could see no obvious source. The cave was empty, apart from a bowl that contained fresh apples and a few coins someone had tossed in. She switched off the torch and turned to start her descent.

When she reached the table rock, she noticed the stones were exactly as she had left them. *What did you expect?* she muttered to herself, as she set off down the path. Although perfect for walking in wet fields on soft ground, her wellingtons kept slipping off as she scrambled down the rocky path. She made her way through the undergrowth until she came to the stream, which seemed to burst from the hillside in a cascade of water, green rocks, ferns and white foam. The shepherd had disappeared, but his flock was still there, their placid presence adding to the beauty of the place, as well as eliminating all possibility of a mysterious young woman appearing. Amaia gazed up at Mari's hill once more and smiled, a little disappointed. But what had she been expecting? Casting a final glance at the sheep, she noticed that they had stopped watering and grazing, their heads raised as if they sensed danger or were hearing something Amaia couldn't hear. Puzzled by this curious behaviour, she stood still, listening. All at once the sheep cocked their heads, their bells rang all at once, sounding like a great gong. The startling silence that followed was broken by a loud whistle. Amaia opened her mouth and took a huge breath as she gazed in bewilderment at the animals, who had resumed their grazing and watering.

She felt an intense sensation of cold on her back, as if someone had draped a wet sheet over her skin. She had heard it clearly, had seen it too. The words of the anthropologist, Barandiarán, whose works she had read a year before while investigating the *basajaun* case, came back to her word for word: 'The *basajaun* makes its presence known to humans through a series of high-pitched whistles, unnecessary in the case of animals, who can sense the *basajaun*; flocks of sheep greet him by making their bells sound as one.'

'Oh, my God!' she whispered.

Seized with panic, Amaia started to run through the trees. Somewhere inside her head a voice begged her to stop, but she replied that she didn't care, she was running because it

409

was all she could do, just as when she used to play that childish game in the graveyard. She sprinted along the path through the woods, clutching her gun. As she approached the abandoned farmhouse, she glanced over her shoulder, disobeying all her cautionary instincts telling her not to. There was no one in sight. Her ears were filled with the sound of her own ragged breaths after the frenzied dash. Touching her brow, which was dripping with sweat, she stared down at the gun in her other hand. Imagining how crazy she must look, she unzipped her jacket and concealed her weapon, still reluctant to holster it. She crossed the field and then the bridge, her fear giving way to irritation, which, by the time she reached the car, had blossomed into a monumental rage.

The *pottoks* had gone, leaving behind a few mounds of steaming dung on the road. She climbed into the car, pulled away and accelerated, her heart still racing. What the hell was going on? What did they want from her? She wasn't crazy! Why was this happening to her? Didn't she have enough problems in her private life, not to mention being a homicide detective? Who the fuck had decided all this mystical shit should be dumped on her?

'Fuck!' she repeated, thumping the wheel.

Her aunt or her sister Ros would have interpreted what just happened as a blessing, but she was a cop, for Christ's sake! A detective, with a rational brain and a high IQ. She excelled at solving problems using logic and common sense, not by making offerings to storm goddesses or sprites with webbed feet. No. Those sheep weren't hailing the lord of the forest any more than *mairu* bones had a narcotic effect.

'Fuck!' she exclaimed, pounding the steering wheel once more: 'Fuck, fuck, fuck!'

That accursed cave was to blame for everything. It was one of those places where things happen, which the universe, with its laws, black holes and stars can't leave alone, making everything in it sting like a damn ulcer.

'Fuck!' she screamed, slapping the steering wheel this time.

Suddenly, out of nowhere, a woman wearing a brown parka with fur lining round the hood appeared in the middle of the road. Amaia slammed on the brakes. The car skidded a few metres, screeching to a halt right next to the woman, who wheeled around and gazed at Amaia wide-eyed, her face pale. Amaia leapt out of the car and started towards her.

'Oh, my God! Are you all right?'

The woman looked at her and smiled timidly.

'Yes, yes, don't worry, it's just the shock.'

As Amaia drew closer to see for herself, she noticed the woman's belly protruding beneath the fur-lined parka.

'Are you pregnant?'

The woman laughed self-consciously. 'Heavily, I'd say.'

'Oh my God! Are you sure you're OK?'

'As well as anyone can be in my condition.'

When Amaia continued to look worried, the woman hastily added: 'I'm only teasing. Honestly, I'm fine. It's my own fault, I shouldn't have been walking in the middle of the road, and I should probably wear reflective armbands or something.' She glanced down and touched the sleeve of her brown coat. 'I'm not very visible in this thing, but it's comfortable.'

Amaia sympathised; towards the end of her pregnancy, she had practically lived in the same clothes.

'No, it's my fault,' she said. 'I wasn't concentrating. I'm the one who should apologise. At least let me give you a lift. Where are you going?'

'Well, nowhere in particular, I was just taking a stroll – it does me good to walk,' she said, glancing at the car, 'but I'll accept your offer, seeing as I'm feeling especially tired today.'

'Of course,' said Amaia, glad to be of help.

She opened the passenger door for the woman and waited

until she was settled. Amaia noticed that she was young, not much older than twenty. Beneath her parka she had on brown leggings, and a long sweater the same shade. Her hair tumbled down her back in a braid, and she wore a tortoiseshell headband that contrasted with the pallor of her face, which Amaia had initially attributed to the shock. The girl was fiddling with a small object in her hand; she seemed to have regained her composure. Amaia climbed back into the driver's seat and set off once more.

'Do you often go out walking?'

'As often as I can; it's the best form of exercise towards the end of a pregnancy.'

'Yes, I know. Not so long ago, I was in the same state as you. I have a four-month-old baby now.'

'Boy or girl?'

'Well, it was going to be a girl, right up until the birth, then I found out it was a boy,' said Amaia pensively.

'Would you have preferred a girl?'

'No, it's not that, it was just a bit . . . disconcerting.'

'If you had a boy, it must be because that was meant to be.'

'I suppose so,' said Amaia.

'It's wonderful!' the girl exclaimed, gazing at her. 'You already have your baby, you can't imagine how much I long to have mine.'

'Yes,' Amaia agreed, 'it *is* wonderful, but complicated too. Sometimes I miss being pregnant, you know, having the baby there with me, safe and calm,' she said, a tinge of melancholy in her voice.

'I understand, but I can't wait to see its little face, to get rid of this,' she said, prodding her belly. 'I look awful.'

'That's not true,' said Amaia.

And it wasn't. Despite her claim that she was tired, the young woman's face showed no signs of fatigue. Her whole being radiated well-being; at a time when women were getting pregnant later and later, such a young mother was a refreshing sight.

'Don't get me wrong, I feel joy every time I see my son, but motherhood isn't as ideal as it's made out to be in magazines.'

'Oh, I know that,' said the young woman. 'This isn't my first.'

Amaia looked at her in surprise.

'Don't be deceived by my appearance, I'm older than I look. In fact, I can't remember a time when I wasn't pregnant.'

Amaia averted her eyes to hide her confusion. A flurry of questions came into her head, none of which she felt she could ask a woman she'd only just met, whom she had narrowly missed running over. Even so, she said:

'How do you manage pregnancy and motherhood? I ask, because I'm having trouble juggling the demands of my job with being a good mother.'

She noticed the woman contemplating her at length.

'I see. So you're one of them?'

The words triggered a memory of that flower-growing harpy saying exactly the same thing; in her mind's eye, Amaia could picture her snapping off the young buds with her nail.

'What do you mean?' she asked defensively.

'One of those women who let other people tell them how to be a mother. You mentioned magazines just now. Look, motherhood is something a lot more instinctive and natural. All those instructions and examinations and advice can overwhelm mothers.'

'But it's normal to want to do things properly,' Amaia replied.

'Of course, but those worries won't go away no matter how many books you read. Believe me, Amaia, you are the best mother for your little boy, he is the son you were meant to have,' she said, fondling the object in her hand, kneading it between her fingers.

Amaia didn't remember having told the woman her name, but decided to let it pass. Instead she replied, 'I have so many doubts, I feel so ignorant. I wouldn't want to do anything that might harm him, now or later on.'

'The only way a mother can harm her children is by not loving them. She may give them everything they need – food, clothes, an education – but if they don't receive her love, the natural, unconditional love of a mother, they will grow up emotionally stunted, with an unhealthy idea of love that will prevent them from being happy.'

Amaia thought of her own mother.

'But . . .' she replied, 'certain things are known to be better, such as breastfeeding.'

'The best way to relate to your child is freely, without following guidelines or bowing to pressure. If you want to breastfeed, go ahead, if you want to bottle feed, do that.'

'What if you can't do what you want to do?'

'Then you must adapt, but in a relaxed way. We can't always have summer, but autumn is good too.'

Amaia remained silent for an instant.

'You sound like an expert.'

'I am,' the other woman declared, unabashed, 'and so are you. I think you should make a bonfire out of all those books, tapes, magazines. You'll feel a lot better, and you can focus on accomplishing your mission.' She said those last words as if she were referring to a specific goal.

Startled by this, Amaia turned to look at her.

'Stop here, please,' the stranger said abruptly, pointing to a place on the road where a path led into the forest. 'I'll carry on walking for a while.'

Amaia stopped the car and the young woman got out, leaning down so that she could see her face.

'And don't worry so much, you're doing fine.'

Amaia was about to say something, but the woman closed the car door and started walking along the beaten-earth track.

When she drove off again, she noticed the young woman had left something behind on the seat. Examining it more closely, she realised what it was. She slowed down and pulled over, contemplating the object without touching it. Incredulous, with trembling fingers, she picked up the rounded chip of stone, turning it over, only to discover the cement on the back that for so long had fixed it in between the paving stones outside her aunt's house.

33

Dawn heralded a rare day of sunshine. The lingering mist would soon evaporate if the sun continued to blaze like that. The sun always had made Amaia feel grateful, but today it also provided the perfect excuse to disguise the bruise on her cheek behind a pair of oversized sunglasses.

Iriarte had driven them to Pamplona, but apart from a few comments about developments regarding the case, he had remained detached and silent, limiting himself to concentrating on the road. She had seen Montes in the entrance. He had greeted her with a timid 'good morning', and she was relieved to see that his face was no better than hers. His lower lip was swollen, and the dark gash in the middle looked like a strange piercing.

A policeman came to usher them into the Commissioner's office. They were all in full uniform except for Montes, who wore an elegant, no doubt expensive, dark blue suit.

The Commissioner was already seated at the long conference table, along with the two officers from Internal Affairs who had taken their statements when the incident took place. Amaia couldn't help noticing the furtive glances the two men gave her bruised cheek, barely concealed by her make-up, as well as Montes's lip.

'As you are all aware, it's been twelve months since Inspector Montes was suspended as a result of the events that took place in February last year outside Hotel Baztán in Elizondo. During that time, Inspector Montes has attended the recommended therapy sessions. I have here the reports, which are favourable to his reinstatement. Detective Inspector Salazar, Inspector Iriarte, you were present when the aforementioned events took place. In your opinion, is Inspector Montes ready to be reinstated?'

Iriarte glanced at Amaia before speaking:

'I was present the day the incident took place and, during the months following his suspension, I have met with Inspector Montes on several occasions when he stopped by the station to pay his respects to his colleagues. His behaviour . . .' Iriarte hesitated long enough for Amaia, but apparently not the others, to notice, 'has at all times been appropriate. In my opinion, he is ready to resume his post.'

Amaia sighed.

'Detective Inspector Salazar,' the Commissioner said, inviting her to speak.

'Inspector Montes's absence has required adjustments that my entire team has had to shoulder, not without considerable effort and personal sacrifice. I think it's appropriate for him to be reinstated as soon as possible.'

As she spoke, she was aware of the ripple of surprise that spread through the assembled hierarchy.

'Inspector Montes?' the Commissioner said.

'I'd like to thank Inspector Iriarte and Detective Inspector Salazar for placing their confidence in me. A week ago, I would gladly have accepted. However, after a discussion with a close colleague, I've decided it would be better if I continued in therapy for a few more months.'

Amaia cut in. 'If I may be permitted, sir. I fully understand Inspector Montes wanting to continue his therapy, but I see no reason why he can't do both. The team is struggling, people are working long hours, doing overtime . . .'

'Very well,' the Commissioner nodded. 'I agree with you. Montes, as of tomorrow you may return to duty. Welcome back,' he said, extending his hand.

Amaia walked out without waiting. She drank from the water-cooler in the corridor, killing time. Montes stood chatting to Iriarte in the doorway to the office, but when he saw her, he took his leave of the others and came up to her.

'Thank you, I—'

'Forget about tomorrow morning,' she interrupted him. 'You're staying in Elizondo, aren't you? I want you to drive there now, and while you're at it, you can give Iriarte a lift. I hope you're in the mood for work, because we have one suspect on the run, two patrol cars staking out a house and a church, a desecrator and something far worse. So, get to it.'

Montes looked at her, grinning:

'Thanks, chief.'

'Let's see if you're still thanking me in a week's time.'

Amaia hadn't been exaggerating the urgency of the situation in Elizondo in the rundown she'd given Montes, though she was almost certain the desecrator was unlikely to pose any further problems. The only reason she was maintaining a police presence outside the church was to placate Sarasola after her refusal to bring charges against Beñat Zaldúa, and to reassure the Commissioner, who'd given her a hard time after learning that the patrol car had been absent when a forklift was driven through the church wall.

She spent the next half-hour driving round Pamplona, killing time before her meeting with Markina. Finally she pulled into the underground car park at Plaza del Castillo and paused to check her appearance in the rear-view mirror, straightening her red beret and smoothing out the red jacket bearing the Navarre coat of arms on the front.

The restaurant in Hotel Europa was one of the finest in the city. Knowing Markina's gastronomic preferences, his choice didn't surprise her. The Europa had succeeded in embracing the popular nouvelle cuisine whilst maintaining the tradition of serving up a hefty slab of meat or fish on the diner's plate.

She noticed people's eyes following her as she entered. The sight of a uniformed police officer in a chic restaurant was as conspicuous as a cockroach on a wedding cake.

'I'm meeting someone,' she murmured, brushing past the head waiter who came to greet her. She headed over to the table where Markina was waiting. He rose to his feet, doing his best not to look surprised. She thrust out a gloved hand before he had time to react.

'Judge Markina,' she said.

Only when she had sat down did she remove her gloves.

'You're in uniform,' said Markina, puzzled.

'Yes, I had an important meeting, where it was obligatory. I only just got out,' she lied.

'And you're armed,' he said, gesturing towards the gun on her belt.

'I'm always armed, your honour.'

'Yes, but not in full view.'

'I'm sorry if it bothers you – I wear my uniform with pride.'

'It doesn't bother me,' he insisted, and as if to prove it gave that smile of his. 'It just took me by surprise.'

She arched her eyebrows. 'You insisted we meet today, even though I told you I had an important meeting at the Commissioner's office.'

'You're right, I requested this meeting, to which you agreed.' Markina seemed vexed, but she didn't care.

'I wanted to thank you for your support, and for deciding to open the *tarttalo* case.'

'You left me little choice.'

'Well, in light of the evidence . . .'

'True, but initially I placed my trust in you,' he said, giving her a meaningful look. 'Have you made any progress?'

419

'We've found another woman who appears to fit the victim-ology. For two years she was imprisoned and tortured by her husband; although living in Murcia at the time, she was born in Baztán. He was sent to jail, but went looking for her when he was released on parole. We've issued a warrant for his arrest. He, too, fits the profile. We also suspect he is being manipulated. The instigator appears to choose a specific type of person. As yet, we don't know how he builds a relationship with them, but we know some time elapses before they are primed and ready to enact his plan. At that point it appears he only has to snap his fingers and they do his bidding.'

The waiter brought over some wine, which Markina had doubtless selected. Amaia declined.

'Water, please,' she said, ignoring the judge's protests.

When the waiter had moved away, he resumed his questions:

'Have you any further clues about the identity of the suspect who visited your mother at the hospital?'

She felt uneasy discussing that subject with Markina, and would have done anything to avoid it.

'Well, I sent the images to the FBI for enhancement . . .'

'Yes, I saw the results. It's interesting that you have such good contacts there, although even with the most cutting-edge technology it seems they haven't been able to achieve much.'

'There was some improvement, but not enough to ID the suspect.'

'Have there been any further attempts to visit or contact her?'

'We've moved her to a completely secure unit, so there's no risk of that. The director of the new centre is aware of the situation and I trust his judgement.'

She wondered to what extent this was true. How far did she trust Sarasola? Certainly not one hundred per cent. She wondered whether Dr Franz might be infecting her with his paranoia.

Amaia had decided not to tell Markina that she suspected the *tarttalo* was behind the desecrations. Nor was she about to divulge that the DNA of the remains left in the church matched members of her own family, with the latest *mairubeso* belonging to her twin sister, a 'cot death' victim who'd been erased from her family history as if she had never existed. She wondered how much longer she could conceal these details from Markina without jeopardising the investigation. *I'll tell him when I have the evidence to link it*, she said to herself. *Not before.*

However, she did bring him up to speed on the metal tooth found in Lucía Aguirre's remains, as well as the antique scalpel the visitor had delivered to her mother.

A fresh group of diners entered the restaurant and made their way to a reserved table nearby. Several of them gave her a funny look, and Markina's discomfort didn't escape her.

She used it to her advantage.

'I think I've told you everything we have so far. We're closing the net on the husband, and hope to arrest him within the next few hours. I'll keep you informed.'

Markina gave a distracted nod.

'I'll leave you to enjoy your lunch.'

He made as if to protest, but thought better of it. 'Very well, as you wish,' he replied, feigning reluctance while actually feeling relieved.

If a police officer in a bright red uniform doesn't scare you off, nothing will, thought Amaia, getting up and proffering her hand.

As she left, everyone in the restaurant turned to look at her. She remembered the day she had met James at a gallery where his work was on display. She had been in uniform that day too. James had walked up to her, handed her a catalogue and invited her to see the exhibition.

Before switching on the car engine, Amaia took out her phone and dialled.

421

'Don't start dinner without me, my love. I'm on my way.'
'Of course,' he replied.

In Amaia's experience, there was always a point, an instant during an investigation that at first sight seemed no different from any other, yet would ultimately prove pivotal. For a detective, solving a crime was like attempting to complete a jigsaw puzzle without knowing how many pieces it contained, or what the finished picture would look like. And sometimes there were pieces that left black holes in the investigation, areas of total darkness that would never reveal their secrets.

People told lies – not big lies, but important ones; they lied about the details. They lied not to cover up a murder, but rather to conceal trivial aspects of their own lives. And because the detective noticed these lies, they brought suspicion on themselves, even though ninety-nine per cent of the time their lies had been motivated by shame, and the fear that their spouse, boss or parents would find out what they had really been up to.

In other instances, the only two witnesses to a crime would refuse to talk: the murderer, for obvious reasons, and the victim, because he or she had been forcibly silenced. In recent years, advanced investigation techniques had opened up a whole new area of forensic science based on the victim, the silent witness, who for too long had been considered of secondary importance.

Victimology threw up multiple lines of investigation focusing on the personality, tastes, as well as behaviour of the victim. And on a forensic level, investigators could now employ new resources such as facial reconstruction from skeletal remains, DNA identification, forensic dentistry. And where the alleged victim was presumed dead, but no body was found, as in the case of Lucía Aguirre, an in-depth study of the victim's behaviour and their private life could provide as many clues as having the victim appear at the foot of your bed, whispering the name of her killer.

But there was yet another piece of the puzzle, the piece detectives were always hoping to find: the key piece that would help decipher the whole picture, helping everything else fall into place and make perfect sense. Sometimes, finding that piece might mean abandoning a line of investigation which dozens of people had been working on for months. On other occasions it was some tiny but brilliant detail that might present itself in myriad ways: a witness who suddenly came forward, a cashier who filmed something, the results of a test, phone company records, or a significant lie that was exposed. Discovering this small piece of the puzzle gave the whole meaning. And in that instant, where all had been darkness now there was light.

It could happen in a flash. The moment that elusive piece was added to the puzzle, the detectives knew they had it, they had their killer. Sometimes that magical insight came even before they had all the evidence; sometimes it never came.

34

There was no sign of the sun which the previous morning had helped lighten her mood and disperse the mist. It was raining in a way that to any seasoned Baztán inhabitant was a sure sign it wouldn't let up all day.

It was early, so she drove over to Txokoto and parked behind the bakery. Amaia pushed open the door and walked into the brightly lit interior, where a few of the assistants were already at work. She greeted them as she made her way to the far end. Rosaura smiled when she saw her sister.

'Good morning, early bird, I thought you were a cop, not a baker.'

'I'm a cop who needs coffee and pastries.'

While Ros was making the coffee, Amaia stood next to the window and contemplated the bakery.

'I came here the other night.'

Ros stood, plate in hand, looking at her solemnly.

'I hope you don't mind,' Amaia added. 'I needed to think, or remember, I'm not sure which . . .'

'Sometimes I forget what a terrible place this must be for you.'

Amaia said nothing: what could she say? She stared at her sister for a few moments, then shrugged her shoulders.

Ros put the coffees and pastries on the low table in front of the settee and sat down, inviting her sister to join her. Without reaching to take her coffee, she waited until Amaia was seated.

'I knew.'

Amaia looked puzzled.

'I knew what was going on,' repeated Ros, in a strangled voice.

'What do you mean?'

'I mean that I knew what *Ama* was doing.'

Amaia leant over and placed a hand on her sister's.

'There was nothing you could do, Ros; you and Flora were too young. Of course you saw the things she did, but *Ama* was so full of contradictions . . . For two small girls it must have been confusing.'

'I don't mean when she cut off your hair, or when she wouldn't dance with you, or the awful presents she gave you. One of the many nights when you insisted on sleeping with me, you clung to me so tight you made me hot, so I waited until you were asleep, then climbed into your bed.'

Amaia froze, cup in mid-air even as her hands started to tremble. She put the cup down on the table, instinctively holding her breath.

'*Ama* came to see me, thinking, of course, I was you. I was about to fall asleep when I heard her voice, close to my ear. There was no mistaking her words: "Sleep, you little bitch, *Ama* won't eat you tonight." And do you know what I did when she had gone, Amaia? I got out of bed and climbed in beside you, scared to death. That's why from that day on, I let you sleep in my bed. I'm sure that somehow she knew, perhaps because she realised I had started to watch her watching you. I've never told anyone this before. I'm so sorry, Amaia.'

The pair of them sat in silence for a few moments that felt like an eternity.

425

'Don't torment yourself. There was nothing you could do. *Aita* was the responsible adult. He was the only one who could have defended me, yet he did nothing.'

'*Aita* was a good man, Amaia, he just wanted everything to be OK.'

'But he got it wrong; that's not how you make a family work. He protected his wife and forced his nine-year-old child to leave home, not to live with him and sisters. He banished me.'

'He did it to protect you.'

'That's what I've been telling myself all these years. But now that I'm a mother, I know one thing for sure: I would put my child's safety first, above that of James, above my own, and I hope that James would too.'

Amaia stood up and, making her way over to the door, picked up her coat.

'Aren't you going to finish your coffee?'

'Not today.'

The rain was lashing down harder than before; even at full speed, the wipers were unable to clear the windscreen fast enough. She drove to the police station, where water was cascading down the sloping base and draining into the specially dug gully that surrounded the building like a small moat. Instead of heading for the front entrance, she drove around the back and parked at the top among the red cars bearing the Navarre police insignia on their side. She went into the meeting room she was using as an office and saw that Fermín Montes was already there. He had rolled up his sleeves and was busy drawing a chart on a new whiteboard they had brought in. Etxaide and Zabalza were with him.

'Morning, chief,' he said breezily, when he saw her enter.

'Good morning,' she replied, registering the other two men's surprise.

Jonan gave a wry smile, raising his eyebrows as he said

426

good morning, while Zabalza frowned and mumbled something that sounded like a greeting. On the table in front of him lay the large heap of documents they had compiled during the course of the investigation. Judging from the mess, and the number of jottings on the whiteboard, she estimated they had been there the best part of two hours.

'Where did this board come from?'

'I found it downstairs. No one else seems to be using it,' said Fermín, turning to look at her. 'I was trying to get up to speed before you arrived.'

'Carry on,' she said. 'We'll start as soon as Inspector Iriarte gets here.'

Opening her email, she found the usual suspects. Dr Franz's hysteria had reached fever pitch, and he was threatening to 'do something'. There was another message from the Golden Comb:

Where better to conceal sand than on a beach,
where better to conceal a stone than on the river bed.
Evil is ruled by its own nature.

Iriarte came in carrying one of the mugs his kids had given him on father's day and placed it in front of her.

'Good morning. Thanks,' she said.

'Morning, gentlemen,' said Iriarte, 'whenever you're ready.'

Amaia took a mouthful of coffee before walking over to the whiteboards.

'As this is Inspector Montes's first day back, we'll go over what we have so far. And since you've started with this,' she said, pointing at the heading 'desecrations', 'we'll go from there. I can see they've briefed you on the early stages of the case, so let's talk about what we know now. We questioned Beñat Zaldúa, a youth from Arizkun, the author of a protest blog about the history of the *agotes*. In the end,' she said, her eye alighting briefly on Zabalza, 'the boy admitted he had an accomplice, a male adult with whom he exchanged emails, and who encouraged him to act on his words. To begin with, Beñat thought this would help to draw attention to his protest, but the appearance of the bones scared him. Arizkun is a small place, word travels fast. Beñat denies all knowledge of the bones and claims he took no part in the most recent desecration, involving the forklift truck. The lad was quite frightened, and positively identified Antonio Garrido,' she said, pointing to the photocopies of Garrido's criminal record that Zabalza was handing to Montes.

'Garrido's ex-wife, Nuría, is the woman who shot at an intruder in her home. This turned out to be Garrido himself, who had tortured and imprisoned her for two years and was coming back to finish her off. Which brings us to . . .' Amaia turned the other board around '. . . the *tarttalo*. So far we have established a link between Johana Márquez and four other murders, all perpetrated by husbands or partners, men close to the victims. These were typical crimes of domestic violence, but with a twist: in each case the woman came from Baztán and had moved away from the region.'

'All except for Johana,' said Etxaide.

'Yes, all except Johana, who still lived here. Each of the victims was subjected to a post-mortem amputation, and each of the killers took his own life and left the same signature: *Tarttalo*.

'All the amputations were performed with a serrated object that we initially thought might be a compass saw or an electric kitchen knife. However, the discovery of a fragment in Lucía Aguirre's remains enabled us to confirm that it was in fact an old surgical saw, used to perform amputations.'

Montes arched an eyebrow.

'Dr San Martín is presently making a mould of the metal tooth to confirm this, but all indications are that this is the type of instrument we're looking for. And it would also make sense, because in the Johana Márquez case, the place where the amputation took place, the hut where her body was found, had no electricity, so an electric kitchen knife or compass saw would have been unusable unless they were battery-operated. There's one other thing . . .' She glanced alternately at Jonan and Iriarte, both of whom were in the know. 'Tests have shown that the two sets of bones left in the church at Arizkun belonged to members of my family and were deliberately placed there,' she explained, without mentioning where the bones had been taken from. That was enough information for the time being.

'Fuck, Salazar!' exclaimed Montes, turning to the others as though seeking their confirmation. 'So this is personal,' he declared.

'It seems so,' Amaia went on, 'especially since we know who told him where to find them. He visited my mother at the hospital where she was detained, passing himself off as my brother.'

'But, you don't have a brother.'

'No, Montes, I don't. I have the two sisters you know, which just shows you how audacious he is.'

'He wormed the information out of your elderly mother, then left the bones there to provoke you.'

The term 'elderly mother' conjured images of a poor, naïve old woman, manipulated by a Machiavellian monster. Amaia gave a faint smile.

'And you think it's this Garrido guy with the missing fingers?'

Iriarte took over: 'No, it's not him. The images from the hospital rule him out as the visitor. Everything suggests that these chaotic, violent aggressors were merely doing the bidding of someone far cleverer. An instigator, a person who manipulates the rage of these men at will, directing it at the women close to them. Someone who has such power over them that

429

he can persuade them to take their own lives once he has no more use for them.'

'I think the first thing we should do is to find out who might have had access to your mother while she was at the hospital,' said Montes.

'Zabalza is working on that.'

Montes was taking notes. 'What else do we have?'

Jonan shot Amaia a questioning look, to which she responded by shaking her head. The fact that the last lot of bones belonged to her twin sister had no bearing on the case; it made no difference whether they belonged to one relative or another. Although she knew this wasn't true: the fact that the bones belonged to her sister was a special kind of provocation, an outrage that haunted her. However, she hadn't shared this information with Markina and she didn't see why she should do so with Montes and Zabalza. As far as she was concerned, too many people knew about it. So, for the moment, they were simply bones found at the desecration site.

'Well, all that remains is for him to contact you directly, then it'll be a textbook case,' said Montes.

'The emails,' said Jonan.

'Yeah, well . . .' she said, prevaricating.

'Inspector Salazar has been receiving somewhat strange emails on a daily basis. We've traced them to a dynamic IP address, but after tracking it halfway across Europe we still have no location, although it's probably a public Internet access point.'

'In other words: impossible to trace,' said Montes.

'Precisely.' Etxaide grinned.

'Well, why not just say so!' exclaimed Montes, also grinning.

'The instigator's profile,' said Amaia, writing on the board. 'A male, with links to Baztán. Possibly born here, or had a wife or partner from here, whom he killed or wanted to kill –

which might explain his hatred towards these other women. As Montes pointed out,' she said, looking at him, 'his actions clearly contain an element of personal provocation towards me. By using my ancestors' bones he has, in effect, contacted me. So, this gives us a fairly clear picture: on the one hand I'm a woman in a position of authority – something misogynists cannot stand. And yet his actions were designed to ensure that I took on the case, which suggests that he's competing with me. Similar profiles in FBI case studies suggest that he's probably five years younger or older than me, so we're looking at an age range of between twenty-eight and thirty-eight. He is young and well-educated. Not all of his followers were thugs; at least two were directors of multinational companies and had university degrees. I'm referring to the two men in Bilbao and Burgos; the guy in Bilbao was also extremely wealthy. It's unthinkable that they would have let just anyone into their circle. He is physically attractive, without being handsome; he has a seductive, charismatic personality, and exudes the self-confidence and poise necessary to enable him to exercise his power over others. We don't know how he ensnares them, but we do know one thing about instigators: their followers do not identify with them. The relationship is one of servitude, not of equals. The instigator never obtains anything by force, but is capable of creating in his followers the desire to please him at any price, even at the sacrifice of their own lives.'

A heavy silence hung over the room, broken at last by Montes:

'And we've got one of these roaming around out there?'

'So it seems.'

'What about this Garrido fellow?'

'You have his file. He fits the profile of the violent abuser, though he seems less chaotic than the others, which is probably why our instigator chose him to carry out the desecrations. Bear in mind that he kept his wife captive for two years in his own house without arousing any suspicion; if she hadn't managed to escape, she would still be there. Before imprisoning her, he had succeeded in breaking off all contact with his own family and with hers. Needless to say, he had no dealings with his neighbours. According to one of his colleagues, he was pleasant, helpful and hard-working, but never socialised outside the office.'

'Chief,' said Montes, 'can I look into this? I'd like to speak to his wife; she must have some idea about where he might be. If he doesn't know the area well, he won't get far, not with the checkpoints on the roads. He must be holed up somewhere, because if he'd killed himself we'd have found him by now.'

Amaia nodded. 'OK, you look into that.'

Montes took the file on Antonio Garrido from the table and flicked through it.

'He's hiding somewhere, I'm sure of it,' he said, holding up a photograph. 'Look at the pigsty he lived in while he had his wife imprisoned.' The image showed a filthy-looking house piled with rubbish; a straw mattress was draped with the chains that had shackled Nuría for two years. 'This guy isn't fussy; he could easily survive in a hut or barn. Can I take a look at those emails you've been getting?'

'Yes. Jonan could you print them out for him, please?'

Jonan returned with the emails and Montes read them out loud.

'"Stones in the river and sand on the beach": I've never been much good with poetry, my ex says I lack sensitivity. What do you think it means?'

Amaia gazed at him in astonishment. This was the first time she had heard Montes joke about his divorce; perhaps he really *was* making progress.

'It's about hiding things in a place so obvious that they go unnoticed. It's a reference to a poem: stones on the riverbed and sand on a beach, something hidden in plain sight.'

'Could it refer to this *tarttalo* guy we're looking for? That would take some nerve, sending us clues about where to find him.'

Amaia shrugged. 'Good. So, Montes, you concentrate on finding Antonio Garrido. Etxaide, carry on with your task,' she said without elaborating. 'And if you want, you can accompany Inspector Montes when he goes to see Nuría. Iriarte, you're with me. Call Lieutenant Padua of the *Guardia Civil*, and ask him if he can come with us. Zabalza, what do you have?'

'A few results, a lot more names to check out, but quite a few overlaps. Right now, I'm cross-checking the staff lists of a cleaning company that had contracts in all three hospitals. There are also orderlies who worked at all three hospitals, as well as doctors and trainee nurses who visit more than one. What with replacements and casual workers, it's time-consuming.'

She gazed at him thoughtfully. 'What about Dr Sarasola?'

'There's no record of him having treated her before now. Do you want me to look into that further?'

'No, Deputy Inspector Etxaide can do that. You carry on with the lists.'

She noticed his look of frustration. The guy was never satisfied.

Jonan seemed pensive; she sensed from his expression that he had something to tell her.

'Stay here, Etxaide,' she said.

He waited until the others had gone, then smiled apologetically. 'Actually, it's just a silly detail about the emails you've been receiving, only I didn't want to mention it in front of the others before I'd told you.'

She looked at him expectantly.

'When I was tracking the IP address, the signal suddenly jumped to a server in the States, Virginia to be exact, before leading me to the source of the messages.'

'And?'

'They come from Baton Rouge, Louisiana. The FBI detected my search and ordered me to cease immediately. They gave no explanation, but the route the signal took suggests either a suspect or an infiltrator.'

'Good. Thanks, Jonan: you were right to tell me about this first.'

35

Amaia hated carrying an umbrella, but it was raining so hard she would have been soaked the instant she stepped out of the car. She unfurled it reluctantly and waited for Iriarte to circle the car before starting up the track. The hut, which a year earlier had been all but obscured by vegetation, was now completely enveloped. Padua was waiting in his patrol car, having driven up to the door. He stepped out when he saw them approach, and they entered the hut together. The bindweed, which once poked timidly through the hole in the roof, had wrapped itself round the rafters, forming a natural canopy that prevented the rain from pouring through the hole.

There was no sign of the old settee, or the mattress that had covered Johana's body; the table and bench had also disappeared. She thought this was a shame. Huts like this were welcoming places, open to all, where shepherds, hunters or hikers could take refuge from the rain, stay the night, or simply rest a while. But Johana's murder had tainted it. The floor strewn with droppings, the bale of hay in one corner, and the unmistakable odour of sheep made it clear that only animals sheltered there now.

Amaia walked to the back of the hut and stopped to inspect

the site where a year before they had discovered Johana's body, as though somehow she might be able to perceive the imprint of that brief life.

'Thanks for coming, Padua,' she said, turning to face him.

The lieutenant played it down with a gesture. 'What's on your mind?'

'Do you remember Jasón Medina's statement when he was arrested?'

Padua nodded. 'Yes, he broke down and confessed between sobs what he had done to his stepdaughter.'

'Precisely. Unlike our other killers, Medina's profile wasn't that of a violent, deeply frustrated man. His wife suspected him because of the lascivious looks she caught him giving her daughter, his excessive control over the girl's comings and goings, even what she wore. The only substantial difference between his crime and that of the others was the rape, which in itself isn't out of the ordinary; many violent attacks on women involve sexual assault.'

'So, what doesn't fit? The similarities are obvious.'

'Yes, they are, but there's something else. All the other murdered women were born in the valley, but had moved away due to circumstance: their parents moved to another province, or they got married, or, as in Nuría's case, because her abuser wanted to distance her from her family as part of his plan to destroy her. All the other killers had a history of violence, or of pent-up violence, the kind of temperament that's like a pressure-cooker. In Johana's case, not only was she not born here, she was the only one actually living here when she was killed. Also, her stepfather had no history of violence and doesn't fit the profile. Jasón Medina was a sexual pervert, who can only engage in violence during the sexual act – and even then only if the victim resisted, which we know Johana did.'

'OK,' said Padua, 'but I imagine you have also established that the instigator has some connection to the valley?'

436

'Yes, of course, only there's another difference: in Johana's case, the crime bore no signature.'

Padua looked puzzled. 'He wrote "*Tarttalo*" on his cell wall, as well as in the note he addressed to you.'

'But not at the scene of the crime. And there are a couple of other details, which may or may not be relevant: in some of the other cases the signature appeared only on the cell walls of the killers, but in each case it was part of a visual strategy. What's more, it was a whole year before Jasón Medina took his own life while in custody, whereas his predecessors did so immediately. The only reason Quiralte took four months was because he had to wait for me to return from maternity leave. Show him, Iriarte,' she said.

The inspector took the ring binder he'd been carrying under his arm, opened it and held it up with both hands so they could see.

'All the murderers killed their wives and then committed suicide, some at the crime scene – like this fellow in Bilbao, you see the signature?' he said, pointing at the photo. 'The guy from Burgos left the house and hanged himself from a tree – and there's the signature. The guy in Logroño topped himself in prison – there's the signature. Quiralte, in prison, just after telling us where to find Lucía Aguirre's body – here's the signature . . .'

'And Medina, in prison, with the signature . . .' said Padua, contemplating the documents.

'Yes, but a year later.'

'Maybe because of his character he was a bit of a coward?'

'Possibly, but if he'd been recruited like his "brethren" he would have done the same. Besides, it takes lot of determination to slit your own throat; I wouldn't describe that as the act of a coward.'

'Where are you going with this? Johana's arm turned up in Arri Zahar along with the others—'

'I'm not disputing that. We're pretty certain that the same implement was used to sever all the limbs.'

'So . . .'

'I don't know.' She paused, glancing about her. 'You questioned Medina. Do you think he was lying?'

'No, I believe the miserable bastard was telling the truth.'

She remembered how Medina sobbed continuously, the tears and mucus running down his face. A pathetic sight. He confessed to having assaulted his stepdaughter, then strangled her with his bare hands and raped her after she was dead. But when they asked him why he had severed one of her arms, he looked bewildered and claimed he knew nothing about it. After killing her on impulse, he went home to fetch some rope, which he placed around the girl's neck to try to disguise it as one of the *basajaun* crimes he had read about in the press. When he arrived back at the hut, Johana's arm was missing.

'Do you remember him saying that he felt a presence?' she asked.

'He thought someone was watching him. He even imagined it might be Johana's ghost,' said Padua, explaining to Iriarte.

'After placing the rope, he went home, waited for his wife to come back from work, and tried to act normal. When I asked whether he'd severed the girl's arm to try to conceal her identity, he looked puzzled and said he thought she must have been bitten by an animal.'

'The guy was an idiot! It would take a very large animal to chew her arm off.'

'That's neither here nor there. What matters is why he thought that: there was a chunk of flesh missing from her upper arm; even an idiot like Medina can recognise teeth marks when he sees them.'

'True, there were bite marks on the flesh,' Padua conceded.

'Again, the bodies in the other cases showed no trace of bite marks, least of all from human teeth. And then there's

438

the matter of the hut itself: it's off the beaten track, you don't just stumble across it, you have to know where it is – like hunters, shepherds, the lads who found the body, local people.'

'Yes, Medina only knew about it because he had a job tending sheep for a while.'

'Also, this was in February last last year, when it rained almost as much as this year.'

'Well, I reckon this year is going to break all records, but yes, it did rain a lot. The paths turned to mud. Only someone who knew the place would venture out here.'

'So, either the *tarttalo* bumped into Medina by chance, or he was following him, watching him. I'll wager it's the latter.'

'Do you think they'd met at that point?'

'I think the *tarttalo* knew Medina. What I'm unsure about is when he started to gain control over him. He must have been a hard nut to crack, because his behaviour doesn't fit the profile.'

Iriarte piped up. 'Do you think he met him first and recruited him later?'

Amaia raised a finger.

'There's the discrepancy,' she said. 'I believe Jasón's crime was driven by his desire. His actions were muddle-headed, unpremeditated, as borne out by the fact that he returned home to fetch the rope in an effort to make it look like the previous crimes. Johana's murder was a crime of opportunity. He said he had taken the girl with him to a car wash, and that halfway there he had the urge to rape her. Driven by brute desire, he acted without thinking about the circumstances, appropriateness or consequences of his actions. Only afterwards, when he had come to his senses, did he start planning; he brought her here, returned home to fetch the rope, then tried to convince the girl's mother that she had gone off, as on previous occasions. A few days later, he even went so far as to remove some of Johana's clothes, money, her ID card, claiming that the girl had come back for them. He was thinking on his feet, he had no preconceived plan.'

'Yes, which suggests . . .'

'That if he acted on impulse, if Johana's death wasn't premeditated, how come our *tarttalo* appeared on cue to take his trophy?' said Amaia. 'In order to recruit acolytes, he has to be expert at sniffing out killers, a specialist in criminal profiling. I'm convinced he knew Medina. And, knowing he was unpredictable, there was only one way he could have been here at precisely the right moment . . .'

'He was following him,' said Padua.

'It wouldn't be easy to tail someone in the valley without them knowing,' Iriarte pointed out.

'Unless you blend in,' said Amaia. 'Unless you're part of the scenery – you're from the valley.'

36

Amaia had been standing at the window for the past twenty minutes. Anyone observing her would have said she was staring into the distance, but the torrential rain outside had reduced visibility to a few yards, so all she could see was the water cascading down the road. A car pulled up outside the entrance and she wondered why the driver hadn't parked beneath the overhang of the building, which was what people coming to reception generally did. She saw a uniformed officer approach the vehicle to enquire, followed a few moments later by Deputy Inspector Zabalza, who flung open the driver's door and, judging from his gestures, became involved in an angry discussion that lasted about a minute. He slammed the door and went back into the building. The car remained where it was for a few minutes before starting up, turning around and driving off.

The police station was quiet. Most of the officers had finished for the day, although the activity on the ground floor was ceaseless. She was the only one upstairs, along with Zabalza two doors down, and the hiss of the coffee machine in the passageway.

Her visit to the hut with Padua and Iriarte had left her feeling increasingly uneasy, suspecting she was missing

441

something obvious in relation to Johana Márquez's death. But what? All she could think of was that it was something obscene.

Johana Márquez was the discordant note in the instigator's composition, and not only because of Medina's aberrant behaviour and impulsiveness. The instigator must have known Medina. She was sure he had identified him from the start as a prospective acolyte. But if, as she suspected, the instigator was an expert profiler, it would have been perfectly obvious to him that Medina was unpredictable, that like all sexual predators he acted on impulse when his desire was aroused, that he was incapable of controlling himself.

So why did he take a risk with him? Why not simply rule him out? He had the wrong profile, his wasn't a sin of wrath, but of lust, his prospective victim wasn't even born in the valley. Amaia was certain that this discordant note was significant, that it wasn't random, and might therefore hold the key to unravelling the instigator's behaviour, to revealing his identity. Why had he chosen Medina? She felt sure the reason was covetousness. The intense longing to obtain what we desire, the seed of our desire, the desire for something that doesn't belong to us, which becomes perverted into a longing to deprive the other of the object of our desire. In Dante's *Purgatory*, the author describes: 'Love of one's own good perverted to a desire to deprive other men of theirs'. The punishment for the envious was to have their eyelids sewn shut, depriving them of the pleasure of seeing others' suffering.

Amaia was as certain that the instigator knew Johana as she was that he didn't know the other victims. He saw the sweet little Johana, he saw the monster who lay in wait for her, and that was what made him deviate from his usual pattern. He coveted her, he coveted her sweetness, her tenderness; it was this urge to satisfy his desire that drew him to someone as unpredictable as Medina, who might explode at

442

any moment. And so he trailed him until he had the chance to obtain what he coveted.

Amaia left her post by the window and grabbed her bag. Before leaving the room, she went over to the board and scribbled: 'The *tarttalo* knew Johana.'

As she approached Zabalza's work station, she decided to tell him to call it a day: it was late, and in any event cross-checking all the names on those lists would take several days. She was about to go in, when she realised he was speaking on the phone. From his hushed monosyllables she knew instantly the kind of conversation he was having. She and James would often joke about the dulcet tone she adopted when speaking to him. 'You're sweet-talking me,' he would say, and he was right.

Deputy Inspector Zabalza was employing the masculine version of that tone, which was the preserve of lovers. She walked past the door without stopping, glancing sidelong at him as he stood by the window, mobile in hand. Even with his back turned, his body language betrayed a pleasurable languor rare in a man who always seemed so tense. While she waited by the lift, she heard him laugh and it struck her that this was the first time she'd heard that sound.

She paused in the entrance, deterred by the rain. The duty officer looked at her solemnly.

'They're saying the river will burst its banks.'

'I wouldn't be surprised,' she replied, pulling up the hood of her coat. 'Who was here to see Deputy Inspector Zabalza?'

'His girlfriend,' said the officer. 'She didn't want to wait inside, and asked me to tell him she was here.' He shrugged.

As she drove down the hill and round the corner, Amaia noticed the girlfriend's car parked beside a bramble patch. She glided past and saw a young woman inside, her gaze fixed on the police station, clearly not talking on the phone to her boyfriend.

Before going home, she stopped off at *Juanitaenea*, put on her boots and, sheltering beneath her umbrella, walked around the outside of the house. She could see that the earth from the disturbed graves had been flattened by the intense rainfall over the last few hours. There were no fresh burrows. She returned to the car and sat inside, contemplating the allotment and recalling the hostile looks the gardener Esteban had given her.

She could hear the Golden Girls' raucous laughter even from outside her aunt's house.

'Ladies, what a din, the neighbours have called the police saying there's a witches' coven in here,' she said as she entered.

'Your niece has come to arrest us, Engrasi!' tittered Josepa. 'Why didn't she send one of those handsome young traffic cops instead?'

'You saucy old thing!' Engrasi laughed. 'Don't think I haven't seen you veering all over the road, hoping you'll be pulled over. You rascal!'

Amaia watched them. Their flushed laughter made her think of mischievous teenagers. It occurred to her that their get-togethers probably weren't so different from the gatherings of Baztán women through the centuries, who would spend the afternoon in one another's houses, stitching wedding trousseaus or making baby baskets for their offspring. Or José Miguel Barandiarán's descriptions of the *etxeko andreak*, those housewives who came together to exchange recipes and opinions, recite the rosary or trade tales about witches. Tales that had left their mark on the valley, striking fear into the hearts of the young women, some of whom had to walk miles to get home afterwards. They probably weren't that different, at least to begin with, from the meetings Elena and her mother had attended. Her face clouded when she remembered Elena talking of *the sacrifice*.

James came downstairs carrying Ibai. When he saw Amaia,

444

he cradled the baby in one arm and reached out the other arm to embrace her.

'Hello, darling,' she whispered. 'Hello, my love!' she said, taking Ibai without letting go of James. 'How was your day?'

He kissed her before replying: 'This morning I went to the studio in Pamplona, to get everything packed up and to talk to the haulage people. It's all arranged.'

'Oh, yes, of course!'

She'd forgotten that the next day James's works were due to be transported to the Guggenheim.

'You remembered, right?' he said mischievously.

'Of course I did. Auntie, can you look after Ibai tomorrow, or shall we take him with us?'

'You'll do no such thing; leave him here. Your sister has spoken to Ernesto, who has agreed to take care of the bakery so that she can come and help me. You two go to Bilbao and enjoy yourselves.'

Amaia made a mental list of the calls she had to make if she wanted to leave everything organised for the next day. The investigation was progressing nicely; she didn't think it would matter if she was absent for one day. She glanced at her watch, then lifted Ibai level with her face, which made him giggle.

'Time for your bath, *ttikitto*.'

37

Nuría was wearing a blue dress and matching jacket. She had swapped her woollen hat for a wide headband, which she wore like a bandana around her cropped head. She didn't have any make-up on, but Jonan noticed that she had painted her nails black. Even before they reached the path, she had opened the front door. With a timid smile she ushered them into the living room, where both men accepted her offer of coffee. Then Inspector Montes asked her about what had happened, whether she remembered anything else. She narrated the same story, only this time with a vehemence that was missing the first time round. She spoke about the incident objectively, as if it had happened to someone else, a different woman, and Jonan realised that in a sense this was true. While Montes was questioning her about how well Antonio Garrido might know the area, Jonan noticed an elaborate flower picture over the hole in the door, which didn't quite cover the gunshot residue at the sides, creating an odd impression. A brand-new double-barrelled shotgun was propped up against the window.

'That gun should be kept in a rack,' Montes commented as they were leaving.

'Yes, I was about to do that when you arrived.'

'I'm sure you were . . .' replied Montes.

It was pouring down when they left the house.

'What do you think?' asked Jonan when they reached the gate.

'I think this Garrido fellow should find something better to do than come after his wife, because next time she's going to kill him and, well . . . there'll be one bastard less in the world.'

Jonan thought so too. He had seen the changes in her attitude and her clothing. The curtains in the living room were drawn back, so that she could see if anyone approached. She had moved the furniture around, keeping a coffee machine, biscuits and a shotgun close by. No doubt she slept on the sofa to keep a lookout. She had exchanged her baggy track-suit for a dress, and had no qualms about displaying her cropped hair, adorning it with a bright bandana; she had covered the traces of the bullet and painted her nails. She was a sniper.

Etxaide shook his head, clasping an umbrella that offered scant protection against the downpour. The fabric was sodden and a fine spray fell on their faces as water dripped down the shaft on to his hand. The two men walked towards the town centre through flooded streets where the gutters weren't draining fast enough. The force of the water hitting the pavement caused it to rain upwards; no umbrella had been invented against that.

Making their way down Pedro Axular, they were instinctively drawn towards the railings at the river bend. The water was level with the path.

'The forecaster was right. If it carries on raining like this, the river will soon burst its banks.'

'Is there nothing they can do?'

'Be ready,' said Jonan, shrugging.

'Will it flood the whole town?'

'No. Where Inspector Salazar's aunt lives, for example, it

never gets flooded. Here, you've got the bend in the river. The Txokoto weir doesn't help either.'

'It must serve some purpose, though?'

'Not any longer. Like most barrages, it was originally constructed to produce electricity. One of earliest buildings in Elizondo is the old mill opposite the arches at the far end of Calle Jaime Urrutia. It was rebuilt in the nineteenth century and turned into a power plant in the mid-twentieth century. If you look carefully, you'll see a fish ladder on the other side of the weir. They've talked about removing it to allow the river to flow more freely, but the locals won't hear of it.'

'Why not?'

'Because they've become accustomed to the weir, to seeing it, to the sound it makes. Also, tourists like to take pictures on the bridge.'

'But if it causes so many problems . . .'

'Not that many. The river floods once a year, if that. Sometimes it doesn't flood for years; it's swings and roundabouts.'

Montes gazed over the steadily rising waters.

'They're headstrong, the people in Elizondo,' Jonan said, as they made their way towards Calle Jaime Urrutia. 'Years ago, there was a terrible flood. Perhaps if the weir hadn't been there it would have made a difference. Look,' he said, pointing at old Serora's house, 'the water rose as far as that plaque. That used to be where the priest's servant lived. The old church was right there,' he said, indicating with a sweep of his hand the square, where all that remained was a fountain. 'The current washed it away.'

'And yet they insist on keeping the weir?'

'On that occasion, the flood was caused by rocks and fallen trees blocking the river upstream. When it gave way, the river descended with such force that it swept away everything in its path. I'm convinced the problem is the bend in the river, it's logical that it floods at this point.'

Montes noticed that shop owners had prepared for the flood, sealing their doors with boards and sheets of foam rubber; some had even piled up sandbags. Most businesses were closed, but a few of the houses overlooking the river were unprotected.

'It's a shame no one bothers about these buildings,' he said.

'Some of them are abandoned; but yes, it is a shame, because they are of considerable historical interest. That one, for instance,' said Jonan, pointing to an ancient-looking structure. 'It's called *Hospitalenea*. For centuries, pilgrims took shelter there after crossing the Pyrenees on their way to Santiago de Compostela; it was a tough route and they would arrive exhausted. Many didn't make it.'

Montes raised his head to get a better look. The closed shutters had the greyish tinge of very old wood, while the long, ironwork balcony on the top floor seemed to be hanging from the wall, attached by three supports. Above the first-floor balcony was an inscription, which Montes couldn't read through the rain.

'What does it say?'

'The year the house was bought and restored: 1811, I think.'

They walked on, then Montes stopped for a moment, passing the umbrella to Jonan.

'Wait here,' he said, retracing his steps.

Jonan stood clasping the umbrella in the middle of the street as he watched Montes hurry back, disappearing from sight at the bend in the river, behind Arizkunenea Palace.

Montes returned to where they had paused to look at the river. The rain had ruffled its mirror-like surface, and the lights shone on the water like moving dots. Gripping the railing with both hands, he counted the houses overlooking the river under his breath. He recounted them even as he strained to see. The rain was coming down in torrents, soaking his clothes and hair, running into his eyes. Shielding them with his hand, he counted once more then waited until he saw it.

449

A shimmering glow, like a dancing candle flame, followed by a formless shadow gliding across the unshuttered window, then darkness. Montes suddenly realised his shoes were full of water; glancing down he saw that the river had breached the wall and the water was moving like a small wave towards the street. He started to run, rounded the corner by Arizkunenea Palace, then sprinted towards Jonan, counting the buildings again as he drew his weapon.

Alarmed, Jonan glanced down both ends of the deserted street.

'What are you doing?'

Montes drew level with him, explaining between gasps as he dragged him towards the door of the abandoned house.

'He's here. What did you say this place was called?'

'*Hospitalenea*,' said Jonan, nodding as it dawned on him what Montes was saying. 'This was an old hospital – he told Nuría: "I'm taking you to the hospital".'

'Are you armed?'

'Of course,' said Jonan, throwing aside the umbrella and taking out his Glock, along with a torch.

'I thought you archaeologists carried a pick and a brush,' Montes said with a grin.

'I'm going to call for back-up.'

Montes put a hand on his shoulder.

'There isn't time, Jonan. If he's watching, which he doubtless is, then he'll have seen us stop opposite the house. I think he had a candle and snuffed it out because he saw me. If we wait for back-up, we'll find him dead – and we need to question him. He's upstairs, first door on the left.'

Montes grasped the rusty handle and turned it.

'It's locked,' he whispered. 'On the count of three. One. Two . . .' He rammed his shoulder against the wooden door, swollen with damp. It opened about twenty centimetres then stuck fast. Reaching through with his arm, Montes pushed hard and managed to open it wider. Etxaide followed him. They were running up the staircase, feeling the wood groan beneath their feet, the banister rail juddering as though shaken by an earthquake, when the body plunged through the stairwell with an almighty crack. They aimed their torches downwards.

'That sonofabitch!' cried Montes, turning back. 'He's hanged himself.'

As soon as Montes reached the ground floor, he took hold of the man by his legs, hoisting him up to slacken the pressure of the rope round his neck.

'Go up and cut the rope!' he yelled to Etxaide. 'Cut the rope!'

Jonan flew up the stairs, waving his torch until he saw where the rope was fastened to the broken banister rail – the source of the noise they had heard. The rope was too thick to have broken his neck or trachea, but would have cut off his windpipe. Jonan tucked his gun into his waistband, glancing uneasily at the darkened rooms they hadn't had time to search. Montes was by this time screaming at the top of his lungs. Jonan tried to wedge his fingers between the knot and the banister, but the weight had pulled the rope taut. He cast about, looking for something to cut it with, while Montes yelled:

'Cut it, cut it, for fuck's sake!'

Grabbing his gun, Jonan aimed at the rope and fired. The cord leapt, snake-like, into the air, then fell limply into the stairwell. He hurried downstairs to find Montes crouched over the man, attempting to unfasten the rope from around his neck. He rose to his feet triumphantly.

'The bastard's alive.' As if to corroborate this, the man coughed then groaned, with a shrill, rasping sound.

'What the hell were you doing up there? Why did it take you so long?' said Montes, spreading his hands and gesturing towards his clothes with a grimace of disgust. 'You make the calls – that son of a bitch pissed all over me.'

Her phone rang as they were sitting down to dinner.

'We've got Garrido. He was hiding in the old pilgrims'

hospital. He tried to hang himself when we broke in. He's still alive, thanks to Montes, but only just. We've called an ambulance.'

A stark image of Freddy hooked up to tubes and paralysed in a hospital bed flashed through Amaia's mind.

'I'm on my way. If the ambulance gets there before me, don't let him out of your sight – and don't allow anyone to approach or talk to him,' she said, before hanging up.

The Accident and Emergency department at Hospital Virgen del Camino in Pamplona was unusually empty, no doubt because of the rainstorm. There were scarcely half a dozen people in the waiting area; it seemed most people preferred to postpone coming in until the rain stopped.

She and Iriarte flashed their badges at the receptionist.

'Antonio Garrido, he was brought in by ambulance from Baztán.'

'Ward three. The doctors are with him now. You can sit in the waiting area.'

Ignoring the woman, they set off down the corridor. Before they had reached ward three, Jonan came out to greet them.

'Don't worry, Montes is in there with him.'

'How is he?'

'Conscious, breathing OK, he has a nasty friction burn around his neck, and he can't talk. I expect he's damaged his trachea, but he'll live. He can certainly move his legs; he was thrashing about when Montes had a hold of him, then afterwards when he was on the floor.'

'What are they doing in there?'

'They X-rayed his throat when he arrived; now the doctors are checking him over.'

The doors swung open; two doctors, a man and a woman, emerged, followed by a nurse.

'You're not supposed to be here,' she said when she saw them.

'Navarre police,' replied Amaia. 'We're here to guard the detainee, Antonio Garrido. How is he?'

The doctors paused in front of her.

'Well, he's alive, thanks to your colleague. If he hadn't relieved the pressure of the rope, the man would have suffocated. Fortunately, he didn't jump from a great height; the banister gave way almost immediately; and it seems he used a thick rope, which kept his vertebra in place. His trachea is in bad shape, though.'

'Can he speak?'

'With difficulty, but enough to ask to be voluntarily discharged, so . . .'

'He's asked to be discharged?'

'The nurse is preparing the paperwork for him to sign,' said the doctor apologetically. 'Look, we've warned him about the seriousness of his injuries. I told him that, although he might feel OK now, his condition could deteriorate in the next few hours. He's requested some sedatives, but still insists he wants to be voluntarily discharged. I've put a cervical collar on him and we've dressed what remains of his ear. In our view, he needs surgery, but he absolutely refuses. So, once he's signed the paperwork, he's yours.'

Amaia looked at Iriarte, puzzled. 'What's this guy playing at?'

'No idea.'

'I'm going to call Markina, then we'll take Garrido to the main police headquarters.'

The interview room at the Pamplona police station was identical to the one in Elizondo: a two-way mirror on one wall, a table, four chairs, and a ceiling camera. A uniformed officer stood by the door.

They observed Garrido from behind the two-way mirror. He had red marks around his eyes and his face was flushed from the pressure of the collar. A thick bandage covered his ear and the part of his head that had no hair; a greasy ointment

453

had been applied where the gunpowder burns flecked his face. Apart from that, he seemed calm, his eyes resting on the table as he fiddled with the bottle of water and the effervescent tablets they had given him at the hospital. If he was in any pain or discomfort he didn't let it show. He gave the impression of someone waiting patiently, aware that nothing he might do would make the time pass more quickly.

Montes and Iriarte entered the interview room. Iriarte sat down opposite Garrido and looked straight at him, while Montes remained standing. Garrido acted as if nothing around him had changed.

'Antonio Garrido, is that correct?' asked Iriarte.

The man looked at him. 'What's the time?'

'Are you Antonio Garrido?'

'You know I am,' he said in a faint voice. 'What's the time?'

'Why do you want to know?'

'I have to take my medication.'

'It's six o'clock in the morning.'

Garrido grinned and his face flushed even more.

'You're wasting your time.'

'Really? Why is that?'

'Because I won't talk to anyone except the star cop,' he said with a giggle.

Behind the glass, Amaia glanced at Jonan and sighed. She had a growing feeling of having seen this before during the interview with Quiralte. It was clear they had been given the same instructions.

'I don't know who you're talking about,' replied Iriarte.

'I mean her,' he said, pointing towards the glass window with the stump of his finger.

'You agree to speak to Inspector Salazar?'

'Yes, but not now, not yet.'

'When?'

'Later, but only with her, with the star cop.' He gave the same silly laugh.

454

Montes stepped in:

'What if I smash your teeth in, you won't have anything to laugh about then.'

'You won't do that, you're my fucking guardian angel! I owe you my life and that makes me your responsibility, did you know that? In some cultures, you'd be obliged to look after me for the rest of your life.'

Montes smiled.

'So, your my responsibility because I prevented you from killing yourself? And how come you're so stupid as to attempt to do that without having completed your task? Your master can't be very happy with your services.'

Garrido's muscles tensed beneath his shirt.

'I've served him well,' he whispered.

'Oh, yes, I forgot: using a poor kid to desecrate churches at night.' Garrido was staring at the mirror; Amaia knew why. 'A poor, abused young lad – aren't you ashamed of yourself?'

'Believe me, he enjoyed it. It's the most he'll ever do. He hasn't the balls to do what he should.'

'And what should he do, in your opinion?'

'Kill his father.'

Amaia took out her mobile and dialled.

'Zabalza, take a patrol car, drive to Zaldúa's house and fetch the son. Garrido has just declared that he's too cowardly to kill his father. Let's hope he's right.'

'Thanks,' said Zabalza.

His answer puzzled her, but then, he was a strange guy.

Montes continued: 'I get it: scared kids, defenceless women – you're a real champ. Or at least, you were. The fact is, you've messed up big time. You failed to intimidate the boy, he grassed you up straight away. As for your wife, that really takes the biscuit: you only need to look at what she did to your face.'

'Shut up,' muttered Garrido.

Montes smiled, standing behind the man's chair.

'I saw her, you know? Very pretty, though a little on the skinny side. How much does she weigh? Forty-five kilos? Probably less, but that slip of a girl ripped your ear off – and she'd rip your balls off, if we let her. She gave you what was coming to you, I reckon.'

A rasping grunt rose from Garrido's throat. Amaia was sure he would pounce, but instead he began to rock back and forth in his chair, murmuring some kind of incantation. He repeated the gesture a dozen times before stopping. And as he did so, he gave a smile.

'I'll talk later.'

Montes gestured to Iriarte and they left the room. Before the door closed, Garrido called out.

'Inspector.'

Montes turned to look at him.

'I'm sorry I pissed on you,' he said, laughing.

Montes made as if to go back, but Iriarte pushed him outside.

They stifled their smiles as Montes walked in.

'You managed to rile him over his wife,' said Jonan.

'Of course, what could humiliate a man like that more than being beaten up by a woman?'

Amaia smiled: the same could apply to him.

'But it wasn't enough,' said Montes ruefully.

'What do you suppose he's waiting for? Do you think he'll talk to you?' Iriarte asked.

'I don't know, but he's clearly playing for time. I think he tried to kill himself because that's what he was meant to do if we caught him, but now his mission has changed. As he said, he served his master well, carrying out the desecrations, but I think this is plan B. If the *tarttalo* allowed him to be caught, it's because he still has some use for him.'

'We could have another go at him,' suggested Iriarte. 'For

a moment there, you almost made him lose control,' he said to Montes.

'Yes, but what was he doing in there, what was he muttering to himself?' asked Amaia.

'I heard,' said Iriarte. 'He was saying: "She doesn't matter."'

'Could you step outside, chief?' said Montes, going into the corridor and taking her to one side. 'It's an anger-management technique they teach you in therapy. They offer them to violent prisoners too. But the fact is, you have to be a hundred per cent committed for it to work; otherwise you simply learn to control yourself outwardly, to appear normal, while inside you're exactly the same. And all that pent-up anger has to come out, it's as simple as that. Despite all appearances to the contrary, I *did* attend therapy, but I swear it only made me feel worse, so I stopped going. I remember after six sessions still feeling I could kill you.'

Amaia stared at him, surprised by his candour. 'Or I you . . .'

'That too,' he conceded, 'but the fact is, I felt anger towards . . . a lot of things, but above all you. And in my experience, those anger-management therapies only teach you how to pretend that you aren't angry.'

38

The heavy rain had eased in the last few hours and morning had arrived, noisy and hectic, in Pamplona. Traffic clogged the streets, pedestrians scurried along beneath their umbrellas, which occasionally vanished amid the branches of the tall trees that surrounded the police station, and were an unmistakable emblem of that green city of stone. Gazing through the windows of the police station, which at that time in the morning smelled of coffee and aftershave, she missed her house in Calle Mercaderes. That made her think of James, and she took out her mobile.

'Hi, Amaia, good morning, I was about to call you—'

'I'm sorry, James, things got complicated last night.'

'But you're to going make it, aren't you?'

She sighed, deflated, before answering.

'James, I won't be able to go with you. We arrested the man responsible for the desecrations in Arizkun yesterday, and this week in Elizondo he attempted to kill his wife whom he had held captive for two years. He probably also dug up the graves at *Juanitaenea*. He's going to make a statement – and I need to be there . . . Do you understand?'

He took a couple of seconds to respond.

'I do understand, Amaia, only . . . You know how important this is to me. We've been waiting for it so long. I thought you'd be here with me.'

'Oh, James, my love, I'm sorry. Go and set up the exhibition. I promise I'll be with you as soon as I can after I finish here.'

She felt like a traitor. Exhibiting at the Guggenheim had to be the high point in the life of any artist, and setting it up was for James one of the most exciting moments; placing the sculptures, the lighting, studying the pieces from every angle, carefully adjusting with both hands the position of each piece until it was illuminated exactly as he wanted. His gestures had a sensual, erotic charge, enhanced by the intensity of his gaze while he was performing them.

'How is Ibai?'

'He woke up an hour ago. Your aunt is giving him a feed. His little eyelids are already drooping.'

'And Elizondo?'

'I haven't been outside yet, but your sister says she saw several inches of water in Calle Jaime Urrutia and in the square. The rain has let up, but it doesn't look like it's going to stop. Provided it stays like this, at least it won't get worse.'

'James, I'm so sorry. I'd give anything to be able to be with you.'

Another overly long silence.

'Don't worry, I understand. We'll talk later.'

After he hung up, she stood staring at her phone, missing his voice, wishing she could say more. They'd been looking forward to today for a long time, not least because, aside from the occasional dinner out, it would have been their first time alone together since Ibai was born. How would she make it up to him? How would she make it up to herself?

The phone buzzed in her hand, telling her she had new emails in her inbox. Dr Franz firing accusations at Sarasola. He

459

repeated his arguments, which, oddly, sounded both more plausible and more desperate. She searched for his number and called him.

Dr Franz's initial surprise at receiving her call lasted as long as it took him to assess whether she had started to take him seriously or not. He decided she had: why else would she call if she didn't believe him?

'I'm so glad you're finally listening to me. Sarasola is a manipulator, that's how he rose to fame. I find it hard to believe that a rational woman like yourself would be taken in by the mystical drivel of a Vatican exorcist.'

Amaia appreciated the compliment, reflecting that the two men's tactics weren't so dissimilar.

'There's no doubt in my mind that Sarasola is behind all this. Think about it: your mother's phantom visitor, her medication stuffed in the bedframe, his opportune appearance as the saviour who whisks her away. It makes no sense otherwise. He doesn't fool me. What I can't work out is his motive. Granted, from a medical point of view Rosario's case is interesting – but it hardly justifies arming a dangerous patient, who, were it not for the alarm system, would have killed that nurse. The only other possibility is that he's mentally unbalanced, or that a desire for notoriety has clouded his judgement, leading him to commit this atrocity.'

Amaia summoned all her patience.

'Dr Franz, there's no way of establishing a link between Sarasola and your hospital. You know him too well; he couldn't possibly have gained access without being discovered. And, frankly, the whole idea is a little far-fetched.'

'I disagree. I'm sure that he's behind the whole thing. What's more, I don't intend to let the matter rest.'

'Dr Franz, I advise you to back off. As things stand, no one else is levelling accusations against Sarasola. I wouldn't want you to get into trouble for making threats. Leave this to us, I promise we'll look into it.'

'Really?' He sounded far from convinced. 'Mark my words – strange as this might sound, coming from a shrink: that man is a devil.'

Amaia returned to the room behind the mirror and observed Garrido. Despite his injuries, he didn't appear in the least fatigued; he sat back in his chair, relaxed, amusing himself by picking the label off his water bottle with his nail. A uniformed officer brought him some coffee in a paper cup and a bun wrapped in cling film, doubtless from the vending machine on the first floor. Garrido chewed each morsel slowly before swallowing. It must have been agony, but he didn't complain. The culture of pain, Amaia reflected. Perhaps, after all, it was more widespread than Lasa III believed. She saw Garrido say something to the officer on guard. Amaia turned on the speakers, but Garrido fell silent again. She poked her head into the corridor and called to another officer.

'Take over from your colleague in the interview room.'

When the first officer came out Amaia asked him: 'What did he say to you?

'He asked what time it was, then said he wanted to make his call.'

Amaia turned to Iriarte and Montes, who were coming back from breakfast.

'Garrido has asked to make a call.'

Iriarte looked puzzled. 'He said he didn't want a lawyer.'

'Well, now he says he wants to make a call. Bring him out into the corridor handcuffed. Don't let him out of your sight.'

'Excuse me, Inspector,' said the officer who had been guarding the prisoner. 'He told me he wanted to call his psychiatrist.'

'His psychiatrist?'

'Yes, that's what he said.'

As she went back into her office, a fresh incoming email made her phone vibrate at the same time as she received a call. It was Zabalza.

'Good morning, chief,' he said, whispering the last word. 'We accompanied social services who removed Beñat Zaldúa from his father's house. I've spoken to a cousin of his in Pamplona, who seems willing to take him in.'

'Good.'

'I've finished cross-referencing those lists. A few of the names come up in more than one. I've just emailed them to you.'

'Great. Anything else?'

'Yes, we carried out an exhaustive search this morning of the pilgrims' hospital where the suspect was hiding out. We found remains of food and provisions, indicating that he had been there for a couple of weeks and probably planned on staying a while longer; waiting, I guess. But what's most interesting is all the old hospital equipment we found on the top floor. Beds, lamps, tables, and cabinets containing surgical instruments similar to the scalpel Dr San Martín analysed. Identical, I'd say. I'll send you some photos now.'

'Damn, of course, the old pilgrims' hospital, that's where the instruments came from. That's why Garrido told Nuria Otaño he was going to "take her" to the hospital, which made no sense . . . Good work, Inspector, well done. Send the instruments to San Martín so that he can compare them. And . . . Zabalza, come to Pamplona – I need you here.'

'Yes, chief,' he replied.

Amaia smiled. This was the first time he had sounded as if he meant it.

After hanging up, she opened the email. The list of names that coincided was longer than she had expected. She read through it, scouring her memory. Some names rang a bell, but that was normal; over the years, she and her sisters must

462

have heard dozens, as they were introduced to doctors in hospital corridors, in Accident and Emergency, not to mention psychiatrists' consulting rooms. Even Dr Franz appeared a couple of times. But not Sarasola. She went over the list again to see if any names stood out. Most were Basque or Navarrese. Nothing extraordinary. She closed the email and thought again about Garrido and what Montes had said about anger-management therapy. She looked up Padua's number.

'Good morning, Inspector, I was going to call to congratulate you. The whole valley is buzzing with the news that you've arrested the desecrator.'

'Thanks, Padua, but he's only a puppet. This is just the beginning.'

'How can I help you?'

'I've had an idea. I'm very interested to know whether the inmate who killed himself in Logroño was having therapy before or during his time in prison. I thought that, since you're on such good terms with the force there . . . As for Medina, I know he received no therapy prior to his arrest, but I'd like to know whether he saw a psychiatrist while he was in prison.'

'Is there anything else?'

'Well, while you're at it, you could also ask about Quiralte. He was in Pamplona, like Medina. Let's see what they say.'

'I'm sure they would have done; the majority of prisoners undergo therapy these days as a way of reducing their sentences. Every prison has a visiting shrink, sometimes even voluntary doctors from charitable organisations.'

Amaia scrolled through her address book for a couple of other numbers and called them. María Abásolo's aunt thought her niece's husband had been in therapy.

'. . . I gave him a serious talking to and he promised he'd

go, but then he gave it up after two sessions. I'm not sure I'd call that being in therapy . . .'

Zuriñe Zabaleta's sister remembered as soon as Amaia mentioned it.

'Of course, that's right, I'd forgotten. I don't know if he actually went, but my sister told me that when she first asked for a divorce he promised he would see a therapist. I don't know why I didn't remember sooner. Perhaps because afterwards it seemed obvious that he never went,' she said sadly.

'Or perhaps he did . . .' whispered Amaia after hanging up.

It was midday when Padua rang back.

'Inspector, they confirmed in Logroño that the prisoner saw a psychiatrist. It's written on his report, but they don't have a name; all it says is "psychiatric services" – the signature is illegible. It occurred to me that we could call the prison. It's been a while, but they might remember. Pamplona was easier: both Medina and Quiralte attended therapy; the psychiatrists come from the University Hospital.'

Amaia felt the hairs on the back of her neck stand on end at the mention of the place where Sarasola worked. Maybe Dr Franz wasn't so wide of the mark after all.

'Does it give a specific name?'

'No, just psychiatric services from the University Hospital of Navarre.'

Amaia left her office and went back to the observation room, where she watched Garrido for a couple of minutes. Iriarte and Montes stood beside her, motionless in front of the glass.

'He's asked the time twice. This guy has no intention of telling us anything. There will be no statement, he's stringing us along,' declared Iriarte.

Amaia frowned. 'I still can't work out why he's constantly asking the time. He's waiting for something. You heard what he said. He's keeping us hanging with a promise that he'll

464

make a statement, but he won't. His work was done when his wife stopped behaving the way he expected – at that moment she ceased to be a target. Then Beñat Zaldúa's statement put an end to the desecrations. Garrido was supposed to take his life before he was caught, but because he failed, he is implementing this plan B you mentioned, Montes, which is to keep us busy while someone is doing something elsewhere.'

'There's no way of knowing where,' said Montes.

'The timing has to be related to you, chief,' said Zabalza, who had just walked in.

She looked at Zabalza without seeing him, as she considered his theory.

'It's possible,' she said, stepping out into the corridor. The others followed her. 'Which telephone did Garrido call from?'

Montes gestured to a phone sitting on top of a counter. She picked up the receiver.

'Who else has used this phone since he made the call?'

'Anyone could have,' said Montes. 'But we might be in luck: these phones memorise the last ten calls.'

She pressed a button, looked at the screen and breathed a sigh as she saw the codes.

'They're all in Pamplona. Jonan, check the numbers will you?'

Turning to Zabalza as they walked back to the two-way mirror, she asked, 'Why do you think whatever Garrido is waiting for is related to me?'

'Because everything about this case is related to you. And to Baztán, but especially to you. Whatever he's waiting for must have something to do with you.'

Amaia studied Zabalza, considering what he'd said. If he could only get over himself, he might make a good cop.

Jonan came running back, obviously excited.

'Chief, you're not going to believe this! Most of the calls are work related or private, people calling home and so on, but look at this one.' Jonan dialled the number on his mobile and passed it to her.

She heard the impersonal voice say clearly:

'University Hospital, Department of Psychiatry, how can I help?'

39

Inmaculada Herranz glared at her with a look of displeasure, her lips all but disappearing into the ugly crease that was her mouth. Amaia checked her watch: either the judge's secretary was doing overtime, or she had stayed behind to be there when she arrived. Earlier, when Amaia had called to speak to him, the woman had put her through without acknowledging her greeting; now there she was sitting behind her desk pretending to read the same file, having not turned a page in ten minutes.

Markina arrived in a hurry. He was wearing a long wool coat, which the rain couldn't quite penetrate, remaining on the surface like strange dark specks.

'Sorry to make you wait,' he apologised to Amaia, as he noticed his secretary's presence.

'Are you still here, Inma?' he said, gesturing at the clock.

'I was just finishing going through these dossiers,' she said, in a singsong voice.

'But haven't you seen what time it is? They can wait until morning.'

'I'd prefer to finish them today,' she demurred. 'If you've no objection, we have rather a lot on tomorrow . . .'

He smiled, flashing his perfect teeth. 'I won't hear of it,' he said, striding across to her desk and closing the file. 'Go home and relax.'

She gazed at him rapturously for a few seconds before remembering her rival.

'As you wish,' she replied, somewhat crestfallen.

Having solved his domestic problems, Markina strode into his office without giving her another glance.

'Come with me, Inspector,' he said.

Amaia followed, conscious of Inma looking daggers at her back. She turned to see a face darkened as if the light had gone out in front of it; lips set in a thin fold and in her gaze the age-old hatred of jealous women.

Amaia poked her tongue out.

The woman's loathing turned to astonishment, then outright indignation. She yanked her coat from its hanger and stormed out. Amaia was still grinning when she sat down opposite Markina. He gazed at her, slightly baffled, unsure where this was coming from.

'I imagine there has been some progress in the investigation, otherwise you wouldn't have come to see me,' he said amiably.

'That's right. I informed you last night that we had arrested a suspect. He is currently in custody at the police station, but that's not what I want to talk to you about.'

During the next half hour, she brought Markina up to date with the latest developments, along with the resulting doubts and suspicions. The judge listened closely, writing down a few facts while she expanded on her ideas. After she had finished, the two of them sat in silence for a while. Markina frowned, tilting his head to one side.

'You want to arrest a man of the cloth, a Vatican envoy whose task is to defend the faith – one of the most senior figures in the Church – because you suspect him of being a serial killer, a cannibal, as well as instigating others to murder?'

Amaia shut her eyes and breathed out loudly through her nose.

'I don't propose to accuse him of anything. I simply want to question him. As head of the psychiatric department at the University Hospital, he is responsible for allocating psychiatrists to these prison services.'

'Services that are offered in a spirit of philanthropy.'

'I couldn't care less how philanthropic they are if the service they offer is inciting violent criminals to commit further acts of violence or to take their own lives.'

'We'll have a hard time proving it.'

'OK, but what I have right now is a series of sketchy prison reports signed off by Sarasola, with no name in the box of the appointed psychiatrist.'

'An irregularity which the prisons in question chose to ignore,' Markina reminded her.

'They were signed by the head of the psychiatric department; why would they question that?'

'Do you honestly think that he'd sign them if he was the one visiting the prisoners?'

'Good point. I'm sure his defence lawyer would agree.'

'I doubt this will get as far as lawyers, because what you're asking me is impossible. The man is a senior representative of the Vatican – that means we'd be going up against the Holy See. Moreover, we're talking about a prestigious hospital run by Opus Dei. You're from around here; I don't need to remind you who they are.'

'I know perfectly well who they are. I simply want to ask him a few questions.'

Markina shook his head. 'I'll have to think about it. The accusations of a resentful psychiatrist whose medical pride has suffered, as no doubt his bank account has suffered too, aren't sufficient to justify interrogating a well-known person like Sarasola.'

'The man who carried out the desecrations and who tried to kill his wife called the psychiatric department at that University Hospital this morning. At least two of the other killers also received therapy from that hospital and I'm sure I could prove the others did too. As for the so-called resentful psychiatrist, his accusations aren't completely unfounded. He makes a coherent and logical case against Sarasola: for a start, his involvement was hardly coincidental. He specifically asked for me to head the investigation into the desecrations at Arizkun, then showed up as if by magic when my mother had to be moved.'

Markina shook his head. 'My hands are tied.'

'Yes, this would take real guts.' Amaia looked him in the eye.

'Don't do this to me, Amaia, don't do this to me,' he implored.

She tossed her head contemptuously.

'You have no right to do this to me.'

'I don't know what you mean, your honour.'

'You know perfectly well what I mean.'

Amaia's mobile started to ring. She glanced at the screen; it was Iriarte. She picked up, holding Markina's gaze defiantly while she listened to what Iriarte was saying, hanging up just as the judge's phone rang.

'You're the duty judge, aren't you? Well, you needn't bother picking up, I can tell you what it's about: you know that paranoid psychiatrist, the one with the wounded pride? He's been physically wounded how. In fact, he's dead. And what a coincidence: his body has been found in the car park of the University Hospital – hours after he told me he wasn't going to let Sarasola get away with this.'

Night was falling fast, aided by the black clouds over Pamplona. The rain had finally stopped, although from the look of the sky it was only a lull. A ghostly vapour floated above the stationary police vehicles and the car park was a mass of puddles. Amaia picked her way around them as she

470

approached the body, a silent Markina following behind. Dr San Martín looked up and greeted her.

'How nice to see you, Inspector Salazar, even if it is in these circumstances.'

'Hello, Doctor,' she replied.

Iriarte came over and showed her a bloody wallet, in which the ID card was visible. She nodded; it belonged to Aldo Franz, Dr Franz.

The body was slumped against a car. Much of the blood had come from a deep but narrow gash in his neck. His shirt was torn in several places where he had been stabbed again and again, and his tie appeared embedded in his stomach, as if the wound there had sucked it in.

'First he was stabbed in the abdomen,' said San Martín. 'Without moving the body, I can see eight stab wounds; the one to the neck came later, possibly to stop the victim from crying out. Do you see he had time to raise his hand to his neck to staunch the flow?' San Martín pointed to the bloodied hand and sleeve. 'With this amount of blood loss, he would have quickly lost strength.'

Amaia glanced at Markina, who looked downcast as he contemplated the blood that had flowed over the damp ground until it reached a nearby puddle, spreading on the surface of the water in random red flowers.

Dr Franz's constant, blatant attempts to influence her opinion had not endeared him to her, but seeing his crumpled frame riddled with stab wounds, abandoned amid the puddles, Amaia couldn't help wondering to what extent her failure to take him seriously made her responsible for his death. It was true that she had warned him against getting involved, but she also knew that, for Dr Franz this had been a personal insult. It was only human to feel justified, compelled even, to settle the matter himself.

Montes was standing to one side, having a word with Zabalza, while Etxaide smiled uneasily at Dr San Martín,

471

who delivered his observations as though determined to gauge how squeamish the deputy inspector was. Stooping over the body, he lifted the dead man's raincoat and jacket with his pen to display the angle of the puncture wounds.

'If you look carefully, you'll see there's a definite order, regardless how close they are. Clearly his assailant attacked him head on, with a concealed weapon, probably placing his arm around him or holding him up while he stabbed him. This wound here, the lowest, was undoubtedly the first. His attacker waited until he was very close, then with his right hand plunged the knife into the victim's intestines.' Looking up at Jonan, he added: 'Incredibly painful, but not deadly.' He held the detective's gaze for an instant before focusing on the body again. 'All the others were sheer savagery: see how the trajectory moves upwards in a ladder pattern as the victim started to double over: liver, stomach and . . . if you'll give me a hand here,' he said, leaning the body forward and palpating the back.

Amaia saw Deputy Inspector Etxaide close his eyes as he propped up the limp form with his shoulder.

'Yes,' San Martín declared triumphantly, 'just as I thought: several thrusts went straight through him.'

'That takes a lot of strength,' said Etxaide, relieved to release his hold on the body.

'Or hatred,' said Iriarte. 'This has all the hallmarks of a personal vendetta. Most of the stab wounds were aimed not at killing, but rather inflicting maximum pain.'

Amaia listened to them, looking from the body to Judge Markina, who a few paces behind her was dictating his report for the legal secretary. He was staring intently at the stream of blood and the endless shapes it cast in the water, without ever completely dissolving. She walked over to him, stepping purposefully into the centre of the puddle, which clouded beneath her feet, bringing Markina back to himself. He caught her eye for a moment, gazed up at the façade of the hospital, then nodded.

472

Amaia wheeled round to face her team.

'Iriarte, you're with me. Montes, send people to cover all the exits, including main doors, emergency exits, kitchen, everything. We're looking for Dr Sarasola.' Suddenly she realised that she didn't know his Christian name. 'He's a priest, so he's usually dressed in black with a dog collar, although in the hospital he wears a white coat. If you find him, ask him politely if he could wait, tell him I want a word with him – don't let him leave, but don't arrest him either, make up some excuse.'

The hospital reception area was quiet at that time in the evening. Amaia and Iriarte walked over to the lift while Zabalza stayed in the main entrance. The receptionist called out to them from behind the counter:

'Excuse me, which floor are you going to? Visiting hours are over.'

Amaia turned her back on the woman.

'Excuse me!' she repeated. 'It's forbidden to go up to the wards out of hours without an appointment.'

Her voice alerted the security guard, who changed his habitual route and started towards reception. The lift doors opened and they stepped inside without a word.

'She'll be calling ahead to warn them,' said Iriarte, as the doors closed.

The alarm hadn't yet been raised on the fourth floor. They strode past the nurses' station towards Sarasola's office. A nurse they hadn't seen stepped out from behind the desk.

'Excuse me, you're not authorised to be here.'

The woman stopped in her tracks as Amaia held out her badge practically thrusting it into her face.

She knocked twice before entering. Dr Sarasola was sitting at his desk. He didn't appear surprised to see them.

'Come in, come in, take a seat. I was expecting you. The

473

incident outside in the hospital car park is terrible: how is it possible for such things to happen in the centre of a peaceful city like Pamplona?'

'Don't you know who the victim is?' asked Iriarte.

Even if Sarasola had played no part in this, Amaia found it hard to believe that the powerful priest didn't know at least *that* much about something that had happened right outside his hospital.

'Well, there are rumours, of course, but who can trust them? I was hoping you would clarify matters.'

'The victim is your colleague, Dr Franz,' said Iriarte.

Amaia stared unblinkingly at the priest, who, aware of her eyes on him, decided not to feign astonishment.

'Yes, that's what I heard. I wish it were a mistake.'

'Were you meeting him?' asked Amaia.

'Was I meeting him? Why no, whatever makes you think that, no . . .'

Too long an answer, thought Amaia, *a simple no would have sufficed.*

'You are aware that Dr Franz wasn't at all happy with the way that Rosario was transferred to your hospital. In fact, this morning he informed several people of his intention to resolve the matter with you.'

'I knew nothing about it,' said Sarasola.

'We can easily check Dr Franz's recent calls,' said Iriarte, holding up the dead man's mobile.

Dr Sarasola pursed his lips and remained like that for a few moments.

'Yes, he may have called, but I ignored him, he rang me several times after the transfer . . .'

'Have you changed your clothes in the last few hours, Doctor?' Amaia asked, studying his impeccable appearance.

'What kind of question is that?'

'It looks to me like you've recently taken a shower.'

'I don't see the relevance.'

'Whoever stabbed Dr Franz must have been covered in his blood.'

'You aren't suggesting . . .?'

'Dr Franz was convinced you had something to do with Rosario's strange conduct and the incident at Santa María de las Nieves; that somehow you stage-managed her transferral.'

'That's absurd! Dr Franz was consumed with professional jealousy.'

'Why did you ask for me to head the investigation into the desecrations?'

'What has that to do with anything?'

'Answer the question, please,' Iriarte advised him.

Sarasola smiled as he looked at Amaia.

'Because your reputation precedes you. I believed, correctly as it turned out, that you possessed both the professionalism and discretion necessary for such a sensitive case; I don't have to tell you that for the Church—'

Amaia broke in: 'Where were you an hour ago?'

'Are you accusing me?'

'I'm asking you,' she said patiently.

'Well, it sounds as if you're accusing me.'

'A murder has been committed at your hospital. The victim came here to see you – and relations between the two of you weren't exactly amicable.'

'Firstly, if relations between us weren't amicable, that came purely from him. Secondly, the crime was committed outside, in the car park. Thirdly, this isn't *my* hospital, I'm simply head of psychiatry.'

'I know,' said Amaia smiling. 'And as head of psychiatry, you authorise any external services, such as the therapy offered in prisons.'

'That's correct,' he said.

'At least two of the patients who murdered their wives were seen by you in prison. They subsequently took their own lives – and left the same signature.'

'What?' Sarasola seemed genuinely surprised.

'Jasón Medina, Ramon Quiralte, and now Antonio Garrido, who this morning exercised his right to make a call and rang this department.'

'I don't know those people. I've never heard their names before. You can check as many call registers as you like. I spent the entire morning at the Archbishop's residence with a visiting prelate from the Vatican.'

'Your signature appears on the treatment log for these patients.'

'That means nothing. I sign lots of documents. And of course I always sign the treatment log. But I never visit patients in prison, that's a voluntary service. Several doctors from my department take part in these schemes, but I can assure you that none of them would ever be mixed up in anything as sordid as this.'

'You've never visited any prison in your capacity as a psychiatrist?'

Sarasola shook his head, his confusion palpable.

'Where is Rosario?'

'What? Your mother?'

'I want to see her.'

'That's impossible. She's currently undergoing a form of treatment in which isolation plays an essential role.'

'Take me to see her.'

'If we do that, we will be wasting days of work. A mind as fragile as that of your mother isn't capable of stopping and starting again later. If we interrupt her treatment now, it could have serious consequences.'

'I take full responsibility. Besides, you raised no objections the other day.'

'You'll need to sign a disclaimer, the hospital declines all responsibility—'

'I'll sign anything you like – afterwards. Now, take me to see Rosario.'

Sarasola got to his feet and they followed him down the corridor, through various doors, which he opened with his ID card and password, until they reached a private room. Sarasola turned to Amaia; he seemed to have recovered his customary self-assurance.

'Are you sure about this? I'm not thinking of Rosario – she'll be delighted to see you, I'm sure – but what about you? Are you ready?'

No! A little girl inside her cried out.

'Open the door.'

Sarasola punched in his password, turned the handle and gently pushed open the door.

'Go ahead,' he said to Amaia, ushering her in first.

Inspector Iriarte stepped in front of her, drawing his weapon as he crossed the threshold.

'For the love of God! There's no need for that,' Father Sarasola protested.

'There's no one here,' said Iriarte, wheeling round. 'Are you taking us for fools?'

Sarasola entered the room, a look of astonishment on his face. The bed was unmade and a couple of padded chains hung from either side.

'How about in the bathroom?' suggested Amaia, clasping her hand over her nose and mouth to avoid breathing in her mother's odour.

'She was catheterised in order to keep her completely immobile, she doesn't need to go to the bathroom,' said Sarasola, observing Amaia's response with a clinician's eye. 'You can't stand her odour . . . Extraordinary. All I can smell is the cleaning fluid they use here, whereas you—'

'Where is she?' Amaia interrupted him angrily.

He nodded as he made his way over to the nurses' station. Sarasola's reputation must have been formidable. The nurse, a woman of about fifty, sat up straight, smoothing her uniform with her hands. She was clearly terrified of him.

477

'Why isn't Rosario Iturzaeta in her room?'

'Oh, good evening, Dr Sarasola. They took her for a CT scan.'

'A CT scan?'

'Yes, Dr Sarasola, it was scheduled.'

'I'm sure I didn't request a CT scan for Rosario Iturzaeta.'

'No, it was Dr Berasategui.'

'This is highly irregular.'

The nurse's face flushed and she started to quiver imperceptibly. Amaia turned away in disgust. If there was anything she detested more than the obsequiousness of people like Inmaculada Herranz, it was this kind of subservience born of fear.

Dr Sarasola dialled a number, raised the receiver and waited, his vexation visibly growing.

'He isn't picking up.' Sarasola turned to the nurse. 'Put out a message to Dr Berasategui on the hospital intercom telling him to call me.'

'Where do they carry out the CT scans?'

'In the basement,' said the priest, walking towards the lift.

'Who is this Dr Berasategui?'

'A brilliant clinician. I can't understand what's behind this decision. He knows perfectly well that under no circumstances is Rosario to leave isolation during this phase of her treatment. There must be some explanation. Dr Berasategui is an excellent psychiatrist, one of the best on my team, if not *the* best. He has had first-rate training and is closely linked to Rosario's case.' He pulled a face, as though recollecting something. 'You met him,' he said, 'although not formally. It was the day of the incident with your mother in the room with the two-way mirror. He was among the group of doctors we bumped into in the corridor. When I saw him, I remembered that he was the one who first showed interest in Rosario's case. I was going to introduce you, but you, well . . . I realise it probably wasn't the best time.'

The memory of that terrifying sensation flashed into her mind, but she pushed it aside, desperate to gather her thoughts.

'So, it was Dr Berasategui who first drew your attention to her case. Was that how you became interested in her?'

'Yes, you asked me about that, remember? I told you I had come across her case at several conventions, but that I couldn't recall the first time someone mentioned her to me. It was only when I saw him that I remembered.'

'His name rings a bell.'

'As I said, he's a renowned psychiatrist.'

'No, not because of that,' said Amaia, clutching at a vague memory that retreated infuriatingly into the mists of her mind.

By this time they had reached the X-ray and scanning department. Sarasola questioned another terrified nurse, while the intercom repeated the announcement in the background. Yes, Dr Berasategui had booked a CT scan, but it hadn't taken place.

'Can you tell me why?'

'I've only just come on duty, but the roster says that he cancelled it at the last moment.'

'What's going on here!' exclaimed the priest.

It was clear from his ashen complexion and his tone that Sarasola wasn't used to events escaping his control. He made one more unsuccessful attempt to reach Dr Berasategui on the phone, before calling security.

'Find Dr Berasategui at once. He is with a highly dangerous psychiatric patient called Rosario Iturzaeta.'

'I assume you have CCTV,' said Iriarte.

'Of course,' replied Sarasola, relieved.

By the time they got there, the control room was in uproar. When he saw them, the head of security addressed Sarasola, standing to attention, as though instead of a priest or a doctor he was reporting to a general.

'Dr Sarasola, we've scanned all the images – it appears Dr

Berasategui took the patient down to the basement, then left through the back door.'

Sarasola was flabbergasted.

'What you're telling me isn't possible.'

The guard played back the sequence of images on the screens. A doctor in a white coat accompanied an orderly pushing a gurney on which an anonymous patient lay hidden beneath a sheet. The next sequence was in the lift, then the basement corridor. After that, the orderly disappeared and the CCTV footage showed the doctor in the white coat helping someone to walk: a figure wearing a quilted coat that reached down to the floor, with a fur-lined hood pulled up over their head.

'He's taken her on foot!' Sarasola exclaimed, incredulous.

The head of security's walkie-talkie crackled and the voice on the other end said something that made his face cloud before he spoke again.

'They've found the orderly in a broom cupboard. He's been stabbed – he's in a bad way.'

Sarasola closed his eyes. Amaia realised he was starting to shut down.

'Doctor, where does that exit lead?'

'Out into the car park,' he replied wearily. 'I don't understand how Dr Berasategui could act so irresponsibly. All I can think of is that she's threatening him: we know how dangerous she is.'

'Look at the images again, Doctor. He's there of his own free will, he's the one leading her.'

Sarasola studied the images of Dr Berasategui as he offered his companion his arm and pointed the way.

'We'll need a photograph of Dr Berasategui.'

The head of security handed her a sheet of paper with a security pass attached. Amaia examined it, picturing him with a pair of glasses and a goatee. There was no question this was the mysterious visitor to Santa María de las Nieves.

The footage showed that, despite having been immobilised

for several days, Rosario walked confidently if somewhat stiffly. Beneath the coat, her legs looked painfully white as she almost dragged her slippered feet across the floor. An image of Engrasi shuffling along in a pair of slippers that were too big for her flashed through Amaia's mind; she wondered if that was the reason for the shuffling gait. Seeing her mother walking upright was a kind of aberration that threatened the mental picture Amaia had built up of her all those years. Fear was on the prowl; somewhere in the depths of her soul, a little girl cried out, 'She's coming to get you, she's coming to get you!'

There's no fear quite like the fear we already know, whose smell, touch and taste is familiar to us. A musty old vampire sleeping entombed beneath a veneer of order and normality that we keep at bay by feigning a composure that's as fake as canned laughter. There's no fear quite like the fear we once experienced, which has lingered on, unmoving, its damp breaths coming from somewhere inside our head. There's no fear quite like the fear of that fear returning. In our dreams we glimpse the red light that reminds us fear isn't vanquished, only resting. If we're lucky it will never come back. But we know that, if it does, we won't be able to bear it; we will either die or go mad.

A shiver like an electric shock ran down Amaia's spine. She swallowed hard, her saliva suddenly thick, then inhaled as much air as she could to compensate for how long she'd been holding her breath.

'Can we count on your assistance?' she asked Dr Sarasola.

'You've had that from the start,' he retorted.

There was a note of reproach in his voice, which Amaia decided to ignore. She understood that being treated as a suspect had left a bad taste in his mouth, but she'd been doing her job. He'd brought suspicion on himself by failing to be honest with them. She drew close, until she was sure no one else could overhear.

481

'I find it hard to believe that one of the all-powerful Dr Sarasola's sheep has strayed while he was asleep under an olive tree. I'm not pointing the finger at you; I believe you were unaware of what your boy got up to when left to his own devices.' By referring to Berasategui as *your boy*, she was making it clear she held him responsible. 'However, I'm sure that, were I to question all of your boys – which would be extremely damaging for the hospital's image – they would confirm that they were encouraged by the head of psychiatry to seek out those special cases which are your area of expertise – those who possess that subtle difference, the nuance of evil. And that the fact that this clinic carries out so much voluntary work in prisons is motivated less by altruism than by your interest in finding this type of patient, who must proliferate in such places – am I wrong? Dr Berasategui may have spoken to you about Rosario's case, but your hunt for "special" patients didn't begin or end with her, did it? Dare I suggest that you gave him carte blanche to continue that search?'

Sarasola gazed at her impassively, but she could tell he was rattled by her suggestion that a member of his staff might be a loose cannon.

'The policy of this hospital with regard to the selection of psychiatric patients is a matter of public knowledge, as is the generosity and altruism of our treatment of prison inmates. And as you so rightly point out, our team is instructed to select cases of potential interest for purposes of research and development aimed at providing a better quality of life for our patients and their families.'

Amaia shook her head, exasperated. 'This isn't a press conference, Dr Sarasola. Were you aware of and did you promote the intake of mentally ill inmates who presented with "the nuance of evil"? Or is Dr Berasategui the real head of psychiatry here?'

Sarasola glowered at her, but his tone didn't change:

'I signed off the visits, as I do with all members of my team, but I was unaware of Dr Berasategui's parallel activities.'

Amaia smiled; ever the corporate manager – or was he the wily Grand Inquisitor? It made no difference; he had made a concession. In return, she would be conciliatory.

'I realise we can't see them, but perhaps you could review the most recent sessions with Rosario to see if anything she said might provide a clue. I'll also need the help of your head of security.'

Sarasola gestured to the guard, who nodded and stood to attention.

Amaia addressed him:

'Provide Inspector Montes with the make and registration of Dr Berasategui's vehicle so we can put out a search. I'll need to see all his records, including his CV, accreditations, professional degrees, his personal file, job application and references, if you have them. And of course his telephone number, his address, and the addresses of his relatives.'

Sarasola nodded, taking out his mobile. 'I'll call my secretary.'

Iriarte chipped in: 'Could you give us a desk to work on?'

'You can use the head of security's office.'

Montes came in carrying enlargements of the photographs of Berasategui. His face was ashen.

'Zabalza says the guy's name appears at least twice on his lists.' He shook his head, clearly in shock. 'For fuck's sake, chief, this guy Berasategui was my shrink when I was suspended. He was the one who gave the anger-management courses.'

She looked at him in astonishment.

'Well then, Inspector, it's no wonder you felt such a strong desire to kill me.'

Using Sarasola's password, Amaia accessed all the files on Dr Berasategui. An outstanding CV, studies in Switzerland,

France and the UK. Born in Navarre, but there was no mention of the precise location and no name or address for his parents.

'He seems to have cut off all ties with his family,' said Montes. 'There's an address for him here in Pamplona, but according to this, he's single and lives alone.'

'Good, I'll call Markina from the car. In the meantime I want you to email Berasategui's photo to the prisons in Pamplona and Logroño to see if anyone recognises him. Tell them it's urgent – if necessary, get hold of the prison governors. I need to know as soon as possible. Also, email it to the police in Elizondo and tell them to send a patrol car to call on Nuría and Johana Márquez's mother to show it to them.'

40

The streets of Pamplona were crowded with shoppers, although it was late and the stores were about to close. Amaia called Markina from the car. He appeared relieved to learn that Sarasola wasn't implicated in the case and that Dr Berasategui appeared to have acted alone.

'We're on our way to his house now, but I'll need a court order to go in and search the place, whether he's there or not.'

'You'll have it.'

'And one more thing . . .'

'Whatever you need.'

'Thanks for authorising me back there.'

'You needn't thank me – you were right. Even if Sarasola wasn't the culprit, he was the key to this.'

Montes and Amaia went up in the lift with the porter, while Etxaide and Iriarte climbed the stairs. Amaia waited until everyone was in position either side of the door, then Montes knocked.

'Police, open up,' he said, standing aside.

There was no answer and no sound of movement from within.

'I told you he wasn't here,' the porter said behind them. 'He spends long periods abroad. He's probably travelling now. I haven't seen Señor Berasategui for at least a week.'

Amaia motioned to Iriarte, who took the key the porter handed him, inserted it in the keyhole, turning it twice. Montes pushed open the door and entered, gun levelled, as the others followed.

'Police!' they shouted.

'Clear,' declared Iriarte from the far end of the apartment.

'Clear,' echoed Montes from the bedroom.

'Good, now let's search the place. Gloves on, everyone,' commanded Amaia.

The apartment was made up of a living room, kitchen, bedroom with en suite bathroom, exercise room and a large balcony; approximately two hundred square metres, in which the overriding impression was of order, enhanced by the austere black-and-white décor.

'The wardrobes are practically empty,' said Iriarte. 'The man seems to have no clothes or belongings of any kind. I haven't seen a computer or a landline.'

Jonan poked his head out of the kitchen.

'The cupboards are bare too. Nothing in the fridge except bottles of water. But we've found a small freezer hidden beneath the kitchen counter. You'd better come and take a look.'

It resembled a wine cabinet and looked fairly new, made of stainless steel. Etxaide took out a couple of trays to show her they were empty. The inside was frost-free and so clean it might have come straight from the store. In the uppermost tray, twelve separate bundles, none of them much bigger than a mobile phone, were lined up neatly according to size. They noticed the care with which the packages had been wrapped in cream-coloured waxed paper, tied up with string and knotted with a bow, which would have given them the air of small gifts, were it not for the labels attached to them. They

486

all recognised them instantly, having seen them dozens of times dangling from the feet or wrists of dead bodies in the morgue. Handwritten on the lines reserved for the cadavers' details, in what Amaia thought was charcoal, were a series of numbers, which she identified as dates.

'Have you brought your field kit?' she asked, turning to Jonan.

'It's in the car. I'll fetch it,' he said, slipping out.

'I want everything photographed, don't touch anything until Deputy Inspector Etxaide has finished processing it.'

'What do you think is in those packages?' a voice behind her asked.

She wheeled round to see Judge Markina, who had entered without a sound. He joined the officers gathered around the open freezer. Every so often puffs of icy vapour wafted out from inside, cascading to the pristine floor, leaving a chill round their ankles, before evaporating.

Amaia had no intention of replying to his question. She refused to allow any space for conjecture. They were about to find out.

'Please, gentlemen, we need room to work,' she said, gesturing for them to clear a space for Deputy Inspector Etxaide, who had returned with the kit. 'Montes, do you have the details of all the murders?'

He took out his BlackBerry and held it up to show her.

Amaia nodded. 'I think these inscriptions are dates. This one, 31 August last year, corresponds to the day Lucía Aguirre disappeared; 15 November the year before, I think that's María in Burgos; six months earlier, 2 May, that's Zuriñe in Bilbao . . .'

Inspector Montes confirmed that the dates corresponded exactly.

Jonan had placed a ruler next to the packages and was taking pictures from various angles. She ran her eye over some of the labels; the inscriptions meant nothing to her, until she noticed one package. It was the smallest, no bigger than a cigarette lighter, the paper had more crease marks than the others. The string with the label attached hung loose, as if it had been tied in a hurry with no pressure applied to the knot. She checked the date, February of last year; it coincided with the murder of Johana Márquez. She sighed.

'Jonan, take photos of this one: it looks as though he's wrapped and unwrapped it several times.'

She waited for him to finish taking photos. Then using two pairs of tweezers, she lifted the package out of the freezer tray and placed it on the piece of canvas spread over the countertop for that purpose. Taking care not to undo the loose knot, she removed the string from the package and delicately used the tweezers to part the frozen flaps of paper, which remained rigid, like the petals of a strange flower. Inside, beneath a fine layer of see-through plastic, was a portion of flesh. It was easily identifiable from the fibrous strands formed by the muscle, which were frayed and whitish at both ends, suggesting it had been subjected to repeated defrosting and refreezing.

Montes shuddered. 'Do you think that's human flesh, chief?'

'Yes, I think it is. We'll have to wait for the test results, but it resembles some of the samples I saw at Quantico.'

She crouched down to get an eye-level view of the end of the piece of flesh.

'Look, those appear to be teeth marks. And that patchy, whitish colouring? That's freezer-burn. I think Berasategui must have defrosted it, taken a bite and then re-frozen it.'

'Like a delicacy he wants to keep, but which at the same time he can't resist,' said Jonan.

Amaia looked at him proudly.

'Top marks, Jonan. Wrap it up and put it back where it was until Forensics arrive,' she said, straightening up and leaving the kitchen.

She took a tour of the apartment, trying to understand

what it was telling her. When she was done, she returned to the kitchen.

'This is a stage set,' she declared.

They turned as one to look at her.

'Everything – the gym, the furniture, this fabulous apartment, where, according to the porter, he barely spends any time – it's a stage set. Part of the mask he hides behind, a necessary image he has to project the successful young psychiatrist. This is merely an address, a place where he might invite a colleague for a drink, an occasional woman – not many, I'm sure, just enough to give the impression of normality. The only real trace of him is in those packages in the freezer. And in something else we can't see, but which is obvious: the absence of dirt or disorder. This place is spotless – and that's not staged, it's genuine. Manipulators like him need to exercise extreme self-discipline.'

'So . . .?'

'He doesn't live here, but he has to spend time here to keep up appearances. Being here is a bore, though; he misses his real home, his stuff, his belongings, his trophies. So he alleviates that by bringing part of his home with him, like an anchor to his real world, to who he really is. That's why he brought these samples – they're fetishes that help him to maintain the pretence of—'

'Inspector,' interrupted Iriarte, holding out his phone, 'it's Elizondo on the line: Nuría says she's never seen the man before, but they're with Johana Márquez's mother now – she wants to speak to you.'

'Yes, I recognise the man, Inspector. He used to come to the garage where . . . where that *devil* worked . . . Forgive me, Inspector, I can't bring myself to say his name after what he did to us, may he rot in hell. Anyway, that man had an expensive car, a Mercedes, I think; I don't know much about cars, but I can tell that make from the star on the bonnet. He brought it in one day, then came back several times, not

489

because of the car, but to have coffee with . . . with *him*. I remember seeing him one day when I walked past the bar, sitting there in his elegant clothes; you could tell he was educated and had money. It seemed strange to me a man like that would come all the way here to have coffee with a simple mechanic. I even asked *him* about it, but he told me to mind my own business. I saw the man a couple more times after that.'

'Thank you, Inés. You've been a great help.'

After ending the call, she used her phone to access the picture of Berasategui they had been given at the hospital. Closing the screen, she dialled her aunt's number, waited while it rang, but no one picked up. She checked the time; it was nine o'clock, Engrasi would never leave the house at that hour. She called Ros's mobile and she picked up straight away.

'Ros, I'm worried. I called home and no one answered.'

'The lines are down. There's a terrible storm here in Elizondo – the power went about an hour ago. I'm at the bakery with Ernesto, you can't imagine the chaos here. We were in the middle of preparing a huge order for a French supermarket, to be delivered the day after tomorrow. Ernesto stayed behind with two of the assistants to oversee the baking, but when the power went, the ovens stopped working. Not only have we lost a whole batch but the dough has melted all over the hotplates. As the self-cleaning cycle runs on electricity, we're working by candlelight to scrape it off with spatulas, praying the power comes back on soon. I'll be here for a while, but don't worry, Engrasi has filled the living room with perfumed candles – the house looks lovely. Why don't you try her on her mobile?'

'Aunt Engrasi has a mobile?'

'Yes, didn't she tell you? That's probably because she doesn't like using it. I bought it for her recently. I was worried something might happen to her on one of her walks. Not long ago a woman from Erratzu tripped and fell on a path and was

490

lying on the ground for two hours before someone passed by. That convinced her, but she's always forgetting to charge it up,' she added with a chuckle before giving Amaia the number.

She called her aunt's mobile.

'Engrasi Salazar speaking.'

Amaia laughed out loud before she finally managed to get a word out. 'It's me, Auntie!'

'My dear, what a lovely surprise, it's good to know this thing has some uses.'

'How are you?'

'We're fine, enjoying the candlelight and the warmth of the fire. The power went off just as we'd finished bathing Ibai. Then Ernesto called and said they've lost a whole batch, so your sister had to go to the bakery. It's still pouring down here – they say there's nearly half a metre of water in the square and in Calle Jaime Urrutia. The emergency services are being called out all over the place. The thunder is deafening, but your son doesn't mind; he's had his feed and he's sleeping like an angel.'

'Auntie, there's something I wanted to ask you.'

'Of course, go ahead.'

'The man who looks after the allotments at *Juanitaenea*.'

'Yes, Esteban Yáñez.'

'That's right, you told me he had a son. Do you remember whether he looked like his father?'

'The spitting image, at least when he was small.'

'You don't happen to remember his name, do you?'

'No, my dear. I was in Paris then; I don't recall ever hearing his name mentioned. You're more likely to know him than I am. He was a couple of years older than you, three at the most.'

Amaia reflected. It was unlikely she'd have known him; two years was a huge difference at that age.

'And, well, as I told you, after his mother's suicide, the poor boy was packed off to an expensive boarding school in

491

Switzerland. He can't have been much more than ten. I dare say they gave him a good education, but he got no affection.'

'OK, Auntie, thanks. Oh, one other thing: is your mobile fully charged?'

'How do I tell?'

'Look at the screen: there should be some tiny bars at the top. How many bars do you see?'

'Wait a minute, I'll put my glasses on.'

Amaia smiled as she heard her aunt rummaging.

'One.'

'Your battery is almost dead, and now you can't charge it.'

'Your sister is always scolding me, but I forget. It's hardly surprising; I never use the thing.'

Amaia was about to hang up when she thought of something.

'Auntie, the woman who killed herself, the boy's mother, do you remember *her* name?'

'Oh, yes, of course. Margarita Berasategui – a sweet woman, such a shame.'

Another call came in. She said goodbye to Engrasi and took Sarasola's call.

'Inspector Salazar, I've been looking over Rosario's therapy sessions, as you suggested. She said very little, but she did seem very excited about the possibility of meeting her grand-daughter.'

'Rosario has no grand-daughter,' she replied.

'Didn't you have a baby recently?'

'Yes, but I had a boy. In any case, I don't think she knows. How could she?'

'It just occurred to me that she was referring to your baby.'

As soon as she'd hung up, Amaia dialled again, glancing about uneasily at the austere décor the killer had chosen for his apartment.

After a few rings, Flora answered. 'Amaia? What a surprise! To what do I owe the honour?'

492

'Flora, did you tell *Ama* that I'd had a baby boy?'

When she replied, Flora's tone had changed completely: 'No . . . Well . . .'

'Did you or didn't you tell her?'

'I told her she was going to be a grandmother. But that's when we still thought it was going to be a girl. When I saw how she responded, I didn't mention it again.'

'How did she respond?

'What?'

'You implied she responded badly. What did she say?'

'To start with, she asked what you were going to call her. I said you still hadn't chosen a name . . . Honestly, at first she seemed pleased, but then she said something . . . I don't know, she started to laugh and say nasty things . . .'

'What did she say, Flora?' Amaia insisted.

'I think it's best I don't tell you. You know how unwell she is. Sometimes she says nasty things, but she doesn't—'

'Flora!' she yelled.

Flora's voice was trembling on the other end of the line as she said:

'"I'll eat that little bitch."'

Panic produces a sudden accelerated heart rate, increased by the elevated secretion of adrenaline. Our mouth twists into a smile, the primitive smile with which evolution taught us to placate our enemies. Our breathing becomes more rapid to meet the demands of the heart. The rush of adrenaline makes our eyes open wide, as if they were bulging, causing us to lose most of our peripheral vision.

'Amaia, what's wrong?' asked Markina, coming closer to her.

Instinctively, she reached for her Glock.

'She's going to kill my son. They're heading for Elizondo – that's why he let her out. They're going to kill my son. This is what Garrido is waiting for. James is in Bilbao and we're busy investigating this crap. He's tricked us: this is all a

493

diversion – he's going to kill my son, they're going to kill Ibai. Oh my God, he's alone with my aunt!' she said, as thick, burning hot tears pricked her eyes.

When they heard her, the others piled out of the kitchen.

'Have you called the house?' asked Iriarte.

She gazed at him with a look of surprise. How was this possible? In her panic she had stopped thinking. She took out her phone and called her aunt's mobile. She heard the ringtone, but just as Engrasi answered, the phone went dead. A familiar nightmare played out before her eyes, as she imagined Rosario leaning over Ibai's cradle, the way she had so many times over Amaia's own bed. A rational thought snapped her back to reality. Her aunt's battery was dead: she only had one bar left, the energy used to make the phone ring had finished it up – she could imagine Engrasi cursing the useless device.

'My aunt's mobile is dead and the landline isn't working; there's been a power cut in Elizondo.'

'Let's go, Inspector,' said Iriarte. 'We'll mobilise everyone, we'll catch them.'

They didn't wait for the lift, but ran down the stairs, Montes and Iriarte speaking on their phones. By the time they reached the car, Amaia had regained some of her composure, but Jonan snatched the keys out of her hand and she didn't object; her head felt heavy, as if she were underwater or wearing a helmet that muffled everything around her. She noticed Markina standing beside her.

'I'm going with you,' he said.

'No,' she managed to utter. 'You can't come.'

He seized her hands. 'Amaia, I'm not letting you go there alone.'

'No, I said!' she exclaimed, wriggling free.

He seized her hands again, more forcefully. 'I'm going with you. I'm going wherever you go.'

She stared at him for a second, trying to think. 'All right, but in a different car.'

He nodded, then hurried over to Montes's vehicle.

No sooner had they set off than Jonan's mobile rang. He put it on speakerphone. Iriarte's voice reached them.

'Chief, I've sent out all patrol cars. The River Baztán flooded yesterday and the water level is rising again with today's storm. More than half the valley is without electricity after a tree fell on the power cables; it's going to take several hours to fix. On top of that, the heavy rainfall has caused a mudslide on the Baztán pass. The N-121 is closed, which could work in our favour. If they've been diverted via the NA-1210, they'll have lost a lot of time; I've been told there's quite a tailback. I've tried to reach the fire brigade at Oronoz, but they must've had a lot of call-outs and I can't get through. I'm going to try a few private numbers, but in any event a patrol car is on its way to your aunt's house as I speak.'

My sister, she thought, all of a sudden, dialling her number.

'It's worse than I thought, little sister,' said Ros when she picked up.

Amaia spoke across her:

'Ros, you need to go home. A doctor has helped *Ama* escape from the clinic – she told Flora that she would kill the little bitch I was going to have.' Even as she spoke, the tears sprang to her eyes. She struggled to hold them back. 'Ros, she's going to kill my baby because she couldn't kill me.'

When Ros answered, she could tell from her voice that she was running.

'I'm on my way there now, Amaia.'

'Ros, don't go there alone. Take Ernesto with you.'

A loud thunderclap reached her through the phone; either the connection was cut off or Ros had hung up. She felt devastated.

The NA-1210 was one of the most picturesque routes you could take through Navarre. Surrounded by idyllic green forests, light filtered through the treetops creating luminous patterns that danced on the ground. But what had once been the main road was now hazardous even at the best of times: the trucks that still favoured this route had left their mark on the surface, leaving it potholed and crumbling; the forest on either side provided occasional obstacles such as fallen branches and the corpses of animals that had strayed into the road. Tonight, with pitch-darkness illuminated only by flashes of lightning, the torrential downpour reducing visibility even further, it had become a hell on earth, clogged with traffic diverted from the motorway.

Amaia paid no attention to the road. Determined not to revisit the nightmare scenarios her mind was projecting, she focused instead on compiling a profile – the profile of a psychopath. Psychopaths cannot empathise, that is their 'design flaw'. They can experience the emotions stirred by envy and longing, anger and satisfaction; they are capable of being stirred by music and art. However they are incapable of putting themselves in someone else's shoes; they have no understanding of what it is to experience pity or compassion; they feel no sense of solidarity, no affection towards others. As a result, they go through life perfectly aware that they are unlike anyone else, seeing themselves as gods in a world of mere mortals – simultaneously chosen and deprived of recognition.

An intelligent, highly educated man. A child torn from his home after losing his mother, rejected by the only person he had left in the world. He plotted, possibly over many years – the vengeance of an adult returning to punish those who failed him. His position as a psychiatrist had given him access to the kind of individuals he needed. An expert manipulator, he had controlled those men like a puppeteer, pulling their strings until he had them exactly where he wanted them. Every detail had been precisely mapped out as he set about harnessing the rage of those brutes and wielding it like a lethal weapon, then disposing of them by having them take their own lives. He'd then ensured Amaia's involvement by orchestrating a series of desecrations. He truly was a master of horror.

She wondered how long he had known about the *itxusuria*. It was possible he'd made use of his own father; the old gardener might have come across it by chance while he was digging. Or did he suspect that such an old house was bound to have one, so he'd gone looking for it? In any event, it had created a magnificent dramatic effect, yet another to add to his catalogue of horrors.

And yet he had made a mistake. Ironically, what had betrayed him was the tiny part of him that was still human. A problem with his car had taken him to the garage where Jasón Medina worked. There, also by chance, he had come across Johana. Amaia was sure that he had initially ruled out Medina; it was impossible to control men like him. Sex attackers are never rehabilitated; despite prison sentences and therapy, they re-offend because they are driven by a desire to satisfy their needs, regardless of the consequences.

Berasategui was too expert a manipulator not to have known that, but his desire for Johana overwhelmed him. That innocent little girl with her firm dark flesh stirred new emotions in him, delicious sensations arising from an unsuspected quarter, the same feeling of exhilaration as falling in love. Johana became his obsession; he was so seduced by his discovery that he made the only mistake a mind like his could make: he allowed himself to be carried away by his greed, departing from his normal patterns of behaviour and revealing the key piece of the puzzle every detective hopes to find. A discrepancy. We are slaves to our habits.

Yes, he was an arch manipulator, but his pretensions to being a cannibalistic god paled into insignificance when compared to Rosario. Amaia had realised this when she saw the CCTV footage of the *tarttalo* accompanying Rosario willingly as they made their way out of the hospital. He might have mastery over ferocious beasts, but if he believed for one moment that he could control Rosario, he was mistaken.

Ama had been driven by one sole aim since the day her twin daughters came into the world and for over thirty years no one had been able to sway her from her path.

41

The storm appeared to have settled over the valley. Although the rain was easing off, it hadn't stopped all day; each subsiding rumble of thunder was followed by an even louder barrage. Without light, Elizondo was almost completely engulfed by the hills, its continued presence betrayed only by brief volleys of lightning and the frenetic dance of torches.

Ros was racing through the streets, carrying one of those flashlights, her hair sticking to her head in the rain, her heart pounding in her ears like a huge drum, drowning out the sound of Ernesto's footsteps as he ran close behind her. Reaching the front gate, she saw that the door was open. The rush of energy that had kept her going suddenly abandoned her, and her legs turned to jelly. As she braced herself against the cold, rough stone around the doorway, she knew that something terrible had happened, that this place, which had always been a safe haven against everything bad – the cold, the rain, loneliness, pain and the *gauekos*, the nocturnal spirits of Baztán – had finally been tainted.

Ernesto caught up with her, grabbed the torch and went in. The house still felt warm, despite the open door, but the flickering lights that had illuminated it earlier had been extinguished, with the acrid odour of snuffed candles hanging in the air. They could see the disarray in the faint glow from the embers. Ernesto swept the torch beam around the living room. A chair was upturned close to the table and fragments from the vase of fresh flowers Engrasi always kept on it were strewn across the floor. One of the wing-back armchairs had been pushed over by the hearth; had the flames been higher, it would have caught alight.

'Auntie,' Ros called out in a voice she didn't recognise as her own.

The torchlight illuminated the old woman spread-eagled on the floor, legs exposed beneath her hiked-up nightgown. The wing-back chair hid the upper part of her body. Ernesto went over and moved it aside.

'Oh my God!' he cried, stepping back when he saw her.

Ros didn't want to look. She was convinced as soon as she walked into the house that her aunt was dead.

'She's dead,' she said. 'She's dead, isn't she?'

Ernesto stooped over Engrasi's limp form.

'No, she's alive, but her head's smashed in. Ros, we have to call a doctor.'

Her phone rang in her coat pocket. She fumbled for it, shakily. She looked at the screen, unable to see through her tears, but she knew who it was.

'Amaia, it's Aunt Engrasi . . .' she wept bitter tears. 'She's as good as dead – her head's smashed in and she's bleeding to death. Ernesto called an ambulance, but they're all out because of the storm. Even the fire brigade aren't sure they can make it.' She was shrieking as she paced about the living room, in the grip of panic. 'The house has been turned upside down – she put up a fight, but Ibai's gone, they've taken him, they've taken the boy!' she screamed, utterly beside herself.

You know when it's a heart attack because you think you're dying.

Amaia's whole body imploded. She felt the weight of an ocean bearing down on her chest, the awareness that her heart had stopped, the certainty that she was going to die, the relief of knowing that it would only take a second and that afterwards the pain would cease.

The sharp aroma of ozone from the storm flowed into her as she gulped for air, or was it some benevolent *inguma*, an invisible creature breathing through her nose and mouth, rescuing her from the embrace of that calm, dense ocean she had almost welcomed?

She gulped for air again and again, with panting breaths.

'I'm stopping the car,' Jonan shouted.

Amaia had the door open even before they came to a halt. She walked round to the front, hyperventilating, her hands on her knees, staring ahead into the darkness of the forest as she tried to calm herself and gather her thoughts.

She could hear Iriarte's car pulling over behind hers, then the sound of running footsteps.

'Is she OK?' he asked Jonan.

'They've all but killed my aunt and they've taken my son.'

Iriarte gaped, shaking his head, unable to speak. Markina stood next to him, also at a loss. Jonan clasped his head in his hands; even Zabalza raised a hand to his mouth. Only Montes spoke:

'They can't get through up ahead. If we close off this road, they won't stand a chance.'

'He was born here, he knows the roads, they could be in France by now,' said Amaia.

'Nonsense,' insisted Montes. 'I'll put out an alert – I'll call Padua and get him to notify the Basque police, in case they're heading for Irun, and the French gendarmerie too, just in case they *are* on their way to France. But I doubt they've had time, chief. If, as you say, he's from around here, he'll know better than to try to go anywhere in this weather. He's more likely to hide out somewhere he knows. Remember, he has an old woman and a baby with him.'

'His father's place,' Amaia replied instantaneously. 'Esteban Yáñez is his father and he lives in Elizondo. If he's not there, try *Juanitaenea*. Esteban has the key to the house,' she said, suddenly euphoric. She nodded at Montes, grateful for his presence of mind, before turning back to the car.

'Let me drive, Jonan,' she said.

'Are you sure?'

She sat behind the wheel, remaining motionless for a few seconds while the others drove off into the darkness. Then she started the engine and turned the car around. Jonan looked at her and pursed his lips in an expression of restrained concern she knew so well. She drove a short way before leaving the main road.

The clamour of the river reached them from the right bank; even in that impenetrable darkness, it had the palpable force of a living creature. She drove at speed amid the swirling mist that seemed to form a second road, a pathway for ethereal creatures who were heading to the same spot as her. Luckily the sheep and *pottoks* had been rounded up for the night, because if they hit one at that speed they would be killed for sure.

To identify a place on a hillside in the dark is hard enough without a rainstorm blurring every landmark. She stopped the car and got out, lighting her way with a torch. Everything looked the same, but as she shone the beam further away, she recognised the wall of the abandoned farmhouse on the far side of the river. She went back to the car.

'Jonan, I have to go somewhere. I can't ask you to come with me because I'm following a hunch. If they're headed where I think they are, they'll go via the road and then the track, but this way I might get there first. It's my only chance.'

'I'm going with you,' he said, stepping out of the car. 'That's why you didn't let Markina come with us, isn't it? You knew you might have to do something like this.'

She gazed at him, wondering how much of her conversation with Markina he had overheard. She decided it wasn't important; none of that mattered now.

The grass on the slope was slippery, but the moist earth made it easier to get a purchase as they made their way down to the riverbank. The water was flowing between the rusty railings on the bridge, which were swaying, about to come loose. They shone their torches downward: to the left, a large pile of leaves and branches had formed a barrage and the cement base was now submerged. Realising the bridge might give way under their wieght, they exchanged glances and set off at a sprint. Even when they were safely across, they still seemed to be wading rather than walking. The river had flooded the entire field, which stood in almost twenty centimetres of water. The earth was still firm, thanks to the layer of grass, but it was extremely slippery and every step had to be carefully negotiated. They passed the farmhouse and came to the edge of the forest. Amaia looked ahead of her with a mixture of dread and determination, which was the only thing keeping her going. And yet the forest came as a relief. The trees had acted like a natural umbrella, so the ground was virtually unaffected by the days of heavy rainfall. They ran through the thick undergrowth, shining their torch beams ahead of them as they tried, amid lightning flashes, to find their way out of that labyrinth. They carried on for a while, aware only of the scrunch of leaves and their own breath, until suddenly Amaia came to a halt. Jonan stopped next to her, panting for breath.

'We should be out of the forest by now. We're lost.'

Jonan shone his torch about them, but the forest gave no clues as to where the exit lay. Amaia turned towards the darkness and shouted:

'Help me!'

Jonan looked at her, bewildered. 'I think it must be a few metres ahead—'

'Help me!' she shouted at the darkness once more, ignoring her companion.

Jonan said nothing this time. He watched her in silence, pointing his torch downwards. She stood motionless, eyes closed in an attitude of prayer.

The whistle was so loud, so close, that Jonan gave a start, dropping his torch. He bent over to retrieve it and when he straightened up again, she had changed. Her despair had evaporated, giving way to a firm resolve.

'Come on', she said, pointing.

They set off again, continuing through the trees until another whistle to their right made them alter their course. A longer, louder one rang out ahead of them as they left the forest. The glade where the sheep had been grazing days before had disappeared beneath the water; beyond, where the *lamias'* stream joined the river, a deafening cascade flowed down the slope like a broad tongue of water, covering the rocks and ferns on either side. They searched for the tiny cement bridge that spanned the raging torrent. Although submerged, it was still the best place to cross. Holding hands, they started over it. Just before they reached the other side a large branch swept along by the river caught Jonan's ankle. He fell forward on to his knees, the water washing over him. Amaia held on tight and, steadying herself, yanked his arm. He managed to straighten up and step out of the torrent.

'Are you OK?'

'Yes,' he replied, 'but I've lost the torch.'

'We're nearly there,' she said, running at the slope. They made their way through the undergrowth and started to climb. Noticing that Jonan was lagging behind, she turned to shine the torch beam on him: the hem of his jeans and his shoe were covered in blood where the floating branch had ripped into his ankle.

'Oh, Jonan . . .'

'I'm OK,' he said. 'You go on ahead. I'll catch you up.'

She nodded. Much as she hated the idea of leaving him on the mountainside, wounded and without a torch, she hurried on. She couldn't wait for him – they both knew that.

Midway up the slope, she skirted round the rock that blocked the cave's entrance. As she did so, she caught a glimpse of light inside. She drew her Glock and switched off her torch.

'Help me, God,' she pleaded under her breath. 'And you, accursed queen of storms,' she added.

As she slipped noiselessly along the small s-bend that acted as a natural doorway, her ears strained to detect sounds from within. She could make out the swish of fabric, steps on the ground, and then, suddenly, one of Ibai's beloved little gurgles. Her eyes filled with tears. She felt so grateful that her baby boy was still alive, she could have sunk to her knees then and there to give thanks to the god who watched over children. Instead, she wiped her hand furiously over her face, rubbing away all trace of her tears. Clutching her gun, she moved forward . . . What she saw next made her blood run cold. Ibai was lying on the ground, in the centre of an intricate drawing traced with what looked like salt or ash. He was surrounded by candles, which had warmed the air, so that, despite only wearing a nappy, he wasn't crying from cold.

Beside him, she saw a wooden bowl, a glass container, and a metal funnel. Vivid images of the sacrifices Elena had described flashed through her mind. Oblivious to what was going on, Ibai was busy trying to grab his own toes. Rosario was kneeling, brandishing a knife over the child's belly, as though tracing invisible figures. Beneath the huge quilted coat, now hanging open, Amaia saw she was wearing a grey jumper and trousers; her hair was scraped into a bun. Dr Berasategui, more of a *tarttalo* than ever, stooped beside her, smiling as

505

though entranced by the ceremony. He was chanting something; it sounded like a song that Amaia didn't recognise.

Her heart beating madly, she raised the Glock. She could feel the sweat running from her palms and trickling down her sleeve. She'd known before she entered the cave that she was afraid, that terror would engulf her when she was confronted with Rosario. But in spite of this there had been no doubt in her mind that she would do what she had to do.

Berasategui saw her first. He studied her with interest, as if she were an unexpected though not at all unwelcome guest.

Rosario looked up, piercing Amaia with her dark gaze. Instantly, Amaia was nine years old again. She could feel the silent pull of the rope, the spider's web of her mother's control, transporting her back to her childhood bed, to the kneading bowl, to her grave.

Then Ibai gave a soft whimper, as though he was about to start crying, and this was enough to bring Amaia back to her senses, to unleash her pent-up rage. She hadn't expected to feel such fury; at once instinctive and rational, it coursed through her body, ringing in her head like a command, overriding her fear and urging: 'Kill her!'

'Put down the knife and step away from my son,' she said firmly.

Rosario's face twisted into a smile, but then she froze, as if something had caught her attention.

'Carry on,' commanded Berasategui, ignoring Amaia's presence.

But Rosario remained stock-still, gazing at Amaia with the wariness of one calculating their next move when confronted with the enemy.

'I said, step away from the boy or I swear to God I'll blow both your heads off.'

Rosario's face contorted as she emptied her lungs in a long howl. Tossing the knife to one side, she leant over the child and tore open his nappy.

She let out a shriek of horror at what was revealed.

Extending an arm, she leaned on Berasategui to heave herself up.

'Where's the girl?' she cried. 'Where's the girl? You've tricked me.' Then she looked straight at Amaia and demanded:

'Where's your daughter?'

Ibai started to cry, alarmed by her shouting.

'Ibai is my son,' said Amaia resolutely. As she did so, she realised that this affirmation was a statement of intent: Ibai, the river child, *the baby boy who was supposed to be a girl but changed his mind at the last minute*. She remembered the words of the girl by the stream: 'If you had a boy, it must be because that was meant to be.'

'But Flora told me it was a she!' Rosario protested, bewildered. 'She was supposed to be a little bitch, she was supposed to be *the sacrifice*.'

Berasategui looked at the boy with a grimace of irritation, then lost all interest and stepped back against the cave wall.

'Like my sister?'

Rosario appeared taken aback, then hissed: 'And you, too . . . Or did you think I'd finished with you?'

Ibai's cries had intensified, resounding inside the cave like needles piercing Amaia's eardrums. Rosario cast a backward glance at the child before advancing towards her.

'Stop,' Amaia ordered, still pointing her gun. 'Don't move.'

But her mother kept coming and Amaia turned slowly, as if the two of them were engaged in a strange dance that brought her closer to the centre of the cave where Ibai lay. The space between them remained the same, like poles of two magnets, repelling one another.

Keeping one eye on Berasategui, who appeared to be enjoying the spectacle, Amaia held her gun steady until *Ama* reached the mouth of the cave and disappeared. Only then did Amaia turn towards Berasategui, who smiled beguilingly, raising his hands as he took a step towards the cave entrance.

507

'Make no mistake,' she said calmly. 'In your case, I won't hesitate. One more step and you're dead.'

He halted in his tracks, giving a resigned shrug.

'Against the wall,' she ordered.

Still aiming at him, she drew closer and tossed him the handcuffs.

'Put these on.'

He obeyed with a nonchalant gesture, lifting both hands to show her.

'Down on the floor, on your knees.'

Berasategui obeyed, seemingly reluctant, as though she might have asked him to do something more enjoyable instead of arresting him.

Then Amaia went over to the child, swept him up off the floor, knocking over several candles, which carried on burning as they rolled on the ground. She clutched him to her, wrapping him in her clothes, and kissing him when she saw that he was unharmed.

'Inspector?' called Jonan from outside.

'In here, Jonan,' she shouted, relieved to hear his voice. 'In here.'

Amaia had no intention of pursuing her mother through the storm. She wasn't going to leave the wounded Jonan in charge of a detainee, nor would she leave Ibai. She checked her phone and glanced at her deputy.

'I have no coverage.'

'It's OK,' he said. 'I had some on the hillside. I made a call – help's on its way.'

She heaved a sigh of relief.

The search operation went into immediate effect, a joint collaboration between the Navarre police and *Guardia Civil*. They even brought a dog team from Zaragoza. After scouring the area for twenty-four hours, volunteers found the quilted coat with the fur-lined hood Rosario had been wearing tangled up in some branches a few miles downriver. After a cursory examination of the garment, which attested to the wearer having received a multitude of blows and scratches, Markina told those heading the search to call it off.

'If she fell into the water last night, with this current she'll be in the Bay of Biscay by now,' said one volunteer. 'Yesterday I saw tree trunks thicker than bodies being swept away by the river as if they were twigs.'

Markina nodded. 'We'll alert the seaside towns and coastal patrols.'

Amaia returned to the house, which without Engrasi was no longer a home. As she watched her son sleeping, she embraced James.

'I don't care what they say: I know Rosario isn't dead.'

He offered no contradiction but drew her close and asked: 'How do you know?'

'Because I can still feel her threat, like a rope binding us together. I know she's still out there somewhere. This isn't over yet.'

'She's a sick old lady. Do you honestly think she got out of the forest and found somewhere to hide?'

'I know my pursuer is out there, James. Jonan thinks she might have abandoned her coat while she was fleeing.'

'Amaia, don't think about it, please,' he said, holding her even tighter.

42

Amaia entered the interview room with Iriarte. When he saw her, Berasategui smiled. She had seen his lawyer many times on TV. He didn't get up when she and Iriarte came in, but instead carefully smoothed his expensive jacket before speaking. Amaia wondered how much he charged by the hour.

'Inspector Salazar, my client would like to thank you for all your efforts to save him. If it hadn't been for you, things might have turned out very differently.'

She glanced at Iriarte; this charade might have been amusing had she not felt so sad.

'Is this your strategy?' enquired Iriarte. 'Trying to make us believe that you were a victim of circumstance?'

'It isn't a strategy,' replied the lawyer. 'With all due respect,' he said, addressing Amaia, 'my client's actions were carried out whilst he was under threat from a dangerous lunatic.'

'Your client visited Rosario at Santa María de las Nieves, posing as a relative and using fake ID,' said Iriarte, placing before the lawyer the images taken from the CCTV cameras at the clinic.

'Indeed,' the man replied pompously. 'My client is guilty of an excess of enthusiasm. He was fascinated by Rosario's case. He had befriended her when they met years ago in a different

510

hospital. He became fond of her. Since she was only permitted to see relatives, my client, without malicious intent, posed as a relative in order to visit.'

'He used fake ID.'

'Yes, he admits to that,' the lawyer said unctuously. 'I'm sure the judge will concede that there was no malicious intent. We're talking six months at the most.'

'Let's leave the calculations for now, shall we? I'm not done yet,' said Iriarte. 'He also provided her with a weapon, which he smuggled into the clinic.' The lawyer began shaking his head. 'An antique scalpel, which he got from the place where Antonio Garrido was hiding.'

Berasategui's smile was snuffed out for an instant before returning once more.

'You can't prove that,' said the lawyer.

'Do you want me to believe that she forced him?'

'You saw what she did to that nurse – and to Dr Franz, as well as to your poor aunt . . .' the lawyer added, glancing at Amaia.

'Antonio Garrido is alive.' Amaia spoke for the first time, fixing her gaze on Berasategui.

'Well, that's purely coincidental,' he said, holding her gaze. 'You know how it is in life: the only thing we know for sure is that we die.'

'Will you make him kill himself?'

Berasategui smiled benevolently, as if the remark were completely obvious.

'I won't make him do anything. He will do it because he's a highly disturbed individual. I've been treating him for some time and he is a potential suicide.'

'Yes, as were Quiralte, Medina, Fernández, and Durán. All patients of yours, now dead. All murderers whose victims were women who were close to them and were born in Baztán. And they all signed their crimes in the same way,' she said, showing him the photographs of the various cell walls. 'After each of these crimes, someone removed a trophy from the crime scene, using a surgical saw taken from the pilgrims' hospital – the same place where your acolyte Antonio Garrido was hiding out.'

'There's an extremely high suicide rate among violent persons. Since I am innocent, I of course have an alibi for each of those occasions.'

Iriarte opened another file from which he extracted six photographs and placed them in front of the lawyer and his client.

'All the limbs amputated at the crime scenes were discovered a year ago in Arri Zahar. Some have human bite marks on them. I don't know whether you're aware of the latest advances in forensic dentistry, a simple cast of your teeth will enable us to establish a link.'

'Once again, I'm sorry to disappoint you. As a child I was the victim of a terrible car accident, resulting on a fractured jaw and the loss of several teeth. These are implants,' he said, grinning exaggeratedly to show off his dentures. 'Similar to thousands of other implants – or similar enough to create reasonable doubt in the mind of a juror.'

The lawyer nodded vigorously.

'Let's go back to your acolyte.'

'Yes, let's,' Berasategui said smugly, to his lawyer's evident dismay.

'Garrido confessed to having carried out the desecration of the church at Arizkun.'

'I don't see what this has to do with—' protested the lawyer.

Amaia cut him off. 'In addition to damaging church property, the descrators left behind human remains that had been removed from a family grave.'

Berasategui's smile was so dazzling that for an instant all eyes were on him, even those of the lawyer, who seemed increasingly disconcerted. But his client's gaze was fixed on Amaia.

'Did you like that, Inspector?'

The others remained silent, contemplating Berasategui's smile and Amaia's face, which was devoid of all expression.

'The discrepancy and the beginning,' she said.

Berasategui leaned in slightly, giving her his full attention.

'The beginning and the discrepancy,' Amaia repeated.

He looked at Iriarte, then at his lawyer, shrugging his shoulders to show he had no idea what she was talking about.

'In a murder investigation, the discrepancy provides the key and the beginning provides the origin; and each origin contains the source of its own end.'

Once more Berasategui raised his cuffed hands in a gesture of bewilderment.

'You don't understand what I'm saying, Dr Berasategui – or should I say Dr Yáñez?'

The smile froze on his lips.

'That's the beginning, the origin. You are the son of Esteban Yáñez and Margarita Berasategui. Esteban Yáñez, a pensioner who tends the vegetable garden surrounding my grandmother's house. He was the one who discovered my family's *itxusuria*, its burial ground. It was Esteban who provided Garrido with the bones. Your father is in the room next door; he claims he had no idea the bones would be used to desecrate a church. He thought they were part of a macabre prank, in retaliation for being ousted from what he considered his land.

'And then there's Margarita Berasategui – your mother, whose surname you adopted as a tribute – a wretched woman who suffered from lifelong depression. It must have been unbearable for a child with a brilliant mind like yours to grow up in such a mournful, gloomy house, plagued with silences and weeping. Like being buried alive, isn't that right? She did her best; she kept her house spotless, ironed the clothes, cooked the meals. But that isn't enough for a child, is it? A child needs love, companionship and affection, it needs to play, but she couldn't bear you to touch her, could she?

513

Perhaps because she sensed the kind of monster you were – a mother always knows these things. She'd tried to kill herself before, several times, swallowing handfuls of tranquilisers, but never quite enough. Perhaps because she didn't really want to die, she simply longed for a different life. Until one day you came home from school to find her semi-comatose, a bottle of pills spilled in her lap . . . then you did the rest. You put your father's rifle to her head and, possibly using her own hand, you blew her brains out. No one suspected a thing, because they all knew about her depression and her previous half-hearted attempts; besides, the region has one of the highest suicide rates in the country. No one but your father, that is. He must have known when he walked in and saw her brains splattered all over the walls and ceiling. Margarita might have been in the depths of despair, but her house was always spick and span. Women rarely kill themselves in such a messy way, least of all women like her. That's why he threw you out of his house and sent you far away. That's why, even now, he still fears and obeys you.

'That's the origin. You renounced your father by erasing his name, but in taking your mother's name, you were actually taking the name of your first victim.'

Berasategui sat completely still, listening.

'Do you have any proof for these allegations?' asked the lawyer.

'And now the discrepancy,' she resumed, ignoring the lawyer, while observing every detail of Berasategui's face. 'The victims were adult females, originally from Baztán. Each was killed by an abusive husband or partner who had been in anger-management therapy – the perfect environment in which to find people susceptible to being manipulated.'

'I'm not a manipulator,' he murmured.

The lawyer had pushed his chair slightly away from the table, erecting an invisible barrier between himself and his client.

514

Amaia smiled. 'Of course not, how silly of me. That's a point of honour among you instigators. You aren't manipulators; the difference being that your victims *want* to do what they do, isn't that right? They want to serve you and they do what they must do, which just happens to coincide with what you want.'

He smiled.

'Then into this picture of order and harmony came the discrepancy called Johana Márquez. I know you tried to manipulate her stepfather, but he was such a brute your control tactics didn't work on him. Yet still you couldn't resist the excitement Johana aroused in you, your desire to take her life, the soft, firm flesh beneath her perfect skin, which that animal was about to defile.' Amaia watched Berasategui open his lips and run his tongue slowly around his mouth. 'You stalked her like a hungry wolf, waiting for the moment you knew would arrive. Your desire was overwhelming, you simply couldn't resist, could you? You took a bite out of Johana in that hut when you claimed your trophy. Dental implants may leave a reasonable doubt, but you left traces of saliva on that special morsel of flesh you preserve alongside the others, like a delicacy you want to keep, but which at the same time you can't resist,' she said, quoting Jonan.

He gazed at Amaia wistfully.

'Johana,' he said, lowering his head.

It hadn't rained for two days and the sun peeping through the clouds made everything look sharper and brighter.

First thing that morning she had paid a visit to the Navarre Forensic Institute. She insisted on going in alone, although James and her sisters were waiting outside in the car.

San Martín came up to her as soon as he saw her and embraced her fleetingly, asking, 'How are you?'

'Fine,' she replied serenely, relieved at the brevity of the embrace.

The doctor led her to his official workplace, which was filled with bronze statues. It was a room he never used, preferring the cluttered table in the corner downstairs.

'It's just a formality, Inspector,' he said, passing her some documents. 'Once you've signed these, I can hand over the remains.'

She scrawled her signature, then all but fled San Martín's friendly attentions.

That had been the easy part. Now, the sun warming her back as she crouched over the open grave, ironically she wished it were raining. The sun oughtn't to shine at funerals; it made them more vivid, more dazzling and unendurable; the warm sun only intensified the horror with all the cruelty of a gaping wound.

She knelt on the ground, still sodden after the torrential rains, breathing in the rich mineral aroma. Carefully, she nudged the tiny bones into the grave, then covered them, patting down the earth with her hands. She turned to look at her sisters and James, who was cradling Ibai in his arms, then her gaze came to rest on the indestructible Engrasi, who wore a hat tilted coquettishly to conceal her bandaged head.

GLOSSARY

CAGOT: one of the oldest names from which the Spanish word *agote* undoubtedly derives.

INGUMA: a malevolent spirit that robs people's breath as they sleep, hovering above their chest and placing its jaws over their nose and mouth.

KAIXO: hello.

MAITIA: darling, sweetheart.

TTIKITTO: little boy.

ZORIONAK, AITA: congratulations [happy birthday] dad.

ACKNOWLEDGEMENTS

I would like to thank all those who, once again, have enabled me through their skill and expertise to turn this fiction in to the physical object you now hold in your hands. Any errors or omissions, of which there will be many, are solely down to me.

Thanks to Doctor Leo Seguín at the Universidad de San Luis.

And to Paloma Gómez Borrero.

A thousand thanks to the Navarre Police, and in particular to the Elizondo Unit: KEEP UP THE GOOD WORK.

Thanks to Mario Zunzarren Angos, Chief Commissioner of the Pamplona Police.

And to the captain of the Guardia Civil Judicial Police in Pamplona.

To Juan Mari Ondikol and Beatriz Ruiz de Larrinaga from Elizondo who set up guided tours of the locations in and around Elizondo where the Baztán trilogy takes place.

And to the Oronoz-Mugairi Fire Brigade, in the person of Julián Baldanta.

Also to the *pelotari* Oskar Lasa, Lasa III, because sometimes a conversation can go a long way.

To Isabel Medina for telling me a wonderful story about Baztán.

And, of course, to Mari.